NOSTRADAMUS REVEALS

Who Will Stand In The Shadow Of Towers

LEWIS PHILIPS

ISBN - 9781645507291

Because of the dynamic nature of the Internet, any web addresses or links contained in this book may have changed since publication and may no longer be valid. The views expressed in this work are solely those of the author and do not necessarily reflect the views of the publisher, and the publisher hereby disclaims any responsibility for them.

This book is written as fiction & reality and the author takes no responsibility for injury if anyone emulates any actions or stunts described in this book. The author does not dispense medical advice or prescribe the use of any technique as a form of treatment for physical, emotional, or medical problems without the advice of a physician, either directly or indirectly. The intent of the author is only to offer general information relating to spiritualism, and there is no guarantee that any outcome will help you in your quest for emotional and spiritual well-being. In the event you use any of the information in this book for yourself, which is your constitutional right, the author and the publisher assume no responsibility for your actions.

Matchstick Literary
www.matchliterary.com
1-888-306-8885
orders@matchliterary.com

CONTENTS

PREFACE

What the author reveals now, is stranger than fiction, and the book you are about read will leave readers thinking, *is it more than fiction*. Much of the book was inspired by actual events and in the end the book became the story.

What happened in April 1996? Well, it's rarely repeated, because it gave the author goose bumps when spoken. These few words are what inspired the author to write, and now's the time to reveal how a phone call set off a chain reaction one day in April, when a young lad got involved in a car accident. Jay was riding his friend's push bike when the brakes failed and the bike went hurtling down a steep hill, even as a van swerved into Pakenham Street, Aroona, causing a high-speed impact, sending Jay smashing into the windscreen. Sirens could be heard from Phil's home one street away as ambulance, police, and emergency services began to arrived.

Jay was rushed to Nambour Hospital and moved quickly to intensive care, where he was placed on life support. His injuries were critical, and his parents were informed that his chances of survival were slim and dependent on the outcome of emergency surgery, but unfortunately, there was no surgeon capable of performing this operation at Nambour Hospital.

To make matters worse, the boy's injuries were such that he could not be moved to Brisbane's major hospital, Royal Brisbane.

That day, while staying overnight on a business trip in Toowoomba, Phil's wife Betty updated him on Jay's condition. Throughout that night, he had difficulty sleeping, tossing on his bed; he remained positive that a strong young lad like Jay would eventually beat the odds. He must know he was in good hands with doctors doing all they could for him.

The next morning, Betty called Phil to tell him that Jay would undergo a major operation which, if successful, would save his life.

When Phil finished seeing his business contacts in and around Toowoomba, he would drive the two and half hour trip to the Sunshine Coast, north of Brisbane. By late afternoon, he was ready to drive back home, first heading west and then north-west, followed by a sharp right-hand turn at Yarraman. That was a shortcut route back to the coast.

Toowoomba happens to be the largest inland city in Queensland, perched high on a mountain range of red soil, which in part is an extinct volcanic crater. From the crater rim at Highfields, one can spot the road cutting eastwards to the coast, the route most travellers followed to the west or east.

Heading west, he turned right to Kingsthorpe on to Goombungee, and from there, left to Quinalow, Maclagan, and Cooyar. He continued along sharp winding bends, cutting a path heading down The Great Dividing Range.

Phil's thoughts were still focussed on Jay, who he hoped would recover fast, while trying to concentrate on his driving. One more dip in the road, and then it was almost a straight drive to Yarraman. The only intersection coming up was one minute away, and as Phil thought of Jay, tears welled up in his eyes.

His thoughts flew back to old school days, when students were taught that God is omnipotent and omnipresent. He recalled a saying from the past: "May the healing spirit of God rest upon you."

At that very moment, something unexpected happened at the intersection, which he had crossed several times before. Seemingly from nowhere, a red sedan appeared, speeding into the junction from left field. Drivers on the main road had right of way. There was also a Give Way sign to remove any confusion. Phil braked hard, allowing the speeding sedan to just brush past without crashing.

A wordy duel followed, when suddenly his eyes fell on the sedan's number plate: JAY16. Phil's first thoughts were, *Oh my God, this could be an omen.* He somehow knew that if he left this sign behind, he would be abandoning Jay.

From that moment on, Phil followed but tried not to shoot past the red sedan. When they started approaching the town of Yarraman, the vehicle continued into town as he turned right to the coast. However, that was not the last time he got a sign.

On arriving home, he shared this incident with Betty. He then asked her, "How old is Jay?" Betty answered, "Fifteen."

"Well," Phil said, "he'll make it to his next birthday."

Lying down, he explained what had happened, and that's when an image flashed before his eyes from a painting hanging on the wall.

From these unexplained events, a mantra evolved, and he settled on the final words based on number 23; twenty-three letters in the first line, twenty-three words in total, delivering within what he called the Scroll.

They dropped in on Jay at the hospital a few days later and found him in good spirits, sitting up in bed and greeting them with a cheerful smile. As with everyone who has had an operation, Jay showed his battle scar. His wound looked almost healed.

Phil reflected back on the chain of events that led to Jay's recovery: how paramedics arrived first on the scene, and how a top surgeon was flown in on a helicopter from Royal Brisbane Hospital to Nambour Hospital; it seemed no less than a miracle.

So the journey begins, to save and deliver the Scroll, but first we have to go back in time. The year 1973.

INTRODUCTION

I think the best way to describe this read is a journey of discovery to find answers to some of the perplexing issues facing the world's population, both physical and spiritual, and our place in the universe. Does this book have the answers? I leave it up to readers to decide.

I Am the One - Lewis Philips was published in 2014 and includes, past publications - *Past, Present, Future - Image of the Past & New Amsterdam, New York, New Babylon Falls*. The new title, *Nostradamus Reveals* completes the series and includes the final chapters in *Archaea Rising*.

ACKNOWLEDGEMENTS

I would like to thank my family for their support over the past few years with my obsession to write, especially Betty, who at times thought I was too consumed in writing these books. For our sons and daughters, we hope they find insight in our journey through life. I acknowledge and thank them for their support and encouragement.

I am concerned about our environment and believe that primates of Sumatra and Borneo need our protection from habitat destruction. A percentage of profits from this book will be made to organisations that protect the orang-utans.

BOOK 1

PAST
PRESENT
FUTURE

PAST

Perched high in a eucalyptus tree two eagles watch over their domain - The Glass House Mountains. The spiritual home of the Kabi Kabi people, custodians of this ancient land. Atop of Wild Horse Mountain, one hundred and twenty three metres above sea level, a lone figure, stands motionless, wearing a black Driza-bone waistcoat and hood. Hands are on the central platform, as he looks to the horizon on sunset bursting into colour. Lightning cracks are seen to the east, and gusts of rain push through the structure without walls. It doubles as a fire observation post, and communication receivers dot the tower roof.

One can only guess what he's doing.

Lightning strikes one of the aerials on the roof, and the eagles take flight heading down the highway that cuts a path through this ancient land, revealing a stream of vehicle lights that leads to an old rundown homestead; better known as a Queenslander sitting on the banks of Enoggera Creek, Brisbane, the year 1973.

Flashes of light reveal a Kombi in a driveway, surrounded by Harley-Davidsons. George the driver, parked the Kombi, being careful not to knock over any of the bikes. He did well, considering his pounding headache from a bender the night before.

As the guys lined up in the back, heads bowed, Bear pushed open the kombi side door with a bang, as lightning cracks. Three guys are about to step out of the kombi as bolts of light flicker as if someone's turning on and off a light switch. Brownie, who knows all things aboriginal, passes a slab of beer to Bear before stepping out. Bear wouldn't be out of place in rugby scrum, and the sort of guy you'd want on your side when your backs to the wall. Cassa slammed the door shut. He liked to think of himself as a chick magnet with his long blond hair; and a sweet talker to boot.

Sloshing their way up damp ground, after getting out the front doors of the kombi - LP, who reckons he can see the future on a good day. Mason who had issues with his Masonic Brethren and one day would become the Grand Master. And George just liked to stir up people with his sarcasm.

Passing an old verandah at the side of the house looked dilapidated and in need of a good reno, and that's when LP started mumbling -

> 'Past-Present-Future
> Captured in numbers
> Enclosed in time
> The thunder we feel and hear
> Happened seconds ago
> Soon it's going to bucket down'
> Bear whispers, "Keep it down with your fortune telling."

The guys - surfers on a mission to reach Bells Beach in time for a surf contest, but first they have to collect their mate, Red - Mr. Fixit, who was about to be evicted form what could be best called - a squat, along with his flatmate Willy. Even Red would have had a hard time fixing the place up. Demolition might be the answer.

Willy was friends with the Bad Meadows Motorcycle Club, and it was obvious they were already there in full force from the number of motorbikes parked along the gravel driveway.

Several bikies turned to see who was entering their turf.

One of the bikies yelled, "Who's these surfie bums?" Luckily, Red was standing nearby and was quick to reply, "I invited them, Porky; they're my mates."

Red's intervention calmed Porky down—temporarily.

As the guys entered the backyard, they saw a raging fire with flames almost as high as the trees. It looked like a sight from Guy Fawkes Night. They all felt a little on edge seeing so many bikies around the fire getting pissed, all arguing and talking loudly.

Bear shouted over to Red in the crowd, "How long has this been going on?"

"It started at three o'clock," Red replied, walking over to the group. "They've got a head start on us, so be careful. They're all pretty drunk."

George, despite being short and stocky, was often a bit of a smart-ass. He struck up a conversation with Porky, who happened to be number two gang leader.

Porky was a tall, large-framed bikie. When he walked, the parts of his body moved and swayed in different directions. He could have done with a crash diet—it didn't even look like his Harley could carry him. His long ginger hair and gingery white beard that touched his chest made him look like someone who had stepped out of an old Western movie.

George looked up at him and asked, "Where did you get a name like Bad Meadows?"

George's question was like a red rag to a bull. The anger in Porky's face could be seen by everyone. The guys all looked at each other and thought, *This is not a good start to the night.*

Porky paused for a couple of seconds, wondering which one he should punch out first for questioning his club colours. Holding back his anger, he looked George in the eye and said, "Well, pal, the short answer is that the name we wanted was already registered. If you say Bad Meadows fast, it sounds like the name we wanted."

George fired another question: "Well, what do you guys do for money?"

Again, Porky paused, now clenching his fists and rocking back and forth. He gave the question some serious thought, reached down to the ground, and picked up a tally of beer. Gulping it down, he burped and then said, "Read the colours on my back, and don't ask any more stupid questions or I'll thump ya."

He turned around; his jacket read:

Bad Meadows
Building and Design
AG Security
Circled around the words were:

"Bad Meadows Motorcycle Club"
Porky added, "We're in building design and AG security. That speaks for itself. Now do you understand what we do for money?"

Cassa thought, *Whatever it means, it's not legal!*

George's thinking was similar: *It's got to be a cover for illegal activity.*

"Well, what do you think?" Porky asked.

George responded first: "Sounds like the type of business we should get involved in." Cassa nodded his head in agreement.

Porky looked at George and Cassa fiercely. "There's only room in this town for one gang in the business, so think again! Now, I've got some business to attend to, so don't leave this fire till I get back, okay?"

"Yeah, sure, we'll be here when you come back," George replies, then mumbled under his breath, "Light travels faster than sound. That's why people like you appear bright until they open their mouth."

Porky and his mate, Nutter, walked away from the fire to conduct a drug deal in front of the house with Conjay, a South African. They would be exchanging twenty-five pounds of pure hashish for twenty-five pounds of gold Krugerrand coins.

Conjay and his South African mate were both dressed in black trousers, white shirts, and dark sunglasses; they handed Porky a bag containing the gold coins. Porky stretched out his right hand and grabbed the bag. In his other hand, he held the block of hashish. He balanced both and declared, "Correct weight; done deal!"

"Where do we put these coins for now?" Porky asked Nutter.

Nutter paused and looked around.

"Stick it in the back of the engine compartment of that Kombi. We'll get it later. If anything goes wrong, those surfie bums will wear it."

Conjay walked back to his hearse with his offsider, opened the back hatch, and pulled out a small coffin. He placed the block of hashish inside.

"What's the go with that coffin?" asked Nutter.

"Who would pull over a hearse, or open a child's coffin in air transit? It's the perfect cover to smuggle drugs, diamonds, and gold," replied Conjay.

Nutter's cold black heart beat poison through his veins. He had no reaction or feeling about seeing a child's coffin, even knowing drugs often played a part in young people's loss of innocence and, worse, an early grave for some.

With the deal done, the South Africans got into the hearse and drove out of the driveway, turning left onto the main road.

The guys around the fire realised they needed to get out of there. The bikies, full of booze and drugs, were descending into tribalism around the fire, and it was starting to get ugly. The fire was dying and needed more fuel; the old Queenslander had plenty of timber to fuel their bonfire, as light rain continued to fall.

The back stairs to the house were falling apart from many years of neglect. As he and Porky walked back to the party, Nutter ordered his brain-dead bikies to pull down the stairs and throw them on the fire.

Nutter was the gang leader. Whatever he said would happen; obey his command or pain would be inflicted on anyone who questioned his orders. Several bikies turned to his command immediately.

Others soon joined in, ripping off the old weatherboards and fuelling the fire higher and higher. Board by board, several crazed bikies ripped apart the old Queenslander.

As the fire grew larger, Nutter took off his jacket to reveal his black, hairy arms, covered in tats. On one arm was a dragon like serpent and on the other, the names of his fallen comrades who had upheld the Bad Meadows code of honour: death before disloyalty.

Meanwhile, the creek, only four yards away from the house, was rising quickly as the thunderstorm approached Brisbane. Within minutes, the flood waters were only a couple of feet away from the Kombi.

Cassa pointed towards the creek and yelled, "Check that out!" Cassa's eyesight was pretty good at night, as though he had night vision without goggles. He had the whitest of white skin and shoulder-length blond hair; he wasn't hard to spot in the dark. His mates were always making jokes about his skin colour and about him tripping over things, and reckoned he was blind as a bat because he was albino.

What he was pointing to was a van floating down the swollen creek, which now looked like a raging river. The guys ran down the driveway. As they looked closely at the rear window panel, it looked like several people banging on the window, trying to get out.

"They're trapped inside the van," said Cassa with panic in his voice.

The guys looked on helplessly as the van, now in the centre of the fast-flowing creek, hit the bridge and went under. Hands were still banging on the rear window, but they didn't see the van resurface.

"What do we do about that?" Mason asked.

"No one could survive those flood waters," said Bear. "I saw a public phone in the hallway back at the house. Red, ring the cops and tell them what's happened."

Red ran back to the house, up the front stairs, and down the hallway. He picked up the red pay phone and dialled 000. While he was explaining to the police that a panel van had struck the Enoggera Creek Bridge and disappeared under the flood waters, Porky noticed him and yelled, "Hey, who are you calling? It better not be the cops, asshole!"

Red dropped the phone, swung around, and grabbed Porky in a headlock. He pushed his head through the timber wall and made sure he wasn't going anywhere fast. He unclipped Porky's belt buckle, dropping his Levi's to his ankles. *Let's see how he explains that to his bikie mates,* thought Red.

The guys headed back to the Kombi. It was dark and hard to see as they walked over the muddy ground. They heard George yell, "Mason, help me. I can't walk. I've stepped in a rabbit hole and twisted my ankle."

Mason turned to help George. He pulled his foot out of the hole, put his arm around his shoulder, and helped him back to the Kombi.

"I can't drive," said George.

"LP, you drive," said Bear. "You know how to handle a Kombi. Hurry up! Let's get out of here."

George was still whining in the back of the van.

"George, shut up," Bear said, turning to him. "Or we'll leave you behind. There's nothing more we can do here; let's get some pizzas from Romeo's, and we'll be on our way to Bells Beach for the surf contest."

"Where's Brownie?" asked Mason.

"Stuff him; he's always late. Have-A-Chat is probably still back with the bikies," said Bear.

"We'll have to go back for him, but let's make it quick. We don't want to be here when the cops arrive. They'll be all over the place any minute."

Mason ran back and spotted Brownie, beer in hand, talking crap with one of the bikies.

"Come on, let's go, Brownie; the guys are waiting," Mason whispered.

Brownie turned and started walking back to the Kombi with Mason, climbing in through the side door.

LP accelerated down the driveway and turned right onto the main road as the police arrived.

The guys in the Kombi speculated whether the cops were responding to Red's call about the van floating down the creek or answering a neighbour's noise complaint. They figured the cops would be more interested in how many bikies they could arrest than looking for a sunken panel van in a swollen creek.

Back inside the house, Nutter found Porky still trying to get his head out of the wall. He helped his mate and then went to the front door to confront the police.

"What do you want?" asked Nutter. "Don't you know we're untouchables? Speak to your boss."

"If you're lucky, you'll still be patrolling the city streets and not sent so far west you'll never be heard of again," said Porky, backing up his mate.

"Get on your two-way radio," Nutter ordered. "Who's on duty? Who's your superior?"

"Sergeant Jack Herbertsin," the constable answered.

"Tell him who we are."

The constable spoke on his radio. "Hey, Sarge, we're out on a noise complaint, and there's a mob of bikies here. They say they're called Bad Meadows bikies. Do you know them?"

The response came back through the radio: "Yeah, let 'em go. Tell them I want fifty red ones in a brown paper bag by Monday." The constable reluctantly passed on the message, adding, "You're free to go."

Once Nutter and Porky had dealt with the coppers, their main concern was to catch up with the surfies and their gold in the Kombi.

2

The flood waters had risen further and were flowing over the bridge. LP made a judgement call, without taking advice from Mason, who was sitting in the passenger seat. With foresight, he visualised himself on the other side of the bridge. Without hesitation, he drove straight into flood waters flowing across the bridge. The Kombi stalled and stopped halfway across. *So much for foresight,* he thought.

"This ain't good," said LP. "Oh well, my mistake. I'll get us out of this mess. Mason, get behind the wheel and press the winch release button, and I'll take it through to the other side."

LP slowly walked through the flowing water. There was a gap of twenty feet where there was no guardrail. If he lost his footing, he'd be like the others who had disappeared under the bridge. Step by step, he slowly pushed through the rushing waters.

"Hurry up," Bear yelled. "You've got company."

The swollen creek had flushed out water rats the size of small beavers, and they were headed for LP. He glanced around and saw six rodents swimming towards him. Teeth gnarling, ready for an evening meal.

"Oh shit!" he yelled. "Do something!"

"Turn the floodlight on, George," said Bear. "Before those rodents start chomping on LP's legs."

"If I do that without the engine running, we'll have one dead battery. That floodlight has the brightness of two million candles."

"Just do it *now*!" Bear shouted.

When George flicked the switch, the brightness was blinding, and the rodents turned and swam off. LP reached the other side of the bridge, secured the cable to a lamp post, and called out, "Mason, press the winch button."

The guys had luck on their side with the auxiliary battery connected directly to the winch, or they would have been stuffed. Mason pressed the winch button, and the Kombi was slowly pulled through the flooded waters.

Bear made his thoughts clear: "That was a close call; if you didn't make it, I was going to kill you!"

"That would be a bit difficult, as you would have been in the Kombi floating down the creek," LP replied, smiling for the first time that night.

Laughter from the guys could have been heard streets away, but it covered their fear of what might have happened.

Everyone except LP got back into the Kombi, glad to be out of the rain. Then, out of the darkness, a stranger climbed up the flooded embankment. He was drenched and wearing only his undies.

"Holy shit who are you?" Mason asked through the side window.

"My name's Bill. I'm from Western Australia. I was sleeping in my panel van across the creek in the park, and I guess the flood waters picked up the van. I still can't believe what happened, but at least I'm still alive. All I've got left is what I'm standing in: *my jocks*."

"Well, mate, we phoned the police; they are on the other side of the bridge. The water is subsiding; head over now and see those coppers. They'll help. Was there anyone else with you?"

"Nope, just me banging on the back window until I kicked it out," Bill replied.

Bill started to walk across the bridge as flood waters receded a little; he finally made it to the police for help. LP hoped he wouldn't get mistaken for another drunken bikie. Otherwise, he'd be arrested for unlawful exposure, vagrancy, and not having a licence, and when they found out he was actually sleeping across the creek bank, they'd most likely book him for illegal camping as well.

By now LP was cold, saturated, and starting to get the shivers from his creek crossing. He dried off his lanky body and shoulder length brown hair and then changed into jeans and his favourite t-shirt: brightly coloured with an image of a wave breaking, and the words "The Bigger, the Better." He climbed back into the driver's seat of George's red Kombi and turned the key to start the engine. It coughed and spluttered a couple of times before finally kicking over.

Looking back out the driver's side mirror, he could see Bill in handcuffs, being escorted over to one of the paddy wagons. With a street light at the end of the bridge, he saw one cop pull out his revolver, point it towards the back of Bill's head, and fire a shot. The other copper opened the back door to their temporary jail, and they both pushed Bill in, face down. LP thought, *Surely that copper didn't shoot him.* What was a more credible scenario: *The cop must have fired at those water rats.*

Using his foresight skills, LP figured the coppers must have seen the *Westie* dead or alive as a ticket to get back to the station early, and get out of the rain, leaving their copper mates to deal with the Bad Meadows bikies. That was the *Westie's* welcome to Queensland. Beautiful one day, in the slammer the next.

The guys left the unfolding drama behind them and headed to Romeo's Pizza Palace in downtown Brisbane, an area known as the Valley. It was the seedy underbelly of the city but had not gained the notoriety of King's Cross in Sydney.

By this time, all the guys had the munchies and were hanging out for a feed.

LP parked the Kombi a hundred yards up the road from Romeo's. They all got out except for Red, who said, "I'm staying with the Kombi. Just bring back a couple of slices of pizza, and don't be too long."

The reason Red didn't get out of the Kombi was that he had cut his toes on some broken glass back at the party, and he needed to bandage them to stop the bleeding. He didn't tell the guys how bad the cut was, because he wanted to avoid wasting time going to a hospital—it would delay getting to Bells Beach.

Romeo's was a great pizza place; not just any pizza, great pizza. The best order was the Godfather's Pizza. It was a true Italian-style pizza, just like the old country.

At Romeo's, you did *not* make eye contact with anyone—it could be taken the wrong way. The Valley was controlled by Mafia heavyweights. The nightclub next door was also under their control. Luckily, any time the guys had been in that part of town, they had never had any trouble. They ordered three pizzas and waited quietly.

Next door, a group of drunken troublemakers were trying to get into Romeo's nightclub, but they were turned away. They apparently took it as an insult that they were refused entry by a faceless voice that came through the door's peephole. In revenge, several decided to take a leak on the closed door, and urine seeped under the doorway into the club.

They had picked on the wrong people to piss on—or piss off. The door opened, and there was an all-out brawl on the footpath. Not one troublemaker was left standing after the bouncers and patrons were done with them.

"No one dishonours this place or our women," said one of the bouncers. He spat on them and turned to go back inside, slamming the door.

The pizzas were ready by this time, and the main man of the restaurant, with a scar from ear to cheek, said, "Boys, don't look left or right; go straight to your car, and leave quickly."

They all thought that sounded like good advice.

Bear said, "Good idea; let's get out of here."

Mason walked out with the pizza boxes in hand. He was a Leo Sayer look-a-like, with his long, black, curly hair. He also had an ear for music, but sometimes what came out of his mouth would be better left unsaid.

Mason made eye contact with Scarface and yelled, "You don't scare me!"

The guys realised they were in trouble and bolted out with the pizzas, avoiding the bodies that lay bleeding across the footpath outside the nightclub.

"Mason, you dickhead, you should have kept your mouth shut," said Bear.

"Can't help myself sometimes," he replied, while running with the pizzas. Bear had a better understanding of why Mason behaved the way he did. He was raised in a Masonic home.

They sprinted to the Kombi. The gangsters were right behind, wanting to inflict some damage to them.

Bear yelled, "Red, move over a bit; LP, get the Kombi rolling!" LP jumped in and tried to start the engine. "Start pushing;

the battery's flat again!"

"Try auxiliary."

"No go; it's flat, too!"

Bear, Cassa, and Brownie started pushing the Kombi, and George, a slow fourth, was still hobbling along, trying to catch up. The mob was gaining on them.

The Kombi finally started. Bear, Cassa, and Brownie ran up to the side door, pulled it open, and jumped in.

"Where's George?" shouted LP.

Mason, who had jumped in the front seat, juggling the pizzas, said, "He's still coming."

LP did a sharp U-turn. Bear reached out, grabbed George by the hand, and pulled him in the side door. LP did another sharp U-turn and left the gangsters in the distance.

With a sigh of relief, Bear said, "Just as well we didn't try to get into that nightclub. I don't think they'd like long-haired surfies, either."

Mason raised two pizza boxes from his lap, and Bear grabbed both, and all the guys started digging into pizza as LP drove.

LP looked down at the fuel gauge and said, "Hey guys, we've got to get petrol soon, or we're going nowhere."

Red came up with a bright idea; they could siphon fuel from a truck he knew was always parked in a back alley not far from where they were.

They headed down the road around five hundred yards and found the truck parked where Red had said it would be.

"There it is; turn the engine off and pull up across the driveway."

Bear and Cassa jumped out with a jerrycan and headed over to the truck. They proceeded to siphon as much petrol as they could in the shortest possible time. Unfortunately, just then, the owner of the truck came out onto the third-floor balcony of a nearby building.

"You bastards, I'll kill you!" he yelled. "Get away from my truck."

It was time to do a runner. Cassa struggled to carry the jerrycan, spilling petrol as he ran. The trucker pulled out a rifle, took aim, and fired. Luckily, it was pretty dark in the laneway, and his bullet missed Cassa. He panicked, dropped the can, and ran, empty-handed, back to the Kombi.

"Let's get out of here," Bear yelled as they climbed into the side door and slammed it closed.

The trucker fired again; lead ricocheted off the bitumen, sparked, and ignited the spilt fuel.

As the guys sped off in the Kombi, they saw a line of flame racing to the truck's fuel tanks. Within seconds, there was a huge explosion; one truck was destroyed, one truckie not happy, and part of the Valley about to be burnt down.

Nutter and Porky had taken a different route to avoid the flooded roads and bridge. Hot on their trail, Nutter's bikie gang were out to recover their coin. They had overheard the surfers talking about Romeo's pizza, so they figured that was where they would catch up with them. They arrived there on their Harleys, with two hundred other bikies following.

As the troublemakers from the nightclub started picking themselves off the footpath, Nutter pulled up and asked, "What happened to you lot?"

"The last thing I remember is some long-haired surfies walking across our backs after leaving the pizza house."

"These guys are tougher than I thought," said Nutter. "Yeah, and I bet that explosion and flames down in the Valley was their handiwork, too," replied Porky.

Nutter and Porky headed down to the back alley and found the truck ablaze. The truckie was soaking down his pride and joy with a nearby fire hose.

"What happened?" Nutter asked.

"Bloody long-haired surfies. If I catch 'em, I'll kill 'em." "No worries; if we get to 'em first, they're dead meat."

The bikies roared off just as the police and fire brigade arrived. Sarge said to the constable, "Looks like we can add this to the Bad Meadows charge sheet: destruction of property and arson. Put a call out to arrest all those bloody bikies; we'll lock 'em up for good this time."

"How low is the fuel, LP?" asked Bear.

"We've got a couple miles left in it. Around the corner there's a self-serve pump at a service station just down the road. I'll pull into the Esso servo, and we'll get fuel there. The coin-operated machine only takes twenty-cent coins. Dig deep, guys, and see how many we have."

"Is that it? Ten twenty-cent coins?" asked Bear.

"That's not going to take us far," added George.

"Two dollars of fuel will get us over the border. We'll fill up in the morning. The servos will be open then," LP said. He stopped the Kombi at the bowser.

Bear took the coins and dropped them into the slot. LP started to fill the tank, but the fuel bowser stopped with still a dollar to go. Bear kicked the bowser in frustration, but that didn't help. It looked like road rage without a road, as Bear's temper boiled over. He walked over to the coin slot in the wall and started thumping it, trying to make it work.

Brownie got out of the Kombi, grabbed the Golden Fleece emblem on top of the bowser, and started rocking it in frustration. That didn't help, either—it broke off. He was left holding a ram in his hands. "Oh shit! I didn't think that would happen."

However, something else happened: The fuel started to flow again and, when it got to two dollars, it didn't stop. After a while, the tank was full.

"Don't stop now; fill the long range fuel tank, too," said George.

"Brownie, put that Golden Fleece emblem on the ground, and I'll fill it up, too," LP said. "We can use it as a plastic jerrycan." LP filled the Golden Fleece, which looked like a small hollow merino ram. He put the hose back, and the self-service bowser stopped.

"You'll need a bung for that thing, or it's not riding in the back with us," said Bear.

"No worries. Grab that footy sock and shove it in the opening. That's it; there will be no fuel coming out now. Strap it on top of the Kombi, at the back of the surfboards, and we'll use it down the track."

3

As LP clicked over the Kombi and pulled out from a well-lit driveway, he glanced back in the mirror and spotted the bikers again.

"How's these guys? They don't give up. I bet they think we called the coppers on 'em," LP said, as he wondered how to lose them.

"I reckon it might be more than that," replied Red.

"Let's not wait around to find out. I know a shortcut, and they won't see us for dust," LP said with confidence. He'd snapped out of his depressive state of mind and had to find a solution to rid them of trouble following.

"What are you doing? This is a dead-end street!" Bear called out.

Looking back, the guys saw the bikies following in the distance.

LP turned off the bitumen and headed for the gutter. This wasn't really a shortcut, but he had a plan.

"Hang on, guys!" LP yelled as he hit gravel, sending George's Kombi fishtailing out of control, just missing some gum trees and heading towards a football field.

Bear screamed, "You're going to kill us all!"

LP took no notice, even though it looked like he was going to run down a team of football players.

Bear said, "That's real bright, LP. Those blokes are not going to be happy with us on their field."

LP steered the Kombi carefully through the footballers training under flood lights and stopped next to a man with a whistle around his neck. He turned and looked at LP, spat out his whistle, and said, "What the hell are you doing on our football field, LP?"

"We need some help, Donny," LP replied. "There's trouble following us. A bikie gang is chasing us. Can you help?"

"Yeah, sure, why not?" said Donny. "The guys could use some extra physical contact to blood them for next week's game. They get sick of running their bodies into these timber scrum rams. You guys piss off now, and we'll sort them out."

LP put his foot to the floor and sped off through the low fog. Donny yelled to his football mates, "Push the scrum rams together and stand in front of them."

It wasn't long before the bikies followed onto the field. The roar of two hundred bikies was almost deafening.

"Stand your ground; don't move yet," commanded Donny. Nutter and his biker mates had one intention—going straight through the footballers.

Low fog hid the scrum rams from sight. The footballers could only be seen from above the waist.

Donny yelled, "Now move!"

There was an opening left for the bikies to go through, but not for long. The lead bikies hit the scrum rams hidden in the fog and went flying through the air, landing with a thud. The rest proceeded to crash or turn to avoid further chaos.

Nutter got up, shouting, "I'll kill the bloody lot of you."

"I don't think so," replied Donny.

"There are two hundred of us, and twenty of you bum-sniffing footballers. This'll be the last game of football you'll train for."

"Give it your best shot, dickheads!"

Donny blew his whistle. To the left and the right, the reserve and B-grade teams finished their one hundred push-ups and rose up out of the fog.

"Let's show these guys some football skills that are not allowed these days on the field. One, the elbow; two, the eye gouge; three, the spear tackle; four, the biff. Go for it, guys! They're on our turf now; don't leave anyone standing."

The footballers charged the bikies from three sides with thumping tackles, spear tackles, eye gouging, and elbows, and they didn't forget the biff.

The training session was over, and the Bad Meadows bikie gang, knowing they'd been outplayed, rode or pushed their bikes off the field and into the distance.

"It's time for drinks. I'll see you all back at the club house," Donny called to his teammates, walking from the field.

The floodlights were turned off, leaving the field in darkness. LP looked in the rear-vision mirror and found no bikies in sight. He thought, *You can rely on Donny to get you out of a jam.* "Floor it; let's get some distance between those bikies and us.

We need to figure out why they want to kill us," said Bear.

"I think I may have had something to do with it," replied Red. "When I phoned the coppers about the van floating down the creek, Porky came down the hallway, and he thought I was calling the coppers on them. That's when I put his head through a wall. That's why they're after us."

"Good one, Red; you should have put Nutter's head there, too." Bear laughed.

The guys all had a good chuckle over that story.

"The south coast road is flooded, so we can't go that way," LP pointed out. "We have to make it to the contest on time. We'll head west and take the inland road, then south to Bells Beach."

"Speed bump up ahead; slow down," yelled Bear.

"Hang on," LP said, and then he sped up. "If they wanted me to slow down, the sign should read 'Slow bump'!"

Bump! Bump!

"Are you happy now?" asked Bear.

"Not quite; there's a roundabout coming up ahead."

"Look out! Everyone lean to the right. LP, don't get stuck on the roundabout again; it's not funny."

"Well, just tell me which exit to take, and no problem."

"Now, now, turn left!" LP kept going around, with a crazy grin on his face.

"Oops, missed it; hang on; we'll go around again."

"I can understand why they call you LP. You're like a broken record that just goes around and around. Now listen carefully, or I'll jump over there and drive myself," Bear snarled.

The direction sunk in, and this time, LP turned left and exited to the western freeway.

The guys settled in for the long drive to Bells Beach. The drive would take three days if they managed to avoid the flooded creeks and rivers along the coast road. Once they crossed the mountain range, it would be as dry as a bone. That part of the country was still in drought.

Eventually, they came to the border crossing. It was heavily lighted, with barbed wire and armed guards. A large spotlight was pointed at the Kombi, and the guys in the back woke up, wanting to know what was happening.

"Calm down," LP said. "Border security. They're going to search the van. Get rid of that weed in the back, quick smart."

Cassa quickly shoved a handful of grass into the shoebox with Wal, their pet cane toad. "Don't eat the grass, or you'll be one stoned toad!" he warned Wal.

The side door opened, and an armed guard lent forward and stepped inside the Kombi, and sat squeezed between Cassa and Brownie. "Have you got anything to declare?" he asked.

Cassa looked at Bear. Bear looked at Red.

"Do we have to declare the guns on the gun rack?" asked Bear. "No, but tell me what's the go with that knife and boomerang?" "Souvenirs, mate," replied Brownie.

The officer eyed them with suspicion. "That's one big knife; where did you get it?"

"It's a ceremonial knife carved from an extinct giant kangaroo jawbone from Dreamtime."

"Don't go walking down any streets with that thing," the officer warned, "or you'll get arrested."

"No problem officer; they're just souvenirs," Brownie repeated. "Now, look outside and see the sign. What does it say?"

Bananas are prohibited
past this checkpoint.

"You have to hand over all your bananas before crossing this security checkpoint. Do you declare you have no bananas? What's that moving in the box?"

"Just a pet from up north," Bear said.

"Well, let's have a look."

Bear lifted the lid of the shoebox, and there was Wal, the largest cane toad you've ever seen.

"What do you feed it, besides that grass?" the officer inquired. "Wal loves chewing on cockroaches for breakfast, and spitting them out, so don't get too close."

"Look, how long is this going to take?" asked LP. "We're on a tight schedule to get to Bells Beach for a surf contest."

"You're right to go. Guns, cane toads, and green grass from Queensland are not illegal. But never try to cross this border with bananas, or you'll all end up in the lock-up, and your vehicle will be confiscated."

"No worries, Officer; there are no vegetarians here." LP accelerated away with a sigh of relief.

"Alright, guys, what's next?" asked Bear. "We're almost out of fuel, and we haven't got enough coin to get us to Bells."

Red had a bright idea. Willy, Red's flatmate, had worked for PMG when it had been split to Australia Post and Telecom. Willy was an IT guy who had helped to design the electronic components for the latest telephone boxes.

"When we see a silver phone box, not the old red ones, we'll stop, and I'll get the coins out. I know the code to press, and the coin box will automatically empty."

"Okay, Mason, look up the map; where's the next truck stop?" asked LP.

"About fifteen miles down the road."

Sure enough, fifteen miles further on, there was a phone box out in the middle of nowhere.

"Red, go make your withdrawal from the phone box. Mason, fill the tank, and we'll be on our way."

Red realised that the wound on his foot, from the broken glass at the party, had started to bleed again. Walking to the phone box to get the coins had opened a large gash.

"You'll need stitches for that cut, mate, or you'll bleed to death," said Cassa.

"It'll be okay. I'll stop at the next town. There's sure to be a doctor's surgery," said LP.

"Yeah, you're right, and we're not far from a good camping site. We can get some target practice in and stay overnight," said Brownie.

The so-called town was not much more than a truck stop, but there was a sign:

LP said, "Red, you'll have to wait till seven thirty."

While they waited, Brownie told the guys about a secret aboriginal site he knew of that was worth having a look at and wasn't too far from the town.

At 7:30 am on the dot, a good-looking girl with blonde hair, wearing a white skirt and white blouse, walked up to the surgery door. She unlocked the door and entered.

"Mason, help Red into the surgery," said Bear.

Red hobbled over to the doorway. "Thanks, mate, I'm right now. I'll be back out soon."

Mason walked back to where he left his mates and saw George sitting on the Kombi floor, rubbing his ankle. "Why don't you have your foot looked out while we're here?

George said, "I'm not going to be the one stopping us from getting to Bells Beach on time. I'll strap my ankle with tape from the first aid kit. Grab it from the back of the Kombi; Good one, Mason. I'll be right now."

Cassa and Bear were up on the Kombi roof, checking that the surfboards and the Golden Fleece, now used as a jerrycan for fuel in reserve, were still securely tied to the roof racks.

Red was inside the surgery, chatting up the young doctor's assistant. Even though he felt throbbing pain from his wound, his instant attraction to the girl dissolved any thoughts of the stitches he needed. He put on a French accent and poured on the charm. When that happened, women melted into his arms.

The girl directed him over to a chair and made him comfortable. It was no ordinary chair; it was a dentist's chair.

"What's a dentist chair doing in a doctor's surgery, Kat?' Red asked as he quickly glanced at her name badge. He was quick off the mark. "My mates call me Red, so can you, darling." Now on first name basis, Red was thinking of other things to do while in the surgery.

"Our Dr. Punjab is multi-tasked in this small town," she replied. "He is also a practising dentist, and the dentist's chair doubles as a surgery table. Now, Red, lie back while I adjust the chair to a more suitable position."

"I could think of a better position, if you know what I mean." Kat walked over to the door, locked it, walked back over to Red, and then said, "The doctor doesn't arrive for another half hour. What did you have in mind?"

Red raised his hand and pulled Kat forward, kissing her passionately. "I think I'm in love," he said.

"We shouldn't waste any time, then," said Kat.

She slipped her knickers down one thigh, dropped them to her ankle, and straddled the dentist's chair. As Kat leant forward, her long blonde hair fell over Red's face. Her greenish blue eyes were mesmerising as she kissed him. Kat's passion engulfed Red like a praying mantis, about to devour its mate.

The guys were getting bored waiting in the Kombi and wanted to get on the move. "What's taking so long?" mumbled George.

"Oh, shit, look at that; the doctor's only arriving now."

As Kat unlocked the door so the doctor could enter, she said, "You have a patient waiting; I've already prepped him."

Red piped up, "Yeah, Doc, your assistant certainly knows how to relax a guy."

"So, how can I help you?" asked the doctor.

"I need stitches under my toes—I cut them on some glass." The doctor took a look and agreed. "Yes, five stitches should do the job. Do you have any feeling in your toes?" "Yes and no. I can't feel two of them."

"I have a surgeon friend in Sydney who could operate to fix the nerve endings. Your toes would be as good as new."

"What sort of specialist is he?"

"Like me, from Bombay. We both got our doctorate at the same time."

He pointed to the certificate on the wall.

Red looked closely and read, "Doctor of Philosophy." "This doesn't say you're qualified to be a general practitioner."

"Not yet in your state, but I'm doing a correspondence course from my old medical school in Bombay. When completed, I can add the letters GP after my name."

"So how can you practice in Australia without the right qualification?"

"Your hospital system is desperate for more doctors, and they just don't check very much. All I have to do is two years in the Outback, and I'll have a luxurious home on Sydney Harbour. Then I'll be sponsoring all my extended family to come to this great country."

"How will you afford to do that?"

"Medicare, young man! Bulk billing is the answer. Whether it's dentistry, veterinary, or medical; it doesn't matter. If they come in here, they're all bulk billed."

As Red walked out of the surgery, he asked Kat, "How can he get away with that?"

"It's simple. When he treats a dog for fleas, it's a child's rash; when he helps deliver a calf, it's a house call for a home birth; if he does a tooth filling, it's a flu injection."

"That's the best get-rich scheme I've ever heard."

"I don't like it, but I've got no choice; I'm stuck here." "Why don't you come with us? We're going to Bells Beach." "It's all a bit quick. I can't, really."

"Look, we'll be coming back through this way in the morning. Be ready at seven thirty, and we'll pick you up."

"I'll think about it, but a word of advice. Don't see that surgeon in Sydney; his nickname is Dr. Death."

Red planted a kiss on Kat's lips and walked out.

"Come on, mate, hurry up," called Bear.

As Red limped over to the Kombi, a few young local cow cockies followed him and gave him abuse for talking to one of their womenfolk.

Red climbed in the side door, and Bear picked up the shotgun and pointed it out the sliding Kombi door.

"Piss off, dickheads, or I'll blow you lot away! Drive now, LP." As they drove out of town, Brownie said, "I know a top spot to camp tonight. It's not far from here. Just follow the road behind that building, and it's about twenty miles."

"You couldn't call this a road; it's just a graded dirt track," said LP.

It didn't take long before Brownie said, "Pull over here." The Kombi pulled up in a cloud of red dust. In the distance, the sun was still rising across a barren dry red landscape. There had been no decent rain for years.

"This is the real Australia, where my ancestors lived for thousands of years. Look up to the left; see that outcrop of rocks? That's a sacred site; it's a female Bora Ring. It has something to do with women's business. Don't move any rocks, or bad shit could happen."

"Okay let's set up camp and have a break. Later on in the morning, we'll see if we can get some food off this land," said Bear.

By mid-morning, the guys were getting restless.

"Get the guns; we're going hunting," said Bear.

At Brownie's request, they agreed to only shoot feral animals, which competed with the local fauna for the little amount of feed in the barren landscape.

Bear grabbed the shotgun, LP took the .243, and Cassa got the .22. They had enough firepower to take down anything.

"Over there, Cassa, it's a rabbit," called Mason. "See if you can shoot it."

Cassa took aim and fired. The rabbit was still standing, so he shot again. It still didn't move, so he fired again, again, and again. He ended up shooting six times, and still the rabbit hadn't moved.

"You're a bloody city slicker," Mason said to Cassa.

"I might be from the city, but I know how to shoot, and I'm sure I hit that bloody rabbit. I'm going over to check it out."

The rabbit was stone cold dead.

"It was probably dead before you shot it. Look at its eyes. I think it's got that disease they introduced to control the rabbit plague: myxomatosis."

"Oh, bullshit. I shot it, and I'll eat it."

Cassa skinned the rabbit and cut it up into pieces to cook later. "I think you'll be the only one eating that rabbit," said George. "By late in the arvo, you'll all be hanging out for a feed, and you'll eat rabbit then. I bet you."

"Shut up," Bear said. "Look, over there by those rocks, about three hundred yards away. I saw something move."

LP raised the .243 with the telescopic sight.

"I'll give a shotgun blast to the left of the rocks. That should get whatever is behind there running on open ground," said Bear.

He fired both barrels. Instantly, two of the largest feral goats they'd ever seen ran across the red landscape. LP took aim and fired. It was a clean kill. One bullet to the back of the neck of both animals. LP felt a little apprehensive, having shot the goats, but it was food and, as Brownie said, they were feral goats, pests, just like the introduced rabbits.

"Okay, what do we do now?" LP asked.

"Get my knife," replied Brownie. "I'll skin one goat, cut off the hind leg, and make us a roast dinner. When we get back to the ceremonial site, have a look around for a dip in the ground. It'll be a fire pit. If you uncover it, you'll find some large stones. Just gather up some dry timber, and we'll start a fire over them. When there's only ash and coals left, brush the ashes and coals between the rocks, then I'll put the goat leg on the hot rocks."

"Hang on a moment," George said. "I'm not going to eat a leg of goat."

"George, you're an idiot. What if I said it was a leg of lamb covered in Brownie's bush tucker secret herbs and spices? Would you be fine with that?" LP said.

"Well, yeah."

"Then it's a leg of lamb. Put it on the hot rocks and cover it with the sheets of paper bark, and it'll be ready in a couple of hours," said Brownie.

Cassa proudly placed his rabbit portions on the stones, too. "Don't go eating my rabbit, you guys! I'm having roast rabbit tonight."

"Grab some potatoes out of the Kombi," Brownie directed George. "Wrap them in alfoil and put them on the side of the hot stones."

George did this, while mumbling to himself something about his sprained ankle and nobody cares about him.

4

"Have you seen Brownie?" Red asked Bear.

"Nope, he's probably back where the goats were shot. Two were shot, one was skinned, and the hind leg cut off. Both would be covered in paperbark. He should know better. This is snake country. I reckon there would be king browns, death adders, and tiger snakes around here. One bite from any of those, and you're stone dead in thirty minutes," said Bear.

Brownie was pegging the goat's hide on a bull ant nest. By morning, the hide would be eaten clean. A little more time in the sun, and it would be a great throw rug. He covered the remains of the goats with paper bark and said a few words of thanks for providing food for the journey.

He walked from behind the Kombi and joined the guys. He then started to tell them about the days when wombats, with their hairy noses, would pop their heads out of their holes in this desolate landscape.

"There are no wombats now; just holes; so, guys, watch where you're walking. Instead of wombats, king browns and death adders live in those holes. If you're not careful, you'll be an Australian reptile's next meal."

"Is Brownie bullshitting? The next thing he'll be telling us is there's crocodiles out there," Red said in disbelief.

"Well, Red, you're not far wrong about the crocs. When the channel country floods, it washes down crocs from up north. When the river system is dry, there are waterholes; aboriginals call them billabongs, and crocs make their homes there, waiting for prey like you. So steer clear of waterholes in dry river beds." Brownie's advice was taken onboard as all the guys nodded in agreement.

Mason butted into the conversation: "Well, I don't plan to find out if you're right or wrong soon. When I take a leak, I'll make sure there are no holes that you talk about. Brownie, what happened to the wombats?"

"Drought, mate; it hasn't rained out here for two years. Look at the ground; it's just red dirt. Only the Mulga trees and a few paper barks are still surviving. It's a harsh environment." He paused and pointed to the ground. "One day, it will look like this as far as the eye can see."

Red scratched his head, wondering what he was on about, while Mason kicked a dead rotted branch out of his way. Red said, "Looks like all I see is red dirt."

"No, look down again at that green grass shoot," Brownie said. "That's what you're on about, the Mitchell grass," said Mason. "When the drought breaks, the dormant roots deep in the ground will shoot up long blades of grass and transform this landscape from a sea of red to an ocean of green," Brownie explained with a concerned look on his face.

Brownie was interrupted by a smart arse comment from Cassa: "Did you run into any ancestors when you were out there at the bull ant's nest?"

Brownie took offence to that comment and answered, "Don't be like George, with more negativity. Have some respect for the people who were one with this land. Don't talk to me until you have some understanding, or I'll be pegging you out on that ant nest, and they'll eat you alive."

Mason, who didn't want to listen to Brownie and Cassa arguing about ancestors, ants, and red dirt, went over to check out what Brownie had done with the goat hide. Standing back at a safe distance, he looked down at the hide, covered in bull ants. He thought, *Brownie was right; anything on that ant mound would be eaten to the bone by tomorrow.*

Looking at sheets of paperbark partially covering the huge goat horns, which were at least thirty-six inches across from tip to tip, Mason had a bright idea: *The horns would make a great mounted trophy.* He picked up a sharp rock and hit the top part of the skull of the skinned goat. The horns dropped onto the red dirt. He picked up the horns and placed them over the bull ants' mound, alongside the hide, and then started to walk back to the campsite. Mason was deep in thought and didn't see the king brown snake curled up in a wombat hole as he walked past.

Bang! One strike to his left leg, and pain like broken glass rushed through his veins, seeming about to tear his heart apart.

Mason yelled, "Help! I've been bitten by a bloody snake." Mason was already becoming delusional as he crawled away from the snake, which had slithered away into its hole.

Bear arrived first. "Don't move," he shouted. He ripped his sleeve off his shirt and quickly tied it around Mason's thigh.

Mason was scared shitless. His heart was thumping, he was sweating, and he had the shakes.

Brownie arrived next. "That won't work," he said. "He'll lose his leg if you cut off his blood circulation. He'll be dead in twenty minutes."

"That's what I was taught at boarding school, so it has to be right," Bear argued.

"Our old professor told me that if you ever get bitten by a snake, wrap the whole leg firmly to restrict movement and blood flow, but don't cut if off completely," said Cassa.

"Do you want to stake his life on the professor's radical ideas, or listen to me?" Bear asked.

"What he needs is a GP," LP said.

"No, they're a waste of time," said Red.

"I'll just trust the professor," said Mason. "What else did he say?"

"Catch the king brown," said Brownie. "Don't kill it, but milk the venom, and then drink it."

"You've got to be kidding. I've never heard of that," Mason responded in a weak voice"

"Well, you've got twenty minutes to decide, or we'll be strapping your body to the roof racks all the way to Bells Beach," said Bear.

"Okay, do it," Mason said, as he closed his eyes.

Brownie went back to the Kombi and pulled out a six-foot length of PVC conduit. He slipped a length of string down the hollow tube, tied a slipknot at the end, and headed over to the wombat hole. He prodded the snake, but it struck out and slithered along the red dirt. Brownie chased after it. He placed the PVC tube and slipknot ahead of the snake, and looped it around the head, pulling it tight.

He caught it alive.

"Red, grab that jar," yelled Brownie. "Get some cling wrap and cover it."

Brownie grabbed the snake at the back of the head, and Red milked the snake's venom as it bit down on the jar.

"Okay, quickly mix it with a little water, and let's cross our fingers that the professor was right," said Brownie.

Red said to Mason, "Open your eyes; can you hear me, Mason? There's not much time left; take this and hope our old mate the professor is right."

Mason looked up, nodded his head, and whispered, "If anyone knows what to do, it's him. I've seen him catch snakes and carry them in his t-shirt against his skin. He was born to be a zoologist." His voice was fading. "I trust him. Let me drink."

Mason took two gulps, coughed a couple of times, and then Bear and Brownie picked him up and carried him back to the campsite. All they could do after that was wait for a miracle.

Sunset approached, showing the most amazing red colours that blended the red dirt with the setting sun.

"Let's eat while we still have some light," said LP. He started to carve the roast and placed potatoes on everyone's plate.

Brownie got compliments on his bush cooking skills.

They only had three six packs of beer, plus a handful of weed left that Wal was looking after; they hoped he hadn't eaten too much.

"I reckon it's time to crack open a couple of coldies and smoke a joint," said Cassa. "We all need to chill out."

Cassa walked over to the Kombi and opened the side door. He lifted up the shoebox lid, thanked Wal for looking after his weed, and then rolled a huge joint and lit it. Taking a puff, he handed it around the fireplace. The guys had thrown more wood onto the hot coals, and the fire gave off enough heat to keep them all warm as the night temperature fell.

Mason's strength started to come back as he blinked his eyes and his vision started to focus. "Don't leave me out; hand me that joint." He slowly stretched out his right arm, taking the joint to his lips and took a deep breath, and soon he felt no pain. He was starting to look on the bright side of life.

"Are you trying to start a new fashion trend, Bear, with a one-sleeve shirt?" asked Red.

Bear realised, after all the panic with Mason's snake-bite, that it looked a bit stupid wearing a shirt with one long sleeve. He grabbed his remaining sleeve and ripped that one off, too.

"What do you think, guys?" Bear blurted out.

"That could be the next outback clothing trend to take off," Mason replied, while drawing in another deep breath of pot.

Bear pointed to LP and said to Red, "Why don't you go over to the Kombi and cheer up LP? I think he's got the grumps for having to do most of the cooking. He's slipping into one of his depressive moods. He must get his brooding from his Welsh ancestors."

"What is it that brings his mood changes on?"

"He thinks too much, instead of living in the present. He says that sometimes things bubble up from the past."

"Like what?"

"LP hates the fact that he can barely read or write. He thinks he's not that smart. His one saving grace at school was that he learnt how to play chess and became pretty good at it. It helped reshape his thinking. Moves on the board are like decisions in life. Plan, anticipate, defend, attack, and win.

"He told me he went to a private school in the sixties, and it was hell. Every day, up to forty students at a time, like almost half the class, would be lined up against the wall, for answering a question wrong. One particular Christian Brother liked inflicting pain, and he would await each victim to step forward and enforced his total control. He dished out his form of education with a thick leather strap, lashing down from shoulder height. He would use all his force to give them one of his best on the palm of their hand. LP always hoped he'd be at the end of the line, so the Brother would be worn out and wouldn't be able to hit him as hard. By the time he was finished, he was red in the face and looked like he was about to explode."

Red butted in, "Hang on, that's not education; that's torture." "Yeah, they were called Christian Brothers, but some would be better titled Brotherhood of Evil. You get my drift. Why not go talk to LP about Double Island and the best surf he ever had? It was during the cyclone, when the swells were thirty to forty feet high and the *Cherry Venture* ran aground. It was a Scandinavian freighter, sixteen hundred ton without cargo. The cyclone pushed it high up on Teewah Beach, just a mile south of Double Island Point."

Red walked over to LP and said, "Hey, LP. LP, I'm talking to you. Answer me."

"Yeah, Red, what do you want?"

"I see you're sitting over here by yourself and thinking too much. I'm here to cheer you up. Think of a song that would lift your spirits."

LP started humming a tune and then sang, "Unchain my mind, let me be free, open my heart, let me be me."

"The tune's right, but I think you've got the words mixed up. It's better than watching you mope, though. Tell me about the best surf you've ever had."

"That would be when we rode out that cyclone at Double Island Point. The waves were up to forty foot high, with tubes you could fit a truck in. Let's hope the waves are as good as that at Bells."

"What else do you remember of that weekend?"

"Dolphins. The dolphins rode the waves with us. It was just unbelievable. It was the most pristine surfing spot in Australia, and no one knew about it. The only way to get there was by four-wheel drive, along the beach on low tide."

"Did you have a four-wheel drive?"

"No, Gordon had one. He would take us up there from Rainbow Beach whenever the tide was low, even if it was two o'clock in the morning. We'd arrive and load up his orange-painted army blitz with surfboards, food, and drinks, and be on the go when he was ready."

"Yeah, I remember that weekend well. They had started mining the untouched Double Island for zircon and RuCon. I guess you could call us the first environmental activists to try to close down mining on Double Island. Kato and I climbed over the dunes like commandos to take out a generator that ran twenty-four hours a day to operate the sand pumps.

"Kato's instincts kicked in that night, and he stopped the generator operating. You could hear the fan blades slowly grinding to a halt; it was such a still night. Kato and I ran from the mining site, down the track to the mine workers' huts. It was bright as day at the camp, with floodlights overhead. We kept running past the miners and over to the sand dunes. There were lots of miners still up drinking, but they didn't take notice of two surfers running past. The workers didn't realise until the next morning what had happened to their generator.

"We knew what we had done was reported to police, because the media got hold of the story, and we heard it on the morning news bulletin. Until then, as far as the government was concerned, there'd been no mining at Double Island.

"Mining was only allowed south of Indian Head on Fraser Island. Most Queenslanders were aware of sand mining on Fraser Island, but not on Double Island. Of course, it turned out that the government did know all along, though—later, the media found minutes from secret cabinet meetings."

"Yeah, Kato and my actions that weekend focussed media attention on what was happening on our beautiful beach. There was a public outcry after the government cover-up was exposed, and the sand mining was stopped immediately.

"Later, there was a blockade on the Noosa River to stop a new generator being transported thirty miles up the beach. That had even more of an impact; without the new generator, the mining was totally finished."

"Hang onto those thoughts, mate, and have a bit of a rest," said Red. "We've got a big day ahead of us tomorrow."

The rest of the guys were sitting around the campfire. Cassa said, "You know, Brownie, you're full of shit. There's no Dreamtime. Your ancestors were just hunters and gatherers who lived off the land. They didn't progress until Europeans came along."

With the ancient sound of a didgeridoo echoing through his mind, Brownie took offence at Cassa's remarks.

He stood up and said, "Forty thousand years ago, your Euro ancestors were still living in caves and gluing their Stone Age tools together, thinking about creating the wheel. By then, my brothers from Dreamtime already understood the aerodynamics of flight. They took a tree branch and reshaped it, not only to fly, but to return to my brothers who launched it into the air."

"Sure, but your ancestors were tribal for tens of thousands of years. So with that know-how, back in Dreamtime, why didn't your people progress like other civilisations?"

"It's like the crocodile. It reached its optimum potential millions of years ago and stopped evolving. It was the same with my ancestors; we had reached oneness with the land, and all was provided for us. We had reached our optimum potential through custom and ritual."

The guys enjoyed the time sitting around the campfire, telling stories, but they kept an eye on Mason's condition. He was going in and out of consciousness and having visions. He didn't know where he was or what was happening to him. Smoking that joint didn't help.

Mason said, in a delusional state of mind, "Turn the spotlight on. The Bora Ring; turn it on. Women! Seven women! Walkabout. You all are chosen."

Bear said, "Brownie, grab that damp rag and put it on Mason's head. See if that'll bring his fever down."

Mason continued screaming, "Chosen ones, undo your clothing. Love; one mind; ecstasy; what's happening? Where are you from? Are you on walkabout?"

The seven women spoke to Mason: "We are from another time and place. Ancient Bora Rings are our time-line markers, transporter; alignment of the heavens, time, and space. The technology of a thousand light-years away will merge with your world. Your scientists are not far off unravelling the mysteries of life. Find future knowledge at your fingertips. Life renewed. When you reach your journey's end, look for guidance from the sea, and you will achieve your aim to be the best."

Silence filled the night air, and LP whispered, "He's sleeping; let's hope he makes it through the night."

* * *

At sunrise, Mason woke up without fever, looking a lot better. LP asked if he understood what he had been talking about the night before.

Mason repeated what he could remember of the visions he had seen and heard.

All the guys connected with his recollection and felt as though they were part of his dream or hallucination. They also talked among themselves, agreeing with recollections of women standing before them, unclothed.

Bear said, "Let's cut the crap and get this show on the road. Pack up; we're getting out of here. This place gives me the spooks." Just before they left, LP pointed over to the Bora Ring.

"What's that standing at the opening of the Bora Ring?"

The stones of the Bora Ring had been placed thousands of years ago to resemble the shape of a woman's womb. This was an unusual shape; usually, Bora Rings were shaped like circles.

The guys looked to where LP was pointing and saw a rolled-up parchment.

Brownie warned everyone, "Don't touch anything; it must be part of this sacred site. Just leave it where it is."

Mason spoke up. "I don't know what happened last night, but you have to take it. Don't leave it behind. It has something to do with the future. I remember the numbers '0101100000; 0101100101' and something about connecting with one and zero."

"Anything else?" asked LP.

"Something about an image and keep it safe."

Bear asked LP to take the parchment, which looked like a scroll, and put it in the Kombi. LP did as he was asked but was of the opinion that they had smoked too much pot around the campfire and it was screwing with their heads.

Brownie again warned them all, "Bad shit will befall us if you remove anything from this site."

"Crap," Bear replied. "We'll leave you behind if that will make you happy. Let's go!"

5

Together, all the guys helped to pack up the campsite, leaving it the same way they had found it. Mason was starting to feel much better. Brownie retrieved the goat hide from the bull ant nest and grabbed the horns for Mason. He threw the hide over the surfboards and roped it down to dry out further in the sun as they drove.

"Brownie, why don't you strap the horns to the front of the roof racks? That'll turn a few heads on the way to Bells."

"Okay, Mason. Anything you say; you're another one of the walking wounded."

They were on the road again. As they left the red dirt track and turned back onto the bitumen, Red said, "When we go back through town, stop at the doctor's surgery."

"What for?" asked Bear. "Have the stitches come out?"

"No, I told Kat we'd pick her up on the way through. If she's coming, she'll be waiting outside the surgery at seven-thirty."

"We'd better pick up the pace after that then, or we won't make it to Bells," said George.

"Oh, George, you're a worrywart," replied Red. "We'll get there and we'll win! We'll take the prize money and be cashed up; you wait and see."

"Yeah, I'll believe it when I see it, and if we don't make it to the contest on time, don't say I was the one that slowed us down at the doctor's surgery," George responded negatively.

When they pulled up at the surgery, Kat was there, waiting.

Bear opened the side door, and she got in.

Kat leant down as she entered the Kombi. She was a tall, slim girl, with an athletic figure. As she moved over to Red, she planted a big kiss on his lips and got ready to enjoy the journey with all the guys.

Bear slammed the door closed and said, "Let's get out of here." As the morning sun warmed the inside of the van, so, too, was the roadway warmed. It became a shimmering heat haze rising from the bitumen. From a distance, the faded red Kombi, covered in bulldust, would have resembled a speeding gold bullet, cutting a path through a desolate stretch of highway, with no end in sight. After a while, Cassa asked, "How about pulling over? I'm cramped and hot. Let me out of this tin can. I'm getting claustrophobic and need to stretch my legs."

LP stopped near a large signpost that read:

Posidimen Mining
Do Not Enter

"Where do you think that gate leads?" Cassa asked.

"It leads you to millionaires," Red replied. "Anyone who bought shares in that company when they were penny-halfpenny shares is now a millionaire."

"That's bullshit," Bear said. "It's all on paper. When the mining boom ends, those blokes will be owing money."

Looking into the distance, they could see heavy machinery hauling coal out of a deep, open-cut mine.

"What do they do with the hole when they finish mining?" George asked Bear.

"One of two things: Either they take out their big sucking pumps and allow it to fill with water to become a large billabong in this desert landscape, or they fill it with garbage from the city."

"If you're waiting for me to give a shit, you'd better pack lunch, it could take time, "George replied.

"Cassa, are you alright now? Are you over your panic attack? Have you got circulation back in your legs? We're wasting time. Let's go." LP started the Kombi and they drove off.

The guys settled in for a long drive to the surf competition at Bells Beach, hoping they hadn't come all that way for nothing.

The hours passed with Brownie doing his weight exercises—any chance to add muscle for the body-building contest back in Brisbane. Cassa was constantly brushing his hair and always looking at himself in his compact mirror for any new zits to pop. Red thumbed through the latest IT magazine, keen to pick up any new ideas. Bear pulled down the guns and cleaned them, making sure they were in working order. Mason sat in the front seat as the pain was starting to come back from the snakebite.

"Bear, can you roll a joint?" Mason asked. "I'm hurting here." Bear slowly rolled one, making sure not to drop a gram of weed; he lit it, took a deep breath, and passed it around. LP was driving and was not happy as the van started to fill up with smoke.

"Keep the windows up," Cassa said.

"It's getting harder for me to see," replied LP.

LP wound down his window, grabbed the front door with both hands, and stuck his head out the window.

"You steer, Mason; I can't see a thing."

Heading towards them was a huge semi-trailer filled with cattle.

"Okay, Mason, straight now; a little to the left," said LP. The truckie couldn't believe his eyes. The vehicle coming towards him looked like it was on fire, full of smoke, and the driver's head and hands were outside the door.

The truckie looked down at his bag full of pills and decided it was time to give up the uppers. As the two vehicles passed in the outback, the trucker thought, *I'm over this shit.* He hurled his bag of drugs out the window.

LP pulled his head back from the Kombi window and was back in control, with both hands steering a course to Bells. He said, "Mason, wind your window down to let the smoke out. Someone reach over and open the side door."

A moment later Red called out, "But it still smells like something burning." He looked back to see more smoke at the back of the Kombi.

"We're on fire!" Bear yelled. "Pull over."

LP pulled over to the side of the road, jumped out, and ran to the back hatch. He lifted the latch open, and yes, Bear was right; one of the batteries had caught on fire. The metal bracket holding it in place had touched against the terminal, and the battery casing was literally melting down. Now flames were spreading over the fuel tank.

"Quick, everyone, grab a handful of dirt and throw it on the batteries," said Bear.

Cassa, Red, and George jumped out of the side door, grabbed some dirt, and started throwing it over the batteries. By this time, the second battery was also on fire, and its casing began melting. Seconds later, the fire was out. Everyone was thankful that the Kombi hadn't exploded while they were driving; they would all have been incinerated in a fireball.

Luck was on their side for now, but how long would it last? The batteries still needed to work. LP jumped into the driver's seat and clicked her over. To their surprise, the Kombi started.

"Red, can you make sure that the brackets are holding down the batteries securely this time?"

"Okay, no worries."

He clamped them down and was about to close the hatch when he called out, "Hey, guys, check this out. There's a bag in here."

"George, it's your van; do you know what it is?"

"It's probably just the jack and wheel brace. Don't worry about it; let's get on the go."

Red grabbed the bag, opened it, and found it full of muddy-looking coins, a bit like old pennies. For a moment, he thought that he'd hit the jackpot. He rubbed the mud from one of the coins, and saw it read "South Africa."

"They're just some foreign coins. So much for a lucky break!" "Throw them in the back," George said. "We should get a few dollars out of them. We could sell them at a flea market as old coins, or make them into medallions. Mason, that's your job. When we stop next, there's a can of silver spray paint rolling around in the back of the Kombi. Clean them up, paint them, and we'll make some money from 'em." "Brownie, what are you doing?" asked Bear. "What does it look like? I'm having a shave."

"Can you do that somewhere else? We don't want to see you lathering up and shaving your legs. Go around beside the Kombi, not in front of us."

Brownie heeded Bear's advice and walked out of sight. A few minutes later, he came back and asked, "Who wants to wax my back? I've got to be hairless for the body-building contest next week."

"You're on your own with that one, Brownie."

Kat said, "I'll do it; where's the wax and cloth strips?" Brownie handed the cloths and the jar to Kat and then took off his tank top.

"How long did it take to get muscles like that?"

"Twelve months of solid workout at my gym. Do you think I've got what it takes to win a muscle building contest?"

"It all looks good to me. Now turn around and lean up against the Kombi. This is going to hurt. Are you going to cry like a baby or grin and bear it?"

"Funny. Ha ha! Just do it."

A few minutes later, there were some grunts and groans of pain as Kat ripped strips of hair off Brownie's back.

Bear said, "I hope you're not having a Brazilian over there. Just keep your boxer shorts on. Otherwise, we're leaving you behind." "Kat, would you rub suntan oil onto my back? It'll reduce the redness," Brownie said.

Kat gently rubbed the oil over Brownie's now hairless, smooth back, using slow, circular strokes. Red noticed what was happening and started to get jealous. He walked over to them.

"You've oiled him up enough; how about my back and shoulders now?"

Kat turned, smiled, and said, "Don't get jealous, Red. I'm with you."

They walked back to the Kombi to declare their love for each other.

LP climbed onto the Kombi roof rack to check out the goat hide.

"Hey, check this out; the mixture of red dirt and sun has changed the goat hide's colour and texture. It's soft and golden. Feels good, too. Brownie, you were right about getting that salt from the salt pan near the Bora Ring."

"I told you, all you had to do was rub the salt and suntan oil into its hide and leave it in the sun; job done," Brownie replied.

"I'll throw it over the seat; it might help my piles. This long-distance driving is getting to be a pain in the butt. There's no time to wait; let's get on the move."

6

"We haven't got much petrol left," said LP.

"Don't forget the fuel on the roof," Mason reminded him. "Yeah, we'll keep that for an emergency. Let's start heading back to the coast; we're past all that flooding and rain now. George, look up the map and see how far it is to the next town." "It's twenty miles, and we won't make it without more fuel,"

George reported.

"I'll take bets on it. This Kombi could run on the smell of an oily rag," said LP.

"Anyway, we've still got fuel up top."

"Don't forget, we don't have any cash until the banks open on Monday morning," Bear reminded everyone.

"Just find me another phone box, and I'll make a withdrawal." Red laughed.

"We'll have enough coin for petrol, and we still have enough time to make it to Bells for the contest on Sunday morning."

"You did pay the entrance fee for the contest before we left Brisbane, didn't you?" Cassa asked LP.

"No, they said to pay at registration on arrival," LP replied. "Well, where are we going to get a hundred dollars to register?" asked Bear.

"We could try getting more coins out of telephone boxes,"

Red replied, "but there aren't enough truck stops out here in the middle of nowhere to find the right silver phone booths."

"It would be a lot simpler if banks made it easier to withdraw money on weekends. Like if you could press the right code and it would spit money out of the bank wall."

"Red, you're completely off the wall with your ideas. There's no way that will happen. That bloody IT mag you're reading sounds more like a comic book. You'd be better off using it as toilet paper," said Bear.

"Mark my words; it won't be only getting cash out of a wall. Unless it's plastic, the only thing you'll be able to buy is lollies with your loose change."

"You mean paper money is going to be plastic?" Bear asked, sounding unconvinced.

"Yes," Red replied adamantly.

"I'll say it again: the only thing that mag is good for is wiping your ass! I don't want to hear any more about that crap. Let's keep rolling; we've a contest to win, and I won't be accepting plastic money when we collect the winnings. I want only paper money … Red, you're dreaming, mate; that will never happen."

"Talk to me about it in thirty years. It's called technology." "Now let's get back to the problem of how to raise a hundred dollars to enter the contest."

"My flatmate, Willy," Red said. "The geek who told me about the code for the telephone boxes; he said he did the same thing with pokie machines at the last place he was working at. He designed and programmed the chip and circuit boards for the new pokie machines.

"The new machines have no handles to pull; you just press a button to play. He told me that, if you find the latest machines without handles, press '1 x 1' till the free spins come up, then

'1 x 1' forty-eight times, and then hit 'Maximum bet,' and the maximum pay line will come up."

"Okay, Red, that's a good plan. Keep an eye out for a sports or footy club; they'll have pokies."

The next town they came to was Eden. There was a footy club with pokies across the road from the surf beach and camping area.

Bear and Brownie decided to go surfing.

"I'm going nowhere," said George. "My sprained ankle is still swollen."

"I still feel pretty weak from that bloody king brown," said Mason. "But I'll go with you, LP, and have a go at those pokies. Let's see if your geeky mate was right."

Mason and LP signed in as visitors at the footy club and went straight through to the pokie room to look for the right machine.

"Yep, that'll do," said LP.

Mason dropped twenty twenty-cent coins through the machine, pressed '1 x 1' several times, and the free spins came up.

"We're halfway there; now hit it forty-eight times."

On the forty-ninth hit, LP changed to Maximum bet, pressed down hard, and the free spins came up, paying out the maximum amount—five hundred dollars.

"We could make a living out of this, LP!" "How long will this last?"

"Not long. The club will remove any machines that are not returning a profit."

"We're ahead of the game. We robbed them before the bastards robbed us."

"These things are nothing more than false idols that people will stand at and worship in expectation of a greater gain," said LP.

"Well, it's bullshit. There's no way to win in the long run, unless you beat them at their own game." Mason thanked LP for the lecture. "Let's collect and get out of here."

LP collected the five hundred dollars, and they headed out of the club and over to the Kombi. By this time, Bear and Brownie were back out of the surf.

"Hey guys, we've got no problem with money now. Red's flatmate's theory on winning on those poker machines was right. LP hit the jackpot at the footy club."

"Great. We'll stay the night here and head off at daybreak. That'll give us enough time to register and win the contest," Bear said. "Let's take the Kombi over to that camping area, and we'll set up. LP, you're cashed up; go grab three pizzas and go back to the footy club and buy a couple of six packs of FourX beer."

"I'm coming, too," said Cassa.

LP returned with two cartons of Resches beer, and Cassa carried the three pizzas.

"That's southern beer. We're not drinking that stuff!" Bear yelled.

"The bloke over at the bottlo said that it would taste like XXXX beer after you down a couple. He said they don't sell that beer in this town because no one drinks it. He reckons it's foreign beer."

"You should have told him he doesn't know what he's talking about. Everyone up north drinks only XXXX or they're not a Queenslander," said Bear.

"Alright! Throw over one of those beers and pass the pizza around."

Most of the guys agreed that it the first decent feed in days. "Well, I thought the roast was pretty good back at the Bora Ring," said LP.

"Yeah, but takeaway is better," said Red.

"Yeah, sure, if you like standing in a line to be served, and waiting another twenty minutes before it's cooked."

After downing another beer, Bear said, "I've got an idea. If you had a takeaway food outlet, where the pizzas are already cooked and ready to go, and there was no waiting, you would make a fortune."

"Bear, if you think that's a goer, let's do something about it when we get back over the border," Red said.

"I'm putting the billy on for a hot cuppa," said Red. "Anyone else for tea?"

"Nope," everyone else replied.

"Cold beer is going down better than a hot cup of tea." "Damn, there's no milk. I'm going over the road to get some." Cassa said, "I'll come with you." He was quick to change into his favourite floral shirt, a real chick magnet. He put on his Levi jeans and slipped on a pair of moccasins. With a couple brushes of his long blond hair, he was ready, rehearsing his best pick-up lines.

They all figured that Cassa's charm came from his Irish heritage.

As Red walked into the shop, Cassa called out, "I'm going into the club to see if I can pick up some women. I'll catch up with you later."

Cassa walked off down the road to the footy club.

Red went to the shop's fridge cabinet, grabbed a pint of milk, placed it on the counter, and searched through his pockets for loose change. He pulled out a twenty-cent piece, placed it on the counter, took the milk, and left.

As he walked out, he was confronted by two coppers.

"We haven't seen you in this town before. Where are you from?"

"It's a free country. I can go where I like," answered Red.

"Are you alone or here with some others?" one copper asked.

"What does it look like? I'm standing here alone. It's pretty obvious," was Red's reply.

"So you're a bit of a smart ass, too," said the other; he had sergeant stripes on his uniform. "Show us some ID."

"I don't have to, this ain't a communist country," Red fired back.

"Do you have any money on you?" the sergeant asked. "Why, do you want to roll me?" was not the best answer from Red.

"You're under arrest!" said the sergeant.

The officers grabbed Red, and the milk spilt over the coppers as they tried to handcuff him.

One officer said to the other, "This guy will be a nice little earner for the magistrate on Monday: resisting arrest, assault, and vagrancy. Walk him over to the station and lock him up."

As the officer walked Red to the station with his hands handcuffed behind his back, Bear said, "Bugger, check that out; the coppers have got Red."

"What are we going to do?" George asked.

"Well, for a start, I'll go get another bottle of milk, and we'll have a cuppa. Then we'll figure out what to do."

As he sipped on his cuppa, George asked Bear, "How come everyone knows you as Bear?"

"George, you almost got your head knocked off back at Red's place for asking stupid questions, so don't go there. It's a long story."

"Come on, tell me. I want to know how you got the nickname, Bear," George insisted.

"Okay, listen and learn. My grandfather's family escaped Russia during the Bolshevik revolution in 1917. They got on a train in Moscow and travelled through Siberia all the way to Vladivostok. There, they managed to catch a steamer going to India. After that, my grandfather joined the Indian army. He couldn't join the British army, because he wasn't a citizen of Britain. His son, my father, joined the Indian navy when he was old enough and rose to commander of the Indian fleet. The ships he commanded during World War II were both sunk. After the war, he migrated to Australia. That's why I'm here today.

"And the question you asked, why am I called Bear? I'm nicknamed Bear after the Russian Bear—Stalin. I'd rather be called Bear than Stalin, thank you."

After all had finished their hot tea, Bear decided that the best thing to do was to go surfing again. They hoped, while out surfing, they could come up some ideas to get Red out of jail before they left for Bells in the morning.

Bear and Brownie changed into wetsuits, picked up their surfboards, and walked from the campsite, over the dunes and down to a perfect reef break. They paddled across a deep ocean gutter. Fishermen with lines cast out made it an obstacle course to reach the surf break. Within thirty seconds, they were waiting for their first waves to come barrelling in.

Bear and Brownie rode their last waves right in to the beach. The sun was setting behind the mountains in the distance as the guys walked up the beach to the camping area.

They helped each other unzip their wetsuits from the back, towelled off, and changed into some dry boardies.

"Did anyone come up with a plan to get Red out of jail?" asked Brownie.

George answered, "I've got an idea. You know when we were all around the campfire at Red's place? Well, those idiot bikies were passing around their latest toy. It's a silencer for a .22 rifle, and guess what?"

George walked over to the Kombi, searched through his backpack, and pulled out what looked like a small metal tube. He said, "I've got the silencer. Those bikies were too drunk to notice me slipping it into my pocket."

"I like your thinking," said Bear. "We take out those streetlights, use the winch to pull out the jail bars, and we're all out of here, first up in the morning."

George said, "I think we need a little more planning than that."

"Yeah, but it's a start. We can work out the rest later."

That night, the guys discussed in detail how they would break Red out of jail.

"Set your watches for 4 am," said Bear.

They all settled into their sleeping bags to get some shuteye. A tarp stretched from the Kombi roof and pegged to the ground gave shelter from the morning dew.

* * *

As Red lay on the bunk in his cell, Johnny Cash's immortalised words echoed through his head: "I hear the train a-comin', it's rolling round the bend."

* * *

The Bad Meadows bikie gang had taken a punt that the surfies would turn up at the surf break in Eden.

Rather than ride into town and attract attention, they stopped at a rest stop just out of town. There was a large, weathered building across from where they were standing.

Nutter ordered, "Tiny, go over and see if the door of that hall is locked."

Tiny walked up a couple of stairs, ducked to go under the large balcony overhang, raised his foot, and kicked the door in. He yelled, "It's open! No one's here; come on over."

Nutter and the rest of the bikies kick-started their bikes in a thunderous roar and rode over to the building.

"Tiny and Jimbo," Nutter said, "go into town and look around the beaches for those idiot surfers. When you find them, come back, and we'll all go sort them out and get our bloody coins back."

Jimbo and Tiny rode out onto the main highway, leaving their bikie mates at the building. They rode into town and checked out all the beaches, but found no sign of the Kombi or the surfers.

As Cassa walked from the footy club with a blonde under each arm, heading back to the campsite, one bikie said to the other, "Well, look over there; ain't that one of those surfies?"

"Yep, let's get him and take him back to Nutter and Porky," Tiny said.

"We're supposed to find all of them and the Kombi, not just one," replied Jimbo.

"Just get him, and we'll make him talk," was Tiny's answer. Jimbo and Tiny pulled up and jumped off their bikes, and Tiny tapped Cassa on the shoulder.

"We've been looking for you," said Tiny.

"I don't know who you are," Cassa replied.

"We know who you are. Get on the back of my mate's bike. You're coming with us."

"And if I say no, what are you going to do about it?" replied Cassa in a defiant voice.

"Well, pretty boy, you won't be so attractive after we finish with you," Tiny said, as he pushed the girls aside.

"Well, that's a reasonable request; just leave the girls alone and I'll come with you guys."

Cassa climbed onto Jimbo's bike, turned to the two blondes, and said, "I'll see you back at the footy club."

With those last words, the bikies rode out of town with Cassa. Ten minutes later, they arrived back at the hall. Along the way, Cassa had hoped to spot some coppers that could make themselves useful and get him out of what fate had in store for him, but he didn't see any.

Nutter asked, "Well, where are they?"

"We've got someone who can tell us where the rest of them are," Tiny replied.

"Okay, tie him up on that chair," Nutter ordered. "Well, pretty white boy, tell us where your stupid surfie mates are."

"Get stuffed; I'm telling you nothing." "Tiny, work him over, but don't kill him."

Tiny gave a left and right punch to Cassa's head. His head fell forward as he was knocked unconscious.

"I wanted him alive," Nutter said.

"I barely touched him."

"You idiot, you don't know your own strength."

The bikies walked away and continued drinking. Tiny said, "When he wakes up, I'll find out where the rest of them are."

"I don't think so," Nutter replied. "I've got another idea. When he's conscious and can talk, I'll let Gena have her way with him. He'll tell her everything. This guy's a sucker for a beautiful woman."

A little after midnight, Cassa started to come around. Nutter and the other bikies were pretty pissed by this time.

Nutter yelled to Gena, the bikie group's girl, "See what you can find out from this asshole surfie."

Gena walked over to Cassa's chair, wearing red, high-heeled stilettos and a long black flowing, dusty, Drizabone waistcoat. The only other clothing she had on was the tiniest red polka dot bikini.

As Cassa looked up, he thought, *Evil eyes, don't look at me, don't play your games with me.*

His heart started pumping a little harder. Gena walked towards him, placed her legs over his, and sat down on his lap. She was as close as she could get to his face. Cassa looked down and liked what he saw.

"Tell me where your surfie mates are. Nutter only wants to talk to them, and you can be on your way."

"Does he want to know whether we called the cops and ratted you guys out about the fire?"

"I'm asking the questions, not you. Now tell me where they are. Where's the Kombi?"

There was no answer from Cassa. Gena grabbed his long, blond hair and pulled his face into her bosom. He thought, *I've got to tell them something other than where we stopped.*

Cassa mumbled, "We're camped on the other side of town at a rest stop."

Nutter yelled to Jimbo, "You guys couldn't have looked too hard. Next time do as I say, or you won't be wearing the Bad Meadows colours."

"Let's go get 'em," said Porky.

"No, we'll wait a while. We'd better sleep off the grog, and we'd make too much noise for this time in the morning. The cops will be on our case, and we'll all end up in the lock-up. We'll get an early start at sunrise."

Gena was finished with Cassa after extracting the info. As she walked away, she asked Nutter, "What are you going to do with him?" "Well, I'm taking no chances; he's coming with us, just in case he's trying to send us on a wild goose chase."

* * *

Around four o'clock, the surfers woke and quietly packed, rolling up the tarp, gathering up their sleeping bags, and throwing them in the back of the Kombi. LP climbed into the driver's seat. Bear and Brownie quietly pushed the Kombi over towards the police station's back wall.

The old stone jail had been built back in the 1800s. Bear figured that the mortar holding the bars into the stone wall would be weak, because it had been built by convicts. They weren't fools. They had known their days were numbered, and they could end up behind those bars, for no reason other than the constabulary mood of the day.

George and Mason were the walking wounded and weren't much help with pushing.

Bear and Brownie pushed the Kombi up against a large gum tree; the bumper bar wedged tightly against it. George pulled out the .22 rifle, attached the silencer, and handed it to Bear.

Bear rested the rifle on the back of the Kombi, took aim, and fired. *Pop, pop, pop;* three streetlights were taken out without raising any suspicion from anyone in the camping ground.

"LP, run over and attach the winch to the jail bars," Bear whispered.

LP signalled the "all okay" by raising his hand.

He stood back from the stone wall as Bear started the winch. Seconds later, the bars popped out, taking half the stone wall with them. Red walked casually out through the rubble and dust, as if he were taking a walk in the park.

"Get over here; there's no time to waste. Let's go," Bear yelled, breaking the morning quiet along with the old stone wall crashing down.

Kat ran over to Red and gave him a hug. "Don't ever leave me like that again," she said as she helped him into the Kombi. "I'll need to re-dress your wound, or it'll get infected."

"That bandage isn't red from blood; it's red from dirt," Red replied.

"Where have you been walking then?" Kat asked.

"I don't want to talk about what happened back at the Bora Ring before picking you up, I'll tell you later. Just re-dress my toes, as soon as we get out of here, and see if they're still attached to my foot," said Red.

George piped up, "I'm next. Kat, can you look at my ankle? It's still swollen and bruised."

"Shut up, George, we haven't got time to look after you right now. Kat can look at your ankle when she's finished re-dressing my toes," said Red.

"Well, she won't be able to help you, because I've got the key to the first aid kit," George replied.

Bear butted into the argument: "Everyone in the Kombi now. Brownie, do a head count; are we missing anyone?"

"Damn! We're missing Cassa. He didn't come back last night.

He must be in bed with some bird," Brownie replied.

"That's bloody great!" George said. "We haven't got time to look for him; we'll have to leave him behind."

As LP drove away from the police station, he looked in the rear-vision mirror and saw Cassa running towards the Kombi. He was being chased by six bikies. LP yelled, "I've spotted Cassa; we can't leave town without him."

LP slammed on the brakes. Driving in reverse, he saw Cassa fall to the roadway. Bikies surrounded him and started kicking him on the ground. Cassa looked up, saw the Kombi coming, and managed to roll to the side of the road, as LP used the van to knock over anyone that got in his way.

LP stopped the Kombi, and Bear opened the side door. Brownie and Bear reached down, grabbed Cassa's hands, and pulled him into the Kombi.

Bear yelled, "Step on it; let's get out of here." He looked at Cassa, holding his left side, "What happened with you last night?" "Well, I was tied up by the bikies but I escaped when they were all snoring, I done a Houdini and wriggled out of the ropes. The bikies were no boy scouts; if they were, they would tie better knots. I slipped out of the hall and done a runner down the road. I'll tell you more later," Cassa said, as he coughed up a little blood.

As they sped away, LP looked in the mirror and saw the bikies in hot pursuit.

George, being George, was only thinking of himself and wanted attention for his swollen ankle; he was not about to hand over the key to the first aid box until Kat helped him.

"Hand over the key, George," Red said.

"No, strap my ankle first," George replied.

"Hand over the key, or you'll have a broken leg, too. Anyway, George, how come this Kombi is fitted out with these extras?" Red asked. We've got a first aid kit, winch, auxiliary battery, floodlight, bulbar, long-range fuel tanks ..."

"I bought it from Shannon's Car Auctions," George replied. "It was an ex-PMG vehicle from out in the bush. It was fitted with heaps of extras, because it was used by the government to lay telephone lines in remote areas."

"That's great; now just give me the bloody key," said Red, who was about to grab it out of George's hand.

George handed the key over to Kat, after Bear said, "Stop the arguing; we've got more serious trouble behind us."

Kat, paying no attention to what might happen next with the bikies in pursuit, started to re-dress Red's toes after unlocking the first aid kit. She pulled out a white bandage and quickly dressed Red's wound.

George said again, "Can you do something about my ankle?" Kat picked up the remainder of the bandage and wrapped it tightly around his foot and ankle. "Are you sure that's not too tight?"

"It's fine; you need to restrict movement."

Mason called from the front seat, "Have a look at this." He pointed to two puncture holes on his leg. "Can you do anything about this infection?"

Kat handed the antiseptic bottle to Mason, saying, "Just dab a little on and around the infected area. Take this bandage and wrap it up, and keep it on for a few days until the swelling goes down."

"Have we all finished *General Hospital* back there?" LP asked. "We need to figure out which is the quickest way to Bells. I want to put some distance between us and those bikies. We gotta get out of this bloody town before the cops arrive and find their jail destroyed; we could all end up back there."

7

George, who knew what his Kombi was capable of, said, "Once we start to climb the mountain range, Nutter and his bikie mates will catch up. The Kombi hasn't got enough grunt with this load onboard. We've got about five minutes before the bikies catch up to us. Any suggestions?"

"Right, I've got an idea," said Bear. "Just climb onto the roof rack and give the Golden Fleece the flick. Before you throw it, light the sock and push our make-do jerry can into the roadway. That will stop them in their tracks."

"It's your idea," said Cassa. "You do it."

"No, we'll be democratic." Leaning down Bear picked up a tooth pick container rolling around on the floor. "We'll draw straws," Bear responded.

Cassa said, "I'm out; I've got broken ribs from the bikies sinking their boot in."

"I'm out," George complained, pointing at his ankle. "I've got a sprain."

"I don't care," Bear answered. "Everyone in the draw." Time was slipping away, and the bikies had made up some distance.

"Right, draw straws … Who's got the shortest?" Bear pointed to George and said, "It's you."

Bear reached over and opened the side door. He dropped his cigarette lighter into George's top pocket, and Brownie handed him his knife.

"Stick this between your teeth." "What about my sprained ankle?" "Tough luck," Bear said.

Brownie and Bear held George by the front of his shirt and helped him over to the sliding door.

"Grab the roof racks; now pull yourself along. We're all relying on you," said Brownie.

George, with the hunting knife between his teeth and the lighter in his pocket, moved one hand at a time and slowly made it to the steps leading up to the roof racks. He hopped up three steps and got ready to light the sock.

"Do it now!" Bear yelled.

George flicked down on the lighter and ignited the sock, grabbed the knife from his teeth, and slashed one of the straps. The rubberised stretchable cord with a hook on either end held down the Golden Fleece in place, now about to release a jerrycan of fuel off the surfboards. George figured cutting one strap would act as a catapult as the surfboards flicked up, and with a bit of luck, they would not lose the boards as well. As the guys looked back, the Golden Fleece, full of petrol, landed on the road in a huge fireball.

They saw some of the bikies run off the road into a ditch. The two lead riders came through the flames and pulled over.

"Well, that stopped 'em in their tracks," Bear said. "Come on, George, get back into the Kombi."

Finally, it looked like they were going to make it in time for the contest.

Cassa said, "One problem: I was our best chance to win, but I've got broken ribs."

"Cassa, you're full of yourself," Bear told him. "We're all good surfers, and any one of us could win the contest. But who's got the best chance? Mason, you're still too weak from the snake bite. George, you've got a rolled ankle. Cassa, you reckon you've broken your ribs."

Bear ruled himself out for reasons only known to him. And so did Brownie, who had bulked up from weight training and his own blend of protein supplement. That made him too top heavy to compete against the agile competition he would have to face at Bells Beach. That left LP and Red.

"You forget, I've got stitches in my toes," said Red.

"That leaves you, LP. Can you do it?" Bear asked.

"I know what to look for in the perfect wave. I can do it," LP replied with confidence.

"What do you think, Red?" Bear asked.

Red pointed to LP and replied, "I think LP's got the balls to beat any upstart, would-be professional; go for it and show us the money." "Decision made," Bear said. "You'll register for the contest. You better pull this off; we've come a long way for that prize money."

"I'll give it my best shot. I've been dreaming of this moment and won't let you guys down. I've seen the future," LP replied as he steered a path to Bells Beach.

Bear had a moment of hesitation at LP's last comment, thinking, *Here we go again. He's having another psychic moment.*

"Well, shit happens. The bikies are still coming. Not as many, but enough to stop us," Red said.

"Right, that's it. Those bikies are really pissing me off now!" yelled Bear. "Hand me the .243."

"There only two bullets left," said Red. "There will be close to one hundred of them still following."

"Well then, that makes us about even." Bear was usually overconfident, but this time, he was just mad as hell. He yelled to LP, "Stop the Kombi. I'm getting out. Anyone else want to help? Don't hold back."

Brownie spoke up. "I'm with you, but first I need to put on some moisturiser and sunscreen. I'll be with you in just a minute." Brownie always the perfectionist when it came to grooming, wanted to look his best, even if he was about to get involved in a brawl.

Bear was mighty angry, and you could hear it in his voice. "LP, stop the Kombi now. I'm getting out. You guys, piss off. These dickheads will not get past me—today or ever!"

Mason grabbed a tape and slotted it in the cassette player. "Surfers Rule, Surfers Rule."

The guys joined in, singing, "It's a golden rule, Surfers Rule." Bear climbed out through the side door, grasping his high-powered rifle with telescopic sights.

He walked from the Kombi and straddled the two white lines in the middle of the road as the sound of the Kombi motor faded in the distance.

On the next turn, Brownie said, "I'm ready; let me out. I'll kill 'em all."

Brownie grabbed his ancestral knife and boomerang, and then he started running back to Bear. By this time, Bear had taken aim. Looking down the telescopic sites, he lined up Nutter, on his not-so-gleaming Fat Boy Harley after coming through the flames. He planned to take out Porky second. Porky and Nutter saw him in the middle of the road, but it was too late for them to avoid what was about to happen.

Bear fired, taking out Nutter's front tyre, then Porky's. Both were laid to the ground, as other bikies turned the scene into a highway pile-up as they smashed into Nutter and Porky's bikes.

Other riders avoided a collision and headed for the culvert. Bear threw the .243 over his shoulder and ran towards them. Anyone who stood up to stop him was laid out by his mixture of street fighting and black belt karate.

By the time Brownie caught up to Bear, he was halfway through the bikies, but Brownie arrived better late than never. One bikie pulled himself up out of the culvert with a hunk of wood in his hand. He raised it behind Bear, about to give him a good whack over the head. Brownie didn't hesitate and threw his boomerang. As it swished through the air, Bear turned around to the sound and saw the boomerang crack the bikie's skull, dropping him, his weapon, and the boomerang to the ground.

"Good throw, Brownie," yelled Bear. "I owe you one. Let's make sure they don't follow us this time. Brownie, cut all their fuel lines. Keep two of the bikes rideable so we can get away."

Brownie and Bear took the two bikes, mounted them, and rode up to Nutter.

Bear said, "There's good news and bad news. The good news is, I am going to let you live. The bad news is that if I ever see you again, I'll kill ya."

Bear took his time rolling a smoke, while Nutter looked around at the damage these surfie bums caused. Bear lit his *rollie*, took one puff, and then flicked it back as he rode off. All you could see was bikes exploding; if that wasn't enough, a semi-trailer came around the bend and ran over more bikes, which were now engulfed in flames.

Nutter yelled as Bear and Brownie rode off, "I'm going to kill you bastards!"

Slowly, the so-called Bad Meadows bikies got to their feet. They looked like a sad, defeated bunch of blokes walking to Bells Beach.

It wasn't long before LP had put some distance between the bikies and themselves.

"Turn on the radio," said Red. "Let's listen for the weather report."

LP switched channels, searching for the news and weather. "*Stop the war now! Stop the war now! Stop the war now!* Ten thousand uni students and protesters have brought Eden to a standstill. All roads are blocked, and nobody can get in or out of town," a reporter was saying.

"We got out of there just in time. I thought the change of government from Liberal Country Party to Labour stopped the Vietnam War," said LP.

"Not quite; it's taking time to get our soldiers out of that mess," Mason replied.

"Well, at least we don't have to worry any more about conscription," LP said. "Gough canned that. He's the best bloke running this country now. You know, Donny, Red's, and my number came up for conscription. If it wasn't for Gough, we'd have been in the firing line to be called up next and deployed to Vietnam."

"Okay mate, thanks for the history lesson. Let's listen for the surf report," said Mason.

"The weather will be fine today, with a light breeze. Surf conditions are excellent, with a rising swell. Perfect conditions for today's Bells Beach Surf Contest."

"That's what we want to hear. Step on it and keep your eyes on the road, LP. Not far to go now," Red said.

By this time, Kat was wondering what she got herself involved in. She had followed her heart, but it had taken her on a roller coaster journey with a bunch of blokes that now seemed messed up in the head.

8

LP pulled into the car park at Bells Beach; he had driven through Torquay and filled up on fuel at the Mobil servo on Geelong Street. Now all he had to do was win the contest. The swells were between eight and ten feet, with perfect barrelling waves— just like he liked it. Wasting no time, LP was first out of the Kombi. He ran across to the registration tent, and was given his competition number. Running back, he heard the sound of motor bikes entering the car park. What a surprise!

Brownie and Bear arrived on their newly acquired wheels, and Bear gave their mates the good news, saying, "We'll have no more trouble from the Bad Meadows bikie club. You could say they've been disbanded."

Brownie thought Bear's opinion was pretty funny, and everyone, including Kat, joined in the laughter, believing they had seen the last of those bikies.

LP was pumped up and eager to get in the water. He changed into a full steamer wetsuit and booties. He picked up his single fin six foot six surfboard and walked down to enter the surf for when his number is called. Waves washed up over his booties that protected him from the near freezing Antarctic current that ran all the way up from the South Pole. Waiting in silence, focusing, slowing his breathing and visualising getting the perfect wave was all that mattered.

He didn't have to wait long before his number was called out over the loud speaker, and his mates cheered him on as he entered the water with the other surfers in his heat. Paddling out together they headed for the point to ride the perfect wave to the winner's podium. The blare horn sounded and the heat was on.

George and Cassa talked about how they could have won the contest, except for injuries, agreeing that the prize money would come in handy.

Kat and the guys sat on a high sand dune to watch, except for Red, who had walked over to another vantage point and could be seen sharing a joint with a dreadlocked local. Bear, hearing George and Cassa's comment about the prize money, said, "Give LP some support out there. Let him know we're barracking for him. Wave your hands. Jump up and down, or just maybe we'll be heading back over the border poorer."

"Do you think LP remembers what was said in Mason's vision back at the Bora Ring?" asked George.

"Remind me," Cassa said, while waving his hands above his head. "Look for guidance from the sea, and you will achieve your aim to be the best."

"George, that's the first positive comment that's come out of your mouth this trip. You better be right," Cassa replied.

LP manoeuvred around his competition, lined up for his first wave, and started paddling for it. He dropped down the face of the wave and positioned himself to be tubed, which should score highly. Out of nowhere, a dolphin appeared on the wave with him.

"Look at that. You never see that happen," Bear said.

Bear spotted a dolphin finding the sweet spot on the wave, as LP worked the wave to get the most power out of it.

LP clicked and thought, *All I have to do is follow the dolphin. It knows more about the sea than I do.*

That wave was the longest tube he had ever been in. The judges' scores went up. Nine points out of ten.

There was some talking; someone asked, "Did the dolphin make a difference in LP's top wave ride?"

From a distance, the judges had no problem with it.

The scoring was pretty close as the heat progressed. LP needed another nine or a ten from the five judges to win the heat. It was going to be a hard call. Again, he dropped down the perfect wave, and again there was a dolphin leading him to find the most power in the wave. He followed it up and down the wave, and then they both disappeared into barrelling white water.

The guys on the beach crossed their fingers and held their breath. Would he make it out of the tube? Fifteen seconds went by.

"He's not going to make it," complained George. "There goes the cash."

"Don't give up yet," said Mason.

Covered by water, with the sun shining through, LP thought there was no way out. The crushing weight of white water was about to end his dream of winning. Just then, the dolphin made contact with LP with the sound of click, click, click. LP thought, *That creature's trying to tell me something. Whatever the dolphin does, just follow.* The wave was about to close down, but before it did, the dolphin took a sharp vertical turn and punched through the top. LP followed. The dolphin had made an opening in the wave lip, enough for LP to flip out and over, still standing.

Not everyone on the beach applauded. His mates were ecstatic, of course, but the supporters of the local favourite were not happy. Someone in the crowd yelled out, "That outsider cheated. He had help from a dolphin."

The judges looked at each other, and one said, "There are no rules banning dolphins from a surf contest." All other judges nodded in agreement.

With that, all judges held up their score cards: "10; 10; 10; 10; 10."

There was verbal abuse from locals directed at the judges for giving LP the top score. The judges didn't care and wouldn't allow their authority to be questioned, and ended the contest declaring LP the winner.

LP ran up the beach with his surfboard under his arm; all the guys gave him high fives. He changed out of his wetsuit and bent down to pull off his booties. When he stretched back up, Kat planted a big kiss on his lips and said, "That was great; now get us back over the border without any more trouble."

That moment of glory ended abruptly for LP, after that comment.

"You beauty!" said Bear. "I didn't think you had it in ya." Now back from finishing a joint with the hippy guy. Red said,

"Let's collect the cash, get a photo taken, and get out of here. We need to be back for work on Monday, and this time, no shortcuts."

Kat's grabbed Red's hand and nodded in agreement.

All the guys had something to smile about, knowing that they had finished what they had started. They had overcome bad weather and flooding, kept one step ahead of the Bad Meadows' bikies, and made it to the contest on time. They also reflected back on what had happened at the Bora Ring, which could not be explained away. The numbers and coin were yet to reveal their true value.

"One problem," said Red. "I've given it some thought, and there's no way we'll make it back over the border in time for work. You know what bosses are like; they're going to be pissed off if we don't turn up on time."

LP said, "Look, we've got enough cash for all of us to fly back and still have money left over. Plus, we still have four hundred dollars from the pokie win. George can fly back down next week, get the Kombi, and drive back. His ankle should be better by then. We'll leave it where it is in the car park. It'll be okay till then." George agreed with a nod.

"Okay, we'll travel light; take just the surfboards and whatever we can fit in our backpacks," Bear directed.

Brownie wasn't leaving his ancestral knife and boomerang behind; he climbed into the Kombi and retrieved them.

"I'll take the horns and put them in the duffle bag," Mason said.

"I'll roll up the goat hide and you take it George," said LP.

"Well, I'm not leaving the coins behind," George said. I'll sell them as souvenirs at the local flea market at home." He placed them in his backpack.

"Add this OK, George you take care of the Scroll," said Red.

George snapped back, "Sometimes I only need what you can provide; your absence. And now's one of them."

Bear, not thinking things through, decided to take the guns; he got them out of the Kombi and started to place them in Mason's duffle bag.

"Are you sure about that?" asked Red. "Think about it. You don't have a permit for those guns. Leave them behind. You'll never get them onboard at the airport."

"You're right," Bear said. "I'll dismantle them and leave them behind."

"Right, let's get everything we're taking and hurry up," said LP. Brownie walked over to Mason and said, "Stick my belongings in your bag. It's big enough for my boomerang, knife, toilette bag, and clothing."

"What about Wal?" asked Cassa. "We can't leave him locked up here for a week."

Cassa, concerned about the toad eating the rest of his dope, decided to roll one last joint before flying out from Melbourne.

"I'll put Wal over beside those rocks. He's one tough cane toad. He'll fend for himself," George said.

Cassa's response was more about him: "Okay, but I'm taking the remaining weed with me. That's all I'm taking to the airport."

Bear made sure nothing was forgotten; he told George, "Check all the doors are locked on the Kombi before we head off, and then we're ready to rock and roll."

Luck was on their side once again; they flagged down a minivan headed to the airport.

The guys and Kat got standby tickets and were booked to depart at 6:15 pm for their flight to Brisbane. After checking din, Red and Kat walked away from the others and sat, arms around each other, cuddling up and being passionate.

Red re-assured Kat, "Everything will be fine when we get back up north. Doctors, dentists, and vet surgeries will be a distant memory. We'll start a new life after we cross the border, I promise you." He hugged Kat tightly as song lyrics played on his thoughts: *Baby, it's breaking my heart, I can't get by without you, and I'm nothing without you.*

Nutter and his bikie mates walked into the Bells Beach car park and spotted two Harleys that looked familiar.

"Over there; that's the Kombi," Nutter said, pointing. "Yeah, but where are those surfie bums? I want to kill 'em," replied Porky.

"That can wait," Nutter replied. His rag tag bikie mates surrounded the Kombi, looking for a way in. The doors were locked.

"Try the back hatch, and see if the coins are still there," said Nutter.

Tiny grabbed the handle and turned it, but it was also locked. The bikies started to rock the Kombi from side to side. Their impatience could be seen by beach goers, and it would not be long before the cops arrive.

"Porky make yourself useful, get a rock and smash that side window," ordered Nutter.

The bikies continued pushing the Kombi from side to side, as Porky smashed the front driver's window. Before he could reach in and open the door, Nutter said, "What's that smell?"

"There's smoke coming from the back of the engine," Tiny yelled. "Bugger, it's on fire. Run!" He still had enough brains after the clunk on the head to get out of there fast.

As they ran from the Kombi, it erupted into a huge fireball from a full tank of fuel, with an explosion that lifted it ten feet into the air. It landed back in the same spot, with smoke billowing out of the smashed windows. Everyone ran for cover, and the local news would report it as a car bomb explosion at Bells Beach.

The bikies watched until all that was left was a burnt-out shell. Nutter looked at Porky and said. "Well, we've got no bikes, except those two over there, no money, and nowhere to go. We can't go back over the border. They've got warrants for our arrest unless we can come up with the fifty red ones, and that isn't going to happen for a while."

Porky reminded Nutter about an old mate of his in Melbourne. "He said if you want to make easy money, Melbourne is the place to be."

"It sounds like our kind of city. Well, it looks like there's no choice," replied Nutter.

Jimbo backed up his leader's decision, saying, "It won't be long before everyone down here knows the name Bad Meadows Motorcycle Club, and the money will be flowing in again."

9

Fast forward… the year 2001, only LP walks through the Brisbane Airport lounge. No mates with him this time. Waiting for his backpack at the carousel after returning from Sydney where he caught up with his old mate Bear. As he waited for his backpack, breaking news flashed on the overhead screens. Something unbelievable happened as he watched an aircraft smash into one of the Twin Towers in New York. If that wasn't bad enough, New South Wales police report and escort the Bad Meadows Biker Club to the Queensland border. They want to make sure none of them are left on their side of the border.

LP had a spring in his step and had no lines on his face, but for a birthmark on his left cheek, and was bald as badger. He exited the airport terminal after collecting his backpack, while thinking, *'What's Nutter and his bikie mates up to?'* Ingrid his wife who was waiting for him, and clicked the boot open. LP dropped his backpack in and slammed it shut. Once he was in the vehicle he gave her a kiss on the cheek and said, "Have you heard the news about New York, and Nutter and his bikie mates heading our way?"

"No, I don't want to know. We have enough problems at home."

As they drove through the suburb of The Gap smashed by a tornado the day before, LP inspects the damage throughout the neighbourhood. When they stopped outside their home LP comments, "That can be fixed, but Nutter could be a bigger problem. I'll give Bear a call and see what he thinks?"

Bear answers his phone after a couple of rings, and responded to LP's concerns, "Who gives a rat's arse about what happens up in Queensland? And those bikies couldn't hold a grudge that long. Don't give it a second thought."

"Well, you'd better take notice. Nutter and his bikie mates are back and it means trouble is coming our way."

Talk to Brownie, our 'Mr. Have-a-Chat.' Get to the point with him, or he won't stop talking for hours about his latest trip to the outback. Ring Red next and get back to me if you still think it's a problem. I reckon you're reading too much into it. You're not in one of those psychic moods again, are you?"

"No I don't think so," said LP. "I've just got this feeling that things are going to turn ugly."

"Well, your hunches are usually right. I'll keep an eye on the news; let me know if you want me to fly up to sort out any trouble."

LP rang Brownie and Red to explain the situation. Both agreed with Bear that it was all well in the past and LP was just being paranoid.

"Everything will be fine," said Red.

The next morning, LP was up early and watched the morning news on TV.

"The Bad Meadows bikie gang are now within an hour of the Queensland border," the reporter said.

Police helicopters were keeping surveillance on a long line of bikers, riding north, two abreast. The reporter then spoke to a pilot, who said he'd radioed Queensland Police headquarters and told Jack Herbertsin, the police commissioner, it was the Bad Meadows bikers heading to the border.

It was reported that the police commissioner said, "If they cross the border, my officers will be waiting for 'em!"

News choppers, police surveillance helicopters, and highway patrol officers had been following their movement through New South Wales. The cops from down south wanted to get them out of their state as quickly as possible. Queensland was welcome to this outlaw bikie gang.

The camera then moved to Herbertsin, standing one foot inside the Queensland border, flanked by some of his high-ranking officers. He made a big show for the camera with his warning to those who thought they were above the law. "If anyone breaks Queensland laws, including bikies, then expect to end up in jail." Jack turned from the camera and thought, *It's not like the old days when protection could be paid for. Now there is the CMC corruption watchdog keeping an eye on us and police activists watching for illegal activity within the force.*

Jack had fond memories of the old days, when Queensland had been known as a police state, where corruption had flourished and the police had wielded total power. He had worked his way up the ranks since then to top dog and still liked to think police controlled everything.

The news report showed Nutter getting off his gleaming Fat Boy Harley onto Queensland soil. He walked over to the commissioner, and they had a brief conversation, out of earshot of the cameras.

The commissioner had brought every motorcycle cop within a thousand kilometres as a show of force, and he took great pleasure in delivering a blunt message to his old mate: "We're the biggest gang in town."

"How's it goin', you old bastard? I didn't expect to get such a big welcome," said Nutter.

"Cut the bullshit," said Jack. "What are you doing back here?" "We have unfinished business in this city. There's some gold coins here that belong to us."

"Well, talking about collecting, you still owe me fifty red ones from when you left town without paying up. I'd say that, with inflation and interest, you now owe me a thousand red ones. Or I'll be dusting off those old arrest warrants, and you and your mates won't see daylight in this state again for a long time."

"Ahh, you're stuck in the old days, Jack. You might have got away with an attitude like that back then, but we both know you can't touch us now, so cut the crap. We'll be on our way, and you'll have a brown paper bag full of money within forty-eight hours."

"Nutter, welcome to Queensland."

Jack raised his hand and waved forward his officers to follow out his instructions. They searched every bikie for drugs and weapons, and issued each and every one of them an infringement notice for excessive noise.

This is good press, thought Jack.

Minutes later, a senior officer came back and reported that they were all clean, no drugs or weapons.

"Okay, let 'em pass," said Jack. "We'll be watching your every move, Nutter."

* * *

Meanwhile, LP watched the events unfolding on his TV screen, wondering what was being said between the Queensland police commissioner and the leader of the Bad Meadows bikie gang. As Nutter and his gang started up their bikes again, the journalist reported on his attempts at eavesdropping. "A heated exchange about red paper bags, collecting gold coins, and arrest warrants."

The words "collecting coins" triggered thoughts of muddy coins stamped "South Africa."

LP realised that his worst fears had come true. He grabbed his mobile and keyed in Bear's number in Sydney. "I know what Nutter is after. It's those coins. They weren't just foreign coins; they're pure gold."

"Yeah, I remember; they looked like old pennies covered in mud."

"That's right, but the fact is that someone's got a bag of gold, and that person is George. He was the last one I saw with the coins."

"Okay, I'll get on the three o'clock flight from here. Pick me up at Brisbane Airport," Bear said.

LP was trying to remember what had happened to the coins. George had had them in his backpack going through security at Melbourne airport. They had been painted silver and attracted no attention, because he had said that they were medallions to be sold at flea markets. They had all been pretty naïve back then, but LP now realised how valuable the coins were.

Bear had figured out the same thing, and that's why he was so quick to get on a flight to Brisbane. He was more interested in finding the gold than helping his mates. Bear was struggling to find enough cash to pay the contractors working on his latest high-rise apartment project in inner city Sydney. His company, Bear Towers, was about to collapse into a financial black hole unless he came up with something fast.

LP contacted Brownie and Red, and filled them in on the unfolding saga. Cassa, however, was off the radar. When last seen, he had been trekking through the jungle in Indonesia, looking for an elusive surf break. He would be no help, as usual.

10

Bear walked out of the airport terminal as LP pulled his car up to the kerb. He opened the back door, pushed his carry-on case in, and got in the passenger seat.

"So, what's the plan?" he asked. "Is everyone at the beach house?" "Red's already there, but we don't know where George is. I couldn't get through to Mason, and Cassa is in Indo."

"Okay, drive. We'll sort this problem out real quick."

They arrived at their old hangout, a low-set, three-bedroom house with four steps leading up to a verandah.

Bear had been fortunate enough to inherit the beach house from his uncle. Bear's generous nature meant that the property was available to his mates whenever they wanted.

They had taken up his offer over the years, to surf, fish, and relax at Teewah Beach. It was only a short walk over the dunes to forty miles of white sandy beach. Multi-coloured cliffs allowed hang gliders to launch themselves off as ocean waves pounded below at high tide.

Red was in the tiny lounge room, reminiscing about Kat, who had left him not long after arriving back in Brisbane from Bells Beach. City life had been more than she expected in comparison to outback Queensland's slow pace. So she left Red and gave up nursing, but kept her uniform and became a pole dancer at a gentleman's club, in an unsavoury part of the city.

Red never got over her and did not hook up with another woman for a long time. His lost love had made him irritable and angry. The roller coaster of emotions affected his body also, creating dry scaly outbreaks over his skin, which often became red and infected.

"Long time, no see," Red said as he stood up and shook his old mate's hand with vigour.

Bear replied, "G'day, shit stirrer. How've ya been?"

LP followed them onto the verandah. He reached out his hand and grasped Red's firmly, smiled, and said, "Hi Red, how's it going?"

"I don't want to bore you with my problems. What trouble is heading our way?" Red said.

"Bear will fill you in," LP replied.

Everyone settled onto the couches like they'd never left.

"Where's Brownie?" asked LP.

"Dunno," Red said. "Late, as usual; he's probably chewing someone's ear off with his outback adventures."

"Hey," said Bear. "We've all got a problem, you know. Those bikies are not going to give up looking for us until they get what they want."

"Well, what they want is to beat us to a pulp because they think we dobbed them into the cops," said Red.

"Nope, that's not the main reason," Bear said. "We've got something of theirs, and they want it back. It's those bloody coins we found in the back of the Kombi ages ago. They weren't just foreign coins; they were gold."

"Oh, yes," Red replied. "You beauty, I thought they were just foreign old coins. We're in the money then."

"Let's just find the gold first," said Bear. "Then we'll decide what to do with those bastard bikies."

Suddenly the guys stopped talking.

They could hear the roar of bikes but couldn't see anything other than a huge dust cloud coming from a gravel road that had been recently built by the local council. Up until then, you could only access the township along the beach at low tide.

Nutter and his mad mates were on their way to Bear's beach house; they had got the address from the bent police commissioner.

"That doesn't sound good," said LP.

As the sound of the engines died and the dust settled, the guys could see around thirty angry bikies in the street, with more still coming. Many got off their bikes and spread themselves out, and then Nutter and Porky walked up to the verandah.

Nutter said, "You know why we're here; hand over what belongs to us, and do it now."

"What do you mean, Nutter?" Bear asked. "I have no idea what you're talking about."

"Don't stuff me around; I want our coins back now," Nutter replied.

Bear said, "We ain't got any coins, so go back to where you came from, or I'll have ya."

Nutter laughed. "There's three of you, and a street full of us. Bear, you're full of yourself."

Bear realised the odds were not in his favour; he needed some time to get his head around this jam.

Porky had been standing quietly, sucking from a tallie he had taken from the fridge, and then he said, "Which asshole put my head through that wall thirty years ago?"

"Don't tell me you've come all this way to find that out?" asked Red.

Porky replied, "We've got long memories. Every one of our mates outside wants a piece of you guys. We've been thinking about paying you surfie bums back for all the trouble you caused for a long, long time."

Red said, "You guys need professional help. I know a good shrink in Melbourne who could help you get over your anger management issues."

"Cut the crap. Who put my head through the wall?" Porky repeated.

Red walked forward and grabbed Porky in a headlock. He marched him over to the nearest wall, pushed his head through the gyprock, and then slowly pulled it out, showering his red hair and beard with white gyprock powder. He looked like a ghost.

"Now do you remember who put your head through the wall?" Red asked.

"You ... you bastard."

"That's right, and if you don't leave now, I'll do the same to your brain-dead mates out there, too."

Bear jumped in to calm things down. "Settle down, Red, I'm sure Nutter and I can work something out. Surely you guys didn't come all this way for an old grudge. What's the real reason you're back in town?"

"I was getting to that before your mate got agro," Nutter said.

Bear said, "He had good reason to, so don't stir him up any more."

"Cut to the chase; where's our gold?" asked Nutter.

"What gold?"

"You bastards better still have it, or the money you got for it, or I'm gonna kill ya."

Bear jumped in again. "We've had this little talk once before, and I said that if I ever see you again, I'll kill you. So think again; the only one who's going to die today is you. Now leave us alone before I lose my cool."

Nutter said, "I've got a street full of bikies backing me up, and they want to rip you lot from limb to limb. All I've got to do is give them the word. I'll give you one minute to change your mind and tell me where the coins are."

"Those coins were just some old foreign coins—worth nothing," said Bear.

"Are you lot still as naïve as back then? Those coins are gold Krugerrands. They are collectors now, worth ten times their face value. I'm talking one and a half million," Nutter said.

Nutter started walking out, and then he turned and said, "One minute. That's it, or my mates will come in and extract from you lot where my coins are."

Bear said, "Nutter, a wise man once said to turn the other cheek. Just keep walking and get on your bikes, or you and your bikie mates will not live to tell the story. The coins are long gone." Nutter reminded Bear, "There's two hundred of us and only three of you dickheads."

"That's better odds than the last time we met; bugger off or you'll get burnt."

As Nutter and Porky went back to their mates, Bear, Red, and LP stood looking out at the sea of bikies in front of them. Bear's confidence was over the top again. Things were looking pretty grim.

Ring, ring, ring. Bear flips open his Motorola phone.

"Hey, Bear, I see you've got visitors. What do you want me to do?" It was Brownie.

"Where are you?"

"At the top of your street."

"Go around to the back street and wait for us." This time, Brownie being late was a bonus.

"Okay. LP, Red, do a runner out the back door and over the fence. Brownie's waiting to pick us up. Turn on the gas on the way out."

Red and LP turned the oven on as they raced through the kitchen and went outside. With thirty seconds left of Nutter's ultimatum, Bear stood stock still for a moment, looking out at the bikies. Then he took a deep breath before gas started to fill the living room; he then followed LP and Red through the rear doorway. He stopped a few metres away and watched as Nutter's bikies entered the house.

Like a herd of cattle smelling the slaughterhouse, the bikies realised that what they smelt was danger. They scrambled to get out, climbing and pushing at each other. Bear opened his metal signature lighter, turned the flame to high and jammed it on, then flicked the lighter through the air like a boomerang.

Bang! All the windows blew out with a huge explosion, and smoke billowed through all the windows and doors.

LP yelled out, "Let's go, Bear, don't just stand there. We've got to get out of here fast. Red's already over the fence."

Bear had opened his mobile phone and made a call.

"Hello? There's been an accident at 23 Mullet Lane, Teerwah Beach. Send police, ambulance, and garbage trucks. There a lot of rubbish to clean up." Bear snapped closed his phone and said, "You go. I won't make it over that fence."

"Come on, Bear, where's the grisly Bear from the old days? We'll be over that fence quick smart. Follow me and do as I do." LP ran along the fence, raised his hands, placed them on the fence ridge, and, in one quick motion, lifted himself from one side to the other. Bear did the same, running full bore, and threw himself over the fence.

"No problem!" LP said.

"Let's get the hell out of here," Bear yelled as he climbed into Brownie's van.

"Where to now?' LP asked as he got into the van.

Red, last in the van, sat in the passenger seat and said, "Let's go, Brownie, we're all aboard, step on it and get us to Mason's. He'll know where George is. We'll find Mason down the road in Brighton, at the Masonic Retirement Home. Head south."

A little over one hour later, they arrived at the gates of the sprawling retirement complex. Brownie parked right outside the main building, and the guys all got out and headed through the entrance.

LP said to the receptionist, "We're here to see Mason."

She replied, "We're all Masons here; this is a Masonic Retirement Home. Everyone comes in here a Mason, and leaves a Mason."

"Cut the bullshit," Bear interrupted. "We're here to see your head shorang, top dog, you know."

"Oh, you want to see the CEO."

Mason's title was a cover for his other role as grand master of all things Masonic, protector of the craft and overseer of secrets passed down from biblical times. He had been anointed by his father as the new leader.

His father passed on the story as his father did, telling him that they were direct descendants of the Knights Templar, an order that was disbanded in 1307. The Knights Templar had travelled across Europe and sailed to Scotland, escaping a death ordered by the Vatican in Rome.

Their secrets crossed the ocean to the New World. From the Boston Tea Party to George Washington, future presidents would influence the course of history, drawing on their connection to the craft.

Mason's descendants not only migrated to America but also Australia. As a remnant of those people, they protected the secret knowledge that they believed would lead them to glorious immortality. This knowledge would not come as a surprise to his old mates, who knew of Mason's family connection with the Masonic Temple in Brisbane.

"Call him what you want; just show us his office."

"I'm sorry, you'll need an appointment. How about Tuesday next week?"

Bear started to get angrier and shouted, "Do I have to jump the counter and rip your bloody head off? Where is he?"

In fear, the receptionist replied, "Down the hallway; turn left." The guys started walking down the hallway and were soon stopped by a security officer.

LP put out his hand and gave the man a secret Masonic handshake, and then they went on their way.

"How did you know their secret handshake?" asked Brownie. LP replied, "Internet, mate; whatever you want to know, just look it up there."

Bear opened the office door, and there was Mason, sitting at his desk. Behind him were the old goat horns, stretched a metre across the wall.

Mason asked, "What are you guys doing here?"

"George has some trouble heading his way, and you know where he is," LP replied.

"I'll give you directions," Mason answered.

Bear said, "No, you're coming with us. Ring through and tell the receptionist you're taking the afternoon off."

Old mates started to rekindle old friendships as they walked back out to the car park, arm in arm with Mason. LP and Bear held him firmly just in case he had other ideas of calling for help from his Masonic Brethren, but there was no trouble as

Red stepped up into the front seat; everyone else climbed in through the sliding door.

"We've got to get to George before the bikies do," said LP. "You're the only one who can help, so which way do we go, Mason?"

Bear followed up, saying, "Get a move on, Brownie. Mason, you're the navigator. Show us where George is."

Brownie replied, "Okay, okay, I'm going as fast as I can. We don't want to get booked."

"When did you start to worry about breaking the law? You've become conservative in your old age. Have you become a Monarchist too?" LP said as he laughed out loud.

"Bullshit, I'm a Kabi Kabi man to my bones," Brownie replied with anger in his voice, while pushing the accelerator down further.

About forty minutes later, Mason pointed to a large mountain top near the road Brownie just turned into on Mason's instruction. "George is up there. After we get through the rainforest, you'll see a banana plantation backing onto state forest; that's where we'll find him."

The rainforest track was dangerous to traverse, becoming narrower as they left the main road behind. The forest canopy swallowed any sunlight. Brownie turned the van lights on as a light rain started to fall. He continued driving higher and higher. Suddenly, the road took a sharp hook turn, overlooking a thousand-metre drop.

Red yelled, "Hard left!"

Too late. Brownie hit the guard rail and bounced off it before regaining control.

"Woooh! That was close," Brownie said, as Bear yelled out, "Keep your eyes on the road or I'll climb over and drive."

By this time, the light rain turned into a thunderstorm, drenching the rainforest and making visibility hazardous as Brownie descended a long, steep road.

They were not far from George now, based on Mason's directions. Rain pounded against the windscreen. Brownie could just see a yellow barrier on the roadway as wipers swished on high. He slowly braked, avoiding skidding off the cliff face. They all got out of the van and realised how close they had come to being washed away. The guys kept going on foot, climbing up the track leading out of the rainforest into an open clearing. The storm clouds disappeared, and sunshine started to warm their drenched bodies.

LP asked Mason, "Are you sure we're going the right way?" He nodded and answered, "Yes."

At the bottom of the hill, the causeway was swollen with flood waters. Mason pointed out George's mountain top retreat and began walking towards George's place.

11

What they saw in the clearing was a packing shed, with no walls, and bunches of bananas hanging from the ceiling. Disappearing down the mountainside were rows of banana plants with hands covered in blue plastic, ready for harvest.

"What a surprise," George said when he saw the group. "What are you lot doing here?"

LP said, "Great to see you again, but where's your house?" George replied, "See that cave?"

It was the kind of thing you would expect to find in Coober Pedy, where opal miners made homes from disused mining tunnels to escape the heat.

George said, "Check out inside the cave; you'll be surprised." The old gang walked inside what, at first glance, appeared to be a ledge overhanging the side of a mountain. George had transformed this hole in the volcanic rock into something very liveable. The floor was covered in large stone pavers, and the cave walls had been sprayed with some kind of glow-in-the-dark pigment, which was recharged by sunlight each morning.

George explained how he had come by this property: "I had a $20,000 insurance payout when the van was burnt back at Bells Beach. Actually, I only had it insured for $2,000, but there had been a miscalculation, and I'd been paying the premium for the $20,000 cover. The cheque arrived in the mail, and that's how I bought this property. I turned it into an organic banana farm. If I built a house first, I would not have had enough cash to start this farm. I spent every cent on starting up this farm. There was just no spare cash to build a house. I made the right call, and now I sell truckloads of bananas over the border. No quarantine restrictions, like in the old days."

George had been motivated to buy the property by the haunting images of the Glass House Mountains and what they represented, told by the Kabi Kabi descendents of an ancient land.

The mountain, Tibrogargan, had once been a man. Coonowrin was his son with a crooked neck, and Beerwah was his wife, the tallest mountain. In Dreamtime, they were giant ancestors that turned to stone and now look down and protected their descendants. What was not well known was that there was an ancient Bora Ring within the state forest. George had discovered its location by accident when looking at buying the property. He had trekked south through the state forest that backed onto the land; to the east was a small remnant of rainforest. That's why he had come to live on the mountain.

"After a few years living in the cave with just the basics, I figured that material things are not what they're cracked up to be." Bear said, "George, you need to get out more. Cut the bullshit; now where's the bloody coins?"

"What coins?" George replied.

"Think about it. Thirty years ago, you had those coins in your backpack when you went to the airport. What did you do with them?"

George paused and thought. "Oh, yeah, I think Mason painted them with that silver line marking paint."

"Yeah, that's the ones," Bear stated. "You didn't sell them at the flea market to get some cash, I hope."

"No, they're here in the cave somewhere. Have a look for the backpack. It hasn't been touched since I came back from Bells Beach."

Bear and Mason started rummaging through the stuff that had been stored away in nooks and crannies in George's home.

Mason yelled, "I've found it!"

Bear replied, "Open it."

As Mason unzipped the backpack, his heart was pumping with the possibility of hitting the jackpot. He pulled out a bag, and said, "This must be it. It's got a bit of weight in it. Hey, what's that Scroll doing here?"

"'Don't open that. I kept it because no one else wanted anything to do with it. Mason, you remember, we found that at the female Bora Ring after you made it through the night without dying on us."

They all started to recollect what had happened that night, nearly thirty years ago.

"I don't know if it's a curse or more a blessing!" said George. "George, you're dreaming. Nothing else happened that night other than Mason being bitten by a snake. The women weren't real, and we smoked too much weed, we all agreed back then." George asked, "Well, where do you think that Scroll came from? The moon?"

Brownie suggested the flea market. Bear offered garage sale, and Mason suggested it might have been a door-to-door salesman.

George said, "Think what you like, but we were told to keep it safe until the word was a process. Has anyone figured that one out yet?"

LP responded after a moment's reflection. "It's a computer, a word processor. We wouldn't understand what they were talking about back then."

Bear said, "I don't care about that; show me the gold."

Red opened the bag and poured the coins out. "Once we clean off the silver paint, these gold Krugerrands will be as good as new."

"Okay, now I understand why you are all here. It's the gold. Not a reunion," George said, with disappointment. "Now that you've got what you want, there's solvent on the bench. Clean 'em up and go and leave me in peace on my mountain."

Bear said, "It's not that simple. The Bad Meadows mob are back in town, and they want their coin back." George replied, "Then give them back."

"Do you know how much they're worth? Thirty years ago, gold was worth $30 an ounce, the same as an ounce of weed. Today, an ounce of gold is $937. I looked it up on the Internet. It turns out they're collector's items, worth ten times their weight in gold. That, my friends, equates to one and a half million dollars— split six ways—that's like winning lotto."

Brownie said, "Nutter and his mad mates are not going to stop until they get their coins back."

"I told Nutter what would happen if I ever saw him again," Bear said. "He didn't listen, so he and his bikie mates were blown away back at the beach house. They won't be following us any time soon."

"Don't you think that was a bit extreme, blowing up our holiday house?" asked LP.

Bear replied, "The old place needed a facelift; we can finish the *reno* job when we get back."

While Bear carried on about how he would fix the place up, George went over to his computer and called up the screen for his surveillance camera. He said, "Those bikies you're talking about … Well, they'll be here soon. Have a look at this."

Although George was a bit of a loner, he did his bit to protect his patch of land from wildfires and was a member of the volunteer State Emergency Service. Also, not far from his property, the dirt road dipped like a roller coaster, allowing flood waters to go over when the drain below could not carry the torrent coming off the mountain. The State Emergency Services had provided George with a surveillance camera, aimed at the trouble spot. It was his job to move the yellow barriers on to the road to stop anyone from driving into a flooding causeway.

Nutter and his bikie mates had stopped at the barriers. Blowing some of them up back at the beach house had only slowed them down.

Nutter told Porky to remove the barriers, which he did. The flood waters had now fallen and were flowing under the roadway.

"Well what's your plan now, Bear? This time, there's nowhere to run. There's only one way off this mountain, and it's back the way you came."

Bear looked down the mountain and asked, "What's that cleared area down there?"

George replied, "That's a small subdivision of three cul-de-sacs. I had to do that to pay for land taxes and rates. I didn't want to but had no choice."

Bear was becoming inpatient and didn't want a lecture about taxation. "Mate, is there another way out?"

"Nope, the road that you drove along ends at the cul-de-sacs. The only way in and out, other than walking back along the track the way you came, is the dirt road down to the subdivision. I suspect Nutter will leave some of his bikie mates at the van. Bear, come over here and look at this!" George pointed out the dirt road on the computer that gave a good overview of their hilltop position.

"Wait, there's more," Bear said with urgency. "Position your camera a little to the right."

"More what?" George asked.

"More trouble coming!" was Bear's answer.

As they looked again at the camera, police vehicles and a Tactical Response van were about to cross the causeway.

LP said, "Ah, the coppers will arrest those bikies at the van, and we can get out of here.

"If Herbertsin's with 'em, forget it, he's in bed with the bikies," Bear replied.

George said. "The coppers may not be after Nutter and his mates, but me. My website has been under surveillance for posting government documents on my blog. I got them through freedom of information. You might think you have free speech in this country, until it goes against the government's slant on things. I had been warned by a whistleblower to be careful or I'd end up in jail."

"George, that's not a crime," LP said.

"Well, tell that to the coppers who are on their way," George replied.

"You're paranoid," Bear blurted out.

"If I am paranoid, who's the other group heading this way in those hotted-up vehicles?"

George zoomed in on the driver, who would not be out of place in Afghanistan, with his long black beard and traditional headwear.

Not far behind was a large group of mountain bike riders wearing black and white lycra.

The guys had more trouble than they could handle. "Okay," Mason said. "I know who the bikies and cops are, but who are these guys?"

George said, "They look like a mixed bag of religious zealots. They'd be after the fleece, the Scroll, or both. They must have tracked me down through the website. Now I regret posting how I came to have that Scroll and fleece."

"Have you got the fleece here, as well?" LP asked.

"You're standing on it."

LP looked down, and memories came rushing back of the goat skin turning a golden colour from being on the roof racks in the blazing heat.

"Well, what a surprise, George, you've still got it."

"Yeah, I use it as a meditation mat at sunrise every morning. It gives me inspiration for the rest of the day."

LP said, "Well, that's easy to fix. Just give those religious nutters what they want."

"Yeah, but we're not handing George over to those coppers, and the bloody gold; finders, keepers" said Bear.

LP made his thoughts clear to everyone, not just Bear. "You haven't thought this through. Give the gold to Nutter, and there's a good chance they'll leave. Give the goat skin and Scroll to those religious fanatics, and they can fight each other over them, and not us. We need some insurance before we give all this away."

He reached down, picked up the Scroll, and placed it face down on George's scanner; next, he downloaded it to a document file.

Bear said, "I'll go down and talk to Nutter. I'm sure I can convince him to pack up and leave."

He pushed the gold back into the backpack, threw it over his shoulder, and started walking down the mountain to the first cul-de-sac.

George yelled, "Come back; tell Nutter something from me." He whispered a message into Bear's ear.

"What's that supposed to mean?"

"Just pass that message onto Nutter when you give him the gold."

Bear confronted Nutter at the first cul-de-sac filled with bikies.

Nutter was first to speak. "Have you got anything to say before we pay you back for the pain you put us through over the years?"

"Just two things. Look across at the cops in the other cul-de-sac. Step out of line, and they'll arrest the lot of you," Bear said with confidence.

"I don't think so. The commissioner is an old mate of mine. When he gets what he came for, I'll have no trouble from them coppers."

"And George said to tell you this." Bear moved close to Nutter and whispered in his ear.

Nutter shook his head and asked, "Is that it?"

"Yep, it's your call. Here's the gold; now piss off." He handed over the backpack.

Nutter called over to the police commissioner, "Hey, Jack." Nutter then threw two gold coins through the air, and the commissioner caught them.

"We're square," he said to the commissioner. Then, to the rest of his gang, he said, "We're out of here."

Nutter's mob of bikies started revving their engines and, two by two, followed Nutter and Porky off the mountain.

Bear looked across to the other cul-de-sac, where Brownie was standing. He had walked down the road with Bear and now confronted a rabble of religious fanatics.

One of the mountain bikers spoke in an American accent. "We are the rightful custodians of the Scroll and golden fleece. It is written in prophecy. Hand them over, and we'll leave."

Brownie held the rolled-up goat skin in one hand and the Scroll in the other.

All eyes were fixed on what they had come for. "Whoever is left standing takes the fleece and Scroll."

The ensuing brawl that erupted between these two highly charged groups triggered a response from a van of coppers, trained in handling riots and terrorist threats. They reacted swiftly, with batons in hand, to break up the rabble and send them on their way. Their mission was to back up the commissioner, who had taken it upon himself to arrest George personally. His aim was to send a message that no one spoke out against the police or the government.

Time seemed to stand still as George looked down from his mountain. What he saw was not the cul-de-sacs, but what they represented: the numbers 666. This was not a good sign. He pointed to several bunches of his award-winning bananas and said to Mason, "Take them down to that bunch of coppers, and give them a taste of my success."

Before George followed Mason, LP asked him what he whispered to Bear. George whispered a response, followed by, "This is my mantra for life."

George and Mason walked down the mountain to the clearing, where the subdivision was.

Mason confronted the coppers first, offering them something to munch on while standing in the hot sun. Two battered and bruised guys stood close to them, from the group in hotted-up vehicles.

George whispered the same message Bear had passed on to Nutter to those two.

One asked, "What does that mean?"

"If your leaders are smart enough, they'll know; pass it on," was George's answer.

He then walked over and joined Jack Herbertsin and his coppers.

"I hope you're enjoying my organic bananas. They've been a nice earner, selling by the truckload over the border."

"This'll be your last day as a banana bender. You're under arrest for inciting terrorism," said Jack.

George replied, "That's bullshit; you're the only one bent around here. Why don't you just piss off."

Herbertsin was dismissive and responded with an authority in his voice, "We're closing down your website. We've got new laws that cover just about everything. It's called the Terrorism Act, so you're under arrest."

"I don't think so; the information on my site has all come from government agencies, through freedom of information. How can it be a crime?"

Jack responded angrily, "It doesn't conform to government policy. Under the new laws, we can arrest and hold anyone indefinitely."

Mason interrupted, "So what is it you don't want the public to know?"

"Well, since you ask, it's about prisons and crime. Eighty percent of all people in prison are directly or indirectly in jail due to illegal drugs, soft and hard, and nothing has changed in forty years. That makes us either incompetent or complicit in the status quo. So give yourself up now, or none of you will be leaving this mountain alive."

"My website's got nothing to do with terrorism. I'm not going anywhere with you. I suggest you all leave, or bad shit will happen to you."

The commissioner said to his subordinate, "Handcuff him. If he resists, shoot him. If you don't, I will."

The officers were bad apples from back in the early seventies. They were the ones who had arrested and almost killed the *Westie* who had survived the flood waters.

George had to act fast. He reached into his top pocket and pulled out a Shu-Roo, put it to his lips, and blew.

By this time, it was dusk, but the sky suddenly got much darker. Within seconds, you could not see the sky. It wasn't night falling, but thousands of fruit bats descending on the law enforcement group.

"Don't panic; they're only here to eat those bananas you're holding. If you shoot, they'll go into frenzy and peck you to pieces."

One day, while driving through his banana plantation, George had discovered that fruit bats were highly attracted to his crop. He had finally realised that it was the two Shu-Roos mounted on his bulbar, which emitted a high-pitched sound that only certain animals could hear. It worked best to scare off kangaroos from roadside grazing when driving in outback Australia, but did the opposite for bats—it attracted them. Flying foxes, the locals called them, now in plague throughout Queensland.

Using this knowledge, he had modified his harvesting to allow 20 percent to be eaten by the bats, using the Shu-Roos to control what the bats ate. One extra bonus was the droppings the bats left behind, which became organic fertiliser. So that's how he had become an organic banana grower.

George spoke with confidence. He had the coppers beat. "One other thing: the bats carry the Hendra virus. There is no cure. It's okay for bat shit to fall to the ground, but don't get it on your skin. You'll have a good chance of being infected," George advised. "Your best chance to survive is to run over to the paddock and jump in that dam. Good luck."

Bear, Mason, and Brownie stood several metres away, watching George control the situation.

George whispered the same words to Jack that he had repeated to the others. Jack pulled out his revolver and pointed it at George. "If I'm going to die, so are you."

The sound of the gun exploded through the valley and caused the bats to take off. Like a squadron of planes, they dropped bombs of droppings as they left.

George fell to his knees, blood seeping through his fingers where he held tightly to his side.

The commissioner turned and ran with the others to the dam and jumped in.

Bear said, "We've got to get you back up the mountain. You're losing a lot of blood."

Bear and Brownie picked up their mate and carried him back up to the plantation. They laid him down as the sun became a huge, orange glow on the peak of Mount Beerwah.

Bear said, "We need to get him off this mountain and to hospital, or he's not going to make it."

Nutter had already left with his gold coins. The religious fanatics had ridden off on the mountain bikes, and those in hotted-up vehicles had left before the bats descended.

LP had remained back at George's property and had watched everything on the surveillance camera.

In the distance, several more uninvited visitors were walking up from the east ridge of the plantation. They came over to the packing shed where the guys were huddled around George.

One of them visitors said, "You need to leave this mountain with us now. There's little time to waste. Your government has ordered the mountain to be destroyed. George will not survive, nor will you."

"I don't know who you guys are, but you've got it completely wrong; the noise you hear are Black Hawk helicopters on a training exercise over the Glass House Mountains," Brownie said.

He was well aware of the ancient legend of the Glass House Mountains and believed Tibrogargan would not allow anything to happen to his family.

"There's no time to explain. Follow us to the Bora Ring. It's just past the plantation, in your state forest."

George was still conscious, but time was running out for him. LP asked, "How do you know George's name? We don't know you guys."

"Don't ask questions; there's no time to waste."

The visitors walked over to Brownie and formed a circle around him. They placed their hands on his shoulders and together repeated these words: "Awake, Tibrogargan; your family is about to be destroyed. Protect them from destruction. Awake from Dreamtime."

Bear was watching George's laptop, which displayed a black cloud heading their way, but he could not make out whether it was a storm approaching or something much more sinister.

Rocks started to dislodge, rolling down the mountain. Tremors were increasing. Brownie yelled out, "Tibrogargan has awakened," and with a mighty explosion from the east face, ash and smoke plumes bellowed out.

LP knew that the mountains were in an old volcanic region, which could explain the tremors and explosion.

On the laptop, Bear saw a rolling cloud of smoke and ash about to engulf the black cloud. A squadron of Black Hawk helicopters were armed and ready to fire. Radar had not picked up the impending danger on board, but visual sight had. The squadron leader gave the order: "Abort. Take evasive action, land immediately."

Bear remarked, "Good one, Brownie; you've got good contacts in Dreamtime. Now tell these guys to piss off. We've got to get George off the mountain quick smart, or he's not going to make it."

LP thought, *Are these guys paramedics and part of the training exercise?*

One of the visitors spoke again. "George will not survive. We will look after him; his time on this mountain is at an end."

Another reached down to pick George up. As he did, George said, "Thanks, son."

At that moment, George realised who the strangers were. What had happened back at the Bora Ring in outback Queensland was not a vision from smoking weed. The women from the Bora Ring must have been real. Bear and Mason also realised they weren't strangers. They were their sons. Words said back then flashed through their minds: DNA; renewed life; keep the Scroll safe; etched in time.

George's son carried him down through the banana plantation to the Bora Ring. Those from another place and time stood within the circle of stones, and one of them said, "What was foretold is almost complete. Protect the Scroll until the numbers align. It will give enlightenment to all who connect with the image and words whispered."

Without warning, George and the others vanished into the night.

Bear, LP, Brownie, Mason, and Red were left to figure out what had happened to George, and what to do next.

The guys now knew what the numbers meant, and that it was a date in time—midnight, January 1, 2010, and 1:01 am, New Year's Day. Although they did not have the Scroll in their possession, they did have it saved on George's hard drive. All was not lost. LP had placed it face down on George's scanner before giving it to those religious fanatics. No one looked directly at it as it was scanned. It would reveal what George's son mentioned: the image within the Scroll, which had been spoken of nearly thirty years ago. There was no problem with loading it onto his computer. LP remembered more about that night. He started to recall what one of the women had said: "In one hand, you will hold the knowledge of thousands of years, and in the other, the light of the world."

Even with the gift of foresight, he could not see what the future had in store for him and his mates. Only when the numbers aligned might light be shed on what the future holds.

The Rev Heads, who loved their cars as much as Allah, were part of a sleeper cell that would do anything asked of them by Al Qaeda. Their leader, clutching the rolled-up fleece, was on a plane to Pakistan, heading for a mountainous region bordering Afghanistan. He believed that possessing the golden fleece would enhance their leader's right to rule over all nations.

The word soon spread that a man from Oz had something important to give to their spiritual leader, and it wasn't long before he was face to face with Bin Laden himself. His devout follower handed him the rolled-up fleece. Bin Laden put down his AK47, reached out with both hands, and grabbed the parcel; he untied a small piece of string and unfolded it to reveal a goat skin.

"Look around, you fool; don't you think I have enough goats? I don't need another one."

"But this one is special. The golden fleece has been used by another man on a mountain on the other side of the world for spiritual inspiration. I considered you the rightful one to possess its power."

"Come closer. Tell me more about this golden fleece."

His follower moved closer and repeated, in a soft voice, the words said back at George's mountain. His spiritual leader became agitated, raised his rifle into the air, and fired a round of bullets, yelling, "No! No! No!"

The words were like daggers to his heart. He realised at that moment that his jihad, delivered by his unquestioning followers to the Great Satan America, had failed. His vision of the future with all nations united under Islam and him being supreme spiritual leader were coming to an end.

As for the Scroll, it ended up in Brisbane in a cathedral built of granite—a testament to the success in bringing new believers to their faith. A man wearing black and white lycra left his mountain bike chained to the front gate and walked in through the large doors. He walked down the long aisle past all the pews and stood before the elder's altar. The elder was anxious to be the first to look upon the image handed to him in the Scroll. He believed it would give him absolute power over his flock.

He wasted no time unrolling the Scroll as the man in lycra stood by. Blinded as if looking at the sun, both fell to their knees as the elder dropped face first to the floor, convulsing. It was as if he'd been hit by a stun gun.

As the Scroll coiled back, the first man picked it up and then started to walk back out through the cathedral doors. He unchained his bike, mounted it, and rode towards the city through rush hour traffic. Outside a ten-story building in the heart of Brisbane, he chained his bike to a lamp post and walked towards the main entrance. After pressing an intercom button, a man answered with, "What do you want?"

The bike rider replied, "I have something valuable to leave with you."

He was instructed to enter through two glass doors and was met in the foyer by a man named Steve. They shook hands and walked over to a wall of lifts. Steve entered a security card at one of the lifts, and they headed down to the basement. The men walked out of the lift into a secured area. Steve told the man to walk through a security scanner, carrying the Scroll. He was instructed to place his thumbs on a small scanner and then filled out some paperwork before entering a vault. As the door was pushed open, he looked around and saw safety deposit boxes as well as rows of gold bullion.

Ahead was another security door. In here, controlled ventilation kept moisture from damaging the valuable works of art inside. He went through the door and placed his delivery on a rack. Now that the Scroll was in a safe place, he turned and exited exactly the way he came in, walking out through the glass doors. He unchained his bike and rode out of the city. His intentions regarding the Scroll would remain a mystery.

12

LP turned and walked away from the Bora Ring, pondering what to do next. Bear, Mason, Brownie, and Red followed him up the track, which wound through the banana plantation back to George's home. LP entered the cave and found the laptop undamaged from the tremors; they then made their way back to the causeway, where their van was parked. Mason asked LP to hand him the laptop and opened it as they walked. He found where the Scroll's image was saved and then set up a password that only they would know.

"This will keep the Scroll safe till the time arrives, when the numbers will align, as spoken back at the ancient Bora Ring," Mason said.

LP took the lead; he climbed into the driver's seat and ordered everyone else to get aboard. He then asked Brownie to throw over the keys. With one turn, he clicked over the van and back-tracked to civilisation, leaving George's mountain hideaway protected by the Dreamtime spirits of Tibrogargan and his family.

LP looked over at Brownie in the passenger seat; glancing back at his other mates, he said, "We should keep George's website up and running to keep the bastards honest—it's what he would have wanted." The guys no longer considered what had happened back at the female Bora Ring a vision from smoking too much dope; it was the real deal.

There was also the possibility of using the surveillance camera to prove that the police commissioner had shot George. Until they could find the footage implicating him, they had no proof and no body. The commissioner and his officers would close ranks and would certainly be tight lipped about what had happened that day. This could work to the guys' advantage; the commissioner would prefer to let sleeping dogs lie, rather than have the truth come out. They suspected he would not trouble them anymore, even if he did survive the Hendra virus the bats were carrying.

It wasn't long before they arrived back at the beach house, which needed serious repair work. Bear instructed LP to organise the insurance claim and get the place fixed up. If there were any problems, they could ring him in Sydney.

Brownie wasn't hanging around; he had an outback tour to finish with his German tourists. They were expecting to shoot and eat wild goat and boar. The Germans were good customers and would pay a bonus of a hundred dollars for any wild goat that had horns over one metre across.

Mason went back to his Masonic Retirement Home, saying, "Don't call me; I'll be there when the numbers align."

Red left Queensland, heading south to Bells Beach to chill out and surf. He decided he wanted no part of what might or might not happen at midnight, New Year's Eve 2009.

After he had organised the repairs to the beach house, LP headed back to suburbia with George's laptop. Over the next eight years, the news media reported the most disturbing events that grabbed headlines. Although the reports were without emotion, just matter of fact, behind the news was sorrow and despair. Over the ensuing years, the world they felt comfortable with started to look and sound like a disaster movie that might be called *The Decade from Hell.*

2002

Widespread drought and wildfires struck the United States, causing billions of dollars in damage.

Rivers of molten lava from a volcano in the Congo destroyed dozens of villages and engulfed the city of Goma. Nearly twelve million people were displaced and fled to Rwanda.

A 7.2-magnitude earthquake struck central Asia, killing hundreds of people in a village in Afghanistan.

Four typhoons swept through Japan and the Philippines in early July, killing about a hundred people.

In August, torrential rains resulted in floods and landslides in south-east China.

Monsoon floods and mudslides hit India, Nepal, and Bangladesh, caused nearly a thousand deaths and destroying crops and livestock.

Sixty-five wildfires around Sydney destroyed more than sixty homes and burnt out 296,000 acres of state forest and farmland.

2003

Two-thousand and three fared no better. January was fatal for hundreds of people dying from cold weather and icy conditions on the border of India and Bangladesh, where millions of people had no heat, electricity, or warm clothing.

A three-week heat wave left twelve hundred people dead from sunstroke and dehydration in the Andhra Pradesh state of India. A similar heat wave had killed a thousand people the previous year.

Another heat wave lasting nearly a month hit Europe, causing fourteen thousand deaths in France. Fires raged in France, Portugal, and Spain. Glacial ice melted in the Alps, violent storms hit England, and nuclear power stations had to be cut back due to overheated water.

Hurricane Isabel caused widespread damage. Storms, tornadoes, and hail required $12 billion worth of repairs. More wildfires erupted in late October. Eight hundred thousand acres were burnt, thousands of homes were destroyed, and dozens of people were killed as fifteen thousand fire fighters fought to save lives and property.

Flash flooding near an orang-utan reserve in Bohorok was a direct result of heavy illegal deforestation, the world news reported.

13

2004

Hurricanes Ivan, Jeannie, Frances, and Charley caused billions of dollars worth of damage, and hundreds of US citizens lost their lives. Record-low temperatures hit Canada and the United States, causing snow storms, and Europe fared no better.

Fifty-two tornadoes struck America's Midwest, causing devastation in their path.

Wildfires in Alaska burnt more than five million acres, the worst season on record.

Floods and more than thirty earthquakes hit New Zealand, causing the evacuation of fifteen hundred people.

On the US Atlantic coast, four hurricanes made land in six weeks, causing more damage than Hurricane Andrew.

Flooding resulting from tropical storm Muifa threatened the World Heritage site of Hoi An in Vietnam. Thousands of homes were flooded, and many lives were lost.

A 9.0-magnitude earthquake caused a powerful tsunami in the Indian Ocean that hit twelve countries. Hardest hit was Aceh Province in Indonesia, where the death toll was in the hundreds of thousands. Other countries, including Sri Lanka, India, and Thailand, suffered a similar fate.

This was the last time Cassa's mates heard from him, via a text message: *Jetskin out for to win huge swell coming to Aceh.*

His latest surfing adventure, which put him in the wrong place at the wrong time, had started out at an unlikely place: the Perth mint in Western Australia. Here, the Australian government produced plastic note currency for sixty-eight countries worldwide.

While Cassa planned his next surfing trip throughout Asia, a plot to smuggle out the latest currency printed for Vietnam's communist government was in play. Gary, one of the insiders, needed a mule to smuggle the currency into Vietnam. An alliance was formed where Cassa would make enough money to fund his next surf trip. He could not see any problem taking vietnamese dong with him. The only difference with the money he carried was that the serial numbers were not recorded.

Cassa's past travels through that country had revealed poverty not seen in Australia. Every other building needed repairs and a good paint job. Aid money from Australia to help the vietnamese people had been constantly siphoned off by corrupt government officials.

That's what happened with the goodwill bridge, built on the outskirts of ho Chi Minh city. A $160 million aid package from the Australian government for a four-lane bridge had produced only a two-lane bridge that you could not drive a truck across. It was a white elephant after the comrades siphoned off cash at every level of the building process.

Gary and his co-conspirators had a surfboard already hollowed out, ready to stash 500 million dong in denominations of two hundred thousand. This was only $50,000 australian, but in Vietnam, it was enough to buy a house and retire comfortably.

The plan was in place. Gary didn't explain how he would get the cash out or why it would not be missed from the Perth mint. Like insider trading, while he could get away with it, he could make a fortune. Gary and a couple of other guys escorted Cassa to the Perth airport. He would be accompanied on the trip by Yong, an Australian citizen who was one of the first boat people to arrive in Australia back in the seventies. Yong spoke fluent english as well as vietnamese and could help Cassa if he was stopped by security.

As Cassa walked from the plane at Saigon airport, Yong followed discreetly behind him. Before he could put his hand luggage on the table for inspection, he was pulled aside by a woman wearing a white surgical face mask. He was escorted to a private area of the airport terminal.

Cassa didn't understand what was happening. The stress of his mission had raised his blood pressure and heart beat to a point where his albino white skin had turned red. That had set off a heat thermal scanner, designed to detect anyone who might have a fever and possible swine flu. Yong walked over to an official and said in vietnamese, "That man over there is an albino; he's just flushed from rushing up the ramp to make his next flight." With that, Yong slipped five 200,000-dong notes into the official's hand. The official signalled and said, "let the white man continue." The redness disappeared from Cassa's face, and several vietnamese women in white masks touched his white skin for luck. Yong kept his distance not to arouse suspicion they knew each other.

Cassa walked slowly back to the arrivals counter, taking deep breaths to remain as calm as possible. He handed over his carry-on bag to be searched and then was allowed to proceed to collect his surfboard and luggage.

He walked out of the airport terminal into a stifling, sticky heat wave. Cassa caught a bus into the city and was dropped off at the Grand Palace Hotel. It was an old building, refurbished in the style of its glory days of French colonial rule during the 1920s.

The plan was to stay at the hotel for three days and wait to be contacted about the money. At nine o'clock that night, as he watched TV, Cassa was startled by a knock on the door. By the time he opened the door, there was no one there, just an envelope at his feet. He bent down, picked it up, closed the door, and sat down to read the note inside: "Take 150 million dong to the casino on level two. Go to the cashier, change it to US dollars, and then gamble a small amount on the tables. Don't lose too much. Then return to your room with the US dollars. Do this for two more nights until all the dong is in US notes. I will contact you in three days. Don't fail or you will never see Australia again. Destroy this note."

Three days passed, and another loud knock was heard at the door. This time, Yong was standing there, ready to collect. There was a quick exchange of nearly fifty thousand US dollars. He handed three thousand dollars back to Cassa. Yong left the hotel with his freshly laundered cash. Cassa waited a little while longer and then booked out of the hotel. He then walked over to the Internet service in the hotel foyer and booked a flight to Bali.

Cassa dumped his hollowed out surfboard in a waste bin next to the hotel. He would replace it with something more suitable for surfing reef breaks in Bali.

His flight didn't leave until 11:30 pm, so he caught a cab across town to visit a war museum.

As he walked through the gates, Cassa saw American jet fighters and helicopters captured during the war. Over to his left, he saw a tank with a red star painted on it. It was the infamous tank that had smashed through the gates of the American embassy in the last days of 1975, during the fall of Saigon.

Cassa walked up a few steps and entered the building. A reminder of colonial days and war; it was now a shrine to those who had suffered so much during that conflict. He didn't stay long; some of the images made him physically sick.

Next he headed out of town to the Mekong River, where he boarded a small junk. The river was huge and fast flowing, reminding him of Enogerra Creek when it was in full flood.

After two kilometres, the guide took a sharp turn and headed the junk up a small inlet. The jungle canopy closed in as the inlet became smaller. Suddenly rain started pelting down. The thunderstorm only lasted a minute, but it sounded like a war zone. Cassa was a bit on edge after seeing the images at the war memorial and was having a little trouble on focusing on exactly where he was. He couldn't help thinking the Vietcong were about to come out of the jungle, firing bullets.

By now the boat had pulled up against a muddy embankment. A board was pushed out as a plank to walk on. Cassa quickly disembarked and followed the path through the jungle canopy, where it opened up to reveal a small building.

This was where he wanted to be. He planned to purchase jade Buddha carvings that could be sold in Australia for five times the amount he was about to pay. He would get an even better deal when the seller saw he was paying with US dollars. Cassa purchased only three Buddhas, not enough to attract attention when going through customs.

The boat that had brought him to this secret location had left, and he would have to travel by foot from here over muddy, mosquito-infested swamp land. Halfway across he met a local with a donkey and cart, who took him the rest of the way back to the Mekong River.

On reaching the river, he gave his new friend one hundred thousand dong. With a loud yell, the Vietnamese man called over another local to help Cassa get to the other side of the river.

Cassa climbed into a two-man dug-out, like a small canoe, and was handed an oar. He started paddling with the current and reached the other side without any trouble and then began to walk to the bus stop.

As he walked, Cassa spotted some old temple remains just off the main road and decided to investigate. Some structures were held up with reinforcing to stop them collapsing; others you could walk through. He saw a plaque which stated, "These ruins are a sixth-century temple site." The area had been bombed by the Americans during the war, and some buildings were damaged or destroyed; bomb craters littered the area. Another warning said, "Do not to walk off the track; unexploded bombs may be present."

Cassa made it back to the main road just in time to catch the last bus to Saigon.

He collected his luggage from the cloak room at the Grand Palace and boarded the commuter bus headed for the airport. It was six o'clock. By the time he arrived and checked in, he had only three hours to wait for his flight to Bali.

After arriving in Bali and going through customs without any problems, Cassa headed for the Bounty Hotel at Kuta Beach, a popular hotel for Australian tourists. That afternoon, he bought a new surfboard from one of the many surf shops and headed down to the wharf area. He organised a boat trip to surf the outer reefs.

Cassa spent several days at sea with other surfers from all over the world, who had come to these surf breaks only the locals knew about.

They also visited two small islands, one noted for its variety and strength of marijuana and the other for its women. Depending on your passion for drugs or women, you could choose number one or number two island. Cassa's choice was number three: staying on the boat so he would have a clear head and strength for a few days of surfing.

Cassa had to be mindful of his delicate complexion, as over-exposure to sunlight would burn and blister his skin. He wore a full-length wet suit even in summer and used heaps of sunscreen to protect him from turning as red as a beetroot.

After enjoying the surf off the outer reefs of Bali, he headed for the island of Java, landing at the airport in Jakarta, capital of the Indonesian archipelago.

Cassa travelled by bus across the south coast of Java, encountering police checkpoints where he would have to show his visa and passport. They passed through the first couple of checkpoints smoothly. At the last checkpoint, everyone on the bus was ordered off at gun point. Cassa was singled out because of his long blond hair. The officer checked his passport and visa and then said in broken English, "Your visa dated incorrectly. Follow me and bring your bag."

Cassa followed his instruction. Inside the police station, his bag was searched thoroughly, and nothing illegal was found. The officer spoke again: "Your visa incomplete, you stay night here." Cassa argued loudly with the official, but it just made him agitated. He drew his pistol, stuck it against Cassa's temple, and started to squeeze the trigger. "US dollars! US dollars!" Cassa yelled desperately. The officer released the trigger and lowered his weapon. Cassa reached into his pants pocket and pulled out his wallet. He grabbed a handful of notes and handed them over. The officer counted 220 US dollars. "You go, you go," he said, pointing out the door.

Cassa picked up his bag and got back on the bus. Finally, the bus reached his destination: a Dutch colonial mansion with six white pillars holding up the roof and a full-length verandah. Looking out through the palm trees to the ocean, you could see your own private reef break just a few hundred metres offshore.

For the next few weeks, Cassa surfed his heart out. Each time he watched the sun setting into the ocean, he became mellower. The stress of the trip to Vietnam became a distant memory.

His next adventure was to Aceh, a province at the tip of Sumatra, a place of danger, high adventure, and insurgency. The Indonesian military had been fighting an underground group there that wanted independence from Indonesia. Cassa would have to be extra careful. He weighed up his options and considered the risk worth it: the beach break had been described as bigger and better than pipeline in Hawaii.

Well, he got his wish, but the incoming swell he spotted on the horizon was more than he expected. An earthquake off the Sumatran coast had unleashed a tsunami.

2005

Nineteen feet of snow fell in the Reno-Lake Tahoe area of the United States, the heaviest snowfall since 1916.

Hurricanes continued to strike the States. The worst was Katrina, with an estimated damage of a hundred billion dollars, the most expensive natural disaster in US history. Eighteen hundred lives were lost.

Extreme winter conditions and earthquakes throughout the Afghanistan, India, and Pakistan region had climate forecasters predicting another Boxing Day-type tsunami. Southern China experienced flash flooding, which swept away a school in Ningan, China, causing loss of life.

In Mumbai, India, thirty-seven inches of rain fell in twenty-four hours, the most ever recorded in the country.

On the African continent, famine caused by drought and locusts left more than 3.6 million people in Niger facing starvation.

Wildfires burnt 37,000 acres in the south-east area of Washington, and other fires destroyed a hundred houses north-west of Los Angeles. Hurricane Beta broke the record for damages by an Atlantic storm, set in 1851.

Another hurricane brought torrential rain and more devastation to Central America. Floods and mudslides killed more than two thousand and buried the whole village of Pan in Baj.

2006

Widespread drought affected the United States, resulting in wildfires burning throughout the whole year; it was the warmest summer on record. Texas alone had two hundred wildfires out of control in a twenty-four-hour period. Storms with strong winds left 600,000 homes in Missouri without power for one week. In New York, 100,000 people were left without power for up to nine days.

On the south coast of Java, a 7.7-magnitude earthquake triggered a tsunami that displaced thousands from their homes and killed many hundreds of people.

Throughout late 2006 and into early 2007, Australian bushfires raged out of control in the Victorian Alps and Gippsland area. One million hectares were destroyed, making those fires the worst in living memory.

14

2007

Parts of the world's rivers and oceans were becoming dead zones, starved of oxygen. Mass fish, bee, insect, and bird deaths were being reported worldwide. Two words were becoming spoken more and more often when describing these events: climate change.

Wildfires in North America throughout summer and fall caused huge losses. Drought on the Great Plains resulted in further losses of over $5 billion.

In the Solomon Islands, a magnitude 8.1-earthquake and ensuing tsunami left property destroyed, and thousands homeless; many inhabitants lost their lives. With earthquakes in the south-east of Lima, Peru, climate experts and geologists were joining the dots and writing a white paper to be released. It would report on a major tectonic event that would occur on the west coast of America.

2008

The United States experienced widespread drought through the entire year. Wildfires, as well as Hurricanes Dolly, Iki, and

Gustav, caused damage estimated at $33 billion. Loss of life totalled 128.

Tornadoes ripped through the US Midwest, killing eighty-eight people and causing property, crop, and livestock losses amounting to $4.5 billion.

Sixty-seven thousand people died, and hundreds of thousands were injured, when a 7.9-magnitude earthquake hit Sichaun, Gansu, in the Yunnan province of western China.

In New England, a state of emergency was declared, after electricity was cut to 800,000 homes for several days after a major storm ripped through the region. National Guard troops helped to restore power lines and control demonstrations against the government.

Stock prices fell dramatically, and comparisons were made to the 1929 Wall Street crash. Markets around the world followed its lead and went into free fall.

Banks and financial institutions in America, Europe, and Asia which were deemed too big to fail, collapsed. Some survived with government intervention.

In Australia, the Queensland government response was to sell all remaining state businesses to private enterprise, but the public outcry caused second thoughts. The people of Queensland were starting to get to know what privatisation meant.

In the couple of years since electricity supply had been handed over to private enterprise, electricity prices rose by 50 percent, with suppliers making further submissions for increases. The reason given for selling the electricity asset was that there would be fewer increases in power bills and a more efficient supply system delivered by private enterprise. This had proven to be incorrect.

Old mate Kato again became the environmental warrior, this time not by taking out a mining generator, but by building a power-saving device called Pool Whisperer. This device reduced power consumption and noise pollution by as much as 80 percent; it was the start of the future wave of energy conservation.

Kato thought that any government would support such a huge saving, and he believed that electricity suppliers would promote it. However, even with the help of a lobbyist, an ex-public servant who knew how to approach government departments, he still would not succeed. The conclusion was that governments and electricity suppliers would not support something that would reduce revenue and profits. However, that was not all. Kato warned a senior government official that if maintenance continued to be reduced, and the latest technology was not implemented in transformers throughout the country, the whole power supply system could fail if a perfect solar storm reached Earth, like the one of 1859. His warning was clear and precise: it could not be disputed.

15

2009

Over four hundred wildfires were recorded in Australia. One of the worst in history, named "Black Saturday" by the media, claimed hundreds of lives and destroyed over two thousand homes in the south-east region of Victoria. Police suspected that the fires had been deliberately set by arsonists.

Red, who hadn't been in touch with anyone for years, popped up on the news bulletin. His catering company had donated food and resources to help the State Emergency Services feed the hundreds of volunteers helping to rescue survivors and clean up after the devastating wildfires.

Clusters of tornadoes ripped through Oklahoma, killing and injuring many.

President Obama declared a state of emergency in Minnesota, as flooding of the Red River caused widespread damage to homes in Fargo, North Dakota.

Floods in Manila were the worst in fifty years. Indonesia was struck by an earthquake again, with a 7.6-magnitude quake in Sumatra, and a tsunami hit Samoa.

Dust storms blanketed the eastern seaboard of Australia for days. Record-high temperatures were recorded through the country in November. Wildfires erupted in Western Australia, destroying hundreds of homes. Drought-breaking rain brought floods to central New South Wales, also damaging homes, farms, and roads.

A meeting of heads of government in Copenhagen failed to bring forward a binding agreement that would reduce carbon emissions, believed to be the cause of global warming. Some scientific dissenters argued the status quo but did not mention global dimming: the yin and yang of the problem.

Governments agreed to focus attention on stopping deforestation, at the rate of one hundred thousand football fields a day being logged or burnt. They also continued to support the Global Seed Vault in Svalbard, nicknamed the Doomsday Vault, deep frozen in the middle of a Norwegian mountain. The noughties were creating a sense of déjà vu, for LP bringing back memories of the war in Vietnam and the communist insurgency in Malaya. The Australian government changed from right to left wing, and weather patterns returned to what they were like in the early 1970s. The war on drugs continued, after forty years. There was a mining and share market boom and bust, similar to 1973. Terrorism by the IRA and Black September was replaced by Islamic fundamentalist terrorism.

Cyclones, wildfires, terrorism, tsunamis, and wars in Iraq and Afghanistan were not enough to shake the resolve of LP and the others, who still believed New Year's Eve would be a fitting tribute to George, if nothing else. However, financial turmoil on the share markets throughout the world continued to have an impact throughout 2009.

Bear had done the best of all of them financially and was highly geared with his property developments. He had ridden out the downturn of 2001, but now his luck had run out. All lines of credit had dried up. He phoned LP for help just days before the new year. LP's answer to Bear's problem was not what he wanted to hear. LP was also cash strapped, and so was everybody else. They were all in financial survival mode. However, there was a long shot.

LP reminded Bear about the dreadlocked, sandy-haired hippy with a glass eye who had shared a joint with Red on the beach back at Bells.

"Think hard, Bear. What did Red tell you about that day?" "He told me on the flight back from Melbourne that the guy got his glass eye after a pool cue was jabbed into his eye in a brawl with a bunch of bikers. He spent his time either surfing Bells Beach or prospecting for gold at a place he called Big River. He had found a gold nugget weighing more than three kilos but was unable to get it out for fear that the other gold diggers would hear of the find and kill him. Billy, the hippy, had described how he planned to get the gold out when he went back to the old mining site, which had slowly been swallowed by forest re-growth. He said that there were several canoes down on the river embankment. His plan was to retrieve the nugget and paddle downstream at night to the next town. If all went well, Red would read about it in the newspaper in the following couple of days. If that didn't happen, the hippy said he would either be dead or the local mining prospectors, who had been there for many years, would have the nugget."

Bear hadn't heard anything in the media about a gold nugget, but he considered a third possibility: that the gold was still where Billy had hidden it: a wombat hole under the dirt road, after a sharp bend, two hundred yards from an old makeshift hut.

Bear thanked LP for jogging his memory and wished him good luck for 2010, as he would not make it back to Queensland in time for New Year's Eve. If Bear didn't find the nugget, it would be another financial black hole for him and his company. This time, there was no escape; his plan had to work.

He checked the *Melbourne Age* newspaper archives for any report of a major gold nugget find. There was no reference to the nugget.

Bear booked the earliest flight possible to Melbourne and arranged for a rental car at the airport. He arrived at six o'clock and carried his hand luggage through the airport terminal. He picked up the keys for his rental car—a VW Transporter, the modern-day version of a Kombi. However, this vehicle was even better than the old Kombi. It was fitted for off-road camping. Bear headed towards Bells Beach. It felt just like old times, with luxury. After a bit of a drive across Melbourne and out to Bells, he arrived at Red's house.

Bear walked up to the front door and pounded on it. "What are you doing here?" Red said. "This is a surprise; you should have phoned me first." Bear's old mate looked angry and agitated.

"No time, mate; you're coming with me to Big River. Remember that story you told LP about a hippy and a gold nugget? Well, we're going to find it. Pack some camping gear, and we're out of here."

Bear and Red carried the camping gear to the van and then headed north-west to the old gold mining site, Big River.

As they drove closer to their destination, the van crossed a large bridge. Bear and Red looked down to see a fast-flowing river wedged between steep gorges. They were not far now from the remnants of the old mining town. After the bridge, Bear took a sharp right-hand turn. The gravel road led into dense forest re-growth from mines abandoned over one hundred years ago. Red pointed out old mining shacks, most abandoned, but a few still liveable. Bear stopped at an A-frame shack built of timber logs and rusted iron. A fire was burning outside the shack.

A few old prospectors came out to greet them, asking how long they would be staying and if they were prospecting.

Red answered, "We are looking for a friend who's gone missing. You guys look like you've been around here a long time. Did you know a hippy called Billy? He had long, sandy dreadlocks and a glass eye."

One prospector answered, "About forty years ago, there was a guy like that, but he stopped coming up prospecting. We haven't seen him since then. Why are you interested in him now?"

"Just following up on a cold case," Bear replied. "We have some new information that might help find this chap. Tomorrow, we'll see if we can find any remains or his belongings."

Red had brought some food from his catering business for dinner. His favourite meal in a can was beef stroganoff. Not just a normal-sized tin, but a four-litre can, enough to feed a company battalion. He placed it on the fire's edge to warm up.

One of the prospectors was named Coxie; he was a Pommy who wanted to be addressed as Lord Coxie. The most conversation you could get out of him was "'er, rather." His mate, Gazza, translated for him when he spoke. Red and Bear picked up that these prospectors knew more than they were saying about Billy.

They were right. Before long, Lord Coxie came up behind Bear with a shovel and cracked it across his shoulders. Bear went down onto the fire edge, knocking the stroganoff can into the fire. Bear turned and grabbed the shovel, shoving it right between Coxie's legs. This bought him to the ground with a loud "'er!"

Bear and Red decided to get out of there. Before they left the campsite, Bear picked up two rocks, walked over to the old bush dunny, and grabbed a roll of toilet paper. Bear handed Red a rock, and they each started winding toilet paper around the rock about twelve times.

"We'll make sure those guys don't follow us," said Bear.

As they left the ramshackle miner's huts in the distance, Bear turned and pulled out his lighter. He lit the rock rolled in toot paper and did the same to the one Red was holding. Twenty metres back, Bear and Red had passed two abandoned mine shafts on either side of the road. Bear knew that these holes would be full of methane gas. In unison, they bowled a perfect line and length, and both flaming rocks landed exactly where they wanted them: down the shafts. All you could see were two giant flames shooting to the sky as the explosion destroyed the road.

As they ran further from the campsite, down the dirt road, they heard another loud explosion go off.

"There goes dinner; they'll be picking tin and strog out of their skin for the rest of the night," said Bear.

Bear and Red eventually caught a bit of shut-eye, leaning against a couple of trees. It wasn't exactly the way they wanted to camp out. As morning light filtered through the dense rainforest canopy, they stood, stretched their legs, and then started walking until they came to a sharp bend. They were looking on either side of the dirt road for wombat holes.

Bear yelled, "I've found one. Go down and see if it opens into a larger cave."

Red slid down the embankment and shone his torch in, and yes, there was a larger cave under the roadway. Together, they started digging to make the opening larger and then squeezed their way through. They were both able to crouch in the small cave. There were two smaller wombat tunnels that continued on. Bear shone the torch up the first one and could see some white bones. This could be Billy. He started digging with his small shovel and made it through to the next cave. There it was! The gold nugget rested on the parched bones, and Billy's glass eye reflected light as though he was looking at them with approval.

They quickly crawled out through the tunnel; the air was becoming harder to breathe, because they were inhaling a mixture of air and methane. With their vision becoming blurred and their strength weakening, they just made it out of the wombat hole in time, gasping for breath. The gas explained what had happened to Billy.

Bear carried the impressive nugget. Red pointed down the road to the river's edge, where two canoes lay on the embankment. They ran towards them. Bear put the nugget in the first canoe and climbed in, pushing himself away from the embankment, and Red followed in the other canoe. They didn't have to do much paddling, as the river was flowing pretty fast, but there was a reason for that: on the next bend, the river dropped in depth, exposing rocks and rapids.

Bear made it through, but Red was nowhere to be seen as his upturned canoe floated past Bear. Several minutes passed, but there was no way of going back; the steep gorge on either side of the river was impassable. Bear's only option was to paddle on downstream, under the bridge they had driven over earlier, to reach the next town, twenty kilometres away. Once there, he pointed his canoe towards a small jetty and reached for his phone, which now had reception. Bear rang 000 to organise a search for Red, hoping he was still alive. Next, he phoned LP to let him know he had found the gold nugget but had lost Red coming down the rapids. He said he would wait till the search party found him, dead or alive.

Bear would not be back at the beach house for New Year's Eve, nor would Red.

Bear, now with time on his hands, made a few phone calls to find a buyer for his nugget. He was put in contact with the owner of the Golden Nugget Casino in Las Vegas. He offered $3.5 million for the nugget. It would be showcased in the casino's grand entrance for all to see.

16

New Year's Eve 2009

The countdown had started: "Ten, nine, eight, seven …" LP moved his hand down to the laptop and entered the password as revellers yelled, "Happy New Year!" again. They were celebrating two New Year's Eves, since they were southerners on Daylight Saving Time. He waited until exactly midnight, Queensland time, and then pressed Enter.

Brownie and Mason were celebrating with some women over at Kato's holiday house, just a couple of doors down, across from a sandy track disappearing into the darkness, leading to the shore. They spotted LP standing alone on his verandah.

Brownie yelled, "Happy New Year! Did you remember to upload the Scroll to George's website?"

"Yes," LP replied. "Where were you? Bloody late, as usual." Brownie ignored the comment and replied, "The only thing left to do is text the guys who aren't here and tell them it's done." LP's response was sudden and abrupt: "*No!* Wait till 1:01 am. That's what the second set of numbers must have meant. It's not just the upload to the web; it must be sent at the correct time. I've already attached the image of the Scroll, ready to be emailed."

Brownie's connection with his Dreamtime ancestors, Mason's secret knowledge going back to the biblical days of Solomon, and LP's visions of the future all gave them a level understanding as to why the Scroll needed to be uploaded into cyberspace.

They all came to the same conclusion: the alignment of the numbers enabled the knowledge from within the Scroll to be revealed. Up until that point in time, technology did not have the ability to connect. But now through the World Wide Web, they could deliver the secret hidden within the Scroll as foretold at the female Bora Ring in outback Queensland nearly forty years earlier. That Bora Ring, weathered and aged over tens of thousands of years, was the birth place of Brownie's ancestors, who had first started counting the number of stars in the universe. Over time, they had realised that there was more to counting using just number 1, and that 0 existed, both in the physical and spiritual world. That connection had started the march to this point in time, where the binary numbers of 1 and 0 would intertwine and unlock what was hidden within the Scroll.

With only minutes to go, the wireless modem's signal started to weaken. The two red lights for Wireless and Send started flashing like a railway crossing. LP was about to lose connection. He yelled to Brownie, "I saved the file of the Scroll to my phone earlier, just in case something went wrong. I'm losing reception here; run down to the beach and send it as a text message, quick smart!"

Brownie grabbed the phone and headed down the track to the beach, where reception was stronger. It was windy, with some light rain, and a bright full moon was breaking through storm clouds. LP pressed Enter on his laptop one minute earlier than he should have, but he had no choice; the signal was about to disconnect. It was up to Brownie to pick up reception from the beach.

Brownie walked back up the sandy track, onto the verandah, and over to LP's cooler. He lifted the lid, grabbed three cold beers, twisted the caps off, and handed them around, saying, "There's nothing more to do now other than knock down a couple of coldies and hope the second decade of the new millennium gets off to a better start than the last one."

Brownie, Mason, and LP raised their stubbies and cracked them together in celebration, knowing that the Scroll, as foretold, was now in cyberspace.

LP took several mouthfuls of beer and then stood motionless, staring out into darkness.

The moonlight disappeared behind a swirling mass of storm clouds, just as, in his mind, darkness had filled him with gut-wrenching panic. What he was now seeing was the future, frozen in time. Ice covered the north, and like the darkness of his thoughts, so too darkness would cross the land for thirty nights.

Mason looked towards LP and asked, "What do you see out there?"

LP blinked his eyes and, with his body trembling, replied, "Brownie, your hope for a better start for this decade will be short lived. What I've seen, I hope will not come to pass. Remember Kato warned authorities about power failures resulting from the next solar maximum? Well, it'll peak on the twenty-third."

Brownie replied, "You're mad and way off with your psychic predictions; don't worry, guys, my ancestors from Dreamtime won't desert us if shit happens. When the time comes, they'll help."

Mason interrupted, "You're both a little crazy with the way you think. How about live the moment and let the future be a mystery."

0101100000001011001010101100000010110010101011000000101
1001010101100000010110010101011000000101100101010110000
0001011001010101100000010110010101011000000101100101010
0110000000101100101010110000001011001010101100000010110
0101010110000000101100101010110000001011001010101100000
0101100101010110000000101100101010110000001011001010101
1000000010110010101011000000101100101010110000001011001
0101011000000010110010101011000000101100101010110000001
0110010101011000000010110010101011000000101100101010110
0000010110010101011000000010110010101011000000101100101
0101100000001011001010101100000010110010101011000000101

BOOK 2

IMAGE OF THE PAST

17

NOVEMBER 4, 2010

LP struggled to sleep, tossing and turning as pain shot up his right leg. His knee cap had been bandaged for over two weeks and was still giving him trouble, making long distance driving demanding. He lay awake, thinking what daylight might bring besides pain.

Morning silence was broken by his son's screeching alarm clock and a pair of kookaburras laughing from a gum tree near their bedroom window. His son had to be up at five, ready for his boss to pick him up at the servo near his home at five twenty-five. LP prepared his son's lunch and dropped him off at the Shell Servo, as he had done for the past four months.

In the New Year, his son would get back his driving licence. He had recently had a brain snap, resulting in him losing his licence for drink driving.

But LP was looking forward to the New Year for more reasons than one.

He finished packing, making quite sure nothing was forgotten. Squeezing down and zipping the cases closed, LP then weighed them to ensure there wouldn't be any excess baggage charges.

Although Christmas was only six weeks away, LP was preoccupied with thoughts of what happened back at the Bora Ring. One thought kept popping into his head: *Go back to the mountain.* He knew it was a mountain in New Zealand, not the Glass House Mountains. A mountain he had climbed back in 1974, where he reflected on what life would deal him after returning with all his old mates from the Bells Beach surf contest.

Around two that afternoon, LP and Ingrid finally arrived at Brisbane Airport, after travelling through painfully slow traffic.

They had travelled by cab with a driver who was a refugee from Afghanistan. The cabbie, trying to avoid the gridlock on the Gateway Arterial, had taken them down a maze of rat runs. These were shortcuts not even LP knew of, and he had thought he knew every back street.

LP wasn't impressed when what would normally be a thirty-five-dollar fare became fifty dollars, including a tip. "Buy a Navman and set the map for Brisbane, not Afghanistan," he had said sarcastically, "and you'd get everyone to their destination quicker."

"All boarding flight 537 for Christchurch now, please proceed to gate 27. Thank you." LP and Ingrid heard the announcement and joined the queue to start their brief seven-day holiday travelling through the South Island of New Zealand.

LP sat in the aisle seat, with Ingrid in the centre; he looked across to the young lady sitting at the window. With a big smile, she said, "Hi, I'm Gwen."

They waited for takeoff. As their flight taxied down Brisbane Airport's runway, LP's thoughts spiralled back to 1974, when he was on the same runway headed towards the same destination: Brisbane to Christchurch.

He didn't want to repeat the hassles that had greeted him on arrival last time. With shoulder-length hair, backpack in one hand, and surfboard in the other, customs officers had pulled him aside. It seemed that profiling had targeted him as a possible drug courier.

LP had been strip searched for drugs, and a knife was jabbed into a crack in his surfboard and twisted to see if any white powder came out. Either cocaine or heroin, he wasn't sure what they were expecting to find.

The border security officers had told him, "We don't like your type here." LP's welcome to New Zealand had been similar to the *Westie's* encounter with authorities in 1973 in Queensland. "Welcome to Queensland" one minute, in the slammer the next.

LP and Ingrid sat chatting about their itinerary. They had calculated that they could travel by camper van around two thousand kilometres in seven days.

Ingrid had mapped out and marked each town with their estimated arrival times. The road trip would take them from Christchurch to Milford Sound and back, crossing through Haast Pass's snow-capped mountains. After walking and climbing Fox and Franz Josef glaciers, they would head back over the Alps through Arthur's Pass.

LP looked around and saw that every seat on the plane was taken. The friendly cabin crew were demonstrating safety instructions, and so he prepared himself for takeoff.

Belt tightened.

Seat upright.

The engines roared as flight 537's wheels bumped along the runway, lifting off and reaching 35,000 feet in no time.

As the seat belt light turned off, LP reached up to turn his reading light on. He loosened his seat belt and then pressed the left arm rest button. He reclined a little and settled in for the three-hour flight.

Time passed as shades of orange reflected off the plane wing tip. Sunset drew a faint black line across a distant horizon, connecting the vastness of space with our blue planet. LP glanced out from his aisle seat and asked Gwen, "Have you been to Christchurch before?"

"No," she answered, "I'm on my first visit, to go to a six-day meeting."

LP asked, "What type of meeting takes so long?"

"It's not quite what you think," Gwen said, while rummaging through her handbag. She handed LP a large business card that read *Avatar: The Compassion Project.*

"Oh, you've got something to do with the movie?"

"No, nothing to do with the film. We had copyright over the name 'Avatar' well before anyone else wanted to use it," Gwen said confidently. "Why don't you call in and join me at the seminar while you're in Christchurch? You'll get a bit of an idea what we're on about."

"Thanks, we'll see how we're travelling, but we're on a tight schedule. Anyway, what are you drinking?" LP asked, as he turned and looked up into the deep blue eyes of the flight attendant.

Gwen asked for water, and Ingrid requested bourbon and cola. LP asked for a coldie of VB.

Virgin's smiling flight attendant handed their drinks across as LP asked, "Which do you prefer, Australian or New Zealand dollars?"

"Doesn't matter to me," she said.

LP did a quick calculation and handed her a New Zealand twenty-dollar note. He had worked out it was like getting a 20 percent discount off the drinks, because of the favourable exchange rate of the Australian dollar. It was currently almost at parity with the US dollar.

A couple of VBs later, the three of them had their own private party going, talking and laughing about life in general. Like time travellers, their journey seemed to take next to no time.

Touching down, the engines roared in reverse. LP breathed deeply a couple of times as he looked out into the darkness.

They had arrived without any drama; it was 10:30 pm, New Zealand time. They said their good-byes to Gwen and made plans to catch up before heading back to Queensland. Like many well-meaning plans, though, things did not work out that way.

Standing up, LP pulled down his and Ingrid's carry-on bags. Waiting anxiously for people to start moving, LP couldn't help the nightmare thought of being strip searched by customs again.

Waiting at the carousel to collect their baggage, Ingrid spotted two cases with red ribbons tied to their handles. LP pulled the bags off the conveyor belt, and they headed over to the customs checkpoint. Security officers were everywhere. One officer stepped forward and indicated to LP to step aside.

Oh, not again, he thought. But the officer pointed to the exit and said, "You're right to go."

LP looked back and saw the queues of people lined up to have their luggage scanned. He turned to Ingrid and said, "Profiling worked in our favour this time."

Smiling, they walked out into a windy, clouded Christchurch night. Pulling their luggage behind them and struggling with their carry-on bags, they made it to a bus stop.

The bus driver, who looked like he might have been Maori, said helpfully, "Where are you going? I'm heading in to the city in five minutes."

They climbed aboard his minibus while the driver placed their luggage in the rear trailer. As he pulled out from the curb, three Asians ran in front of the vehicle, waving and yelling in a foreign language. You didn't need to speak their language to understand what they wanted.

The driver braked suddenly and gave them a mouth full of expletives. Using his own brand of sign language, he pointed to the side door to enter. They were carrying only backpacks and so didn't need to put any luggage in the trailer. Ten minutes later, the minibus pulled up outside Best Western on Riccarton Road.

LP stepped out first, helping Ingrid down the step. Walking over to collect their luggage from the driver, LP handed him three ten-dollar New Zealand notes and said good-bye.

The keys to the motel room were under a potted plant outside the sliding front doors, just as arranged. LP unlocked their room door and dropped down onto the double bed in exhaustion.

He looked up at Ingrid and said, "I'm stuffed, and my knee's aching. Give me ten minutes, and I'll help unpack."

Ingrid wasn't tired. Her watch was still on Queensland time, so it was only 8:30 pm. She was keen to do some late-night sightseeing in the city and check out the duty-free shops to buy gifts for their sons and daughters.

"Okay, wake up; your ten minutes are up," Ingrid said after a while.

He slowly opened his eyes and said, "I wasn't asleep, just meditating and relaxing."

The technique had been passed on to him in a secret ceremony at a Buddhist monastery in Vietnam. That knowledge allowed him to transcend time, where past, present, and future become one. It could be described as an out-of-body experience that takes him to a place that cannot be described in words. The meditation technique also invigorated LP and made him ready to take on the world.

"Okay, I've got my second wind," he said. "What are we waiting for? Hand me two painkillers for my knee, it's aching again, and we're on the go. What do you want to see first?"

"Duty-free shops," she replied.

"Fine, after that we're goin' to the casino." LP stood up, stretched, and walked to the door, opening it for Ingrid. Then he closed and locked it.

LP figured all they had to do was start walking and hail a cab, and they'd be shopping in twenty minutes. There didn't seem to be any cabs about, though, and in the distance, they saw a fish and chip shop with a public telephone outside.

"I'm phoning for a taxi if we haven't caught one by the time we reach that takeaway place," Ingrid said. LP agreed, as his knee was seizing up again.

While LP made the phone call, Ingrid made conversation with a gentleman carrying a wrapped-up burger and chips.

He introduced himself, "I'm Graham. What's your name?" "Ingrid," she responded, "and that's my other half, trying to book a cab into Christchurch's Cathedral Square."

"I'll take you. Climb in," Graham said, as he opened his front passenger door.

LP heard the conversation as he waited on the phone and said, "Look, you don't have to do this, we'll wait for a cab."

Graham insisted. He could have been an axe murderer, thought LP, but his experience of New Zealand folk from his previous visit was they were very friendly and helpful folk.

LP took up Graham's offer and opened the rear passenger door for Ingrid to hop in. He sat in the front, next to Graham, for a guided tour and commentary of the city. Even though he was from Invercargill, he was used to the drive, as his job was to transport race horses from the North to the South Islands. His love for Christchurch was biased, though, as it was the capital for horse racing.

Graham put his takeaway on the dashboard as he did a u-turn and headed towards Cathedral Square. Driving along a straight, four-lane main road, they passed many houses and shops destroyed by an earthquake only eight weeks earlier.

The destruction had happened on his birthday, the 4th of September 2010. Graham pointed out vacant lots that were once homes and were now completely destroyed. The debris had been removed by the council, and now dark holes were left around the city. Daylight would reveal the true extent of damage to Cantabrians' lives.

Tears welled up in Graham's eyes as he described what he went through the morning of the quake. His first warning came out of the still of night. The horses were neighing and kicking up a ruckus in his stables. Before he could even get out of bed, the house he rented had started to shake, tossing him onto the floor. After picking himself up, he ran outside to settle the horses in his charge. He said it was the scariest moment he had ever experienced.

Graham continued talking about what he loved most: his horses. This week was a big one for him, being Cup Week. He had just transported two race favourites; Monkey King and Smoken Up.

Now smiling, he said, "I'll give you a tip. Put some money on the Monkey, it's a sure bet."

With that advice coming from a bloke with good connections in the horse racing industry, the words struck a chord with LP as a "Shaw bet."

When those words came to mind, LP's gambling instincts kicked in. Shaw was the surname of a family of gamblers. They successfully bet against the odds by growing sweet potatoes and making a profit where others would fail.

Graham pulled up outside the brightly lit Christchurch Casino. He said, "Have a good holiday. You'll love travelling through the centre of Kiaoroa."

LP thanked him for his generosity and went to hand Graham a twenty-dollar note. Graham refused the offer, but as he drove away, LP crunched up the note and dropped it through the passenger window, saying, "Thanks, Graham. Hope you back a winner on Tuesday."

Walking towards the large staircase in the foyer of the casino, LP and Ingrid caught the lift to the poker machines. Hundreds of machines lined the walls, corralling gambling tables crowded with gamblers. Ingrid and LP decided to play the pokies first and try their luck on roulette later. Every machine they touched either paid out mini jackpots or gave them free spins. Luck was on their side tonight.

After pocketing several hundred dollars in winnings, LP said, "I'm going over to play my favourite table."

Ingrid responded, "I need a drink first. I'll see you over there in a minute."

LP was standing next to other punters, all looking for a win on roulette. He muscled his way in, pushing three fifty-dollar notes across a green felt table and changing them for five-dollar chips. The spinner was Asian, very pretty, but with a serious look that glared out across her table.

LP was ready to beat the odds with his winning strategy. He was a counter, a numbers man. Looking at the computerised record of past numbers recorded, he calculated the probability of his favourite numbers coming up. Now, he was ready to play.

He pushed a five-dollar chip onto number twenty-three and then split five dollars over zero and double zero.

With the red ball rolling and the wheel spinning in the opposite direction, LP watched as the ball bounced past his numbers.

"Thirty-five winner," said the spinner, while raking the losing bets towards her. LP placed ten dollars on his same lucky numbers, this time doubling his wager, but without a win again.

He wasn't at all perturbed, though, as he continued to increase his bet to fifteen dollars each, split over zeros and twenty-three. After two more spins, there were no five-dollar chips left in front of him.

Twenty-five dollars split over zero and double zero and twenty-five dollars on twenty-three. LP had crunched the numbers, and probability dictated that this was the winning spin. To make sure luck was on his side, he whispered a chant, "Angel of light, protector, let me see zero."

As he did this, he was stretching and arching backwards and forwards, with his arms pointing to the wheel. To the security cameras, it would look like he was just having a stretch. He held his breath as the ball stopped on twenty-three.

"Winner," called the spinner, pushing a mountain of chips over number twenty-three. LP thought to himself, *Bloody angels weren't listening.*

Pushing twenty chips as a split bet over zero and double zero again, LP waited for the wheel to spin. He repeated what looked like stretching exercises.

"Double zero," she called. All eyes turned to LP as he dragged in $1,700 in chips.

LP now pushed across his chips to be changed into higher denominations. Collecting his winnings in one hand, he waved to Ingrid to meet him at the cashier's counter. She spotted LP pushing a wad of notes into his wallet and asked, "How much did you win?"

"Twenty-six hundred! Let's get out of here quick. Those cameras above may have triggered a profile on me and directed security officers to throw us out for working together to rip the casino off."

As they made their way to the lifts, LP spotted two security guards heading their way. As the lift doors opened, they scampered in and watched the doors shut out their pursuers. At the ground floor level, they hurried towards the exit to the taxi rank. Ingrid climbed in the back seat, and LP sat next to the driver.

"Where to, mate?" the driver asked,

"Best Western on Riccarton, make it quick, thanks!" "What's the hurry?" asked the Maori cabbie.

"I don't think this casino likes people like me," replied LP.

"What do you mean, mate?" the driver asked.

"Casinos throw counters out," LP replied. "Surveillance cameras must have picked up on how I was playing the roulette table, and security followed us. I have a winning system that works most of the time."

The cabbie responded, "Most guys who come out of the casino at this time of night are flat broke, drunk, or both. They barely remember where they live or what their name is. You did well."

"Yeah, we're from Queensland; maybe our good luck followed us." "Look out the window, what do you see?" the driver asked. "Wind, rain, and darkness," LP replied.

"Darkness, you're right. What you can't see is what shook this city and left behind painful memories and rubble to clean up."

Their cab driver slowed as grating wheels scraped against the gutter. "That'll be twenty-two dollars fifty; thanks, mate."

LP pulled out a handful of notes, giving them to his new friend.

"This is more than a tip. I can't take all this," said the cab driver.

LP said, "Give this to your family and friends who have suffered from the disaster."

As Ingrid and LP entered the motel entrance, Ingrid asked, "How much did you give that guy?"

"You can count what's left when we get back to our room," replied LP. When they got up to their room, he handed his wallet across as he fell backwards into bed. "Wake me for an early start in the morning. I'm stuffed," he said.

Ingrid slowly counted what was left in LP's wallet. $1,985. Ingrid was first up at seven o'clock. She made a cup of coffee, showered, and dressed; after putting on her make-up, she was ready to see Christchurch in daylight. Even though it looked like an overcast, windy day outside, she was still keen to get going.

"Wake up, lazy bones, I'm ready to go. We'll be late for picking up our camper."

LP sprang out of bed, shaved, brushed his teeth and showered; he was ready in less than seven minutes. With their hand luggage packed and suitcases in tow, they paid for the room and left.

They stood out in the motel's driveway, waiting for the cab that had been booked at reception. Ten minutes passed, and when their cabbie arrived, it was none other than the Maori driver who dropped them off at the motel only hours before.

"Hey bro, where do you want to go? I'll take you all around my city, no charge today."

"Thanks, mate, but we've got to head back to the airport."
"Leaving so soon? You just arrived. Is security still after you?

Do you want your money back?"

"No, that's all fine," said LP. "We're picking up our camper from a place near the airport and heading south."

"I know the place. It's called Backpacker," said the cabbie. Their new friend dropped them off outside a large glass plated entrance. They went inside and approached one of several kiosks, handing their Internet booking form to a young woman standing behind her desk.

After filling out all the details, they watched a safety video on how to drive a 6.6-metre campervan, and then Ingrid and LP were ready to hit the trail.

When they walked out, to LP's surprise, there was a VW symbol on the campervan. He couldn't believe it. He was about to drive an oversized Kombi packed with all the extras for camping. What a bonus! It was just like the old days, but this time with luxury; he was stoked.

He thought it might take a while to get used to driving a vehicle like this, but to his surprise, his old Kombi driving skills had not deserted him. The campervan was now a dream machine, taking him back in time. Ingrid reached down and picked up LP's wallet, saying, "Stop in at that Pack'n'Save supermarket. We'll pick up some food and drink supplies. You're cashed up, so you're paying."

As she opened up his wallet to reveal a stack of $50 notes, she looked across at him and said, "How much cash did we have when we walked into that gambling den?"

"About $150," said LP.

"So you're well up, even after giving that cabbie a pretty good tip. What do ya want to spend it on?" asked Ingrid.

LP replied with confidence, "I'm gonna reinvest on a Shaw bet: Monkey King."

"You're not going to put all that money on a horse, are you?" "Maybe half," LP replied. His idea was to keep some cash for an emergency, or even a treat to surprise Ingrid.

Her final words on the matter were, "I don't like what you're thinking, but your winning hands back at the casino worked magic."

LP did as he was told and pulled in to the Pack'n'Save car park. He drove around the packed car park, waiting for someone to leave, until Ingrid pointed to a car backing out.

It wasn't as easy as all that though; 6.6 metres of van wouldn't fit into a regular car space. Luck was still on LP's side. The spot he was about to drive into was next to a KFC drive-thru, with a concrete dividing barrier the length of their van. He was able to park perfectly without blocking the traffic.

As they ran through the rain to the shopping mall entrance, LP started limping. His knee was giving him trouble again.

Once inside the Pack'n'Save, LP grabbed a trolley to use as a crutch. Moving down the first aisle, Ingrid commented on how the prices were pretty similar to back home.

LP put it down to independent food outlets in New Zealand having a greater share of the grocery industry, unlike Australia, where Woolworths and Coles controlled 80 percent of the market. He figured the competition must be good for locals and visitors alike.

Another plus was that you could purchase alcohol while grocery shopping, all under the one roof. Pushing their trolley through the checkout, and paying and packing their own groceries, they headed back to a drenched road and van. LP unlocked the sliding door and put the groceries away, putting a couple of beers in the fridge to chill down as they drove. They were now ready for their adventure.

With the Navman connected, they directed themselves out of Christchurch's city traffic. Their first destination was the Mount Hutt ski area, where LP wanted to have another photo taken after thirty-six years.

Ninety-one clicks later, LP turned off the main road, following a sign pointing to Mount Hutt. Rain drizzled down as the wipers clicked back and forth, making visibility dangerous as he drove up the winding gravel road. Climbing higher into low cloud, watching the rain water running off cliff faces, he decided to turn back. His luck had run out.

"We'll try to climb that mountain on the way back if the weather is better," he said to Ingrid, as they drove back onto the main road.

They slowed down on the outskirts of the next township. Geraldine was the birthplace of Phar Lap, the most famous racing horse in Australian history.

LP pulled into the first gas station they came to. They could see mechanics working under the bonnets of cars in the rear of the building.

After filling up, LP parked at the back of the servo and walked through the light rain, which was making mud stick like glue to his runners. He asked a mechanic if he could have a look at a problem with the van.

The Kiwi asked, "What sort of trouble needs fixing?" LP said, "Don't laugh, but it's the cigarette lighter. If I don't get it fixed, my wife's going to kill me."

"Heavy smoker, huh?" the mechanic laughed with much disbelief.

"No, we're running the Navman and a thing called Cruse, which gives a running commentary via satellite. It all runs off the cigarette lighter," LP replied.

Because the van was insured for breakdowns, the bill for the repair was charged to Backpackers in Christchurch.

Half an hour had passed by the time the repair had been completed. LP was feeling tired, and his knee was playing up. He took off his boots and scraped the chunks of mud off them, then swapped into his old Ugg boots as they headed the campervan out of town.

By four thirty, they had travelled less than two hundred kilometres. At that snail pace, they wouldn't make it back to Christchurch for their return flight to Brisbane in six days. Both Ingrid and LP were feeling tired. It was possibly jet lag, but maybe closer to the truth was that they had only had four hours' sleep in the last thirty-six hours. Stopping at a park with a statue of Phar Lap, they climbed into the rear bunks for a bit of shut-eye.

An hour and a half passed before they stirred again. There was still daylight, and LP figured they could continue on to the next town and stay there overnight. He said, "You drive. I'm going to take a painkiller for my knee. It's only forty-six clicks to the van park at Fairlie."

Before climbing into the passenger seat, he went to the bar fridge and grabbed a coldie. As he put his seat belt on, he said, "Let's get going before it gets dark."

It was nearly seven o'clock, and rain was still falling. The dull remains of daylight gave them an eerie, creepy feeling. Goose bumps quivered down their bodies, but they weren't caused by the cold. It was something else.

Driving past the van park where they were going to stay, Ingrid continued to an intersection and turned left, parking on an angle outside some shops.

It was time to do some sightseeing in the main street of Fairlie. There was about as much excitement in town as you would find at a nursing home as residents waited for their Friday night menu special of tripe with white sauce.

They soon headed back to the van park, but Ingrid felt apprehensive. Her earlier feelings still unsettled her. Reluctantly, she drove into the van park, with the dimming twilight giving the place a spooky feeling.

By eight thirty, they had booked in and Ingrid backed the campervan up to a small stream flowing through the park.

Their new home was not yet crowded with other travelers, although other campers arrived through the night, setting up their camp sites. Fishing rods were laid against trees, indicating they planned to be up at first light, fishing.

The facilities were second to none, with spotless amenities for showering, another for preparing food, and a TV room with a fireplace. They took advantage of the warmth of the fire, watching an hour-long special of *Faulty Towers* with John Cleese, just as politically incorrect these days and just as funny as when they had first seen it many years before.

As they watched TV, a loud explosion startled them. The first thought that came to mind was about their earlier hesitation in staying at this particular camping ground. LP jumped up, ran over to the door, and looked outside.

It sounded like a gas explosion coming from the communal kitchen direction. Another loud bang soon followed, and he was becoming concerned, until it finally clicked.

This was Cup Week, and the townsfolk were watching fireworks at their local park. Wind and rain hadn't dampened their enthusiasm, as the temperature dropped to near zero.

LP said to Ingrid, "Come on, let's get some shut-eye, and we'll be on our way by early morning."

Ingrid poured herself a bourbon and cola nightcap. LP grabbed himself a cold beer from the fridge and sat in the passenger seat to listen to the weather forecast on the van's radio.

The ten thirty news bulletin reported more rain to come, along with gale force winds.

Their trip was off to a slow start. They were already behind schedule, and now the weather was worsening. Unless the weather gods smiled on them, they would find it difficult to complete their journey in time.

Mount Hutt was looking like being off the radar. They needed to travel more kilometres each day, otherwise LP would miss out on climbing the mountain, and they would even risk missing their flight home.

LP's knee was still giving him trouble. He had intended to do all the driving, not knowing if Ingrid was confident to handle such a large vehicle. He might have to rethink that. He would decide what to do in the morning. Right now it was time for bed.

First light filtered through the rainforest trees, and a pure mountain stream flowed past their van. It was an idyllic setting.

Standing outside the campervan door, LP smiled and said to Ingrid, "No wind or rain in sight, and there's clear sky above. The weather gods have been kind!"

He drove out of town, heading west. Lake Tekapo was their next stop, forty-eight clicks away. They drove down a narrow winding roadway that opened up onto a bright blue lake.

Looking up from an empty car park, they saw a small stone church. Ingrid and LP walked up a slight incline, cameras in hand. They entered through open timber doors and were struck by the beauty of the scene.

A large plate glass window framed Lake Tekapo, a masterpiece of creation in all its beauty and wonder.

Travelling through Omarama, and then Cromwell, LP stopped at a BP roadhouse to fill up with diesel. They had travelled 194 clicks. With only sixty kilometres to go, they were making good time and would arrive at Queenstown by 4:00 pm.

Arriving at what LP remembered as a small ski resort town, they found something quite different. Queenstown was not at all as he recalled it from 1974. The traffic was grid locked, and the streets were crowded with tourists.

This was not the quaint town he remembered. In the past, up high behind the township, was the gondola that took you up to a restaurant overlooking Lake Wakatipu, with Queenstown below. Looking out through huge glass panels, watching the snow fall, it was an unforgettable sight. But now what he saw, he would prefer to forget.

After crawling through the traffic, he dropped Ingrid off outside the Tourist Information Centre. With nowhere to park, he went around the block slowly so he could pick her up when he got back.

Maps and tourist pamphlets in hand, Ingrid opened the door and climbed in. As LP drove off, he said, "We're not staying here. It's over the top, just like Noosa's Hastings Street; full of boutiques, shops, and tourists."

Ingrid replied, "We're tourists as well, though, and I like shopping. Park over there."

He refused, so instead she showed him a pamphlet on Arrowtown, an old gold mining town. He said, "We'll head over there. It's only ten minutes away. You can decide where we should sleep tonight."

Arriving at Arrowtown, LP parked across a bay and a half in a shady car park opposite an alley way. They walked up the main street, lined with historic buildings from the gold mining days of the 1800s. If you took the bitumen away and added horses and carts, you could call it Nostalgia Town.

Walking around a corner, they stumbled across the local boutique beer establishment, where a plaque stated:

> *BEER—*
> *It is the drink of folk who think*
> *And feel no fear nor fetter*
> *Who do not drink to senseless sink*
> *But drink to think the better*

LP asked for two beers. "Pints or schooners?" the barman asked.

"Well, I'm pretty thirsty, so make it pints."

LP paid; pizzas were on the menu, so he decided to order a wood-fired supreme pizza to share as well. He walked back outside, sitting down at a round plastic table with Ingrid. The sky was a clear blue, so it seemed that the weather was improving as they travelled further south.

Drinking beer and eating pizza, they talked about what to do next. They decided that Ingrid would drive first, since she had only one beer. LP was concerned about driver fatigue and suggested alternating hourly, if they wanted to make it to Te Anau by eight thirty, while there was still day-light.

He finished his pint and Ingrid's. Walking back to their vehicle, LP felt his knee was coming good. Ingrid was window gazing and spotted a table at the side of a closed shop. There was a sign: *Free Food,* so they helped themselves to ham and salad rolls and bread sticks.

This generosity reminded him how he survived backpacking down the rugged west coast of the South Island in 1974. Many of the pubs down the coast would put on a free supper at nine o'clock, before closing.

One particular pub grub he remembered fondly was saveloys with tomato ketchup sauce, which would be set out in a large stainless bowl placed on the bar. LP would buy one beer and wait for a feed.

Ingrid commented, "I'm not cooking dinner tonight or making lunch tomorrow."

They climbed back into their diesel-powered VW van. It hadn't missed a beat, hugging every bend with ease. LP thanked his lucky stars for what they were driving. Entering Te Anau with daylight to spare, LP drove to the van park they had booked, overlooking Lake Te Anau.

They were now ahead of schedule in their mission to be at Milford Sound by Sunday. Stopping for fuel at Omarama and checking out old gold mining sites along the Kawarau Gorge had not caused any unnecessary delays.

LP waited for sunset to finally arrive at quarter to ten, with cold, gale force winds blowing again. He snapped a couple of awesome photos of the sunset descending behind snow-capped mountains.

Walking back, he was secretly disappointed that Ingrid had discovered the free takeaway meals. He had been hoping she would prepare his favourite meal, chicken wings in a delicious homemade marinade. It was a quarter cup of soy, two squeezed lemons, and a teaspoon of bottled crushed garlic. Mix, then turn twice while cooking at 180 degrees, and you've got the best tasting chicken you could ever savour.

They were up early, before anyone one else stirred. Fog filled the cold air and dew covered the grass as LP pulled his jacket tight, rubbing his hands to get warm. He was ready to leave as soon as Ingrid finished freshening up over at the amenity block.

He started the engine and turned on the heater and radio, listening for the weather report. Ingrid hurried over to climb into the warm van.

LP drove out of the van park at a snail's pace, driving as quietly as possible. He didn't want other overnight campers following him.

Turning onto Te Anau's main street, a large road sign pointed them in the right direction: *"Milford Sound, 121 km."* LP had been warned about road conditions by other tourists travelling in similar Backpacker vans. They said to ignore maps about distance and time when it came to getting to Milford. Allow for two and half hours, and be careful when entering the tunnel.

This knowledge encouraged LP to make an early start. He was preparing himself mentally for what was ahead.

He wished he'd had a similar warning about the dangerous road they'd travelled yesterday to reach St John's Observatory.

It was a steep winding road with only enough room for one car. LP had started having a panic attack, struggling with thoughts of another van coming down towards them. There would be nowhere to go but over the edge, crashing to the valley floor one thousand metres below. He quickly blocked out that possibility, gripping the steering wheel so tightly that sweat dripped from his palms.

Once they reached the summit, they parked next to another VW campervan from the same hire company.

They walked up to the observatory with the drivers of the other van and passed a sign that read:

During your visit, please remember No Littering—
No Aliens—No Smoking Thank you kindly

One of their new friends commented, "Even aliens wouldn't land here, it's too bloody dangerous."

LP agreed, saying, "I'll follow you guys down; I get shivers up my spine just thinking about the descent."

18

Travelling north alongside Lake Te Anau, the sun was rising above a snow-capped mountain peak, shimmering across still blue water. They started to climb steeply as the roadway cut a path through the snow-covered peaks of Fiordland National Park.

They were making good time. If they could make it to the Homer Tunnel before nine, they would have a clear run through to the other side. If not, they would have to wait for the traffic lights on the tunnel to change. The lights were set to allow traffic to head in one direction every twenty minutes.

He was grateful for the warnings given by those who preceded him, and they made it through in the nick of time.

High on the mountain ridge, LP looked down to the snow-covered gorge. It was breathtaking and frightening at the same time as he navigated a hairpin turn. He took several deep breaths and avoided looking over the cliff face. The winding road was just wide enough for two cars to pass each other. Who knows what he'd do if a semi-trailer was coming in the other direction.

At Milford Sound's car park and terminal below the rugged snow-capped mountains, LP parked the vehicle. Several vessels sat in the distance, waiting for passengers and tourists to board.

LP locked the van, and he and Ingrid started walking towards the rainforest track leading to the terminal. The air was damp and cool in the forest. A thousand steps later, they emerged at the terminal. He had a habit of calculated distance when walking by counting, and knew it was a one-kilometre walk.

Entering through the boat terminal's automatic doors, they rushed to the front counter. As they were ahead of schedule, LP enquired whether they could board the ten o'clock departure to Milford Sound rather than their booking at eleven.

The receptionist said that they needed two more passengers in order to take a boat out at ten; she asked them to come back in twenty minutes to check if anyone else had booked. They sat down to enjoy the surreal landscape through the plate glass windows. This was one of the rare places where mere mortals could experience a once-in-a-lifetime magical beauty.

Ingrid couldn't believe that a tourist boat operator would take four passengers out cruising, when the boat could carry one hundred and fifty.

Twenty minutes later, LP approached the counter again to ask if any more passengers had booked. As he waited, the receptionist was trying to help three German tourists, who were struggling to understand the Kiwi accent. "Book now, the captain departs in five minutes."

She was trying to explain to them that this boat would not be crowded with Japanese tourists, whereas bus loads would be arriving soon for the eleven o'clock departure.

The captain, who had been leaning on the counter, looked across and said simply, "Private tour. Let's go." LP backed him up, saying, "Private tour, private tour."

It finally clicked, and the Germans booked their cruise. On the dot of ten, the captain manoeuvred his vessel from port, headed towards the Tasman Sea through Milford Sound.

From then on, picture postcard scenery absorbed their thoughts. Nothing else mattered, as reality was distorted by breathtaking beauty as they motored alongside sheer cliff faces.

"This is your captain speaking. Please pay attention to my crew members demonstrating safety instructions … No, I'll cut it short. If we run into any trouble, hang onto a crew member. Thank you."

LP and Ingrid were standing on the top deck, which was big enough for a helicopter to land on. They laughed as they listened to the briefest safety instructions they had ever heard.

LP left Ingrid taking photos and climbed down a steep stairwell to the boat's bar. A smiling crew member waited to serve LP a cold stubby of beer. "That'll be four dollars fifty," she said, as she placed his liquid amber on the bar.

LP saw that Ingrid had climbed down from the top deck and entered the captain's bridge, even though it was roped off. He joined them in conversation but hesitated to step into the chained-off area.

He suddenly had a flashback to a time when an American aircraft carrier had docked at Fisherman Island in Brisbane. The Harrier jump jets were roped off with a sign saying "Do Not Enter," plus a yellow security line. Taking a step across that line would create trouble.

But that's exactly what had happened. Protesters were mingling with sightseers, and from within the crowd, three long-haired hippies had removed their jumpers to reveal t-shirts emblazoned with the slogan "Ban Nuclear Power." They stepped over the yellow line on the aircraft carrier's deck.

Marine MPs arrived within seconds to remove the intruders. To avoid a scuffle and media attention, the security officers carried stretchers for the unexpected protestors to be placed on. One of the protesters must have put up a struggle, because another Marine arrived soon after with bucket and mop in hand to clean a pool of blood off the deck.

Stepping over the rope, LP politely asked the captain if he could have a picture taken sitting in his chair. Waving him though, the captain said, "Go right ahead, that's fine, the boat's on autopilot."

He sat smiling, high in the captain's chair, for Ingrid to take his photo. All of a sudden, without warning, the captain collapsed, hitting his head hard on the deck floor. Panic set in. Ingrid yelled out to the other crew members to help. The second mate arrived from below deck. He kneeled down, rolled the captain over, and starting to give CPR.

LP asked, "Is there anything I can do? I've got a licence for boats like this." The first mate replied, "Switch the autopilot off and turn this boat around." LP was suddenly captain, preparing to steer back to port.

"Radio ahead. Ask for a helicopter to take the captain to the nearest hospital."

Five minutes seemed like an hour as they waited for the sound of chopper blades to mark the helicopter's arrival on the top stern deck. The crew carried their captain upstairs to the waiting helicopter for evacuation.

After Milford's flight care helicopter departed with the captain, the second mate took the helm. As soon as they arrived back in port, Ingrid and LP left the terminal.

Questions would have to be answered if they had stayed any longer. They didn't have time for long-winded explanations. Knowing the captain was in good hands, they headed back through the Homer Tunnel.

At this time of the day, they would have to wait for traffic lights to allow them to enter the dark, two-kilometre tunnel that seeped water.

As they waited in the traffic queue on a steep fish hook turn, LP hesitated to look down to the thousand-metre sheer drop to the mountain floor.

Finally, green signalled a long drive ahead to reach Wanaka before nightfall. Factoring in stops for fuel and taking some photos, as well as changing drivers every couple of hours, they figured they would be there by seven o'clock.

They arrived at Lake Wanaka, and LP parked their campervan near some picnic tables. The large grassed area that led down to ripples of water washing up gritty sand was reminiscent of Shelly beach in Caloundra, but they were inland, cradled below snow-capped mountains.

Ingrid prepared a dinner of hot dogs, using fresh bread rolls smothered with tomato ketchup sauce.

"You know, if we go up that gravel road again to Mount Hutt there's no certainty we'll make it up the mountain. Its nickname is Mount Shut," said Ingrid.

"Well, what else have you got in mind?" LP asked. "Let's book a helicopter to take us up the mountain."

"Okay, but we'd better check how much it'll cost first."

LP used his mobile to phone the Mount Hutt helicopter company and found a friendly and helpful receptionist.

"Mount Hutt is closed," she said. "The season finished last week, so the gates are locked." LP was disappointed, but the receptionist continued, "You've phoned the right place to get there though. We're still available for charters to land on the mountain. It would be $420 and take about fifteen minutes to get there."

LP turned to Ingrid and said, "Four twenty." She replied, "Just do it."

"Okay, book us in for Wednesday," LP said to the receptionist. Once he hung up, he said to Ingrid, "I'm going back to the mountain after thirty-six years. I can't wait."

Ingrid was anxious to book in at Wanaka's van park that overlooked the lake. It was already eight thirty and would be dark soon. She commented, "Without twilight being so late, we would never have made up as much time."

LP nodded his head in agreement as they drove up the steep driveway.

He slammed the door behind him and walked in to the reception office. A tired-looking woman booked them in and they found their site, which backed onto a grazing paddock full of sheep. So typically New Zealand, with sheep anywhere you could see green grass.

The next morning, the sun warmed their camper as they awoke to a postcard outlook. Sheep meandered by their van, separated by a high fence line. Shade awaited them in the corner paddock.

Ingrid was up first and went over to the communal kitchen to make a cup a tea and some cereal.

LP rose and moved to the driver's seat. He switched channels to find a news bulletin for today's weather. It seemed fine for now, but he wanted to find out how dangerous conditions would be driving across the Haast Pass. Their aim was to reach Fox and Franz Josef glaciers early enough to see both before dark.

The news confirmed his fears, with sunshine throughout the morning, but overcast skies and rain expected in the afternoon.

LP suddenly wasn't hungry and wanted to get on the move before the bad weather set in. He asked Ingrid, who was finishing her cuppa, if she was up to driving again. He was planning to change drivers once they reached the Haast Pass, so he would be fresh to drive through the pass in the event of bad weather.

Driving out through town, they stopped for diesel and then left behind Lake Wanaka and its township. One could understand why blockbuster movies were made there. Crystal clear streams shadowed by snow-capped mountains reflected in deep blue lakes throughout the region.

In contrast, when they crossed over to the rugged west coast, they would find it similar in some respects to the Kimberley region on Australia's west coast and the Great Ocean Road in Victoria, with sweeping bends and spectacular scenery.

Looking ahead, a warning sign indicated to slow down to 25 KMH, with a sharp bend ahead. What actually confronted them was Haast Pass, a snow-covered mountain range they had to travel over.

"Sit back and take in the views," said LP, taking over the driving.

He had to concentrate now, ignoring sheer cliff faces as the road cut its way through to the other side.

LP was also cautious about the changing weather conditions: sunny one minute and then raining the next. He steered around every bend with apprehension. Road signs gave some clue of impending dangers, and the Navman helped and hindered at times. Finally, they climbed to a point level with and flanked by New Zealand's snow-covered Alps.

As they descended the other side, they stopped by a stream that would be changed by spring's melting snow into a river, flowing through an unspoiled valley.

LP snapped a couple of pictures, saying, "You can drive; my knee is playing up again."

They swapped seats, clicked on seat belts, and continued their journey. After a short distance, LP unlocked his belt, went to his bar fridge, and grabbed one of the coldies that he now called painkillers.

Sitting back down, beer in hand, he and Ingrid argued with "the other woman" (the Navman) about which turn to take.

He was in the navigator's seat, remembering the road from travelling across the region years ago. He wasn't going to let the electronic voice tell him where to go. "In one hundred metres, turn." The voice stopped as LP ripped the cord out from the cigarette lighter socket. Ingrid calmed him down before he chucked the Navman out the window.

Although Ingrid had many years of driving experience, she'd found driving such a large campervan more difficult than she had expected. With trying to take in breathtaking scenery while heeding traffic signs signalling danger ahead, she needed a second pair of eyes to warn her of trouble, which could be around any twist and turn. Those eyes were LP's, her navigator, not a voice in a box. It was up to him to coach her through the unfolding terrain.

Unsafe road conditions were not the only danger they were to face. On the news came a report of police arresting a thirty-two-year-old driver, who admitted to smoking two bongs to stay awake, while in control of his forty-tonne dangerous goods truck.

The driver had said that one hand was on the driving wheel most of the time. "Bloody hell," LP said, "just as well he's in the North Island. You wouldn't want to have him coming towards you."

LP had a flashback moment, remembering his close encounter with another truckie on drugs. He and his mates had passed him travelling in the outback, on their road trip to Bells Beach in 1973. He shook his head to get back to reality and concentrate on navigating.

Talk back radio was all about the big race tomorrow. They were expecting capacity crowds to flock through the gates at

Addington racecourse by early morning, even though overcast windy conditions would ruffle a few feathers and hats.

Still, 26,000 race goers were expected to scream the winning trotter across the line. Reputations would be won and lost at Christchurch on Tuesday, and the whole country would come to a standstill as the trotters passed the winning post at Addington Raceway.

LP was keen to place a bet on Graham's tip, Monkey King, for a win. He was still cashed up with the casino winnings and figured luck wouldn't desert him now.

Ingrid's driving skills were improving, and she clutched the driving wheel with growing confidence. Gripping bitumen as they accelerating along straight stretches of highway continuing west, the spinning wheels spat out gravel on tight turns overlooking a steep riverbank.

First stop on the west coast was Haast, a small cluster of houses and one shop. This was the crossroads to the coast, where at last LP could get mobile phone reception.

He stepped out of the van to make a call back to Australia. Using his Queensland TAB betting account, he put $800 on the nose for Monkey King to win.

Ingrid called out, "Hurry up. We need to get to the glaciers before dark." LP climbed back in and buckled up as Ingrid started driving again.

The sun glistened over the expanse of ocean that Kiwis and Aussies call the ditch, otherwise known as the Tasman Sea.

Stopping occasionally to take photos along the road, which hugged the coastline, they kept an eye out for somewhere to stop for a snack break.

LP looked at the map and said, "Lake Paringa is around the next bend. There should be a picnic area overlooking the water." Leaving the ocean outlook behind and motoring along the lake foreshore, LP pointed out a dirt track. Turning off, they drove through thick bush land. Ingrid parked opposite a picnic table overlooking the lake.

On a glorious summer day, they sat looking out over crystal-clear water as they dined on leftover free salad rolls.

Suddenly, a swarm of blood sucking insects attacked them. Jumping up, they ran to the van, opened the sliding side door, and quickly slamming it shut behind them. Not fast enough, though; half the critters follow them inside. They were the notorious sand flies of the South Island. Those blood suckers were squashed with open palms, until they thought there were none left.

In a panic, LP said, "I'll drive before this place devours us." They headed back out onto the west coast's main highway towards their next stop, Fox Glacier.

LP's right knee was giving him trouble again, but the pain was different now. He looked down to see more of the blood suckers leaving red welts on the side of his knee.

He drove with one hand and whacked them with the other as he tried to keep their van heading in the right direction.

LP swerved left, hitting loose gravel and losing traction. He stopped just in time to avoid going over the cliff face to Jacobs River. He finished squashing the last remaining suckers and then battled on, with an aching, itching knee.

Driving north along the west coast road, they came to a small tourist stop. To the right was a boarded-up building that had been a pub in another era.

Opposite, they saw a gigantic bug protruding from another dilapidated building. This had to be some sick joke by warped locals. Using the notorious west coast sand fly as a tourist attraction was not in good humour. In Australia, plenty of tourist locations had giant replicas of what their region was proud of. There was the Big Pineapple, the Big Banana, and the Big Prawn. Everywhere you went in Australia, you'd find a big something the locals were keen on showing off.

The Big Sand Fly of the South Island you wouldn't think was something to boast about. Stopping to investigate, they entered a gravel car park in front of a high wire fence corralling five large-horned goats. LP thought, *You can't go anywhere without reminders of the past.*

They walked over to an old timber hut, probably built back in the 1800s. Inside, animal skins lined the walls and hung from above.

To the right was an eating area with tables and chairs spread inside as well as on a wide verandah. On the menu were possum and venison pies. LP ordered venison and Ingrid asked for possum.

Next to the warming trays, a sign read:

Due to government regulations,
eating possum is illegal.

LP wondered what substitute they would use. He didn't have to think too hard and didn't say anything to Ingrid as she munched on her pie.

A guy in gumboots, looking like he was straight out of the comic series *Footrot Flats*, bounded around acting like he was in command. He grabbed a loudspeaker and started lecturing everyone about the government ruining his business.

He said they had poisoned the surrounding pristine streams and rivers with a chemical called Ten Eighty, by laying baits to kill the possums that were declared feral animals. The government wanted to eradicate ninety million of the buggers, otherwise they'd soon out-number sheep.

This policy had created a mad anarchist who placed large anti-government signs out front of his establishment for all the highway traffic to read.

LP and Ingrid didn't stay long after finishing their pies. Walking back to their van, Ingrid pulled out her camera and snapped a couple of photos of a few goats standing on a manmade outcrop of rocks. LP didn't want to say that they were destined for the next batch of possum pies.

With less than twenty-five clicks to go, LP was anxious to get to Fox Glacier, which he had not had a chance to climb when he was in New Zealand last. He had climbed Franz Josef Glacier with some experienced mountain climbers who had carried their own picks, while he had to hire his.

He was keen on at least walking to the base of those glaciers this time, no matter how much pain he was in.

LP drove into Fox Glacier's car park. It was five in the arvo, overcast with low clouds and a light drizzle falling.

He unfolded his Drizabone oil skin riding coat. They were designed for the high country of Australia in winter but were also ideal in these wet and windy conditions.

An eerie feeling filled the air. Words couldn't explain the goose bump sensation. LP was gob smacked at what he was seeing, walking to the base of the glacier with Ingrid. He looked up in awe at a mixture of white and turquoise colours and saw climbers descending with picks in hand.

That could have been me, if only we had more time, he thought. Walking with a limp, he followed Ingrid back to their van the way they came, along a stony, uneven track.

As they walked, they felt the spray coming off an impressively high waterfall. They stepped carefully on the not so steady stones that had been placed to cross the small stream.

Hundreds of tourists created a continuous line, filing two by two back and forth to the Fox Glacier.

Ingrid volunteered to drive, as LP struggled to lift his leg up into the van.

She accelerated from the Fox Glacier car park, leaving behind majestic beauty.

Next on their itinerary was Franz Josef Glacier, a twenty-seven-kilometre drive through Westland National Park.

On arrival, the rainforest blocked the view of the glacier with only a sign showing a path through the thick vegetation.

It was six thirty and still very overcast. They walked for fifteen minutes, winding their way up and down through the rainforest canopy, until suddenly the view opened up to the sight of Franz Josef Glacier in the distance.

This was as far as they were going. LP's leg was giving him too much trouble to attempt the hour's walk to the glacier and back. And they didn't want to be too late to book into the van park.

While standing on the observation deck taking pictures, LP struck up a conversation with some young backpackers. "Where are you girls from?" he asked.

"The United States, Minnesota," one of them said. Her name was Sarah. "We've been backpacking for ten days. Have you walked down the track to get a good look yet?"

"No, but I climbed it in '74. It was fantastic, although the glacier has retreated since. It's further to walk now."

"Us girls will walk it tomorrow," Sarah said.

LP was curious and asked where they were staying. He wondered how much a night's accommodation cost these days.

"We're staying at Glow Worm Backpackers in Cron Street," Sarah said. "It's twenty-three dollars a night, which is about average."

"You wouldn't believe this. When I was last here, it cost fifty cents a night to stay at a backpacker place."

"My dollars could stretch a lot further if I could find places like that," she replied in amazement.

Sarah snapped a couple of photos of Ingrid and LP with Franz Josef Glacier as a backdrop. They headed back to the van and turned right onto the main road towards the township. As they drove, moving clouds gave an occasional glimpse of an ancient glacier.

LP's memory of the place was vague. All he could remember was a road with lots of trees, extreme cold, and dampness filling the air.

Entering the township, Ingrid seemed to be driving around in circles, looking for the Rainforest Holiday Park. LP reached up and turned on the Navman, which told them where to turn. In less than a minute, Ingrid drove through the van park entrance, opening up into a rainforest area dotted with campervans.

It was eight thirty by the time Ingrid booked in, as low clouds pushed across the mountain backdrop. LP waited in the van, contemplating how far they had come.

There were 450 kilometres to go before he would stand on the mountain to snap the picture that would connect him to the past.

19

LP wrote in his journal while he waited for Ingrid. He penned how he felt about returning to Franz Josef Glacier after all these years and finding the glacier had receded further than he expected. He circled the words "Global Warming" and then glanced up when he heard the jingle of keys near his ear. Ingrid had the amenity keys and their site number.

"You drive," she said. "I'm not confident reversing this RV into a parking spot."

"Okay, no worries," LP replied.

He found site number 26 and reversed the van without any drama. After shutting off the engine, he ran out the power cord and connected it to their pole. Ten minutes later, they'd settled into their new abode and were snacking on corn chips and cheese and downing a couple of cold beers. That night, they headed over to the van park's bar, grill, and pool room, all under the one roof. Sitting opposite the large fireplace, which gave enough heat to warm everyone, they started to relax after their long day of sightseeing.

They ordered dinner and then looked around while they waited to pick it up. Ingrid said, "What I'd give to be like these young ones, fancy free and without a care in the world."

"Sure, that can happen one day, and we'd be called the Grey Nomads. Retirement, my dear, is not far off," replied LP.

Their buzzer sounded, vibrating across the timber table to indicate their food was ready. They walked over to the servery and picked up two plates of grilled barramundi covered in white sauce.

After they finished the succulent meal, a waitress collected their plates and revealed the Westland secret for making white sauce. She said, "This is how you do it: half a cup of milk, a tablespoon each of margarine and flour, plus a pinch of pepper, oregano, and Cajun spices. Simple as that." They talked about their journey so far and said how they found the west coast was living up to its reputation of great food and great hospitality, while the fireplace glow made for a romantic setting.

The evening's entertainment was aimed backpacker travellers. This van park encouraged younger folk to stay by providing their kind of music and a pool competition. The game was called Killer Pool.

Those who played put two dollars in the kitty for the winner. LP decided to enter, but his pool skills were a bit rusty. He was out-played by pool sharks and was eliminated in the third round.

The final game was between two young blokes. Tensions rose and rivalry could be seen on the faces of these mates who had been backpacking together. The cash prize was like striking gold for the backpackers, who counted every cent they spent. Friendships could be broken over the next shot.

After the winner sank the final ball, his mate, with a pool cue in one hand, took three steps forward and raised his right hand. He gripped his mate's right hand, shaking and congratulating him.

Finished for the night, LP and Ingrid headed back to their van to snuggle, preparing to be up for an early start the next day.

The next morning, the clouds had cleared, revealing the highest point of Franz Josef Glacier between the mountain peaks. LP rushed to grab his camera but too late. It became overcast and raining within moments.

He said to Ingrid, "Let's book out before this downpour gets any worse." His knee was feeling a little better, so he would drive as far as possible until the pain returned.

Passing Lake Mapourika as the roadway climbed and twisted its way along its shoreline, they were overshadowed by tall stands of dense rainforest.

Over two hours of constant driving followed, before they arrived at their next destination: Ross, where historic gold fields could still be panned.

They stopped outside Ross's tourist centre to shop for gold jewellery. Checking out the beautiful pieces hand crafted by locals, Ingrid decided on a gold nugget costing $445. She planned to add it to a gold chain she had bought in Vietnam.

They walked out into the main street. An old gold-mining sieve leaned against a wall. You could imagine the hustle and bustle of another time, but now the streets were quiet; it was a ghost town. Even the local pub was empty.

LP continued to drive on to Greymouth, where he would refuel for the journey over Arthur's Pass. Hugging the coastline with blue sky above, a sign pointed to Shantytown, ten kilometres before Greymouth.

LP turned off, following a winding road to an old abandoned township restored to its former glory. They looked at the entrance to the town, decided that they had seen enough old towns, and turned back the way they had come. There was something unsettling about Greymouth.

Approaching the intersection, indecision filled LP's thoughts, confusing him. Knowing he would need more fuel to cross the snow-capped Alps, he turned left. Driving back to the Arthur's Pass turn-off, he gambled on getting over the snow-covered Alps with what fuel he had left. Even if he ran out of fuel, he thought he could simply coast down until he found a fuel stop. His gamble paid off.

In the valley below, beneath snow-capped mountains was a street with a few houses and a gas station. LP turned in, filled up with diesel, drove past a couple of run-down houses needing some repair, and stopped. He made a phone call to the Mount Hutt helicopter company they planned to use and confirmed their flight for Wednesday.

The call was answered in a pleasant and friendly manner:

"Good morning, Kathy speaking."

LP replied, "G'day. I'm checking that everything's right for our booking tomorrow for going up to Mount Hutt. What time do we have to be there for our flight?"

"Your flight's booked for two in the arvo, but there's a slight problem. If you still want to land rather than fly over, a government permit is required because it's off season. That will be an extra $120."

LP turned to Ingrid and repeated what was said.

Ingrid had read a newspaper article about a plane crash in early September that had killed nine people, including two Australians, on Fox Glacier. This was eight weeks before they flew to New Zealand and the same day the earthquake had struck. She was not fazed, though, and was excited about taking her first helicopter ride. "Just do it. We've come this far. Let's finish on a high note."

LP told Kathy that they would pay the extra money for the permit. She confirmed their booking for two o'clock, saying, "Phone again tomorrow morning to check on weather conditions." LP pressed End, put down his phone, and started driving through Arthur's Pass National Park.

Winding their way past ski slopes that were closed for summer, they drove for nearly three hours before being stopped by road works.

Looking right, LP spotted a pub, the Springfield Hotel. The mobile automatic traffic lights signalled LP to move on, but he turned across into the pub's car park. He wanted to find out if his bet on Monkey King had paid off.

The town was playing up to their connection with Homer Simpson's Springfield. To the right of the pub entrance was a large glass window with a cartoon mural of Homer and his family. LP stood beside it while Ingrid snapped a photo.

They walked inside to a bar celebrating Addington Cup Day.

Today was the biggest day of New Zealand's trotting horse calendar.

It was four thirty in the arvo, with a bright blue sky. The warm sunshine was tempered by gusty winds coming off the snow-covered mountain peaks in the distance.

LP leant against the bar, looking at the list of beers on offer. To his surprise, Duff beer was on tap. "Pour me a pint of Duff beer and one for my wife, thanks," he said.

They sat down on a low couch to drink their beers and watch a repeat news report of the New Zealand Trotting Cup presentation on TV.

Monkey King's owner, Robert Famularo, and Ricky May, the driver, were all smiles, with winning accolades and the prize money of $750,000. LP waited to hear how much he had won on his bet, but nothing was mentioned about the odds.

LP looked around at the patrons dressed for Cup Day. Ladies in big hats and men in ties and sports jackets celebrated their wins or drowned their losses. Maybe he could get an answer out of one of them about Monkey King.

They finished their pints, and as they left, LP asked someone how much Monkey King had paid.

"Big win, mate," the punter said as he knocked down the remainder of his schooner of beer. It seemed that they weren't going to get much sense out of this lot, so they headed back to their van.

Ingrid volunteered to drive this time. It had been a long haul over the Alps for LP, and their next stop Methven was only seventy kilometres away; the gateway to Mount Hutt.

They had made up time now, with one day set aside for their helicopter flight, then in to Christchurch for sightseeing and duty-free shopping. The pace had slowed, and they could start to relax.

As they drove down Methven's main street, it could have been any sunny day in Queensland. Ingrid turned left and entered the van park at seven thirty. Their van was the only vehicle there, not counting a bicycle leaning up against a timber fence next to a two-man tent. It looked like there wouldn't be a queue at the amenities block tonight.

They poured a drink and settled in to relax at the timber table and chairs provided at their private camping area. They talked about where to eat that night, as Ingrid wanted to go out for dinner.

She was tired from driving but figured she'd get her second wind after sipping on her bourbon and cola. As she finished her drink, she said, "I'll get changed and freshen up. Let's go up to one of those pubs we passed coming in to town."

LP said, "I'm havin' another coldie; when you're ready, we'll go."

They walked out through the security boom gate at nine fifty and crossed the road towards a blue painted pub in the distance. As they walked, they passed shop fronts that were boarded up, damaged by the earthquake that had shaken the region in September. They were still feeling aftershocks and sympathised with those who had lost loved ones, whose property was damaged, and whose incomes were disrupted.

There were two pubs in town. The blue pub was for tourists, while locals frequented the pub across the road. They walked into the blue pub through two large timber doors, solid enough to withstand snow and blizzard conditions.

The first thought that came to mind was that it was like the foyer of a mountain lodge ski resort. LP ordered a schooner of beer and a bourbon and cola for Ingrid.

As it was so late in the evening, LP asked the waitress if meals were still being served. She replied, "No problem. Take a table, check out our menu, and I'll be over in a minute."

He seated Ingrid facing the fireplace, and they talked about their plans for tomorrow: returning to Mount Hutt after such a long time. LP had a photo of him looking up to snow-capped mountains. His memory was cloudy on when he actually went there, or how he got up to that height at Mount Hutt. Only the photo, taken thirty-six years ago, confirmed that he was there.

Their waitress came over to ask for their order. "Fish and chips, plus garlic bread and a Margarita pizza, thanks," said LP.

While they waited for their meals, they looked at the photos on the walls of the pub. In one photo, snow was a metre deep at the front doors.

After dinner, Ingrid suggested they grab a couple of bourbon and colas to take back to the van with them. As they walked to the drive-thru of the locals' pub, a woman having a smoke outside called out, "Where are you from?"

She could tell they were tourists. "Queensland," Ingrid replied. The women wanted to have a chin wag, but LP was rubbing his hands and beginning to shake from the cold. "Come on, let's get going," he said.

Their new acquaintance, who introduced herself as Stacey, said, "Come inside and meet my partner and some of the locals." They decided to pop in for a quick drink and were introduced to Stacey's partner, Randall, a hunter who stalked wild deer from helicopters across the high country.

Other locals welcomed them and called the barman over so drinks could be ordered all round. More locals soon arrived, and the loud laughter and voices sounded like an approaching stampede of wild animals, pushing and shoving their way through a narrow walkway.

That crowd of partygoers were all returning from a race meet at Addington Raceway, in a jovial mood because Ricky May, the driver of the winning horse Monkey King, was a local. He was a home-grown talent and winner many times over of the New Zealand Cup.

Ingrid decided they should leave before it got any rowdier. She didn't bother with getting any takeaway drinks, and they headed straight back to their van for a good night's sleep.

The next morning, LP's wish for a perfect day was granted. He stood outside their van, looking out over the snow-capped mountains; the sky was blue, without a cloud to be seen nor a breath of wind to be felt.

He went back inside and said to Ingrid, "It's the best day outside so far. We couldn't have wished for better."

LP phoned the helicopter company to check how soon they could take their flight up to the mountain. The receptionist wanted to check with Blair, the pilot, and asked LP to phone back in five minutes.

He phoned again, and this time the answer was that if they arrived at the helipad by ten thirty, Blair would be ready.

They quickly packed up, disconnected the power, and left the amenity keys at the front desk, and then they were ready to climb a mountain.

LP switched on the Navman, punched in the street address, and headed out of Methven.

Thirty minutes later, he was driving across a cattle grid into a large paddock. There were no sheep, just a big hanger with a blue and white helicopter ready for takeoff. They left their vehicle and went inside, informing the receptionist they had arrived.

Kathy said, "Just wait a minute and Blair will be with you." Footsteps down the hallway heralded the arrival of a large man in blue overalls.

"I'm Blair, your pilot for today. What exactly do you want to do: fly over the mountain or land somewhere?"

"Land," replied LP. "I want to land at Mount Hutt." As he spoke, he pulled out a photo taken thirty-six years earlier. "I just want to have a picture taken in the same spot as this one."

"Mount Hutt is closed," Blair said. "The season finished last week. The gates are chained, and you can't fly in without an authorised government permit," said Blair. "Also, that photo is not Mount Hutt."

LP was taken aback. The only other place it could have been taken was at Coronet Peak, near Queenstown. He recalled that trip, driven up by taxi with three other backpackers as drizzle turned to snow. They had had to put on snow chains as they drove up the road overlooking a cliff face, but no picture was taken.

Blair must have been mistaken. LP didn't want to comment that he probably hadn't been born then, but he kept a tight lip.

Blair remarked, "Look, I'll do one better for ya: I'll take you to a mountain peak where it's good to land. You can have your picture taken on top of the world." LP liked that idea.

Cameras in hand, the pilot and tourists walked over to the helicopter with its blades swirling. It was becoming harder to hear the safety instructions as the noise grew louder.

Ingrid was helped up onto the back seat. LP seated himself next to Blair. The takeoff was smooth as they rose above green farmland paddocks dotted with sheep. Tall wind breaks created a checker board of farms below.

LP asked, "How fast are we going?"

"One hundred miles an hour," Blair replied. "You'll feel the speed as we go low over that mountain ridge."

Thirteen minutes later, after climbing 7,500 feet, Blair said, "We're going to land on that snow field, saddled between two peaks. Hold on, it could be a bit bumpy as we set down."

With rotor blades ending the silence of a clear calm day, LP and Ingrid were in awe of standing on what felt like the top of the world.

Blair snapped a couple of pictures of his passengers and asked, "Do you want to climb to the peak?"

LP looked up to the summit and answered, "It's there to be climbed, let's do it."

They all started the ascent, but after a while, Ingrid stopped and said, "I won't make it. You go ahead."

Blair and LP kept climbing on the east face, where the snow had melted. Loose shale slid off the mountain edge as each footstep guided them to the summit.

LP reached the mountain top and stood on a small flat area no larger than half a square metre. He watched his footing; one mistake and he would be freefalling to the valley below, without a parachute.

He positioned himself for the photo he'd travelled so far for. Even though his memory was challenged to exactly where the old photo was taken, in the end, he couldn't have wished for a better outcome.

He stood looking up, hands at his sides, legs apart, straddling the peak. "Blair, take the picture now," he yelled out.

"Got it," Blair said, smiling.

"After thirty-six years, I have returned to the mountain. Hello, world," LP said proudly.

As he looked down, words came to mind:

Download, download, download.

He put that thought to the back of his mind to contemplate later, wondering if it had any meaning or was just a random thought.

LP stepped down off the mountain peak, and he and Blair descended back to Ingrid and the helicopter. Absolute silence filled the air.

LP had no fear, no pain, just sheer pleasure. He had accomplished what he had set out to do.

He gave Ingrid a big hug, which soon turned into a snowball fight on the picturesque mountain.

It was time to leave, and they took off, circling the summit called Old Man Peak.

By the time they landed back at the helipad, fifty minutes had passed. Considering the flight was only booked for fifteen minutes, Blair had looked after them very well; he charged the original price quoted without the additional $120 for the permit. LP and Ingrid thanked Blair for an experience they'd never forget.

20

Leaving the helipad in the distance, LP was high on adrenalin as they sped out through the entrance gate. The noise of the cattle grid scattered sheep in front of him, slowing him down. Heading directly for the east coast was the quickest way back to Christchurch in their reliable campervan; there, they would catch their flight back to Australia. Entering the city outskirts, LP pulled into one of many Top Ten van parks dotted around the country.

They drove up to a window covered by an awning, feeling like they were about to place a take away order. LP asked for one van site with amenities close, and they were given keys and a map showing where to park.

He reversed into their site, directly facing a building housing shower, toilets, and cooking facilities. The backdrop, a paddock of sheep and a shady tree was the perfect spot to set up.

Ingrid started reorganising the back of their van for sleeping. LP grabbed a cold beer from his bar fridge. Sitting outside at the white plastic table and chairs provided, he started feeding the locals. Ten ducks quacked for food as LP broke up bread for them.

"Don't feed the ducks, or they'll be quacking all night for more," Ingrid said from inside the van. "How about a hand setting up? You know I'd like a drink too, but this has to be done first." LP finished his stubby and helped set up the bed. Next on the agenda was shopping in Christchurch.

They crossed the busy four-lane highway outside the van park and sat down at a bus stop. Traffic zoomed past while Ingrid studied her tourist map, circling where they could go for duty-free shopping.

Ten minutes passed before the bus arrived. LP jumped up and raised his hand, signalling the bus to stop. They choose a seat at the front for a clear view as they headed for Cathedral Square. What they saw in full daylight revealed the damage from the recent earthquake.

Aftershocks still rattled the city, and many buildings were closed and boarded up. Other buildings and houses were surrounded by yellow tape, marked for demolition. Vacant blocks marked the places where homes had been swallowed up by nature's fury. For those that withstood the earth tremor, they all shared the mark of collapsed chimney stacks, while the homes remained intact.

Canterbury folk were getting on with their lives, and every other aspect of city life seemed normal. It was peak hour, and the traffic jam gave the city a sense of urban normality as people headed home from work.

The bus driver opened his door onto Christchurch's main street, lined with several duty-free shops. Ingrid stepped out of the bus and straight into the first shop. LP was keeping up, looking for new Ugg boots. It was the one thing he wanted to buy before he flew back to Brisbane: Canterbury sheep-skin boots, size twelve.

Shop after shop, Ingrid noted what she wanted to buy, and then they took a break for a drink at a café overlooking Cathedral Square.

They looked up at the steeple tower, resting on grey blocks of stone, unshaken and unmoved by the earthquake. A house of worship standing firm over its city. LP could not have foreseen that another earthquake would hit Christchurch again, destroying the cathedral and much more.

At an information kiosk, they found out how to catch the tourist tram that did a circuit of the Cathedral Square district every twenty minutes. Ding, ding the tram bells rang as it arrived. Passengers disembarked, and LP and Ingrid hopped on board with all the other tourists.

Ding, ding, the tram driver pulled a lever overhead, and the tram rolled ahead on old steel tracks that had carried passengers down the centre of the road for over one hundred years.

Three stops later, they stepped off, visiting another café for pizza. The pace of the city had slowed now. Twilight was dimming, and their journey was almost at an end.

LP was itching to give the casino another crack at paying out. He said to Ingrid, "Let's go to the casino. I'm feeling lucky." "Give it a miss," she said. "You don't know how much you won on Monkey King, and there's not much cash left in your wallet. We need money to buy gifts for us and the kids. I don't want you to lose it in there."

"Trust me; all I need is twenty minutes. We'll be in and out in no time," LP said with confidence. He'd have to be quick before security cameras picked up that he was in the building again.

"Okay, but I'll kill you if you lose." She looked at him with her lips pulled tight.

They entered the casino at 9:55 pm, and LP walked straight to his winning roulette table. He studied the history of the past numbers dropped. Before placing his first bet, he moved his gambling chips across in front of where he was standing. He followed his previous winning pattern, except he started with a ten-dollar bet on twenty-three, and a split bet across zero and double zero. On the third spin, with sixty dollars placed on the table, LP called on his angels of luck to intervene, as the red ball bounced over the numbers.

"Twenty-three winner," was the call. Wasting no time, LP collected his chips and cashed them in at the cashier's desk.

Ingrid asked, "How much did you win?" "I'm up $1,940."

Luck followed him as they walked past poker machines going off with free spins and mini jackpot wins as players sat with their eyes glued to their machines. LP wanted to stop, but security was heading their way. The last machine they were about to walk past was an oversized, old-style one-armed bandit. Above the machine flashed "Jackpot $23,000."

With his lucky numbers scrolling above, LP couldn't resist dropping a dollar down its throat. He turned to the woman at the next machine as he pulled the handle and said, "I can't wait. If it wins, you collect." Glancing over his shoulder, LP saw security officers still heading their way.

Ding, Ding, Ding. Three gold bars stopped on the centre line. Jackpot!

Everyone crowded around, blocking security as LP and Ingrid left the building.

They stepped straight into a waiting taxi and headed back to finish their duty- free shopping.

After buying presents and LP's Ugg boots, Ingrid asked, "How much cash is left?"

"About seven hundred dollars" he replied.

"Why don't we give some of those winnings to the Salvo's rattling their can in front of the cathedral? They're collecting for the earthquake appeal" Ingrid suggested.

LP agreed, and walking over, pulled out a wad of notes. He counted out five hundred dollars and squeezed the cash into a slot accustomed to loose change. He had about two hundred dollars left for a cab ride to Christchurch Airport and some duty free alcohol.

Arriving back at the van park for their last night in the land of the long white cloud, they walked along a floodlit path through the van park's entrance. Tired, carrying bags of presents, they headed back to their campervan for a good night's sleep.

Up at six, LP sat outside talking to his new-found friends. Short on a conversation, they offered just a few quacks, waiting for him to throw some more bread.

Thick fog filled the air as aftershocks from the recent earthquake rumbled beneath his feet. No alarms were needed that morning as nature shook travellers from their campervans. Ingrid started cleaning and packing the van to return it by mid-day, leaving enough time to make their flight.

LP made breakfast at the communal kitchen while Ingrid finished packing. They returned the keys through the takeaway-style window and motored leisurely away, leaving behind fond memories of the van parks they had stayed in.

They turned north, heading towards the epicentre of the region's recent earthquake. They had about an hour to spare to visit Merv and Rita Smith, parents of one of Ingrid friend's, who had survived the quake.

Driving out of town, debris still lay around, waiting to be removed by council workmen. At Kaiapoi's main intersection, the local hardware shop was half demolished, with rubble strewn into the roadway.

Turning right, they followed instructions from the other woman, Navman. After a while, she announced, "Perform a U-turn. In fifty metres, stop at destination."

Merv and Rita came out outside with a warm welcome. Kisses were shared between the women, and LP stretched out his left hand to shake, aware that Merv had lost his right arm in an industrial accident.

Rita brought out scones and poured tea, hospitality not uncommon in this part of the world. Later, Merv showed LP around their property, viewing the extent of damage caused by the earthquake. Concrete slabs were cracked open like biscuits, oozing out a black gunk from deep below the surface. The lounge room, situated at the front corner of their house, had subsided and could be noticed from the road.

LP sympathised with the trouble and danger they found themselves in. Merv had done a great job restoring their home to something that almost resembled what they had before disaster struck. Now they just had to wait for the National Insurance Fund to organise contractors to fix their property or demolish it.

LP borrowed a hammer and pliers to make repairs to the campervan. A sliding drawer had slid out as they went around a sharp bend at Milford Sound, breaking into pieces. He needed to repair the damage before returning the van. It only took a few minutes and was as good as new.

While they were out at the van, LP opened his bar fridge and grabbed two cold beers. He handed Merv one, saying, "Cheers. We've made up a relief package of all the food we have to leave behind when we go home. There's a half a carton of beer, fruit, and groceries for you."

Merv was grateful for the gift, and LP carried the box of goodies into the house and placed it on the kitchen bench.

Merv wanted to pay back LP's generosity. He said to his new mate, "Sit down and I'll bring you a top up." LP dropped himself down into Merv's favourite recliner and asked, "What's that in the soft drink bottle?"

Merv twisted the screw cap off and poured what looked like ginger ale into two glasses. "What do you think of this? It's our local town brew. All I do is walk down into town, hand over a two litre plastic bottle, have it filled up, and walk back home again. It's good value at six dollars fifty a bottle."

Merv continued, "Tankers that look like stainless steel milk transport vehicles fill up the pubs with beer every week." LP felt a sense of déjà vu, remembering seeing tankers pull up outside pubs, rolling out a large long hose to deliver beer, back thirty-six years ago. Nothing had changed.

"So how do you buy beer in Queensland?" Merv asked. "Cans, bottles, or on tap," LP replied. "It's delivered in stainless steel kegs by truck. Pity breweries don't implement your system of delivery. It could keep prices down."

Before leaving, LP showed Merv the photo of him standing on Old Man Peak. Merv, choked up and a little emotional, walked over to a photo hanging on the wall of him, also standing on a mountain ledge overlooking green pastures below, with snow-capped Alps in the distance. It was before his accident.

Merv reminisced about his old climbing days "You guys had it easy; in my day, with two good arms it would take all day and the next morning to reach some summits. You say it took you twenty minutes. I guess that's progress. Even so, I think if you climbed a mountain the hard way, you'd get far more satisfaction."

"You are probably right. If I had the time to train and bring my fitness level up, I could have done it, even with my crook knee. Times have changed, Merv. The pace of life has quickened, and you need to seize every opportunity before it disappears."

"Granted, I'd like to do more, but since the accident, I'm limited in what I can achieve," Merv said.

"Well mate, next time I'm back in New Zealand, we're going to climb a mountain together. How about that?"

"That'll be great, can't wait," Merv replied.

LP finished his beer, and Ingrid put down her cuppa.

They thanked their hosts for the hospitality and said to call if there was anything they could do to help, before taking some happy snaps in front of Merv's prize-winning roses on the way out.

Their drive back to Christchurch was uneventful, just the usual heavy city traffic. They turned into Backerpacker Van's depot and joined the queue of vehicles waiting to be checked over for damage. He hoped his repair job held up to inspection.

LP was reluctant to hand back the keys to the campervan.

Their seven days of driving reminded him of driving the old Kombi to Bells Beach in 1973.

After staff had checked their van for damage, it was given the all clear. They joined another queue out front of the entrance and waited for one for the shuttle buses to take them over to the airport for the last leg of their journey.

On arriving at the airport, they removed their luggage from the shuttle bus, checked in, and spent the last of their New Zealand money on duty-free alcohol to take home, leaving just five dollars in LP's wallet.

Ingrid still had one question to ask of LP: "How much did you win on Monkey King?"

"I'll keep you guessing until I check my betting account when we get home." Three hours later, they landed back at Brisbane's International Airport. Collecting their luggage, they walked through customs without being searched and exited through the automatic glass doors into the humid air. Leaving the airport by cab, they headed for LP's folks' place, where he had parked their car.

Peak hour traffic was crawling along, made worse by road works for two new overpasses connecting the city and airport. You couldn't get a worse combination for chaos.

He turned to Ingrid and said, "I forgot how bad Brisbane traffic had become. I think i want to go back to new Zealand already."

"Sorry, love, you're back to reality now," Ingrid replied. "There's work tomorrow. Kiwiland is off the radar for a while."

They paid the sixty-dollar cab fare by credit card and thanked the kiwi cab driver. He said he had left New Zealand fifteen years earlier because the blood-sucking sand flies of the south island had driven him crazy.

LP agreed, "been there done that, but we'll leave that part of the country off the radar next time."

21

Weeks passed as LP and Ingrid settled back to work. Their holiday became a distant memory, unless they were asked, "How was New Zealand?"

LP had hundreds of photos printed off at the local electrical goods store. He got a good deal on prints at five cents each and showed them to anyone who wanted to hear about their trip. Those fond memories would carry him through to his next holiday break in December. With six weeks' holidays owing and four months' long service still to use up, he was planning many more adventures.

Since returning from Christchurch, they had only had three sunny days. All the others were overcast or raining. He hoped this pattern would change so he could go fishing and crabbing up the beach, not far from Double Island Point.

His thoughts also wandered back to repeating their trip over the ditch, as Kiwis fondly called the ocean between Australia and New Zealand. He thought next time they could head north from Christchurch and head up to Picton, where the ferries docked after leaving windy Wellington, capital of New Zealand. His plan would be to drive down the rugged west coast, taking in the breathtaking scenery they'd been told about by tourists they had met in their travels. February or over Easter would be a good time to head back. He would run the idea past Ingrid and see what she thought.

Meanwhile, news reports told of further aftershocks in Christchurch, rattling the nerves of city folk.

More disturbing news from around the world reinforced LP's attitude about natural disasters occurring in Indonesia, Pakistan, Haiti, and Chile, to name a few.

He was beginning to believe that the prophecies of the Bible and *I Ching,* the Chinese *Book of Changes,* were merging. Within a short time, they would bring either destruction or enlightenment.

There was also Nostradamus's secret writings to consider, and the Mayan long count calendar, calculated to end after 5,125 years, on December 21, 2012. The future was looking gloomy if he believed everything he watched on the nightly news.

Continuing news bulletins didn't help his attitude, with reports that the worst aspect of man-made pollution may not be carbon in the atmosphere, but methane. Both went hand in hand.

With methane building up in the atmosphere, the title of a book by Bill McKibben, *Earth under Fire,* could well come true.

ABC-TV's *Four Corners* reported on the drilling and capping of hundreds of coal seam gas wells in Queensland. Prime cattle grazing country, as well as cotton and grain fields, had been adversely affected.

Seeping methane gas bubbling up into the atmosphere, as well as chemicals used in fracking to extract coal seam gas, were poisoning the land and threatening to compromise Australia's greatest natural asset.

The Artesian basin's underground water resource, the size of Europe, continually provided fresh water to Australia. Thousands of windmill water pumps positioned through the land provided drought relief for marginal land that would not otherwise be suitable for grazing cattle or sheep. Consequently, it had turned a barren landscape into a profitable venture for the first European settlers, who came to the area in the early 1800s.

Watching ABC's *Four Corners* programme stiffened LP's resolve and only reinforced his concerns that things weren't getting any better. He felt he was becoming a prisoner to an environment spiralling out of control.

He concluded governments that could make changes for the well-being of future generations were slow to act in turning the tide of environmental destruction befalling our way of life. This had also endangered other species to the point of extinction.

Big business, through lobbying politicians at all levels of government, had influenced decision making adversely on our planet, allowing carbon to increase beyond what the planet can cope with. Furthermore, it was reported the rate of deforestation had not abated.

Bloggers, highlighting habitat ruination affecting the survival of orang-utan populations in Borneo and Sumatra, stated that millions of acres of rainforest habitat were cut down each year to make way for palm oil plantations.

That rate of logging and burning could only lead to the extinction of orang-utans in the most horrible way, as witnessed in 1997–1998's uncontrolled burning, which killed nearly eight thousand of the primates.

What happened to those creatures may well mirror how things could pan out for mankind, destroying the ancient forests of their dwelling place and thus, in the not-too-distant future, destroying the planet we know.

Those primates were like the old canaries in the underground coal mines, LP realised: save them, and we save ourselves.

For a species to claim intelligence and rule over its domain, they must also take responsibility to look after and protect that environment and its inhabitants.

At stake was our place in the universe as a sustainable biosphere for future generations. The time to take a stand was approaching, where one voice, echoed by billions, would create change. That day was coming, by LP's reckoning.

LP was becoming increasingly worried about the natural disasters being reported throughout the world. Now events were happening closer to home.

Unprecedented flooding along the eastern seaboard of Australia, bush fires over in the west, and more predictions of cyclones in coming months, might bring more devastation to parts of North Queensland. This would keep State Emergency Services on alert for extreme weather conditions to come.

His mindset needed some clear thinking, as events unfolded as foretold. To get his mind off things, he opened his unread emails.

Bear's was the first he read, bringing a smile to his face as he scrolled down. Bear wrote about the stupidity of some politicians, stating what he would do if he could get hold of the buggers that gave the Communist government in Vietnam $160 million to build another bridge across the Mekong River. You'd think once bitten, twice shy.

He reckoned what he'd do is grab hold of the politicians responsible and give them a good shake or two to see if any intelligence rose to the surface. They should be treated like working dogs, he felt: if they didn't perform, they shouldn't get tucker and instead get the bullet.

LP could understand why Bear was so pissed off over the government sending $4.5 billion overseas as foreign aid, while the country he loved was left wanting for a disaster fund set up like the one in New Zealand.

In his email, Bear wrote, "For every dollar that's sent offshore, one dollar should go into an Australian disaster fund, to help those affected by flooding, earthquakes, wild fires, and cyclones in this country.

LP agreed but emailed back to him that shooting the dog seemed a bit over the top.

Christmas Day started out for Ingrid and LP like any other at their home of thirty-one years. All the presents were piled around a green pine tree, adorned with tinsel and covered in gold bells and a star atop. Flavours filled the air as the food was spread over two large glass tables.

LP's blue cooler, packed with dry ice, was overflowing with festive spirits.

Glancing across at his temperature gauge, he saw that it was thirty degrees already, which at nine o'clock was making for another hot and humid Christmas Day.

The sunrise hour passed, with kookaburras laughing to set the morning theme. Family and friends would arrive mid-morning.

In the meantime, he packed their four-wheel drive. Teewah Beach was on his mind. Tomorrow, they would drive up to Tewantin and cross the flooded Noosa River by barge.

As everyone arrived for lunch, more presents were placed around the tree for all to see. After all the gifts were opened to great enjoyment, the feast was devoured.

LP pushed his chair back, stood up, and said, "What a great spread this was. I think we should thank Ingrid for the food, and I'd like to thank everyone for being here."

He walked inside and flicked on a local news channel for the latest news on flooding in Queensland. A reporter stood at a Brisbane intersection and reported, "The Bad Meadows biker's club, numbering close to two hundred riders, two abreast, is causing traffic chaos." The reporter pointed to gridlocked traffic and continued, "Nutter, their leader, a reformed drug dealer and standover thug, has now ordered his mob to follow him in single file, zigzagging through the traffic chaos they caused."

Nutter rode his gleaming Fat Boy Harley, holding the handle bar with his right hand. In his left, he waved a huge brown teddy bear. The other biker club members also carried Christmas presents for sick kids at Brisbane's Royal Children's Hospital.

LP called out, "Nutter's got a mention on the midday news!" "Yeah, so long as he and his brain-dead bikers keep on riding south, then that's good news," said Ingrid.

Nutter and his band of followers made an impressive sight for TV viewers. They entered the hospital precinct still in single file, and Nutter parked his bike just past a double glass door entrance. Carrying the giant teddy bear under his arm, he walked over to the doorway and handed the bear to a nurse. He then waved through all his other bikers to deliver their presents also.

The head matron said, "Four of you can take your gifts in with the nurses to Ward 7B. But be quiet."

Nutter waved over Porky, Jimbo, and Tiny. All four entered a large foyer area, where their riding boots squeaked on the gleaming polished floor. They were guided to a wall of lifts on either side of a pale green hallway.

Matron pressed the lift button, and the doors opened instantly. Nutter and his men, dressed in black, with their colours emblazoned across their leather jackets, marched down the hallway to Ward 7B. For doctors and nurses, this was the hardest and most rewarding ward to work on. Children being treated for cancer looked up from their beds, and huge smiles greeted the bikies bearing gifts.

Nutter glanced down at the chart on the bed end and said, "Hi Cory. My mates call me Nutter, but you can call me Bruce," to which Cory replied, "I like Nutter better."

Nutter's bikie mates covered their laughter at hearing his real name for the very first time. Smiles continued to fill the ward, as one by one they laid their presents on the beds.

Nutter said to Cory, "I was once like you, in pain, until a man whispered some words to me." He knelt down, placing his head next to Cory's, and whispered the same words Bear had said at their last confrontation, in the shadow of Brownie's ancient Dreamtime ancestor, Tibrogargan.

As Nutter spoke, a tear drop fell on Cory's forehead. "This is your mantra for life," Nutter said. "Make it part of your future." Nutter looked over to the matron and said, "Cory looks very pale. Maybe some sunlight will put colour back into him."

She responded, "We're the professionals. Your point is noted." Nutter turned again to Cory and said, "Find the strength within, and bathe yourself in the morning sunlight reflecting off the Glass House Mountains when it comes through the window at the end of this hallway. And listen to what these hard-working doctors and nurses tell you."

The bikers said good-bye and wished everyone a Merry Christmas. Before walking out, Nutter grabbed hold of the matron's arm and asked quietly, "What chance has he got of beating cancer?"

She replied, "Without Medicare he would have no hope. The latest cancer fighting drug we're using costs $1,925 a shot. He needs one every day. At this hospital, it's free."

Ingrid called out, "Turn that bloody TV off. We're trying to enjoy Christmas Day."

"Yeah, I'm coming. Spare a thought for those that can't spend Christmas Day with family, and the police who have to work today," LP said, as he returned to the smorgasbord feast for seconds.

Police Just Want to Have Fun, Too

Independent police polling highlighted their good work and congratulated them on a job well done. Their culture of looking after each other in difficult times put many Queenslanders off the good work they did in towns and cities around the state.

This created a mentality of "them and us," which persisted from the days when police were used to squash anti-war demonstrations and street marches, such as the one against the South African Springboks rugby team playing matches in Brisbane in 1971, and street marches condemning the Vietnam War.

Joh Bjelke-Peterson the then Premier of Queensland declared a state of emergency that delivered more power to the police commissioner. That gave newspaper cartoonists plenty to draw about back then.

Recently, the ghost of Joh had returned, with police acting badly.

One newspaper cartoon depicted two football teams, Morningside and Wynnum, in police uniforms. The score was 59–72, playing for a side bet. Their prize was to street check two little old ladies who stood outside a barbed-wire fence. The winner would curry favour with senior police, who were competing to clock up the highest tally of random street checks.

Another cartoonist sketched five off-duty cops jumping out of a slow-moving van and doing a quick run around their vehicle, completely starkers, during peak hour traffic. Any civilian carrying on like those fellows would be arrested and charged immediately. Not so in this case; senior police waited on a report before action could be taken or charges were laid.

Another cartoon sketched an officer wearing one glove, knee pads, a bucket hat, and, for the ladies, a short tie. These were the latest suggestions coming from grassroots police on the beat with a flair for fashion or just the ridiculous. Those suggestions would be taken seriously if it meant boosting police morale.

But wait, there was more. LP recollected a cartoon of Blitz and his handler, looking forlorn, with their heads sticking out of a large dog box. The caption read, "We were only doing our job." Blitz and his handler had been suspended for fifteen months for overzealous police work. That crime fighting duo accounted for 23 percent of all arrests made by the dog squad's sixteen members. It all came to a head when Blitz took down a workman by mistake, biting him on the leg.

Blitz's hard work had landed him in the dog house at the Oxley police complex. His handler was suspended indefinitely and had to explain why he and Blitz had made so many arrests.

Blitz was now off duty and being fed tinned rations. His handler had to account for every morsel of dog food given to his crime-fighting partner. That cartoon prompted senior police to handle Blitz's case proactively, to achieve an outcome in line with public opinion.

Next was a cartoon of the premier of Queensland in bed with the police commissioner. The government's Criminal Misconduct Commission (CMC) was the overseer, fighting corruption within the public service and police departments. Seeming to be above the law, ready to prosecute breaches of the law, all were accountable to the inquiry's judgment, including the police commissioner. But Queenslanders were sceptical of any government stopping Queensland police, being a law under themselves, with their own code of conduct, just like the bikies: don't rat on your mates.

Another cartoon depicted senior police as snails, slow to investigate the death of an indigenous inmate on Palm Island, which resulted in rioting that burnt down the only police station, barracks, and court house on the island.

The commissioner had to explain why proper police procedures were overlooked at watch houses throughout the state.

This resulted in pay-outs of hundreds of thousands of dollars to victims of police brutality. That cartoon was not very funny.

Queenslanders could be heard to say that the ghost of Joh had returned. In his day, it was not uncommon for brown paper bags filled with cash to land on his desk. In return, the police would turn a blind eye to illegal activity. It just seemed normal at the time. That's how business was done in the Sunshine State of Australia.

Even with bad press, the police had the full support of the government, and the commissioner retained his position, no matter what the CMC signed off on. He felt confident, because internal polling showed that 63 percent of Queenslanders were happy with his boys and girls in blue. That also meant that more than a third of Queenslanders had a not-so-pleasant experience with his police force, which would not improve their public image.

Tony Fitzgerald echoed those views, saying "The culture of the past has returned since 1987, when I headed the Royal Commission into police corruption in Queensland."

These views of a southerner from over the border were not welcomed in Queensland. His comments were quickly rebuffed by the premier in support of her police force.

Those cartoons jogged LP's memory of how small local football clubs raised money for the upkeep of their fields and clubhouses back in the early seventies. Cops would turn a blind eye to some illegal activities in return for the odd carton of beer that came their way.

That knowledge came in handy one particular time at an Aussie Rules football club trying to raise cash to support their players. Club organisers put on an invite-only night for the blokes. A lady with the stage name Lana would be performing her highly publicised routine, while the audience enjoyed beer and prawns.

The stage act that everyone paid money to see was banned in Queensland, being classed as lurid. If vice squad officers knew where she was performing, they would raid the venue, arresting her and everybody else.

Although the legal age limit for alcohol was twenty-one at the time, that didn't faze bar staff serving any young bloke who placed his money on the bar mat.

LP had asked his friend Donny, "What's the chances of been raided?" to which he replied, "None, look over there." Two coppers were standing at the bar's back door, being handed jugs of beer with glasses.

"Stick your head out of that window and tell me what you see," said Donny.

LP looked out into the darkness to see two police vehicles lit up from nearby streetlights, blocking the Wilston Grange Football Club gate entrance. The two officers walked over to join their fellow constables for a few drinks while still on duty. It looked like no one was coming in or out until the performance was over.

"I see what you mean; if they were arresting anyone tonight, they should arrest themselves first," LP replied.

LP turned around as loud music signalled the beginning of the performance. He was about see why Lana's act was banned.

Back then, police made up their own rules of behaviour, and this persisted up until the Royal Commission brought down senior police and politicians, sending some to jail.

Their belief that they were untouchable and the culture of payoffs and bribes continued during the inquiry of 1987. One blatant example was the Vanuatu Gala Ball.

This wasn't the kind of event that the name suggested. Topless waitresses served beer and prawns. Entertainment was provided by well-endowed women mud wrestling, which could be seen by surrounding neighbours in broad daylight.

Northy Street, where the ball was held, was listed on police monitors as "Do not enter, road works in progress." Local police officers closed off the road until the charity fundraising function finished. This only reinforced LP's view that little had changed in the force in Queensland.

22

**NEW YEAR'S EVE
DECEMBER 31, 2010**

LP rolled his head towards the window and opened his eyes to see sunlight breaking through storm clouds over the horizon. He could hear ocean waves as they broke on shore, washing away vehicle tracks made at low tide, returning Teewah Beach to its pristine beauty.

Flood waters gushed out through the Noosa River mouth to the south of Teewah Township. The water on the shoreline turned brown, with ocean foam rolling along a normally pleasant outlook. Storm water spreading out along the foreshore and strong south-easterlies would prevent any early-morning swimmers coming down for a morning dip on Teewah's normally white sandy beach.

Ingrid moaned. "What time is it? I want to sleep in. Pull the curtains closed."

LP rolled over and placed both feet on the cool polished floor boards. He closed the curtains and went out into the living area, quietly closing the door behind him.

He clicked on the TV and flicked through the channels until he saw flood waters flowing down Queensland's Fitzroy River. ABC 24 Hour News was reporting on flooding throughout

Central Queensland, west to Theodore and St George and back to the coast, an area the size of Texas.

The Fitzroy River flowed through the heart of Rockhampton, a major city in the region. Two large bridges looked like they were holding the city together as residents braced themselves for the full onslaught of flooding upstream.

The airport was already under water, and within days all roads leading to town would be closed. Rocky would become isolated, with only volunteer State Emergency Services and police personnel continuing to evacuate locals to higher ground as the river peaked. Those men and women also had to battle rising waters and avoid deadly snakes and crocs that had been flushed out of their dens and water holes.

He sympathised with those affected up north; to some extent, flooding was also increasing in Queensland's capital of Brisbane. LP and Kato's places were high and dry, and flooding would not affect them, although a rising Noosa River might shut down Tewantin's two barges, which were their only way back south across the river.

LP had seen enough bad news for now and switched the TV off. He headed over to Kato's place, overlooking Teewah Beach. Brownie was due to be staying there tonight for New Year's Eve, if he could get through. Bear's old place was just around the corner as well, but no one was staying there this year. It had no plumbing while the bathroom was being renovated.

LP strolled up the sandy track to Kato's front yard, which was covered by bush and shrubs, creating a private courtyard.

"G'day, mate," LP said when he saw his neighbour. "Getting the rods ready for fishing on the other side?"

"Yep, with a bit of luck there should be a small wave to ride as well."

"Have you seen the news about up north and Briso?" LP asked.

"No, what's happening?" Kato said.

"Well, your mate in Kiwiland was right," LP said.

"What, you mean Ken Ring, the long-range weather forecaster? I'd given up on him," said Kato.

"Don't be too hasty," LP said. "His forecasts were based on the moon going through its thirty-six-year cycle. That means the weather is repeating the pattern of the early seventies."

"Yeah, you're right, it sure feels like that. All we need is a couple of cyclones to come down the coast and cross between Gladstone and Fraser Island, and déjà vu 1974."

LP left Kato contemplating the possibility of worse weather to come and walked back around to his place, where he found Ingrid making breakfast. Her omelette recipe, prized and passed down through family generations, called for a hand full of chopped bacon and shallots, four eggs, quarter milk, plus a pinch of salt and pepper. Adding a teaspoon of flour made the mixture fluffy, just like her Nana's. Pour into a hot saucepan and heat for a few minutes, and then fold and turn once.

He sat down on their verandah, poured himself a large glass of orange juice, and looked out at the dark storm clouds bucketing down torrential rain just offshore.

LP called out to Ingrid, "Better hurry up with breaky, or we're not going to get up to Double Island before this rain comes."

She replied, "If you want it any quicker, come in and help, or make it yourself."

LP was only trying to point out that they needed to leave soon. Not only because of the weather but also to beat the rising tide, otherwise it would be hard going driving on soft sand.

The last hundred meters before going over the blow would be blocked by waves pushing up against the high sand dunes.

If that happened, they'd have to wait there for the tide to turn, which could take up to three hours.

LP went inside and opened up his laptop to check his emails, the latest being from 350.org, McKibben's website. It commented on Queensland's floods, claiming climate change had caused the deluge.

Up until that time, LP had thought Bill McKibben's theories on climate change, based on the amount of carbon in the atmosphere, had some foundation.

McKibben said that if carbon climbed above 350 parts per million (ppm), the planet we know would become unrecognisable. His assumption was that carbon would continue to rise above 350ppm. Then we would all have a problem to solve. Current carbon pollution measured nearly 400ppm and continued to climb higher.

However, LP was now questioning the validity of McKibben's theory. Natural disasters throughout the world were being pointed to by over-zealous followers of McKibben, often without any independent scientific evidence to validate their data.

If they bothered to check flood records on the Brisbane River for the past 180 years, they would have seen that nine major floods had occurred in that time.

On average, then, severe flooding could be expected in Brisbane every twenty years.

LP wouldn't call it climate change, but a climate pattern already understood by Australian scientists.

Australia's climate cycle was said to go through dry and wet centuries. This fact had been proven correct by core samples from the Great Barrier Reef.

McKibben's bloggers wanted to blame flooding in Queensland on climate change; they might as well blame the government for the downpour.

Since 2007, the government had paid a consultant $7.6 million to facilitate cloud seeding over Brisbane's two main dams, Wivenhoe and Somerset. After cloud seeding started, the heavens opened up, and seasonal rain returned. By the end of 2010, all south-east Queensland dams were overflowing.

The question could be asked, did the Queensland government cause Brisbane's biggest flooding since 1974?

LP closed his laptop and they ate breakfast; he and Ingrid wasted little time in organising food and cold drinks for lunch. They packed them into LP's big blue cooler box with a bag of ice.

LP drove down a sandy track and out onto the beach. Thirty-five minutes later, they could see the blow ahead, as waves washed against the sand dunes. "You're too late. You won't make it through those waves," Ingrid said in a cautious tone.

LP planted his foot hard on the accelerator, changing from first to second gear in four-wheel drive. He ran the gauntlet and won with seconds to spare. Turning hard left, he continued up and over the sand dunes. Ingrid gripped the dashboard, bouncing up and down as the vehicle hit ruts in the sand tracks.

LP slowed down as he steered through the rainforest track and sunlight filtered through the greenery overhead. He could see sparkling blue water ahead. Suddenly, the rainforest opened out to Double Island, Ingrid and LP's Shangri-la.

Double Island's northside was protected from the forty-knot south-easterlies, and the ocean was calm with pristine blue water, compared to the other side of the headland. With no rain clouds overhead, it was a welcomed change to all the bad weather that surrounded them.

This destination was a well-kept secret but had been rediscovered. Visitors from throughout the world were starting to come see this special place under the sun. And to their surprise, there were no islands. The name came from Captain James Cook, who had mapped the east coast of Australia way back in 1770. He gave the name to the Glass House Mountains and mistakenly named the point further up the coast, Double Island Point.

Obviously, it was only a headland.

LP stopped his four-wheel drive in front of a large lagoon. He looked up along the shoreline of high sand cliffs leading to Rainbow Beach.

Memories flashed back of forty years past, of Gordon Elmer with his orange ex-army vehicle, loaded up with LP and his mates, as well as food, drinks, and surfboards. Elmer had driven them on the beach to Double Island. They would spend their weekend there until he returned for them on Sunday afternoon. Back then, you rarely saw anyone else. Now, you almost had to reserve a spot on the beach to park.

If you ignored all the other vehicles, fishery inspectors, national park rangers, and police patrolling the beach as if it was a highway, Double Island was as pristine now as back in the early seventies.

LP found a sense of tranquillity and freedom here, even with the unwanted crowds. It was still better than the city life.

LP spotted Kato and parked close enough for them to rope a tarp across both four-wheel drives to protect against the sun or rain.

Once they were unpacked, Kato looked at LP and said, "Look over there, Brownie's finally arriving. He'd be late for his own funeral."

Brownie parked his Toyota Landcruiser next to LP's vehicle. The trayback had a canopy cover with everything inside for camping and with enough food and water to survive three or four weeks on the beach or in outback Queensland.

"How come ya just arriving now?" Kato asked. "We expected you days ago."

"Bloody tourists and flood waters; felt like tellin' 'em to swim back to where they came from. They expected to see the dry arid outback and do some hunting. They're lucky they weren't the hunted. Between the crocs and snakes, we just made it out of there in one piece.

"I got 'em back to Rocky and dropped 'em off at the Fitzroy Hotel for a counter lunch," he continued. "I'd gone into the city to get a radiator hose to replace the one that was hissing steam and losing water.

"By the time I headed back, the police had closed the road, and I couldn't get back in. So here I am. I got out just in time, before the whole town was cut off by road, rail, air, and sea. I'll go back for 'em when the road opens again. That won't be for another two weeks.

"Anyway, where's the surf? It reminds me of when Nat Young and his surfing buddies were here in the early seventies. They said the place had the smallest waves they had ever seen, that had the potential to be the longest wave ever ridden."

"Yeah, just as well it was small that day, or by now it would be packed with surfers, like Noosa National Park on a big swell," Kato said.

LP butted in, "You won't be surfing here today. The only action you'll have is if I take you out on my jet ski. Come on, Brownie, jump on. I'll take you around the front of Double Island. Put that vest on and hang on."

LP pushed his jet ski from the shallow water and climbed on, with Brownie following. One quick squeeze on the throttle trigger gave a burst of power that sent Brownie lurching backwards, gripping tightly to the back of LP's vest.

Thirty seconds later, they reached the headland point, where swells rolled in, producing perfect waves that could be ridden for up to two kilometres. Out here, dolphins imitated surfers with skilful manoeuvres, jumping forward down a wave face and doing a bottom turn just like a seasoned surfie.

They continued out to the next point break. Forty years ago, that break was only the haunt of fishermen. Over the years, sand had built up, making a pretty impressive barrelling break. The only problem was, you had to jump in off an outcrop of rock, called Flat Rock, into rolling swells. Once in the water, you looked straight up at a sheer cliff face as the waves washed up onto large boulders.

The trick to riding those waves was not to get caught in white water, which could push you up onto the rocks. If that happened, you could expect your surfboard to be damaged and to get cuts and abrasions trying to retrieve it. Climbing the cliff face was a challenge, even for an experienced rock climber. You didn't want to find yourself in a position like that. When Flat Rock was pumping, the best option for coming in was to paddle back around the headland.

That was the only safe way to go, allowing the inshore rip to push you along. Eventually, you would reach a sandy cove and could leave the water, looking like you knew what you were doing.

Suddenly, a loud noise overhead broke through Double Island Point's tranquillity. They looked up as rotor blades blasted a path around the jagged headland. Someone in the helicopter was motioning for them to head back to shore. LP acknowledged their instruction, waving back with his left hand. They couldn't tell if it was fisheries, national parks, or police, but they followed the helicopter back as it landed.

Sand pushed up and away, swirling like a sand storm, as the big red and white helicopter set down.

LP slowed down and then beached his ski. Brownie jumped off first and started walking towards an expected confrontation with whichever government agency they were.

LP was still pulling his jet ski further onto dry sand, with his back turned. He had a nightmare thought, that it could be Jack Herbertsin.

He glanced over his left shoulder as a familiar voice bellowed out, "G'day, ya bastards, bet you didn't expect to see me here."

Brownie shouted over the whirling rotors, "Bear, you sure know how to make an entrance!"

"Well, I had no choice. The flood waters have cut all the roads from the airport to here. So I just hired a chopper; no drama, didn't want to miss New Year's Eve again."

"Huh, Kato's sure gonna be surprised," Brownie said. "He reckoned you were too tied up in Sydney to get up here."

LP opened up the front compartment of the jet ski and grabbed another life jacket. He handed it to Bear and said, "Climb on, there's room for three. Let's go."

Bear signalled thumbs-up to his chopper pilot, and the swirling blades churned up sand as the helicopter turned sharply and disappeared out of sight around the headland.

They headed back down to the camp, and with a turning tide, LP drove his jet ski as far up the sand as possible. He reversed his RV and put his ski onto the weather-beaten trailer, ready for the run back over the blow, down the beach, and back to their house.

Bear helped Kato untie the ropes holding the tarp up, then they rolled it up and packed it away for another day. Bear climbed into Kato's Cruiser, and the vehicles drove in convoy back along the beach to their holiday houses.

Bear asked, "Was there anything special happening for New Year? No trouble from coppers or bikers, I hope!"

"The only thing out of the ordinary was two undercover coppers turning up at a wedding at a neighbour's house. I was there having a couple of drinks with them," Kato said.

"How did you know they were coppers?" asked Bear.

Kato said, "The next day they were in uniform doing random breath testing, but I wouldn't make much out of it. I think they were just off-duty cops looking for a late-night party to crash."

"What's LP up to?" Bear asked. "He phoned and said there was one more thing that had to be done with the Scroll. He didn't say what was on his mind, just to be here this time. So what do you know?"

Kato's response was hesitant. "LP believes that the Scroll has to be downloaded at midnight this New Year's Eve. The positioning of the three beach houses, each with a laptop, one of which is George's old one, will form a triangle, pointing directly to Mount Beerwah in the Glass House Mountains, the home of Brownie's ancient ancestors from Dreamtime."

"Get real," Bear said. "I'm havin' a break from Sydney's rat race. I don't want to hear any more about images, aliens, downloads, and bent coppers."

"Okay, but that's not all. He's convinced that the axis of the pyramid that the laptops form when pointed at Mount Beerwah will create a direct link to a planet one thousand light-years away, rotating in the opposite direction to its sun," Kato said, shaking his head in disbelief.

"If he wasn't a mate, I'd think he's completely nuts. Is he using his fortune-telling skills again?" Bear asked, while scratching his head.

"Look, there's no harm in humouring him," Kato said. "All he asked is that at midnight, George's old laptop, his PC, and Brownie's simultaneously download the Scroll. That's no great drama."

"Okay, I can't see a problem with that, but it had better be the end of it all," Bear said. "I don't want any more trouble from bikers, police, and religious fanatics turning up again. Tell me, what happened with that footage implicating the commissioner shooting George?"

"We found it, but it was only recently that we could copy it. We had to run the footage on George's laptop and film it with LP's new video camera. Now it's ready to upload to YouTube," Kato said with a grin.

"Hang on," Bear said, "if Herbertsin gets wind of what you're doing, he won't let sleeping dogs lie any longer."

Kato, still smiling, responded, "Jack Herbertsin ain't the commissioner any more. He now heads the counter-terrorism agency in the federal police in Canberra. He wouldn't give us lot a second thought these days, so don't worry about that."

"Come on, Bear, let's knock down a few beers and talk about the old times," Kato said, "and we'll see the New Year in with some fireworks."

"How did you get hold of fireworks?" Bear asked. They're illegal."

"Banger Bob," replied Kato. "I bought the last lot two years ago, before he was arrested and thrown in jail. I've still got a couple of mortars left from last New Year's Eve; they should be pretty spectacular."

Bear said, "That'll make New Year go off with a big bang, but what I want to do now is go crabbing."

Bear was keen to pack in as much holiday time as he could in the twenty-four hours before he had to head back to Sydney. He really wanted to go fishing and crabbing along the Noosa River. He didn't eat crab meat but liked the challenge of catching them and avoiding their vise-like grip.

It was late afternoon when they returned, and a bright orange sun was setting over the horizon, with dark storm clouds moving above.

Bear spotted LP's crab pots stacked against the house and said, "Come on, we're wasting time. Throw those pots in the tinnie, let's go crabbing." Pots, rods, and bait were placed into LP's boat, and they headed back towards the barge on the Noosa River, where they would launch their crabbing mission.

LP manoeuvred the boat trailer down a small cement ramp next to the Noosa barge and slid his fourteen-foot tinny into the murky brown water. Brownie climbed in, while Bear held the boat.

LP parked his four-wheel drive away from the boat ramp, locked it up, and got into the boat. Bear pushed the tinny away from shore, jumping in while LP motored in reverse.

After turning the tinny, he accelerated downstream, past a small island with a wooden jetty jutting out from mangroves that surrounded the island, and headed towards the river mouth.

Minutes later, LP turned hard to port into a mangrove-covered inlet that only a few locals knew about. He yelled, "Duck!" as he entered.

LP slowed his boat to a punt as it pushed through into a huge lagoon, saying, "This is where we're fishing, out of the wind and current."

After they anchored, Bear threw out three crab pots and proceeded to cast out their lines and wait for a feed of fresh fish, whiting or bream, that they could cook up on the barbie later.

The stillness was broken by Bear's rod as it twanged and bent sharply. He gave it a quick pull backwards and had his first fish jagged. It was a big one and put up an enormous fight, coming to the surface twice before Bear could pull it up and over the edge of the boat. It was a huge Grunter bream, around fifty-five centimetres long and probably weighing in at nearly five kilos. Bear's monster catch would win any fishing contest on the coast. Even so, this was going on their barbie for a feed tonight.

After an hour of fishing, it looked like Bear's catch would be the only fish for dinner. He stood up with the oar in both hands and started moving the boat slowly over to their floats, pulling up three empty crab pots.

Bear was not happy and said, "There's muddies in this river, and I'm gonna find 'em. Pull up anchor and head back upstream." Bear, being not shy to solve a problem, continued, "Head over to those couple of floats near that island. We'll see if they'll give us a feed of muddies."

No one wanted to remind Bear that there were laws against raiding someone else's crab pots. They knew his answer: "How many times have my pots been raided? I'm just returning the favour."

LP motored slowly alongside the first float as Bear pulled up a rope to reveal two captured muddies, one large buck and a small female.

Bear tipped the pot on its side, and both crabs dropped out. He reached down to grab the green female by its back flap and threw it overboard.

He then moved in on the agitated male mud crab, which reared up, snapping its two giant claws. Bear avoided the claws and grabbed the crab from behind.

The mud crab liked wrestling but didn't stand a chance against Bear's quick reflexes. He placed his prize in a blue bucket and then grabbed two VB beers and put them in the crab pot, sinking it back in the river.

That was his payment as well as a bit of a joke. Whoever owned that pot would think it a southerner had raided its contents. Queenslanders would have used the local brew, XXXX.

Moving along, Brownie pointed his torch at the next float. He quickly pulled up another pot and gave a thumbs-up: another large buck. He shook the pot, and the crab dropped directly into the claws of his first capture.

Brownie said, "Drop the pot quick smart, and just punt around to the other side of this island."

"What for?" Bear asked.

"Some of the locals use the dense bush area along the mangroves to grow their own weed," he said. "We'll help ourselves to a few leaves."

As LP pulled up against the small jetty, he asked, "What's the name of this island?"

"Makepeace Island is its name now. It used to be called Pig Island. When the owner, a Miss Makepeace, passed away, she left the property to a woman shopkeeper she had befriended. She sold it to a local artist, who used it as his home and studio. He organised the name change to Makepeace Island and then years later sold it to a high-profile executive, who now allows it to be used for conferences and recreation for his airline staff. It's rumoured he paid four million for it."

As they approached, lights were on and people were standing on the verandah.

Brownie said, "I won't be long. Cut the engine and hand me that torch." LP and Bear watched him disappear into the darkness and waited quietly, not wanting to bring any attention to their ill-gotten booty.

Brownie walked close to the well-lit verandah; moths attracted by the light swarmed so thick you almost had to cut your way through them. He noticed a woman standing on the verandah, as he brushed several moths away from his eyes. She had bright red hair, pale white skin, and freckles.

He thought, *I know that woman*; walking up several stairs, he tapped her on the shoulder and said, "Hello, Riverina."

Startled at first, the woman turned and then recognised the voice. She looked into his face and said, "Brownie, what are you doing here?"

"Ah, a bit of crabbing and fishing. Just stopped to use your toilet."

"Funny, ha ha," she replied.

"So, how you been? Keeping well, I hope." "Yeah. Good, good, real good," she said. "Anyway, where's the loo?" he asked.

She grabbed his hand and led him down a hallway, opened a door, and pushed him in. She followed, closing and locking the door behind her. They were about to repeat their mile high encounter, when they had last met on a flight from Alice Springs. Fireworks were going off early for Brownie at ground level.

23

As they waited for Brownie to return, LP and Bear grew anxious about why he was taking so long. Bear turned to LP and said, "He's taking his bloody time. Hope he hasn't run into any trouble." "Yeah, like the night before goin' south to Bells Beach, when we had that bit of a punch-up with that skinhead mob on the top floor of Lennon's Hotel."

While waiting for Brownie, they reminisced over what had happened that night: LP had downed a schooner of beer before walking down a narrow pathway between table and chairs. He had told Brownie and Bear, "Keep an eye on my back. Those dickhead skinheads could be trouble."

LP squeezed his way past one bloke blocking the entrance to the men's room. As soon as he walked back out, seeing nothing had changed, he pushed forward a white chair with an angry skinhead gasping for breath as his chest was pushed into the corner table.

Brownie and Bear, seeing what was erupting, started running towards their mate. Four tattooed chrome-dome blokes jumped up from their chairs, and one slid across the table towards LP. LP raised his arm and gave him a right upper cut to the nose, with enough force to splinter bone, piercing his forehead.

Brownie, with the force of his Dreamtime ancestors surrounding him in spirit, raised his left leg and kicked another opponent in the head, sending him smashing to a floor soaked in spilt beer.

Bear nabbed another skinhead and gave him three quick jabs to his ribs, plus one almighty punch to crack the bloke's jaw. He fell down, blood trickling from his mouth.

Bouncers pounced, restraining Bear, Brownie, and LP. They quickly pushed them towards Lennon's top floor foyer of lifts, to be sent down out onto Brisbane's Queen Street. Bear was agitated and itching to finish the fight.

He figured those skinheads would be ejected pretty soon. They started walking down a well-lit pavement when Bear pointed to a dark laneway, indicating that this was where they should wait for their prey. From where they waited, they could keep surveillance on the King George Square car park, where Bear's Charger was parked.

After waiting twenty minutes, Bear finally decided that they should call it a night and head back to his car. They walked out of the alleyway and crossed the street to the car park.

Brownie called out, "There they are, walking across the road." Bear and his mates stood around a corner, down a ramp at the first level of the car park. The ramp spiralled down seven levels with no other vehicle exit.

Four bloodied skinheads entered the heavily lit car park; Bear jumped out in front of them, screaming, "Okay, bastards, I'm gonna show you what a modern day warrior would do to you arseholes." Like cornered animals, they stood motionless. Bear started poking their leader in his chest to get a response. He didn't want to throw the first punch; instead, he raised both arms, and then, like a giant grizzly bear, he shredded and ripped the shirt off his prey. At that moment, laughter could be heard at the car park entrance. Two constables stood watching what was happening. LP and Brownie had also spotted the police entering the car park.

The laughter stopped suddenly as a voice yelled out, "You've got just thirty seconds to get in your cars and leave. Otherwise, two paddy wagons are waiting outside to take you all to the city watch house."

The constables stood to attention as the sergeant in charge stood utterly silent, waiting for his command to be heeded.

Bear looked over to LP and Brownie, saying, "That's a reasonable request."

They got into Bear's V8 Charger, giving a couple of revs that echoed throughout the underground car park. With wheels screeching and smoking, they drove out onto Adelaide Street.

LP said, "Look over there. Sarge wasn't bluffing." Two paddy wagons were indeed awaiting them.

As he finished reminiscing, Bear said, "That's a good story; I like that one. Pity the cops aren't as reasonable now as back then. These days they'd book ya or throw you in jail over almost anything."

Several minutes later, Brownie returned, with a two-metre-high marijuana plant covered in flower heads. He had literally pulled it, roots and all, out of the ground. "What took you so long?" Bear asked.

"It was a little cramped where I ended up," he replied. "Took a wrong turn, but it's all okay now. Let's get out of here."

They motored back the way they had come. LP had placed the plant under the boat's flooring. If they were stopped by fisheries or water police and the plant was found, they'd be in the lock-up for New Year's Eve.

They arrived back at the boat ramp under cover of darkness. LP climbed out, ran across to his vehicle, and backed it over to retrieve his boat.

Bear opened the front passenger door and climbed in. Brownie sat in the back seat, keeping an eye on the boat as it was pulled from the water.

Brownie asked LP about last New Year's Eve: "Have you figured out what was meant by saying that ice would cover the land for thirty nights?"

LP replied, "My interpretation is that it had something to do with a severe winter in the northern hemisphere. Major blackouts would follow throughout the north for up to thirty days. Even so, it could be something else."

"What do you mean?" Brownie asked.

"If what happened in 1859 is repeated, that would be a worse case scenario. The fact is a solar flare that occurred in the late sixties has decayed back into the sun, like a lava lamp bubble rising to become another solar flare, the second largest ever recorded. In the past, that occurrence would not have raised an eyebrow."

"However, now that we are dependent on satellite communications and power generation, things have changed. If they were knocked out, planes and ships could not navigate. Mobile phones, computers, and the like would fail. Cities of the world would come to a standstill. Panic would set in, and police and emergency services would have to restore order."

Brownie looked shocked, shaking his head in disbelief. He said, "What can be done?"

LP replied, "Hopefully, the power grids have been upgraded.

New circuit breakers needed to be installed in old transformers.

That's the weak link that needed to be fixed."

Brownie said, "I'll go back to the mountain and ask for help from my Dreamtime ancestors."

"Wishful thinking there, Brownie. That worked once, but you had help on the mountain that day," LP said.

Ten minutes later, they were back at LP's house, cleaning up their catch. Bear walked over to an outdoor bench to scale and gut his monster fish.

Brownie lent a hand, taking the bucket of mud crabs over to the bench. He turned the bucket on its side, revealing two claw-snapping mud crabs. He grabbed his shovel and quickly pushed it through the middle of each crab's hard back shell, killing them instantly.

This was how he prepared crab for cooking. Brownie considered it far more humane than boiling them alive.

LP had water boiling on the stove upstairs, and Brownie placed four cleaned pieces of crab into the boiling salt water.

Bear followed them upstairs, placing his prize fish on alfoil, already buttered, peppered, and seasoned. He gave it a good squeeze of lemon juice and wrapped it up before placing it in LP's oven.

Ingrid turned from watching TV and said, "Smells good. About time you guys did some cooking. Why not make it a habit, instead of only at your barbies?"

The guys grinned as Brownie replied, "We are hunters and gatherers. We won't be making this a habit."

Seven minutes later, Bear's crabs were cooked, the shells changing from a dark green to orange. He removed them from the boiling hot water with tongs and placed them on a plate to cool. Bear grabbed three coldies from the top shelf of the fridge, twisting the tops off and handing them around.

After knocking down a stubby each, Bear opened the oven. As he removed his prize catch, an aroma filled the air, with flavours that made everyone's mouth water.

He placed his Grunter bream and the mud crab pieces on the outdoor table. Like vultures, the guys swooped down, devouring everything in sight.

As they stood around the table, Bear said, "Anyway, where's Mason? I thought he'd be here."

LP replied, "No, I spoke to him on the phone this morning. His night shift staff, and their fellow Masonic brethren, wanted him to celebrate New Year together, so he won't be here. Even if he wanted to, flood waters would stop him from making it up to us. I explained to him what needed to be done at midnight, and he agreed to be ready to download.

"You know I went back to New Zealand six weeks ago?" LP added.

"Yeah, and?" Bear said.

"Well, it's been thirty-six years since I was last there. I found an old photo of me taken back then, standing on a mountain looking pensive; it got me stirred up to head back over the ditch and have another photo taken again in the same position."

"Back in August," he continued, "Virgin Airlines offered cheap Internet flight tickets, so I booked two return flights to Christchurch for a seven-day holiday. On the second last day, we took a helicopter ride up the mountain."

"Not long after returning from Christchurch, I realised there was one more thing to do with the Scroll to complete the sequence. That was to download it and save it."

Bear, now understanding what LP wanted to do, weighed up the situation and asked himself a question: Was the triangular configuration coincidence or design? Bear wasn't taking any chances but wanted to have some fun too.

After the download, he decided to fire off Kato's last batch of fireworks. Those mortars should light up the night sky. He got a kick out of blowing up things.

Everything was now in place for midnight. Brownie, LP, and Kato's family and friends were arriving to celebrate the old year and welcome the New Year in. While everyone was arriving, Bear slipped out the back and went down to his house to check on the bathroom renovation. He also wanted to visit his gun safe, which was hidden behind a wall in the built-in wardrobe.

He walked up three steps onto a wide-open verandah and went through to the bedroom. He opened a large wardrobe door and removed a back wall panel to reveal the gun safe. Bear took out his licensed pistol and shotgun. He used both weapons for hunting and protection when riding his bush bike on outback properties, and he had shortened the barrel of the shotgun, finding it safer.

Placing the pistol in the back of his red board shorts under his jacket, he wrapped his shotgun in a towel and started walking back to LP's holiday house.

Bear slipped up the stairs and went quietly down the hallway to the main bedroom. He placed both weapons under LP's bed and rejoined the celebrations, opening LP's cooler and pulling out a six pack of coldies to hand around.

Over laughter, talking, and the beach house juke box blaring out Jimmy Barnes's gravelly voice, Bear picked up on a noise that was out of place. It sounded like a helicopter overhead. He went outside and looked out over the balcony; he saw nothing unusual, only low-lying, dark storm clouds.

He turned and walked inside, past the juke box pounding out lyrics. Suddenly, over the blaring music, there was a loud bang as glass shattered downstairs. He looked down the stairwell to see several men dressed in black wearing balaclavas and carrying weapons. In single file, they started cautiously moving up the stairs.

Without thinking, Bear's survival instincts kicked in. He took three quick steps, grabbed hold of the juke box, and pulled it across to the stairs. He raised his left leg and gave the jukebox an almighty boot, sending it catapulting down over their New Year's Eve party gatecrashers.

If he were bowling, he would have marked himself down for a strike and scored maximum points. As Bear turned, he saw that those on the balcony had been unaware of what was happening inside until the jukebox music stopped.

He yelled out, "We've got trouble!"

As confident as ever, he took five quick steps back to LP's bedroom and then knelt down as though praying.

He reached down and pulled his shotgun from under LP's bed; he unrolled it from the towel and grabbed his pistol. He pushed it down the back of his board shorts and walked back out to the crowded balcony.

The laughter and music had stopped. All eyes were fixed on Bear. He yelled out, "Everybody inside! Brownie, out the back door now. Get down to Kato's place to download."

LP asked, "What about George's laptop?"

Bear replied, "Forget about his old laptop, it won't work. The reception drops out too often down there."

Out of the darkness, four ropes dropped from above, followed by more black-clad men, faces hidden by balaclavas.

Bear didn't hesitate; he shouted out, "Take this, you bastards!" He discharged each barrel and reloaded at lightning speed. As four sets of eyes looked down, their ropes snapped, sending them plummeting into the thorned rose bushes below.

Not knowing where, or how high, the helicopter was, Bear picked up one of Kato's mortars that were to be part of the midnight fireworks.

He placed it in the firing cylinder, angled between two hand rails, and lit the fuse.

With a sizzle and a bang, exploding fireworks broke through the low cloud in a show that a pyrotechnic would be proud of. The light revealed a chopper positioned above LP's holiday house. Bear was about to pick up his shotgun and give the pilot a warning blast. Suddenly, the swirling blades headed in a southerly direction and soon could be heard landing over at Teewah Beach's helipad, which was the only way in and out in an emergency at high tide.

Bear figured Jack Herbertsin had orchestrated this clandestine, unsanctioned mission for his own personal benefit; now he had to call it off.

He had failed to retrieve George's laptop, which contained the evidence that would incriminate him in the shooting. Intel from those undercover cops didn't help.

Little did he know that if his men had walked into Bear's house, they would have found George's laptop on the kitchen bench.

Jack's men were instructed to pull back to the helipad for evacuation and destroy the log books of their mission. There was to be no record of this incident.

LP looked over to Bear in shock and said, "Bloody hell what just happened."

"Don't worry about it, it's all sorted."

Everyone suddenly turned their attention to the radio. "Ten, nine, eight, seven, six …" The countdown had started. LP was ready to press Enter to download and save the Scroll. "… five, four, three, two, one!"

He pressed Enter and then said, "Let's not forget zero. Without one and zero, this could not happen." Voices yelled out, "Happy New Year!"

Brownie had stripped the leaves off his stolen plant and dried the potent heads in Kato's oven. He removed them after downloading the Scroll.

He used six *rollie* papers to make up a giant joint with leaves, heads, and resin, making it a potent reefer. One puff would get anyone stoned.

He returned to the others to share the joint with LP and Bear. Bear grabbed it from Brownie's hand, stuck it between his lips, and lit it, taking a deep puff before handing it around.

LP said, "I think I just saw George at your place, Bear."
"You're seeing things again. You can't see my place from here.

It's the joint, mate. It's good shit."

"I think I saw something too," Brownie said.

"Right, I'm going to finish this, and we're going down to my place to check out what's happening down there," Bear said.

All three walked along a sandy track to Bear's old beach house, laughing over nothing along the way.

They looked around for any sign of movement before walking up the stairs and entering the kitchen.

Looking over to George's laptop on the bench, they saw the Scroll displayed as a screen saver.

LP said, "I told you guys something like this would happen when the laptops were aligned with Mount Beerwah. Now do you believe me? There should be no reception here. The only possibility is Brownie got reception. Brownie, did you come in here and download this?"

He replied, "No, definitely not, I was too busy rolling that big fat joint."

"Alright," Bear said. "Check where it was saved. It might give us a clue." He pressed Enter and opened up the file.

They all started to read: *Hi guys, couldn't stay long. Your triangular configuration allowed time to fold in, creating a three-dimensional portal to open up a crack in antimatter, like the timeline markers of old at the ancient Bora Rings. That's given me enough time to let you know I'm doing all right, and to enlighten what is to be achieved when the image within the Scroll and words whispered are combined. It will allow you to connect to the greatness within that will go back to the creator, and at that moment, you will know your immortality. The Scroll is saved; knowledge and wisdom are at your fingertips. Equinox, the end is the beginning, life renewed, Omega and Alpha.*

BOOK 3

NEW AMSTERDAM
NEW YORK
NEW BABYLON FALLS

24

FRIDAY, MARCH 31, 2012

Quatrains from Nostradamus haunted LP. He couldn't get those words out of his head. It was bad enough with his view to the future described by Bible prophecies and the *I Ching*. However, now the Mayan long count calendar, which said the world would end on December 21, 2012, played on his mind.

LP struggled to come to terms with all that had happened over the past four decades, which culminated in saving the Scroll in cyberspace. He wanted nothing more to do with it. As far as he was concerned, he and his mates carried out what was foretold at the ancient aboriginal site in the outback, one thousand clicks west of Brisbane, in Queensland.

He only wanted to get his life back to normal, spend time with his family, and finish a project he was working on that would put him in a position to retire early and do the things he loved: go fishing and camping, spend more time with his family, and travel around the world.

With the global financial crisis still affecting retirement funds, however, his retirement plans were on hold—unless he could get a windfall like what happened back in 2003. He had an uncanny ability of reading the future, which he put down to being born, according to the Chinese horoscope, in the year of

239

the snake. He now understood how to use this gift of foresight, which had then netted him a hundred thousand dollars. That windfall went into renovating their run-down old home.

He tried to warn friends and relatives about the looming global financial crisis back then, but some declared he was crazy, and others were dismissive of his prediction of the financial upheaval.

However, acting alone on his hunch, he changed his retirement fund to a conservative investment mix, six months before the first crisis struck in September 2008. Around the world, stock markets went into a tailspin. Fortunately, his retirement fund was not significantly impacted, continuing to produce returns of 5 to 9 percent each year.

Still, this good luck would count for nothing if he could not shake off the feeling that there was one more thing left to be done with the Scroll, even though he didn't have it anymore. What he did have was a ghostly image within the Scroll, which could be printed out on canvas with his colour copier. Connecting with the image, which he named Zero, and whispering George's mantra instantly transported him to a higher level of thought. This, coupled with his gift of foresight, tapped him into visions of the future, helping him avoid disaster and benefit financially by gaining deep insight on where to invest in and when.

He had to make up his mind one way or the other to follow through on the vision. After those thoughts dogged him for months, he decided to visit New York City. Exactly what he was going do there was not clear yet, but one reason for going to Manhattan was meeting with publishers about future book releases. He was not going to mention any other reason for wanting to be in New York to anyone. The real reason was, he believed, he was the one mentioned in Nostradamus's writings foretelling of a man travelling from the East and entering the new city of Babylon. The description fitted LP, now aged: bald, a mark on his face, and a gap between teeth.

Decision day arrived, marking the tenth anniversary of 9/11. In his line of business, three-quarters of the selling season for promotional calendars passed with incentives for introducing new clients to the benefits of the company's products. The prize: an all-expense-paid trip to a conference in Las Vegas, with plenty of time for sightseeing. The timing of the conference was yet to be announced, but it was expected to be held before the end of June 2012.

LP needed to write up as many new orders in three months as he had done in the earlier part of the year. This was a big call, but he knew that if he won, he could to leapfrog from the east coast of Australia to the West Coast of America.

"All passengers, please proceed to boarding gate 52, flight 7 for Los Angeles now boarding," the voice of a flight attendant boomed.

LP turned to Ingrid and said, "I didn't think we'd make it six months ago."

Surprise: he'd achieved his sales target with one day to spare and didn't learn that he qualified for the conference until December.

Ingrid responded, "Banish all thoughts of work. We're having a holiday, and if we don't catch up with anyone from your office in Vegas, that would be great."

"We can't be rude," LP said. "There's the company dinner and a show already booked, plus the sales meeting; other than that, we have time to do what we want and when we want." He smiled, hiding his true intentions after leaving Vegas.

Their chat got interrupted by LP's mobile phone, which vibrated in his jeans pocket. He reached down and flicked it open. It was Rick, the company CEO, calling from Sydney

Airport, asking if everything was fine with them and if they were on time to connect with their flight to LA. LP would be the only company person on flight 7. Everyone else was flying out from Sydney Airport.

"See you in Vegas," was LP's last comment to Rick before flicking closed his phone and slipping it back into his pocket.

LP and Ingrid lined up to board and slowly walked to the final check-in counter. They presented their boarding passes and proceeded down the long walkway before entering the plane. Welcomed by two Virgin Airline hostesses, they were directed down the aisle for sitting.

LP thought, *This is good: two seats back from the toilet with an aisle seat, you beauty.*

That meant he had more leg room and wouldn't feel cramped in. Plus he could have a couple of beers and not be climbing over passengers to go for a wee walk.

However, things did not go to plan. He had worried about bad weather and a rough flight, but he had no idea he would have an altercation with a fellow passenger. He hadn't even mentioned his fears of bad weather to Ingrid, not wanting to worry her unnecessarily.

Two hours out from Brisbane, the captain announced, "Passengers and all crew, be seated and fasten your seat belts."

As the warning light above came on to buckle up, the captain continued, "All flights to Nadi, Fiji have been cancelled due to bad weather, and we are now changing course, heading north to skirt the storm. There could be some turbulence, so please remain seated until the seat belt lights go off."

Well, it was no more beer for LP for a while, so he settled back to watch a movie on the back seat screen.

Before the seat belt lights went on, LP looked over to the main screen, plotting the course travelled. They were nine hours and thirty-five minutes from landing at LA Airport, flying at an altitude of 30,998 feet, and travelling at 937 MPH.

Ingrid nudged LP, pointed to the toilet, and whispered, "Got to go."

He stood up to let her pass and sat back down. There were two ladies waiting to use the rest room, just two seats forward of where they were seated. So Ingrid walked across and past three passengers in the centre row in front of the toilets and waited on the opposite side for the restroom sign to light up.

LP didn't sit down for long. Knocking down the last mouthful of beer, he then followed Ingrid, stepping around three sets of legs, and waited behind her for the toilet to get vacant. When the next passenger exited the toilet, she went back the same way Ingrid came and was about to step around a set of outstretched legs. Of course, common courtesy would allow her to pass when those seated would move their legs if they were blocking the passageway. But the man seated on the far aisle seat had moved his feet up and placed them against the back toilet wall, thus creating a barrier.

The passenger, a woman in her mid-fifties, looked down at the guy. He just ignored her and didn't speak. She turned around and walked up the aisle to the back of the plane and back down to where she was sitting one row back from LP and Ingrid.

As Ingrid entered the small restroom, LP commented, "He's a smartass, but he better not try that on me."

"Settle," Ingrid retorted, "or security will be escorting you off this flight as we land."

"I'm not about to make a scene, just hurry up. I'm busting," he replied.

Ingrid didn't take long and proceeded to walk back the way she came, but again this guy, who looked like he could be part of the Japanese Mafia, with long black hair and olive complexion, appeared cross and a trifle intimidating. His legs were pushed hard against the wall. Ingrid indicated she wanted to pass, and again he ignored any request to put his feet down.

The guy was undoubtedly acting like a petulant child. This was his space, and he was going to control and defend it. Ingrid turned around, so as not to create an incident, and walked up the aisle and back down to their seat.

LP entered the toilet, thinking, *that arsehole isn't going to do that to me.*

When he was done, he slid open the door and walked past two passengers without any conflict. Standing before a barrier, the two legs presented an obstacle. Overhead, the "fasten seat belt" sign was on, and LP wanted to sit down quick smart.

He looked at the guy straight in the eye and said, "either you move your legs, or I'm coming through them."

There was a moment's dead silence as they eye-balled each other. LP glanced over to Ingrid, who was shaking her head, and then raised his right leg and stepped over the man made barrier. A few expletives were exchanged, but it didn't come to blows.

LP sat down next to Ingrid and said, "just as well he didn't jump up, or i would have laid one on him.

"Settle, settle," she said in a soft whisper, "or we won't make it to Vegas."

He pushed his seat back, placed his headphones on, and started watching a movie to take his mind off the altercation, which could have ended his mission to reach New York by good Friday.

Almost two hours had passed since the cabin lights were dimmed. The cabin crew were seated, and except for a baby crying, the only noise that could be heard was the dull roar of the aero-engines. Some turbulence could be felt as the plane skirted around the storm ahead.

The pilot fiddled with the scheduled flight path on the overhead video screen. He had changed course, heading north for about hour, then LP felt the plane changing direction again, now heading in the south-easterly direction. Passengers were able keep track of the altitude, the speed, and the number of hours it took them before landing at LA International. The pilot made up for the time lost from diverting off course, eventually putting him only twenty minutes behind schedule.

Ingrid and LP were the first to stand up after the seat belt sign went off. He needed to stretch his legs, and she was busting to use the restroom again. While Ingrid rushed forward to beat everyone to the toilet, on their aisle side, two seats forward, not create another incident as earlier. LP reached up and opened the overhead luggage compartment, pulling down their carry-on luggage. He shuffled along with the other passengers and met up with Ingrid, who then helped him wheel their belongings off the plane.

It had been a long flight. Although the plane had departed Brisbane Airport at 11:20 am, March 30, they touched down in LA at 7:20 am the same day (albeit different time zones). They had little sleep throughout the flight, but the excitement and adrenalin kept them wide eyed and keen to connect with their flight to Las Vegas.

LP's colleagues going to the conference wouldn't be hard to spot: Just find a bar in the airport, and he was pretty sure that's where he'd catch up with them.

Ingrid and LP collected their luggage from the carousel and headed towards customs and border security. American airports had taken airline safety to a level not experienced in Australia.

Even ten years after 9/11, the fear of hijacking still presented a clear and potent danger to Americans.

LP passed all the checkpoints; after his hand luggage and bags were scanned, his pockets emptied, his shoes and jeans belt removed, he entered the full body scanner. He was called forward and asked to follow the security officer for further scanning.

LP called out to Ingrid, "I'm over here, just gotta go with this security guy. I won't be long."

She looked concerned, thinking, *What has he done now, to bring such attention to himself?*

A security officer escorted him behind a partition and asked, "This is a random check for explosives residue. Have you been in contact with explosive materials?"

Surprised, LP answered, "No."

"What is your reason for entering America?"

"Holidays and to attend a conference in Vegas," he replied. "Well, you're clean to go, have fun in Vegas," said the officer. LP walked around the partition, grabbed Ingrid's hand, and said,

"Let's get out of here before they find something else to hold us up." The airport's main terminal was like entering a massive shopping mall, dotted with eateries, bars, newsstands, and souvenir shops.

LP spotted one of his colleagues and waved to Trev, who had only recently retired as company sales director but wanted to go to one last conference. He had initiated the first one, when he started with the company, about twenty-seven years ago.

"G'day, mate, see you made it on time to connect with the flight to Vegas," Trev said.

"Yeah, only had two problems that could have put a stop to that," LP replied.

"What's that, mate?" asked Trev.

"I'll tell you over a beer when we get to Vegas," LP said. Now there was eleven accounted for. Another eight delegates would arrive from Sydney flying Qantas, arriving at two o'clock. They would catch up with them at Planet Hollywood, where they were all staying.

Trev, always the leader, led the way to the transit terminal. He had been here many times before.

They entered a corridor and went down a flight of stairs opening out onto a large platform. Here they would wait for a light rail commuter train. Five minutes later, the train arrived and they got on board with their entire luggage. They were shuttled to their next departure area.

When the commuter train stopped, Trev was first off, waving his hand in one direction and quipping, "More security checkpoints; follow me and it won't be long before we land in Las Vegas."

The LA domestic terminal had the same security procedures, and all their luggage went through the security checks once again.

Despite the delay, they were on schedule to board Delta flight 201 to Vegas at eleven o'clock. Looking out through the large glass window, LP commented to the group, "We couldn't wish for better weather: blue sky and hardly a cloud in sight. This is going to be a smooth flight, great for sightseeing."

What they hadn't expected was the small size of their aircraft. As they walked across the tarmac, LP saw it was just a fifty-seater commuter plane—an overbooked one, at that. Whoever arrived last would miss this flight. Trev's group was lucky. Seat allocations were done earlier, and everyone boarded together.

LP ducked his head as he entered the plane. There was only one stewardess, who pointed to the rear end of the plane for him to be seated. LP leaned over as he walked up the aisle to avoid hitting his head. This was the smallest plane he had ever flown in, other than his helicopter flight on New Zealand's South Island. He wondered if this plane would fly any higher than that.

Their only stewardess was multi-tasked. She welcomed everyone aboard, shut the plane door, checked that all seat belts were fastened, and demonstrated the safety instructions for an emergency.

When all was ready for takeoff, the pilot said, "This is Captain Roger Smith. Perfect weather conditions ahead, ideal for viewing the snow-capped mountain ranges to the south. We will be arriving in Las Vegas a few minutes ahead of schedule, so I'll circle the city once for passengers to snap some aerial shots before landing."

After an uneventful flight, with no passengers giving LP any reason to get stirred up, he was pretty relaxed. He turned to Ingrid and said, "When we've booked in, let's check out what this town's like during the day."

Ingrid looked like a concerned parent as she said, "You might be looking for excitement in Vegas, but what you are really saying is you want to gamble. Think about it: we have had no sleep for nearly thirty-six hours. Stop and have a rest for an hour or two." "I don't think I can. This is such an adrenalin rush," he replied.

"We'll talk about this later, after we get to Planet Hollywood." When they all walked out from the terminal, they were greeted by a cold nip in the air and two limos waiting to take them to their hotel.

Driving through traffic was not dissimilar to commuting in any Australian city. It was like Surfers Paradise in Queensland, which followed the coastline from Southport to the border, dotting the skyline with high-rise buildings but with just one casino to indulge LP's appetite to gamble. And the city was also nicknamed the Strip.

Driving down the Vegas Strip, the limo driver dodged in and out of the congested traffic lanes, ignoring the blaring horns of the other drivers.

LP looked past the casino buildings and saw a clear blue sky, without a cloud in sight. What a contrast to the chaos on the street and sidewalks, as partygoers got an early start to the night life.

Planet Hollywood was only one set of traffic lights away. The driver hit the accelerator, just beating a red light, and turned down a side street, entering a basement drop-off area. They all chipped in and gave the driver a thirty-dollar tip. Then they grabbed their bags; to their surprise, the ones that had been roped down in the boot were already waiting to be lugged away.

LP was the first to line up to check in, while Ingrid went to the restroom to freshen up. She needed a toilet urgently. LP waited in the line for almost twenty minutes and then got their keys to room 1883.

They headed over to the lift area, pulling their carry-on luggage past rows of poker machines; LP could see these were not like the ones in Australia. Looking across the pathway, he spotted the casino tables, and his heart started to beat a little faster. He also got goose bumps from the sound of slots calling out to him to play.

"Don't get any ideas about gambling until we unpack and do the tourist thing," Ingrid said. "We're going to walk through some of the other casinos before you feed any of those one-armed bandits." As far as LP was concerned, this was a once-in-a-lifetime chance to experience Vegas, both the good and the bad. He couldn't pass up the opportunity to play machines he'd never seen before. Seven days in Vegas would indulge his senses to gamble and drink, anytime, anywhere. He could even walk into a casino with a cold beer in hand, without having to dump it in a trash can. Ingrid looked out the window of their eighteenth-floor room, which was filled with Hollywood memorabilia, and remarked,

"That's the Bellagio across the road. We're going in there first." "Yeah, sure, but what do you think of the Marilyn Monroe photo under the glass coffee table?"

"It reminds me of my younger days," she replied. "Whatever you reckon, I'm picking up a six pack of Bud and some snack food to munch on later," LP countered. "Okay, let's get out of here." She gave in, smiling.

They entered the lift foyer. LP pressed the Down button and waited. With a "Ding," the lift doors opened. Seconds later, they were walking through the casino, once again flanked by rows of poker machines. Ingrid kept a watchful eye on LP. She wanted him to pay attention to what she wanted to do in Vegas: shop. There was going to be a conflict of interest, no matter what LP said. Eventually, he would have to do what Ingrid asked for. Later, he would have permission to indulge himself.

They walked to a nearby mall, turning left onto the Strip. A burly African American caught LP's eye and said, "Hi, would you like free tickets to a show and $200 poker money?"

"What's the catch?" LP replied.

The man directed Ingrid and LP over to a kiosk in front of the main entrance to a casino. There, they were introduced to Marty, who explained how to get money to play the pokies and free tickets for shows and dinners.

It didn't take long for LP to click on what they'd have to do to get these freebies: it was a time share offer. They would have to sit through a ninety-minute presentation, and only then would they be eligible for the $200 to play the pokies, two dinners, and tickets to a show. LP figured a couple of hours out of seven days in Vegas wouldn't be a problem. All they had to do was say no to the sales presentation. They had been through such presentations before and knew what to expect and how to control the events, without being taken for a ride.

Their mind made up, they agreed to the offer and were issued a card, bearing a time and date when they would be picked up in the basement foyer area of Planet Hollywood.

LP thanked Marty and said, "See you then."

Ingrid led the way, keen on getting out onto the Strip and soaking up the atmosphere.

They walked down the main entrance stairs onto the busy sidewalk; tourists filled the walkway as they dodged other pedestrians.

LP and Ingrid waited for the lights to turn red.

"Cross now," LP yelled, as he grabbed Ingrid's hand and led her off the sidewalk as a green "Walk" signal flashed. They headed up Bellagio's driveway and entered through large glass doors, to be greeted by a gold statue of Caesar with his right hand stretched out.

"Come on, stand over here, and I'll take a shot of you and Caesar," Ingrid offered, as she pulled her camera from her handbag.

LP obliged by standing in the same pose as the statue, as tourists and patrons walked by. One click and she had her first photo from Vegas. They then entered the main gambling den, where Ingrid spotted a machine titled "Sex in the City."

She walked over and said, "Let's play this."

Ingrid liked that machine and had a win when the free spins came up, collecting a ticket for $60. LP went over to the cashier and exchanged it for cash. After that, they went back across the road to the Parisian-themed casino next to Planet Hollywood.

There they bought tickets to go to the top of the forty-three-story replica Eiffel Tower. Not as high as the original, but scary enough for a tourist with a French accent to be overheard saying he was not going up in that thing.

The 360-degree view from the viewing platform was worth the twenty-minute wait to go up in the lift. You could see the old part of Vegas, called Freemont, and snow-capped mountains across the desert plains. The Las Vegas skyline looked like a beacon that would light up at night, attracting swarms of tourists to feed on what Vegas had to offer.

LP and Ingrid were now starting to feel the effects of jet lag and needed to get some rest. They headed back to Planet Hollywood, but before going up to their room, LP picked up a six pack of Bud and something to munch on. Back in their room overlooking the Strip, LP twisted off a screw cap and savoured his first taste of a Bud in Vegas. It was cold, with a light refreshing taste, similar to the beers he liked in Australia.

Ingrid placed some savoury biscuits and an avocado dip on the coffee table. They didn't feel like going back out for a meal, staying in their room to finish their drinks and calling it an early night.

The next morning, LP phoned up Rick to confirm the conference time. Ingrid made plans with the other women to go shopping at the discount shopping district in the Freemont area, while the sales people discussed shop.

That night, everyone met up in the foyer and headed across the street, passing the beautiful fountains in front of Bellagio's resort. Every half hour, the water spouts would go off with a spectacular display best seen at night, as coloured lights choreographed a symphony in water, delivering a performance that drew hundreds of tourists to fill the sidewalk. What everyone didn't know was a team of divers and technicians underground made it all tick.

LP and his group had no time to stop now, as they were going to see one of the most popular shows in Vegas: "O," the Cirque du Soleil show. Performers entertained their captive audience with acrobatic, jaw-dropping precision.

Before leaving Australia, the company had bought tickets for the event, and Rick handed them to everyone in his party. LP and Ingrid were seated down close to the stage, five rows back to the left. The performers used ropes and swings, but no safety nets, and kept the audience on edge. They could sense that one mistake could cost a performer serious injury, hurtling any one of them across the stage. When the final curtain fell, they all gave the performers a standing ovation.

LP and Ingrid left the venue, promising to see his colleagues at the company dinner the next day. LP's mate and his wife, Bill and Sandra, would be flying in the next morning, and they would also be staying at Planet Hollywood. From there, the four were scheduled to travel by bus to the Grand Canyon on Monday.

Tuesday morning was set aside for the time-share presentation for the freebies, followed by a visit to the casinos on the Strip. Wednesday was also set aside for free time.

On Thursday, they had plans to catch a bus to the famous Golden Nugget Casino in Freemont, the old part of Vegas. This casino positioned itself as the iconic landmark of another era. It was ticked high on LP's agenda.

The Freemont district was a part of Vegas and the original strip for gamblers past. Even fewer tourists knew of Freemont, except for the presence of a huge shopping precinct, where one could buy designer clothing, perfumes, and almost anything else at throwaway prices.

25

LP started to stir as sunlight filled through the room. He was wide awake, thinking about everything that could happen when they arrived in New York with the Scroll. He had brought not one, but several copies. Although they were not the original, LP thought they would deliver a powerful message for anyone who connected with the image.

His knowledge of the Dreamtime spirits of aboriginal folklore, influenced by Brownie's connection to the Glass House Mountains, continued to shape his thinking. What he struggled with, as their room warmed up, and before Ingrid awoke, was who would receive the Scroll? And exactly where was its final resting place?

His vision of being in New York over Easter seemed to be on track with the flight tickets booked before leaving Australia. Departure from Vegas Airport would be at eleven thirty Thursday evening. Still, the vision of what might unfold in that city was unclear, except that it involved water.

His thoughts wandered back to his childhood days, mixed with pleasure and pain, taking care to recall only the good old times and banishing any negative thoughts of the past.

His thoughts flew back to how all this started, when he was barely twelve years old and had his first vision of the future revealed to him, as he lay in bed, looking out his bedroom window at the stars twinkling in the night sky above.

In that moment, his destiny was summed up in just a few words: "You will be a leader of men." At the time, it seemed impossible, because he struggled with keeping up with his school education and could not imagine that happening.

He left school at fifteen with a level of learning that was barely enough to land him his first job in the printing industry. Here, his interest in printing and sales started to grow. He learned a lot on the job, laying the foundation for his career in sales and marketing.

He thought it funny that fate would have him laying in bed in Vegas on April Fool's Day, thinking of what lay ahead for him in New York. He asked himself if it was all a joke; was his mind playing tricks on him? The answer undoubtedly would come in New York.

"Are you awake?" Ingrid asked gently.

"Yes, I can't sleep, I'm wide awake," LP replied, dogged by his concern for the future. He bounded out of bed, trying to focus on the moment and enjoy their holiday destination.

"Okay, I'm up for a big day," he announced to Ingrid. Then he rang up Bill to catch up and check out Vegas with their wives. Bill answered the call with, "You old bastard! You couldn't let us sleep any longer?"

"Cut the crap," LP responded. "We'll be at your room in fifteen minutes. Let's not waste any more time. There's a lot to do and see."

The first thing Sandra said after LP came into their room was, "I'm starving. I saw that Harley-Davidson Café as we came down the Strip, let's go there for breakfast."

Everyone walked out together and headed for the lifts. They rode to the ground floor and walked through the main casino area. LP struggled to blank out the sounds of the machines as they went past.

LP pointed left, saying, "I saw the same place on the way in. It's just up to the road."

They walked two blocks past construction sites with high safety barriers, then up stairs, along an elevated pathway crossing a road below. Buskers performed their routine along the walkway, looking for tips to be thrown their way. LP stopped and dropped some small change into a guitar case as a bearded old guy played his guitar; he looked like he needed a good feed. They then took the outdoor elevator stairs and rode them down directly to the Harley-Davidson Café.

They were shown over to their table by the hostess and sat down, looking out onto the main Vegas Strip as the morning unfolded. Under a bright blue skyline with casinos as far as the eye could see, they looked over the menu and decided what to get. LP ordered an omelette and a beer. Bill ordered the same, and the women went with croissants first, followed with bacon and eggs.

It was ten o'clock. What started out as sightseeing in the morning would turn into a lazy afternoon, if their waiter didn't hurry up with their meals and drinks. LP asked the waiter how long it would be before their food was served and ordered another beer. The first ice-cold can of Budweiser went down as smooth as silk. The second not so good, as the waiter tripped and spilled a glass of water onto LP's jeans and shirt. He immediately apologised and returned with napkins to soak up the water on his wet clothes, plus a complimentary beer to bring a smile back on his face.

Breakfast was served a few minutes later, and by the time LP had finished his third beer, he was pretty relaxed and keen on seeing as many casinos as possible through the rest of the afternoon. They walked past souvenir shops selling clothing so cheap, it prompted Ingrid to buy four t-shirts for ten dollars, and as they passed the big yellow arch of Mc Donald's, a sign in the window read, "Burgers ninety-nine cents."

LP commented, "How cheap is that? We should have gone there, and it would have been quicker."

In sight was the MGM Casino, just a short walk down the road. They entered through a large foyer, with slot machines that were hard to avoid. The women said they were going to walk around, while Bill and LP had a beer at the bar. LP looked around at the machines, wondering which one was ready to payout big time. He pointed over to one that a woman had just left and said, "I reckon that one's about to pay."

They picked up their beers and walked across; Bill sat down in front of the machine that LP chose. He watched from the adjacent chair as LP took turns on pressing twenty by five, a one-dollar bet each time. It wasn't long before the free spins came up, paying out $240.

In their excitement of having a good win, LP walked away, leaving his small backpack, holding his cameras, next to the slot machine. When LP realised he'd left his backpack behind, he panicked. He turned and started to run back, declaring to everyone, "I've left my cameras next to that poker machine; wait here for me."

His worst fear was realised. No backpack—only two empty beer bottles. He stopped a waitress as she collected their empties and asked if she had seen a backpack.

"No sir, but you could check with the lost and found," she said, pointing in that direction.

LP strode off to the "Lost and Found" sign just around the corner of a row of poker machines. He walked up to the desk and inquired, "Has anyone handed in a small backpack with two cameras in it?"

"When did you notice it missing?" the woman at the counter replied.

"Three twenty-five," replied LP.

"Nothing has been turned in," the attendant said. "You can fill out a lost property report over at Security. Head over to that glass door and speak to someone there, and they will help you." LP did as instructed. By this time, he was already having a panic attack. He could feel his face going red as he wiped beads of perspiration from his head. He stopped in front of the doorway, taking several deep breaths and thinking to himself, *Calm down.* He opened the door and proceeded to the security desk, where he was given a form to fill out.

After he finished, the head of security escorted LP back to where his backpack had disappeared. While walking back, LP asked if the security cameras could identify the thief, but the official's answer was not hopeful. When he finished his part of the report, he handed it to LP to sign. LP asked again about the security camera overhead; he said,

"Surely, you could identify who picked up my backpack. The woman sitting in front of my machine was dressed in a bright blue outfit. She would have been captured on camera and would be easy to identify."

"Easier said than done," the head of security said nonchalantly. "Las Vegas is the city for opportunists. She is long gone, and the video footage will not identify who she is."

A disgruntled LP shook his hand and walked over to where the others were waiting for him; he said, "No luck; the cameras are gone, and Security can't help. Let's get out of here."

Ingrid replied, "Insurance might cover it. We'll put a claim in through travel insurance when we get back home."

LP blanked out any thought of the incident until they arrived back at their room, and then he phoned the police to report his property stolen.

They continued to do the tourist thing; walking in and out of casinos while nursing their drinks was a common practice in this city. To see more of Vegas in the shortest possible time, they would have to ditch any opened bottles of alcohol before catching one of the red buses that travel up and down the Strip.

LP commented to his friends, "Let's do some more sightseeing by bus and put our up feet up for a while." Ingrid nodded in agreement.

When the bus pulled up opposite Planet Hollywood, Ingrid and LP hopped off, leaving their friends to do more sightseeing, while they headed straight back to their room to have a rest before the company dinner at six o'clock.

Bill said, "See ya in the morning," as the bus continued along the Strip.

Everyone from work met in the foyer of Planet Hollywood, before heading off together to a Japanese restaurant that Rick had picked. The site for the company's eightieth anniversary dinner had been a secret that he still kept close to his chest. Like a regiment of troops following their commander, they marched behind Rick into the restaurant.

Entering a small ramp made of cedar, LP looked up to the arcade, which created the illusion of broad daylight. LP commented to Ingrid, "Look, the domed ceiling is painted sky blue with patches of white clouds." She nodded in agreement as the hostess showed them to their seats, which were to the side and in front of a large metal cook top that was part of their table.

Everyone mingled, chatted, and generally had a good time at the company's expense. LP and Ingrid, however, soon grew tired and were the first to leave. They needed to get some sleep, or they wouldn't be up and about for the big day tomorrow, travelling out to the Grand Canyon.

26

They met Bill and Sandra at six o'clock the next morning and headed out to wait for their ride to the Grand Canyon.

They didn't have to wait long before a van pulled up, and the driver jumped out and held open the side door, saying, "Are you folks booked for the Grand Canyon? I'll just tick your names off my list, and we'll be on our way."

The driver helped Ingrid in, and she sat down by the window, followed by LP and their friends; as the driver got behind the wheel, he commented, "There aren't many people going to where we're heading."

Ingrid replied. "We can't wait, even though this is only the transit van to our air-conditioned coach."

She was right as always. She pointed out the window as they pulled up against a luxury coach, already packed to capacity with an eager set of tourists, waiting to get on the move to the Grand Canyon.

Mark was their driver and Gary, the tour guide. Mark looked like someone out of a punk-rock band, with spiked blond hair and dark sunglasses. Gary, on the other hand, looked like he had been a game-show host in a past life. Together, they delivered a flawless performance, engaging their audience for nearly three hours before they arrived at their destination.

Eleven passengers on their bus were dropped off first, including LP, Ingrid, Bill, and Sandra. The forty other tourists continued to the edge of the Grand Canyon West, home of the Hualapai Nation, where a tourist attraction had been built with a glass viewing platform that extended well over the gorge.

LP led the way for their small party to enter the helicopter departure shed. They were excited about flying to the canyon floor and then rafting down the Colorado River. However, first they were herded like cattle to be weighed before they could fly on the chopper.

LP and Ingrid were separated from their friends and escorted over to the first helicopter. Bill yelled out, "See you down there," as they got ready to board the other helicopter waiting for takeoff. Both choppers' engines roared as they rose from the helipad, angling forward, moving low across the arid landscape, dotted with little vegetation. LP looked down from the rear seat and held his breath. Suddenly, their pilot entered the canyon and pointed the chopper down, giving everyone on board a sense of free falling.

Obviously, the pilot knew how to give his passengers the thrill of their lives. After they landed on a cleared dirt patch, LP and Ingrid started climbing down what looked like a mountain goat track, twisting down to the embankment, where boats skippered by Native Americans were waiting to take tourists down the Colorado River.

In the middle of nowhere, halfway down the track, they were stopped by a long queue of people waiting for their turn to be helped onboard the pontoon. Although it was moored with ropes and tightly secured to two posts, the boat still moved up and down, jostled by fast-flowing water. Their skipper, named Jerry, reached his hand out to help his passengers climb aboard.

Ingrid and Sandra chatted while Bill and LP took turns playing shutter bugs. LP was using his iPad as a camera, since his other camera had been stolen. Ten minutes passed as they slowly made their way down the towering walls of the canyon gorge and boarded their ride. Jerry motored them across to the other side of the river, close to the cliff face and away from the current; he idled his motor as he spoke of his ancestors. He told the story of how they lived under the shadow of a great eagle, captured in stone. LP knew what he was talking about because Gary had pointed out the rock formation when the bus stopped to let them off.

LP asked Jerry if he would take a picture of him in the driver's seat, cruising along the waterway. Jerry obliged, cutting short his story and taking LP's iPad, saying, "Don't push the throttle; it's dangerous to try for someone new on the river."

After the picture was taken, Jerry regained control and continued his tour. Fifteen minutes later, they disembarked and moved quickly up to their waiting helicopters. LP and Ingrid boarded the first chopper, while Bill and Sandra followed in the second. It was a coordinated shuttle service, timed with army precision. Land and water were connected to get as many tourists on board on time to connect with their bus drivers.

It was a thrilling ride back to the helipad; as the helicopter ascended out of the canyon, the pilot banked into a tight right-hand turn, going around a bend in the gorge. The suddenly-flat landscape zoomed by with the landing site only minutes away. Their Grand Canyon experience was almost over, signalling them to take their last photos.

After landing, they thanked their pilot and followed the cement pathway back to a white domed tent, opposite where they were weighed in for takeoff.

Inside the building, Ingrid and Sandra walked around, looking through souvenirs to remind them of this part of their exciting holiday. The women settled on jewellery pieces—earrings bracelets—and perfume that symbolised their spiritual connection to the Navajo people.

Bill and LP were more practical, buying t-shirts with four Navajo Indians on the front and the phrase "Homeland Security since 1492." The Indians were outfitted in European clothing from that bygone era, holding rifles close to their chests with bullet belts casually slung over each shoulder.

LP continued to browse, stumbling on something called a dream catcher. The trinket could be hung by the bed rest or window sill. One part caught the bad dreams in its web, while the other part allowed the good dreams to sieve through. Feathers attached allowed the good dreams, akin to dew drops, to evaporate to the Great Spirit, resting in the morning sun. Prayer beads trapped all the bad dreams and burned them up.

LP got goose bumps as he read the story of the dream catcher, and then he decided to pick one off the rotating display stand, taking it with his other purchase to the pay counter.

After making his purchase, LP caught up with everyone else outside, and then they all walked to their bus to connect with the other passengers at the main tourist site. As Mark drove along the dusty dirt road, Gary once again pointed out the rock formation depicting the Eagle Spirit. It was like viewing a Magic Eye picture. You needed to look beyond the rock to see what Gary was pointing to. When all the tourists on the bus agreed with Gary they had got the picture, LP felt he also had connected with the Navajo Dreamtime spirit.

Mark stopped and parked the bus, while Gary pointed to a queue standing in the blazing heat, outside a tin shed.

Gary said, "Grab some grub to eat over there, and I'll see you all back at the bus in one hour."

LP, Ingrid, Bill, and Sandra lined up for their meal and then sat down at a table that provided a panoramic view of the Grand Canyon.

After they finished, the men left the women chatting and walked to the edge of the gorge. There were no barriers to stop anyone from hanging their toes over the edge for a once-in-a-lifetime photo. Bill did exactly that, while LP stood back and snapped the picture. LP then jumped across a crevice in the rock edge, going down three thousand feet. Bill walked over to LP while looking at his pictures he had taken on his iPhone.

His next step would have been his last, if not for LP's quick reflexes. Bill stumbled, not seeing the danger before him. As he lost his balance and was about to fall down to certain death, he grabbed LP's right leg just above the knee. LP's foresight had him just a nano second ahead of what was unfolding. He reached out and grabbed his mate's right wrist, pulling him across the two-foot gap dropping to the canyon floor.

Surprisingly, Bill didn't drop his phone. "Bloody hell mate, where did that come from?" he said, while looking back down to what could have happened.

LP replied, "Keep your eyes open or the Eagle Spirit will take you away, and it won't be by bus."

The tour coach was ready to depart, as everyone met back at the bus as arranged; Gary was standing outside the door, waving and saying, "Hurry up."

LP and Ingrid were the first on board and sat down where she left her handbag. Bill and Sandra sat opposite for the journey back to Vegas. Bill leant back, closed his eyes, and said, "Wake me when we're in Vegas.

The trip back went quickly, as most passengers caught a bit of shut-eye.

"Wake up, Bill, we're here at Planet Hollywood," said Sandra. Bill stretched his hands high above his head and said, "I flew on the wings of the eagle above the canyon and saw that my time to depart this world is not now."

Sandra replied. "We're not leaving Vegas until Friday. What are you talking about?"

"Nothing, it's just a strange dream I had," whispered Bill. "Nothing to worry about."

They all thanked Gary and Mark for a safe and entertaining trip. Then they shook hands and left tips in the jar next to the steering wheel as they departed.

Bill and Sandra said they were going to play the pokies, while LP and Ingrid went back to their room to freshen up. At eight, they planned to check out the night life of Vegas.

Before leaving their room, LP phoned Bill and said, "Meet you down at the roulette wheel." LP wanted to gamble on at least one table while still in Vegas. He figured he had a few minutes left to win or lose until Bill and Sandra arrived. He changed five twenty-dollar notes for fifty two-dollar chips.

He did his usual thing, placing one chip on number twenty-three and quarter bets on the surrounding numbers. Luck was not on his side tonight. By the time their friends arrived, his wallet was one hundred dollars lighter. Ingrid was not impressed, but LP reminded her about the next morning, hoping he wouldn't hear any more about losing money. Free poker money was on the table if they sat through an hour-and-a-half presentation about buying a time share accommodation.

"Hi guys, winning or losing?" Bill called out in a loud, baritone voice.

"Don't want to talk about it," LP replied. "Let's get out of here." He turned, took Ingrid's hand, and led her out of the casino.

LP led them next door to the Parisian casino with its own Eiffel Tower. Once again, before they could get in the lift, they had to wait in a queue for about twenty minutes.

It was well worth the wait as they looked out over the lights of Las Vegas. The neon lights adorning the Strip made it a magical sight, contrasted by the dry brown land they had seen in daylight.

They didn't stay long. It was getting cold as the breeze picked up. When they walked out of the lift, they could hear an announcement being made: "The tower is closed due to the strong winds. Please keep your tickets and return tomorrow."

"That was close. We made it up and down just in time," LP said.

Ingrid replied, "I don't think I can walk another step. My feet are swollen, and I need to put them up somewhere."

LP responded, "I'll go back with you to our room."

Ingrid gave Bill and Sandra a hug, and LP took Ingrid back to their hotel. There was still three days to cram more of Vegas in before their flight out. An early night would help them be on the ball to receive their freebies after the time-share presentation.

LP dropped his head on the pillow, and it wasn't long before he was snoring as Ingrid fell asleep watching TV.

27

Up bright and early, they showered and dressed for another day in Las Vegas. They headed down to the foyer and walked over to where they would be picked up for the presentation.

While they waited LP, said, "When the sales guy asks for an acknowledgement to a question, say either, 'No, I'll have to think about that' or 'I'll have to just run it past my accountant first." Ingrid agreed, as a transit van pulled up. The driver jumped out from behind the wheel and opened the side door. He asked, "Are LP and Ingrid here?"

LP answered, "Yes."

"Climb aboard. I have a few more passengers to pick up, and you'll all be on time for registration," the driver said.

After filling his van with eleven passengers, their driver drove two blocks and pulled into another basement, stopping outside a large metal door. Ingrid had a worried look on her face, thinking of a worst-case scenario. *Could this be a con*, she thought, *a hostage situation, or are we about to be robbed?*

Their driver pushed open the sliding door for everyone to exit.

"Follow me," he instructed.

The metal door opened to reveal a flight of stairs, beyond which lay another door. The driver opened that too, and a sudden bright light lit up the stairwell. Ingrid had no idea where she was and started to panic. She liked to think she could control every situation and give orders on what to do, but not this time. She had a sinking feeling they were caught in a hostage situation.

Her fears were unfounded, as they walked out through the doorway onto the Strip.

Ingrid got her bearings and suddenly said, "I know where we are, that's Planet Hollywood," as she pointed down the street.

She took a deep breath and started smiling, saying to LP, "I was getting a bit worried where all this was going to lead us to." Out of one door and into the next adjacent doorway, they stood waiting for the lift doors to open. The wait wasn't long before they were walking past twelve small round tables to the reception desk.

After registering, they were introduced to James, who would deliver the sales pitch to convince them to buy what they had on offer. He showed them over to a table and seated Ingrid and LP directly facing him. He had a sales folder that would keep him on track throughout the presentation, as each page turned would lead to a decision to buy. That was his plan. For LP, it was the opposite: resist the sales pitch and say no and receive the gifts offered.

LP knew all the sales tactics that would be thrown at them and responded with answers that would not lead to a decision. After an hour and a half of playing this game, James conceded defeat and called over a young woman for a debriefing. She asked how they felt about the presentation, and if there were any more questions they would like to ask that would change their mind. She reminded them again that buying into a lifestyle dream that only the rich and famous indulged themselves in was within their reach.

Still, their answer was no.

She reached into her folder and pulled out two free tickets to a show, coupons for dinner for two, and a $200 voucher to redeem for poker money to gamble on slots. Her last words were, "Have a nice day."

As she escorted them over to the front desk, LP said, "We won't worry about a ride back to our hotel. We'll walk, it's not far." The young woman showed them to the lift, and one minute later they were back on the Strip.

It was lunch time as they zigzagged their way across a packed sidewalk with people going in either direction. Although Planet Hollywood was in sight, Ingrid decided to take the bus, as her feet were still aching. A red bus arrived at the stop, and LP helped Ingrid up the first step. They moved down the aisle and held on to the nearest pole.

The bus stopped outside Bellagio resort, and from there they headed back to the café outside Planet Hollywood on the opposite side. They walked to the reception, without having to stand in a queue for the first time. LP commented, "You beauty, no line up, can't beat that."

They were shown over to a table for two. As tourists walked past carrying their alcoholic drinks in souvenir bottles hanging from their neck, LP looked down onto the Strip and got a sense of what made Vegas tick. It wasn't buildings or the bright lights. It was the freedom to do what you wanted to do—be it drinking, gambling, or phoning a number flashing on a billboard truck, as it drove up and down the Strip, flaunting images of scantily clad, beautiful women.

Sin City was the name Vegas had well earned, but in the end, the state of Nevada followed their relaxed laws relating to forbidden sins. Forty million people visited Las Vegas every year, which speaks volumes for itself. *They must be doing something right, and it seemed to satisfy a need within the human psyche,* LP thought to himself.

Their waitress walked over and smiled, saying, "How are you enjoying your day?"

Ingrid answered, "We're having a great time."

"What would you have to drink?" the young woman asked. "We'll have a Bud and a bourbon and cola please," LP replied. When she returned, LP ordered nachos to share. They were by now starting to soak up the atmosphere that was Vegas under a bright sunny day. After lunch, LP said he was going to play the pokies, whether Ingrid liked it or not. This was Vegas, and he was going to try his luck and see if he could hit the jackpot.

Ingrid left him to play on his own. She knew he was a risk taker and did not wish to cramp his style when he gambled.

She declared, "I'm heading back to the room."

LP left their waitress a ten-dollar tip and walked over to the mall entrance to Planet Hollywood, leaving Ingrid to go her way.

LP was like a kid in a candy shop, wanting to taste all the sweets. But what attracted him the most was something he had never seen in Australia: a large video screen depicting a battleship theme gaming machine. LP sat at one of four seats in front of it and looked up and across, as three other people pushed notes down the throat of their machines that were all linked to other jackpots.

LP slipped twenty dollars in his machine but found no luck. Before walking away, he pressed a five-cent bet. Suddenly, the sound of cannon fire had LP turning around and looking to the screen above as it went into action, depicting a battleship flotilla at war, firing shots across their bow. He quickly walked back to the machine he was playing and waited to see if he was the winner of the battle, which would win him eleven times his bet. *That'll be fifty-five cents*, he thought, *big deal*.

To his amazement, he won all the bets accumulated by the other players, amounting to $265. LP looked over to the losers and said, "That was a bit of luck. My last bet was five cents, and I was walking away. Tell you what: when I collect, I'll come back and give you twenty bucks each." He did just that, to the amazement of the other players who lost when the feature finished. He then headed back to his room, exiting the lift on floor eighteen.

He turned right and walked to the end of the corridor, pulled his security card out of his top pocket, and pushed it in the slot below the door handle. There were no bells and whistles as he pushed down the handle and entered the room. He thought he would hear, "How much did you lose this time?" but he was in luck: Ingrid was snoring.

Actually, no matter what answer he gave his wife, he would be the poorer for it. If he said he won, Ingrid would want to share it, to buy presents and souvenirs. If he said nothing, he'd get, "I told you so, stay away from those one-armed bandits."

A third option was to say, "I didn't stay long and broke even." LP decided on using this option.

He tip-toed into their room and quietly laid down on the bed without waking Ingrid. After awhile, LP gave Ingrid a wake-up call with a gentle nudge on the shoulder. She stirred and asked, "How long was I asleep?"

"Not long, I followed up soon after you left and had a snooze too," LP replied.

No more questions were asked as they got themselves ready for a night out in Vegas on the cheap. They decided to take in a show and dinner in the same mall area, not far from Planet Hollywood.

The show they picked to see was the Ultimate Variety Show. It started at eight, and they arrived an hour earlier to find two queues with a long line up of people already waiting to get in. To their surprise, the Mexican restaurant they had tickets for was directly opposite the theatre. From there, they could sit down, grab a bite, and watch when everyone started moving inside. This would be their cue to leave a tip and follow the line to their seats for the comedy show.

When the performance ended, the entertainers stood near the exit for autographs and photos. LP and Ingrid thought the show was fantastic and had photographs taken with some of the performers. Their talent to entertain with comedy, magic, and stunts few other people in the world could duplicate made it one of the best shows they had ever seen.

It was now getting late, so they headed back to their room for an early night.

28

Looking out of their hotel window as sun rose, LP watched as once again Vegas transformed from a desert city of coloured lights, peppered with stars on a dark horizon. The city, now awake with gray shadows moving across the road below, slowly heralded in a new day. LP had an eerie feeling. He thought how strange this place was—a city born of the desert and nourished by water and power from the Hoover Dam, and fed by tourists, day after day.

Wednesday was reserved for a bus ride to Freemont. It was the original Vegas Strip before casinos sprang up closer to the airport. It still had a few famous casinos, like the Golden Nugget, which LP aimed to visit before leaving Vegas.

Ingrid and LP freshened up and headed for the bus stop directly opposite Planet Hollywood. They had to wait only a few minutes before their ride arrived. The staff and tourist guides told them to stick to the Strip if they didn't wish to run into any trouble. They weren't too sure what they meant by that peculiar statement.

However, LP had received a similar warning on their trip to Hawaii, twenty years ago. That time, it was another offshore conference, celebrating sixty years in business. They had hopped on a bus bearing a "Honolulu" sign. The driver advised them to take another bus, as they were going in the wrong direction, but LP ignored his advice.

He paid for two tickets, and they sat down on an empty bus that took them off the tourist route and headed for the centre of the island. Inhabited by the locals, it presented a stark contrast to the polished part of Waikiki.

They began to worry upon seeing the dilapidated houses that dotted the poorer part of the island; some houses had tarps over their roofs and cried out for repairs. Some front yards had car wrecks as a welcome sign to their property.

However, what they also saw when they looked up was a mountain peak covered in green vegetation and moss. A cloud hung above, as they experienced a light mist of rain. It created its own microcosm that leant a magical air to the island.

Upon recalling that incident, LP and Ingrid braced themselves. Were they about to experience something similar in Vegas? Once their bus left the Vegas Strip, it followed the motorway directly to the old section of town. This was their first glimpse of suburbia, and there was no sight of any run-down part of town.

The bus halted opposite the Golden Nugget Casino, and LP and Ingrid crossed to the other side of the road to enter the casino. He pointed over to a couple of machines where they could sit down and try their luck.

It wasn't long before a waitress walked over and asked, "What would you have to drink? They're free if you're playing."

LP ordered the usual. He was in a serious mood, determined to win on the pokies and find the whereabouts of the 3.6-kilo gold nugget that was sold to some guy from Vegas. That deal was done in Melbourne, and he expected to find it here in this casino.

They finished their drinks and collected a ticket from the poker machine to redeem his small win. When LP went over to the cashier, he asked if a gold nugget was on display. Her answer was, "Yes, come back tonight and see the light show outside; we have a guided tour of the casino, and you'll see the gold nugget."

The cashier exchanged his ticket for cash, and then Ingrid and LP walked through the foyer, exiting the way they came in.

LP's theory on how to win on the pokies was starting to pay off now. After many years of observation and insider knowledge, he figured he knew how to win more often than lose. The trick was he spent no more than twenty dollars on a machine. He avoided sitting down and didn't stay at one machine for far too long. That way, he had more wins than losses.

They decided to head back to Planet Hollywood and rest up. Later that night, they would return to see the light display and take the guided tour through the Golden Nugget Casino.

By the time they returned to their room and caught up on some sleep, they were ready for another night on the town. Ingrid phoned Reception to book a taxi before leaving their room. They headed down in the lift and walked out through the foyer to a waiting cab driver, who asked, "Are you guys going to Freemont?"

LP answered "Yes," and they stepped in for a twenty-minute ride to the Golden Nugget. The cabbie stopped opposite the casino, and said, "That'll be twenty-one dollars."

LP handed him five dollars extra as a tip and said, "Thanks." The driver politely held open the rear door for his passengers. The sidewalk was abuzz with people jostling past each other. Suddenly, the music started rolling as they pushed their way through the crowd.

Standing at the corner intersection of the casino, they looked up to a huge canopy that covered the two street blocks.

They watched a video clip of the band Queen, with Freddie Mercury, belting out "Bohemian Rhapsody." It was the most amazing light and sound show, and they arrived just in time to catch the nine o'clock spectacle.

Next was the tour. LP was on the hunt to find where the gold nugget was showcased. Walking past rows of poker machines, LP spotted a waitress and asked her, "Where do we find the tour?" She pointed to a group of people and said, "Wait over there with them."

They did as instructed. A few minutes passed before they were greeted by a young woman named Melody. She briefly explained what parts of the casino they'd be going through and made a point of saying, "Stick together, or you could get lost in here and not find your way out."

Melody started walking, and like a little flock of sheep, everyone followed her. She gave a history lesson about the Golden Nugget and its chequered past when the Mafia mob were forced out of the other American states for racketeering. They found a safe haven in Las Vegas, where gambling, alcohol, and prostitution were legal. These welcomed visitors set up legitimate businesses that created the foundation for the city to flourish and become what it is today: the tourist capital of the world.

After walking past dozens of gambling tables and hundreds of slot machines, they found themselves before a large glass cabinet.

Like everyone else in the group, LP was pretty impressed with what he saw. Melody started to explain how the nugget came into their possession. It was found in Australia in the early seventies and named the Hand of Faith. It was bought by casino management to attract tourists to their casino.

LP suddenly turned to Ingrid and said, "I've seen enough, let's get out of here. This isn't the 3.6-kilo nugget sold to a bloke from Vegas, as I suspected."

It was ten o'clock when they finally walked out and hailed a taxi to take them to their hotel. Arriving outside Planet Hollywood, LP and Ingrid walked up the stairs and entered the mall entrance, where LP bought two Buds to take to their room.

LP said, "Let's head back to the room. We can catch up on what's happening in the world on TV."

LP entered the room first and turned on the TV. Ingrid followed and walked into the bathroom, where LP had left Ingrid's bottle of cola and bottled water on ice (not where you would expect, but in the sink) before leaving for Freemont.

They both sat down and relaxed while watching the news and weather report. Sightseeing and shopping were on the agenda for tomorrow, and the sun was supposed to shine all day. New York would also have fine weather; they would be leaving Las Vegas Airport for New York at eleven thirty that night.

The next morning, they were up at seven and started packing. They would leave their luggage in Bill and Sandra's room later in the morning and book out at ten. Their plan was to return to the room around five, have farewell drinks, and then catch a taxi at eight to catch their flight to New York.

All was going to plan as they stepped onto a bus back to Freemont's shopping precinct, travelling along the same route as the night before by taxi. LP and Ingrid's bus stopped directly outside the main entrance. As LP stepped off the bus, he looked at his map of the sprawling shopping precinct. It was shaped like a horseshoe and led to another exit opposite another bus stop, which would take them back to Planet Hollywood.

They walked towards the first shops offering discounted products. LP wanted to buy a pair of Levi Strauss jeans, and

Ingrid looked for some perfume; it was less expensive than in Australia. It wasn't long before LP spotted the Levi factory outlet sign and left Ingrid testing perfume at an outdoor kiosk.

He walked inside and couldn't believe the prices. At $32, they cost half of what he would have had to shell out in Australia. He tried on two pairs and bought both, thinking, *What a bargain!*

After he read the inside label, he found his new pair were made in Egypt, and the other pair in Bangladesh. He understood why they were priced so cheap.

Ingrid joined him and chatted about the bargain perfumes she had bought. After paying for his jeans, they headed for the food court and sat down to a shared meal of nachos. All the meals served were so large, they made a habit of buying a meal for one and sharing it. When they finished, they headed for the bus stop. They crossed the road and waited for the next bus that would drop them off at Planet Hollywood. They waited only for a few minutes before the bus arrived.

This was the end of their shopping and sightseeing. By the time they got back to the casino and went up to Bill and Sandra's room, it was already five in the afternoon. LP knocked on their door and was greeted with a beer, twisted opened by his mate. "Get this in ya," said Bill.

Time passed by quickly, and before they knew it, they were in a taxi heading for McCarran Airport, booking in at eight twenty-five. They were taking no chances of missing their flight to New York. The airport and flight would be their accommodation overnight, as they were landing at JFK Airport at seven twenty the next morning. During the flight, LP and Ingrid got some sleep in.

"We are now an hour and half out from New York," the captain announced. "Breakfast will be served soon."

That was the end of any further shut-eye for Ingrid and LP, as the plane's interior lights came up from dull to bright, with flight attendants flitting about with breakfast trays.

Landing on time, they collected their overhead carry-on cases and slowly walked down the aisle, exiting from the plane's front door. All the other passengers were heading in the same direction to collect their luggage from the carrousel, so they followed the herd.

Airport security officers were everywhere as they looked around to find signs on how to get out of the terminal. It didn't take long before they were standing outside, taking in the cool air of New York on a fine sunny day. They waited at the commuter rank for their shuttle service, which was to arrive at eight o'clock and take them to their hotel.

29

LP grew anxious as they waited for their ride to their hotel on Eighth Avenue, verging on another panic attack; he could hardly hide his excitement. He wanted to soak up as much of the atmosphere of the Big Apple, and it couldn't come soon enough. He planned to cram a lot of things on his hit list into his schedule. Ingrid had her own list of places to visit. Four days were not going to be enough to do it all, but they were going to give it their best shot.

Ingrid turned to LP, interrupting his silence, and said, "Let's hope this is our ride to Manhattan."

The driver stopped and wound down his window to inquire, "Are you LP and Ingrid?"

LP replied, "Yes, are we the only pickups here?"

"Yes sir," the driver said. "Let me put your baggage in the back. It will be a quick trip to your hotel."

One hour later was not a quick trip, but it was just as good as any tour guide could give of his city, so that came as a bonus. Before they were dropped off at their hotel, he took them through the back lanes of Manhattan after a detour to explore the narrow, mean streets of Harlem. LP looked up at the towering skyscrapers as they made their way to their destination: the Hilton Garden Inn on Eighth Avenue.

He turned to Ingrid and commented, "We just got our first tour of New York for free."

She nodded in unison.

When they arrived at their hotel, the driver helped them unload. They entered the foyer, pulling and struggling to carry their luggage to the reception desk. It was too early to get their keys for their room, so the young clerk let them store their luggage in the cloak room behind the front desk. They were told to return at two o'clock, by which time their room would be cleaned and ready. They tipped their help two dollars and walked back onto Eighth Avenue. They walked a short distance and went into the building where they would get their tickets to ride the red double-decker tour bus. They then left the building and strolled along, passing their first subway entrance on the corner of Eighth Avenue and Fourteenth Street.

Ingrid commented, "We have to catch the subway before leaving New York."

LP nodded in agreement.

The bus stop was only twenty paces away. Standing in a queue, they waited to board the next red bus going to Central Park, as a chill wind channelled through the skyscrapers and tenements on either side of Eighth Avenue. Their bus ride would give them some ideas on what attractions to see and where to go before heading back home to Australia.

Several hours passed, with the wind picking up, chilling the air down to ten degrees. LP's ear lobes were a barometer on how cold it was. He figured it was freezing cold compared to the temperatures in Brisbane. It was a hot steamy day with a heat haze almost blocking out the Glass House Mountains.

They sat on the top deck of the double-decker bus, which looked exactly like London's red buses except they were without a roof. That's why LP was feeling the cold on his ears and his bald head. He and Ingrid talked about what they wanted to visit: the observation deck of Rockefeller Center, Ground Zero, the Metropolitan Museum of Art, the Statue of Liberty, and Times Square, plus, if time allowed a Broadway show. He also intended to meet up with publishers for his books.

The Easter break would make it hard to do all that. However, they wasted no time in getting out and taking in the sights, sounds, and smell of spring in New York. Before returning to their hotel, they picked up some snack food from the corner store. The basement level opened up to a mini supermarket, and LP grabbed a six pack of Buds to knock down in their room and relax.

He returned to Reception and was handed their key cards for room 709. The duty manager greeted them with a smile and said, "Your luggage will follow in a few minutes. Enjoy your stay with us, and anything you need, please ask."

They proceeded to their room, entering the lift to the seventh floor and then walking a long corridor to the last door on their right. LP pushed the security card into the door's slot, pulled down the handle, and entered the space that was going to be their home away from home for the next four days. Their luggage arrived within minutes, announced with a loud knock on the door. LP tipped the young bloke and asked, "How long have you been working in New York?" He proceeded to fill LP in on his life story, before closing the door behind him.

LP opened two beers and placed them on his bedside table. He sat down on the edge of their bed and handed one to Ingrid, saying. "We made it to New York on time. All we've got to do is fit in everything planned, and we'll be fine."

"Good luck on that one. You'll need another seven days to do what you want to do," she quipped.

"No problem," he said. "We'll just come back again, but travel east to west via India, Europe, and onto New York, travelling on around-the-world tickets. I'll just have to score another off-shore trip paid by the company and tag on a couple of extra weeks."

LP stood up and looked out their window. Down the road, he could see two Broadway theatres a short walk around the corner from Eighth Avenue, and directly across from them was a church. There was no queue for the Friday night gathering at St. Malachy's, compared to the hundreds of people lined up to see *Chicago* and *The Book of Mormon.*

LP turned to Ingrid and said, "Let's go visit that church. It's Good Friday, and I haven't been inside a church since the towers fell on 9/11."

Ingrid freshened up, and they then walked around the corner and entered the church. They were late and sat in the back pew. LP remembered the rituals of past but didn't recognise this service. It wasn't as such a Mass, but the priest's acknowledgement of their saviour's death on the cross: their saviour, their deity, and his promise of life renewed! It brought a tear to LP's eyes. They stayed only ten minutes and then stood up quietly, turned, and walked out of the church; LP pulled out ten dollars out of his wallet and dropped it in the donation box on the way out.

After walking out of St. Malachy's, they walked past all the theatre goers lined up on the sidewalk. Both sides of the street were blocked with a restless audience keen on catching the next performance. They turned right into Broadway and towards Times Square. LP commented, "Jet lag is starting to kick in. We won't stay out much longer. I think we need an early night to make a big day of it tomorrow."

As they got closer to their destination, they could see that the roads leading to Times Square were closed, with New York police officers manning yellow barricades. He wondered if there had been a terrorist threat. It turned out to be nothing that serious, just Nicky Minaj giving a free performance in Times Square.

LP and Ingrid watched her perform two of her best-selling singles, and then they walked back to their room, leaving thousands of fans cheering and applauding the singer. Finally, after returning to their hotel room, LP changed into his warm track suit, fell into bed, and pulled up the bed cover.

He then said, "I'll be first up in the morning. I'll wake you for an early start."

30

LP bounded out of bed early, as light filtered through dense morning fog into their room. He reached for his glasses on the side table and walked over to the window looking out to the street below.

Not all would appreciate another day, he thought, as he looked down and watched a homeless African American man trying to keep warm, sleeping on the top stair with his back leaning against the door of St. Malachy's. Here was a man who needed shelter and help, but the doors were closed to him. Those behind closed doors seemed to fail this man, while those of faith slept safely. An irony, LP thought.

The sound of clanging woke the homeless man, who slowly stood up, unsteady on his feet, and started walking towards Eighth Avenue. New York's garbage trucks were the first sounds of a city coming back to life.

LP made a cup of tea for Ingrid and then shaved, showered, and put on some warm clothes for an early start on New York's landmarks. Ingrid freshened up after LP and put on some makeup. He suggested she wear jeans, since it would be freezing. It could be even colder if the wind blew as strong as yesterday.

As they left the room on the seventh floor to take in the sights and sounds of New York, what they didn't expect to encounter was a fire alarm. When LP went to press the lift button, an alarm blared. As the fire doors closed automatically, Ingrid started to panic and exclaimed, "Oh my God, what's happening?"

LP calmly walked over to the doors and pushed them open. In the corridor, other guests were sticking their heads out of their doorways with concerned looks on their faces, most likely thinking. "Could this be a bomb or terrorist attack?"

LP came back to Ingrid and gave her a reassuring hug. He glanced over her shoulder and saw a phone on a small desk.

"I'll phone reception and see what's going on," he said.

He called up the duty manager, but there was no answer.

He looked over to Ingrid and shook his head.

"Ring again," she pleaded.

This time, someone answered, and before LP could speak, the duty manager said, "Someone set off the fire alarm on floor seven. Did you see anyone acting suspicious?"

"No," he answered.

"Wait a couple of minutes and press the lift button," the manager said, "and everything will be working fine."

He was right. While LP paced up and down, the lift lights came on. He pressed the lift button. The doors opened, and they descended to the ground floor.

Walking into the foyer, they were confronted by a bunch of burly fire-fighters, one carrying an axe and another pulling a fire hose through the entrance. They figured everything was under control as they walked past New York's finest, onto Eighth Avenue, past the fire truck, double parked out front of where they were staying.

They headed for the bus stop. LP and Ingrid joined the queue. They didn't have to wait long before it arrived. First on their agenda was the Rockefeller Center, which was twenty minutes away. Hopping off the bus, they followed the crowd to enter the building that would take them up to the observation floor towering above New York.

LP bought tickets for eighteen dollars each and was told to come back in twenty minutes. LP suggested a drink in the café, just three shop fronts up from where they were standing. They walked up a small incline leading to the coffee shop. Ingrid stood in front of the cashier and ordered coffee and a Budweiser for LP. Seated, they chatted about what to do after going to the Top of the Rock, as New Yorkers liked to call it.

They decided the Metropolitan Museum of Art would be next on their hit list. Ingrid finished her short black first and said, "Knock that beer down quick; we've got to go."

What they hadn't expected was a long queue with security, as they have it at the airport. This would take another fifteen minutes before being escorted to their lift, where they were packed in shoulder to shoulder for what felt like a ride to the top of the world. When the lift doors opened, LP and Ingrid pushed their way through the crowd and walked out onto an open-air area with high glass panels acting as guard rails, stopping anyone from falling seventy floors to the street below.

Looking out to the Empire State Building and other towering structures reminded him of early Bible lessons. One passage from Revelation came to mind: *"Upon the head will be the mark of the beast."* What LP was seeing was not one, but many symbols of corporations wielding more power than individual governments.

He had a vision of the future as he stood looking down at the most powerful city in the world, which could be renamed "New Babylon," where the anti-Christ would be chained and brought to kneel. He thought, *When that happens the serpent with many heads and its creation will fall and obey the will of the people; it won't be the other way around.*

"LP, snap out of it," Ingrid said. "You're daydreaming. Take a photo of me with the Empire State building in the background." Ingrid's voice shook him out of his daydreaming mood. He held up his iPad and snapped a few photos. They walked around to another viewing area with Central Park in the backdrop. LP took another photo with Ingrid smiling.

He then turned and said, "Follow me. We've been up here long enough."

He was getting impatient to move on to the Met. Pointing over to the lift area, he took Ingrid's hand and pushed through the crowd to wait in another queue to go back down to street level. Exiting the lift, they walked past a large cafeteria, looking to the back glass panels, where children and parents enjoyed a bright sunny day on an outdoor ice-skating rink.

LP commented, "Just shows how cold it is out there, when you can skate on the ice that doesn't melt under the midday sun." The headed back to the bus stop and waited to go to their next destination: the Metropolitan Museum of Art. The red double-decker bus stopped almost at the steps of an impressive sandstone building. Looking up at a wide flight of fifty or so stone steps leading to a huge entrance, Ingrid and LP proceeded to climb. Entering the building, they were greeted by the giant skeleton of a dinosaur. LP walked around the display and bought tickets to cover the museum at the three levels.

They spent two hours walking through as many exhibits as possible. Really, they needed two days to take in everything. But time was limited, and Ingrid was developing blisters on her feet. She couldn't walk for much longer, and LP realised that they would have to cut the tour short.

Nonetheless, unable to resist the temptation, he said, "We'll go after seeing two more displays; I've come halfway around the world to see them." He had a keen interest in the Mayan culture and the Big Bang theory. Here, he hoped to find answers to questions that dogged his thinking.

His interest in Mayan culture dated back to his days at school, when he received as an award a book on Mayan and Aztec people. Thereafter he knuckled down and studied up on as much as he could about these two civilisations.

As they entered the Mayan display, he felt awe-struck. He was now standing in front of a large round stone tablet, twenty centimetres thick and measuring over two hundred centimetres in diameter.

It looked like a sun dial. He eagerly looked around for another stone tablet that had twenty-three cogs and could predict sun spot activity. Mayan high priests used that calendar to make long-range weather forecasts before planting crops. They were very knowledgeable when it came to mapping the stars and drawing up calendars for ceremonies and crop planting.

When Hernán Cortés arrived in Cuba, he set his sights on the Yucatan Peninsula. He had gathered an armada of ships and named his flagship *Capitana*. With his fleet of Spanish galleons and 550 men, 16 horses, and 12 cannons, they anchored off the coast of the Yucatan Peninsula. After landing, he found the Aztec culture in some ways was far more advanced in understanding how the sun affected the weather, but on the down side, human sacrifices and tribal warfare weakened them, leading to their conquest by Europeans.

Cortés used this to his advantage siding with the native Totonac Indians to settle border disputes. This strategy enabled him to strengthen his *conquistadores* with one thousand native warriors and two hundred porters. He left a small number of men to hold the fort at Vera Cruz and then led his party two hundred kilometres inland to reach the Aztec capital, where he was welcomed as a god by their ruler, Montezuma.

That's when, LP believed, Cortés discovered the importance of their calendars. After entering the city, they were copied. When he returned, he laid siege to the city. After eighty-eight days, he and his men entered the capital and burnt it to the ground; they also caused massive destruction to the stone temples.

Most of LP's work life revolved around calendars and the passage of time. Yet this exhibit would not shed any light on the coincidence of a photo taken two years earlier, and a measurement relating to twenty-three. The photo of Mount Beerwah with the setting sun on its peak was a once-in-a-lifetime shot. That photo was taken from the observation tower on Wild Horse Mountain, 123 meters above sea level. A cement path wide enough for a vehicle to drive up made it an easy climb.

LP looked for a deeper meaning to the photo. When he had it blown up, he thought, *What if I drew a triangle bordering the sun?* He was amazed that the calculation came to be an equilateral triangle measuring twenty-three millimetres.

The number twenty-three continued to be everywhere he looked. His street number was 23, his credit card expiry dates added up to 23, and his email address had the number 23 in it. He also discovered the largest recorded solar flare was in the year 1859, and when he added up those numerals, the result was 23. To an extent, LP was fixated on that number, imagining that one day it may deliver something important.

The Mayan exhibit was giving no further clues on his question: what would the number 23 possibly deliver other than coincidence?

Nor was there any sign or mention in the exhibit of the Mayan long count calendar that ended in 2012 after 5,125 years.

His interest in the history of calendars dating back to the Julian calendar led him to believe in conspiracy theories. The truth of how the Gregorian calendar came into existence as the modern-day calendar in use throughout the world was answered, after the discovery of the Maya calendars.

The Julian calendar had gone out of sync with the rotation of the Earth and sun. In 1582, it was replaced by the Gregorian calendar, endorsed by (and named for) Pope Gregory XIII.

LP's theory was that the Vatican deciphered the Maya sun stone, giving us the current calendar as we use it today. At first, many countries didn't act on the pope's declaration that urged them to expel ten days from the 5th of October, as some people thought they were going to miss out on more than a week's rent or taxes. The reaction to the proposed change was mixed.

It was a bit like Daylight Saving Time, where some people couldn't get their heads around winding back their clocks by an hour.

In 1918, however, Russia caught up with the rest of the world by changing their calendar at the end of January: the 31st was followed by February 14. That made Russia's calendar more accurate than the Gregorian calendar. Indeed, some argue that the Iranian calendar is even more precise.

At this point, LP turned to Ingrid and said, "Let's check out the science exhibit and then we can get out of here."

They walked down a spiral ramp, experiencing the birth of time, reaching the present, measured with a blink.

Next they waited in line to enter a dome chamber that simulated the Big Bang. It lasted five minutes, giving all those standing around a darkened sphere a sense of being god-like. Cosmic dust formed burning suns, and a multitude of planets and moons created the galaxies that are beyond counting; it was an experience of a lifetime.

As Ingrid and LP left that exhibit, he stopped and said, "Take a picture of me touching this meteorite."

Ingrid obliged as she focused the camera.

LP smiled and said, "I've just touched something that has been hurtling through space for billions of years. How's that?"

After she snapped the picture, they then back-tracked up a spiral ramp and walked out of the Metropolitan Museum's large doors.

Before walking back down to the sidewalk, LP's thoughts wandered back to the words George whispered and how they had become part of the Scroll. LP had a life-changing moment when whispering those words connecting with the image that changed how he lived his present-day reality. Since that day he touched his immortal soul, the question that eluded him - when would he shed his mortal body?

He found he could flit in and out the past, present, and the future and had to work hard to stay at this level of reality. His gift of foresight, coupled with George's whispered words, heightened his extra-sensory perception.

LP and Ingrid walked down the stairs as bright sunshine beamed down, without a cloud in a blue sky above. LP said, "I'm fading. I think we should go back and rest. You probably need to put your feet up before we take in a show tonight."

"Yeah, I agree," she replied. "I need to get off my feet, or I won't be walking anywhere else soon."

Instead of catching the bus back to their room, they headed over to the nearby subway entrance and went down a steep flight of stairs. Ingrid then joined a queue to buy two tokens at a metal caged window.

Standing back from the platform edge, they talked about buying tickets for a Broadway show. They decided to see *Chicago*, just around the corner from where they were staying.

They got on the train and got off at the Forty-Ninth Street station; they headed down one block and bought half-price tickets for the show they wanted to see. LP led the way back to their room, as Ingrid struggled with blisters on her feet, wishing she was already there.

Back in their room, they watched TV while resting up on their bed. LP breathed a sigh of relief after trying to pack too much in one day. Finally, they could take a breather from doing the tourist thing.

His thoughts started to wander; he was not really watching TV, imagining what tomorrow might bring.

The next day, LP would deliver the Scroll to its destination. Ingrid knew they were not leaving New York until he visited Ground Zero, but she had not been told what LP's intentions were when he got there.

Ingrid gave him a shake and said, "We'd better freshen up and get on the move for the seven o'clock show, or we'll be late." The queue to get into *Chicago* stretched half a block; the show had been running for eight years and still drew huge crowds. The show went for two hours. During the interval, LP went to the restroom and then came out to stand in another queue to buy a beer and coffee. He was starting to dislike one thing about America. Everywhere they went, they had to wait in a line for food, tickets, transport, everything. He figured if there were no queues, they'd have a lot more time to see New York's famous landmarks.

Anyway, after the show, they could say to everyone back home that they had seen a Broadway show. Leaving the theatre, they walked down to Times Square for another look around. LP could now understand why New York was called the city that never sleeps. The sidewalk was crammed with locals and tourists alike, taking in the sights and sounds of New York at night.

They left Times Square after LP hailed a taxi. Although it was only a couple of blocks back to their hotel, Ingrid's feet were killing her. The blisters were getting much worse, and she needed to get off her feet, or she'd be going nowhere soon.

Back at the room, he cleaned and dressed her blistered toes, hoping she would be up to another big day.

31

LP was awake for hours before sunrise, unable to sleep, tossing over in his mind all the possibilities that might occur as the day unfolded. He heard a bang outside and was glad it didn't wake Ingrid; he got up and took a couple of steps to their fogged-up window. Rubbing it clear with his hand, he saw a Dumpster emptying garbage bins. It looked cold out, as a U-Haul van pulled up alongside a "No Standing" sign. A woman stepped from the vehicle wearing gloves and a fleecy padded jacket she quickly zipped up. To keep warm, she rubbed her hands as she went inside the building opposite. A police car pulled up behind her van, and an officer proceeded to issue her a ticket. When the woman came back to confront him, they looked like two characters in mime; the woman's body language said it all: she was not amused.

LP and Ingrid gathered what they could to take with them for the day's outing—camera, iPad, band aids, tissues, and wallets. Her handbag carried everything a woman would need to go shopping. LP, on the other hand, travelled light, using a small backpack that carried his diary and two copies of the Scroll, rolled up and sealed in shrink wrap.

They walked out into a cold breeze and headed down to the bus stop to wait for the double-decker tourist bus, to go north, this time travelling around Central Park and taking in historic landmarks such as St. Patrick's Cathedral. It was an impressive structure reminiscent of gothic cathedrals from the thirteenth century.

Inside was the largest pipe organ he'd ever seen, and the greatest church he'd walked through in his life. He found it unusual to see was a display inside, denouncing coal seam gas exploration. As he read the two page script about what mining companies were doing to good farmland, and how farmers had no rights to stop them from exploring and contaminating the land, he thought it was unusual for a church to take a position against mining.

LP sympathised with them and asked someone why this was placed inside a church. The older gentleman whispered, "Politics and religion go hand in hand these days."

It was more political than religious, LP thought.!

LP asked another question but got no response. He thought he must have taken a vow of silence. That's all he was going to get out of him.

LP caught up with Ingrid, who was admiring the huge stained glass panels that adorned the church.

He said, "Come on, are you finished looking around? I don't want to be arriving late at Ground Zero."

Before leaving, LP pushed some change into a donation box and said, "I think this church is getting more paying tourists through its doors than a Sunday service."

They walked out the way they had come in, through two giant wooden doors, held back with black ropes. They stepped down an expanse of stone steps and waited for their bus to arrive right out front of the cathedral.

They didn't have to wait long before their ride to Ground Zero arrived. Ingrid stepped on first and led the way up the narrow curving metal stairs. Seated on the open deck, the tour guide described New York's landmarks and told the passengers where the rich and famous lived.

They reached their destination by three o'clock. LP thoughts turned to what he would do when he stood on the ground where the Twin Towers once dominated the skyline. It felt as if the city's heart had been ripped out. And now growing from the old heart were four arteries fuelled and powered by the desire for renewal.

LP had two copies of the Scroll printed on canvas, shrink wrapped and water tight in his backpack. Although he had no idea what to expect at Ground Zero, he had the premonition that somehow water was involved. Months earlier, he had heard on a radio show that a water feature was being included in the Ground Zero memorial. He had a vision of a high-wire barrier and did not expect to be able to access the area.

The bus stopped not far from their destination. LP went down the spiral stairs first and then watched Ingrid follow, just in case she missed a step. His fear was unfounded, as they both said thanks to their driver.

Walking down the street past a small old church, they spotted another queue.

"Should have expected that," LP said in a dismissive tone. "Everywhere we go involves waiting in a queue."

They stood behind two young people, and Ingrid asked, "Is this the queue to get to Ground Zero?"

One bloke turned and said yes. The other continued texting on his phone.

LP tapped Ingrid on the shoulder and indicated what he thought of this unfriendly chap, sticking two fingers behind his head. She grabbed LP's hand and pulled it down, saying, "Don't be a grumpy old man."

The queue moved slowly past vendors selling all sorts of memorabilia of Ground Zero. Ingrid bought a booklet describing the day the towers fell. Its content had disturbing colour pictures with heart-wrenching eyewitness accounts.

Twenty minutes passed before they could enter from the sidewalk, and then they went up five steps into the building to receive free passes to proceed to where the towers once stood. Before doing that, they walked around the exhibit of photographs taken of that infamous day. Inside a large glass case, a mobile phone played over and over the voice of a distressed mother's last words to her family before it went silent. She knew she was about to die, but her last words were about love and family.

Ingrid turned to LP and asked, "Are you alright?"

LP wiped his teary eyes and said, "I'm going outside. You get the tickets. I'll meet you out there."

She came out a short time later with the tickets, but they would have to return in a half an hour before proceeding to Ground Zero.

She understood why he left the building without her but thought best to say no more about the exhibit.

With some time to spare on their hands, they walked to an old timber church adjacent to where they were standing that had a small graveyard with headstones dating back hundreds of years.

Inside was another reminder of what happened on that fateful day in September.

LP glanced at his watch and said, "Time to go or we'll be late." They walked out, leaving behind walls depicting the harrowing and heroic events that unfolded on the day.

By three thirty, they returned to memorial and stood outside with a group of about thirty people. They all headed together down the road, turning left at the first set of lights, and continued two blocks. On their way, they passed several construction sites, with high chain link fences covered in green matting, blocking the view of what lay behind those barricades.

Ingrid inquired, "Are you sure we're heading in the right direction?" to which LP replied, "Let's just follow the crowd, and we'll get there."

He was of course right. Everyone started turning down a narrow lane and then abruptly stopped. LP commented, "Should have expected this, another bloody queue." They slowly moved forward and entered a security area where bags were being scanned, like at the airport. LP placed his small backpack on the rollers and emptied his pockets, placing the contents in a tray.

He had travelled halfway across the world, carrying the scrolls without breaking open the seals. This looked like the final obstacle to overcome before completing his vision of the future that had taken four decades to save and deliver the Scroll.

Again, he was cleared to proceed without anyone questioning what may have looked like two sticks of dynamite when scanned. If he had been asked to open the shrink-wrapped items, the watertight seals would have to be broken, thereby putting an end to his quest to reach Ground Zero and deliver the scrolls intact.

"Step aside and follow me," a security officer suddenly instructed.

LP walked behind a partition and was told to spread his legs and stretch out his arms as a wand was waved over his body.

LP thought his worst fears were about to come true. *This is the end*, he thought.

"You're clean. You haven't any bomb-making residue on you," the security guard said.

LP collected his belongings and proceeded to walk out of the building opposite Ground Zero with Ingrid, who had little trouble going through security.

Everything seemed to be moving in the right direction, as they continued to walk along a narrow walkway, turning right into bright sunshine beaming down from a clear blue sky.

"We made it, but this is not what I expected to see," LP said.

"What did you expect?" she replied.

"A lake," said LP.

They were now walking towards one of two square inverted waterfalls. Two bronze plaques, bordering both waterfalls, inscribed the names of all those who lost their lives in the terrorist attacks on 9/11/2001.

The bronze plates reflected sunlight in every direction as the waterfalls cascaded, flowing into a small central square. It looked like a bottomless black hole as water disappeared.

It felt like they were on sacred ground, as they thought of what once towered out beneath their feet.

Ingrid looked at LP, as rays of light struck his face, and said in a concerned voice, "Put your cap on or you're bald head's going to get sun burnt; are those two moles on your cheek getting larger?" "No, I've had them checked over the past forty years, since they became raised starting out as two freckles, and their okay," LP replied.

Ingrid pulled out her camera to take a few snaps as LP contemplated what he was going to do next.

He believed this place was where the Scroll had to be delivered, and it was to float upon water. Reaching into his backpack, he grabbed one of the scrolls and got ready to place it beneath the bronze plate, where it could cascade down and disappear into the black hole. But he stopped. Something was not right.

He turned to Ingrid and said in a dismissive tone, "Something is out of place. I think the timing is not right. Let's go."

As they walked back the way they had come, he stopped to greet a New York police officer standing opposite the first waterfall and said, "Take this, it belongs here."

The officer had dark skin and a stocky build; he was leaning up against a metal light pole and didn't understand what LP was saying. Although his strong Australian accent was hard to decipher, the officer stretched out his left hand to take LP's gift.

The African American man nodded, in silence, as he touched the shrink-wrapped Scroll. LP's skin broke out in goose bumps at that moment as static electricity grounded through his body, giving both a small electric shock. In a split second, he realised he was still on track and being guided to finish what destiny had in store for him in New York.

Across the road was an Irish bar. Surprisingly, it still stood after the Twin Towers fell, over ten years earlier.

LP stopped at the menu board outside the pub and said to Ingrid, "Let's get something to eat and have a drink. This is as good a place as any."

Ingrid agreed and pushed open the wooden bar door to reveal the full décor of an Irish pub. They pulled up a stool each and sat down at the bar, where they were served by a young lass with an Irish accent. She had the whitest skin he had seen in America. It was radiant, without a blemish, freckle, or makeup.

She asked, "What would you have today?"

LP ordered a pint of Guinness, and a bourbon and cola for Ingrid. They looked around, sensing a lot of pain and sorrow that filled the walls, with badges from all the district fire stations. Lost mates, husbands, and wives were honoured and remembered there. Children's photos, sadly, were also displayed.

They finished their drinks, and LP said, "We've still got time to see the Statue of Liberty, if we hurry."

The Staten Island ferry was only a short walk away. It was the best way to get close enough to take photos of the statue, since the old girl was closed to tourists. The fear was it might also get blown up by a crazed terrorist.

They kept a steady pace in passing a subway station, as LP commented, "We'll get back to the hotel using this subway after we finish our trip across the bay."

Ingrid agreed, "Sooner the better. My feet are killing me." Waiting for the next ferry, they stood shoulder to shoulder with hundreds of other sightseers in the ferry terminal.

Five minutes passed before the sound of a fog horn announced the arrival of their ride. Passengers disembarked, and the next group of visitors were waved in by the steward.

It would take thirty minutes to dock at Staten Island. There, they would disembark and wait for the next ferry to take them back to the terminal on Manhattan Island.

LP positioned himself on the outside deck with other tourists waiting to take a picture of the Statue of Liberty. He was ready to fulfil his vision of the Scroll floating on the water. And that place was now the mouth of the Hudson River, with the icon of New York just across a windy, choppy waterway. He asked Ingrid to take a photo of him holding the most important thing in the world, he thought, wrapped in watertight shrink wrap. LP was now ready to let it slip from his raised right hand, ignoring everyone else around him.

With his back to the Statue of Liberty, he smiled and then gently released his grip, allowing the Scroll to fall below the bow's wake. Ingrid snapped the picture, thereby ending, she hoped, LP's obsession to deliver the Scroll.

LP contemplated how the numbers 1 and 0 enabled the Scroll to be uploaded to cyberspace for all to download and save. Now Ground Zero would connect with the new tower, "One," in a spectacular way as light reflected off the angled roofline. Beaming bright sunlight would strike hallowed ground on a new Memorial Day. That moment would give reflection on all those who had lost their lives on that day in September.

LP's hoped this gift would deliver a message of peace and healing. He thought anyone could connect with the image within the Scroll, tapping into universal thought and opening up another level of possibilities to contemplate.

Why Ground Zero and the Hudson River was the final destination for the copied Scroll was still a mystery to him, but it was finished now. He could get on with his life, and that meant visiting one more landmark tomorrow morning. Before flying out from JFK Airport onto LA and then back home to Australia, they would catch a taxi at five thirty in the morning and visit the TV studio of NBC's *Today Show*.

Arriving back at the ferry terminal, Ingrid and LP jostled with other passengers to get off first. Their motive was to get on the subway as soon as possible, returning to Forty-Ninth Street so they could reach their hotel before it got dark.

They entered the subway down a steep flight of stairs to a ticket window. LP was thinking, everywhere they went required a ticket, as Ingrid pushed ten dollars through the cashier's caged enclosure. They walked through the turnstile after pushing their tickets into the ticket slot. Standing back a couple of paces from the platform edge, they waited for the train.

LP was on edge, looking around for anything unusual. He'd seen too many movies that ended badly on subway stations. But his anxiety was unfounded as the zooming noise of their approaching ride calmed his nerves.

Entering through the open carriage doorway, they headed towards two empty seats. Although this was their second experience of travelling on a New York subway, it was still eerie. Sitting down, LP glanced around at the other commuters to get a feel of what they were thinking. There was absolute silence. No conversation, no eye contact, only those with heads down reading or texting. LP made sure not to make direct eye contact with anyone, knowing that it could be construed the wrong way. He figured violence could erupt over the most trivial issue, and the best way to avoid it was to ignore everything around him. It was a primitive response to avoid conflict, but it worked.

Twenty minutes passed, with the loud clanging of the subway train making its way to each station. More New Yorkers crowded on, and soon the car was standing room only. Considering the peak hour they were travelling in, Ingrid and LP were lucky to get seats.

The next stop was Forty-Ninth Street. They stood up, pushed their way to the centre doors, and waited for the train to come to a screeching halt. The doors opened, and they stepped onto the old subway platform, which needed a good makeover.

LP indicated, "Walk this way." They headed for a flight of stairs leading out to the heart of New York.

Back in their room, they decided to pack up to be ready for an early start the next morning. They wanted to be outside NBC's studio by six o'clock and back to the hotel by eight, to be picked up for transit to the airport at eight fifteen. Their flight was scheduled for eleven thirty that morning.

32

It was still dark outside when LP showered and changed into his new light gray Levi's. He added a long-sleeved Van Heusen striped shirt and pulled on a hooded fleece-lined jacket bought in Vegas.

LP called out to Ingrid, "Better rug up, it's going to be cold out there."

Ingrid showered and did the usual thing women do before getting dressed, and they left their room by five thirty, requesting a taxi at the front desk. By the time they walked from the foyer onto the sidewalk, their taxi pulled up, with the cabbie inquiring, "Where to, sir?"

LP answered, "NBC, mate," as he held open the back door for Ingrid; he slid into the back seat and snuggled up to her, saying, "It's freezing out here."

Pulling away from the curb, the driver turned at the lights and took the first right at the next intersection, before the arrow turned red. After driving past Times Square, they were just a short walk away from the TV studios at Rockefeller Center Plaza. Low metal barriers restricted access, with a few station hands milling around.

One guy holding a clipboard directed LP and Ingrid around the next corner, past a silver food van, where they found—you guessed it: another queue!

"That'll be right, another bloody line to stand in the freezing cold," LP quipped sarcastically.

They walked to the line-up and edged close to the building to take shelter from the wind. LP expected more people, but when he commented this to the woman in front, she replied, "Wait until seven, when we're herded to the barriers. You'll see the queue stretch beyond the next block."

It suddenly dawned on LP that they were at least an hour early. The show was slated to start at seven, not six in the morning. Well, the one advantage of reporting early, LP figured, was having the pick of where to stand.

Ingrid rubbed her hands, trying to stay warm, while LP walked over to the food van. Complementary coffee and croissants were available. He joined another queue and received his free coffee and snack. When he returned, Ingrid carefully held her coffee in both hands to warm up.

She sipped on her flat black, as she slowly stopped shivering, saying, "LP, how did we get the time wrong?"

"Don't know, but we'll get the best position right out front of the entrance doors."

Sheets of whiteboard were made available to those who wanted to write a message for folks back home. LP took advantage of the extra time before the show started. He went over to the silver van again and asked for a pen and a sheet of whiteboard, after waiting in another queue for the umpteenth time.

Around six forty-five, the guy with the clipboard called out and waved everyone forward. He directed them to walk up to where the metal barriers were and wait for the show to start.

LP and Ingrid positioned themselves right out front of NBC's main entrance glass doors. It was the best position to be noticed. Matt Lauer, the anchorman, came out and greeted his outdoor audience, saying, "How are you all feeling? It's a big show this morning and even better after seeing so many smiling faces. Welcome!"

He walked back through the glass door entrance and prepared himself for going on the air. LP positioned his sign with their message for family in Queensland.

It read, "Hello Australia! Hi Nate, be home soon, guys; love you."

After waiting for three-quarters of an hour, and having the best position to be seen and spoken to, time finally ran out.

They had to leave.

LP turned around to a young couple Ingrid had been chatting to and said, "We got a plane to catch, take our spot up front."

They pushed their way back through the crowded sidewalk and briskly walked back to where they had queued earlier; LP waved his hand to flag a cab. They had little time to spare. If they missed their flight, LP would consider he failed in his mission.

Luckily, a cabbie stopped on Forty-Ninth and Fifth Avenue. LP and Ingrid ran over and climbed in the taxi. Time was their biggest enemy now.

LP directed, "Hilton Garden Inn, Eighth Avenue. Make it snappy, we're running late for our flight at JFK."

Their cabbie wasted no time, and they quickly arrived at their hotel. LP opened his wallet to give his cabbie twenty dollars, as Ingrid quickly started walking back to their room. LP ran to catch up, as the lift doors opened. Thankfully, there were no dramas happening this morning.

They entered their room and double-checked that everything was ready to go. There was no time to wait for a bellhop. They started wheeling their luggage out of the doorway and back down to the lift. LP checked out at the reception desk and followed Ingrid, standing in front of the hotel.

He placed his hand around her shoulder and said, "Have we got everything?" as their transit van arrived right on time: 8:15 am.

Their driver loaded their luggage in through the rear doors. LP and Ingrid made sure to hold on to their hand luggage when they stepped inside the van. Forty minutes later, they were dropped off in front of the airport terminal.

LP was feeling pretty happy with himself. Everything was on schedule. He couldn't spot anything amiss. They stood in line to check in their luggage. As they waited, LP couldn't help eavesdropping on a piece of conversation between one man dressed as a rabbi and another bloke with cufflinks that identified him as a Mason.

In a heavy French accent, the Mason asked the rabbi, "What is God? Where is God? And what does God look like?"

After a moment's reflection, the rabbi answered, "I can't answer your first questions, but God must have a sense of humour, since we are the chosen people."

LP had a quiet chuckle to himself as those two characters sparred off with each other.

"Next, move forward," said an unseen voice. Pulling their luggage behind them and stopping at check-in counter number six, LP lifted Ingrid's bag to be weighed in first, suspecting it might be overweight. The young woman suggested that LP place his bag on as well. Together, their weight turned out to be just correct. The woman said, "Save yourself an excess baggage charge, just repack your bags, so they're equal and underweight."

They did as requested and proceeded through security. LP didn't want to say what he saw ahead, but Ingrid did: "Don't get the grumps, more queues ahead." LP just shrugged his shoulders and murmured, "Huh!"

He looked up at the overhead monitor, showing what fights were boarding. Flight 863 on Delta Airlines was on schedule. They could spot the departure terminal on the left, just a short walk away. LP went ahead and approached the front desk, while Ingrid limped along, nursing her blistered toes. It had been a struggle at times with her feet, but she would soon be able to put them up and rest.

LP presented their tickets for seat allocations but was told to wait until the flight was boarding, because they didn't have priority seating, and their flight was overbooked.

LP turned to Ingrid, who had caught up, and said, "Things are not looking good to get out of New York today."

"What do you mean?" she asked. "Don't tell me our flight's cancelled?" Ingrid glared at him as her lips tightened.

"No, we have to wait, and they'll let us know if we can board. They're overbooked."

LP then pointed over to the airport café and suggested, "Let's grab something to eat. I'm having a beer to take the edge of things."

Ingrid ordered eggs, bacon, and toast to share, a Bud for LP, and cappuccino for herself. They were seated with a clear view of what was happening with their flight, across the walkway. LP walked over and spoke to the airline assistant on several occasions, with no luck. What he found out was there were seven other passengers before them, waiting to board the same flight.

Chatting about how far they had travelled, Ingrid thought, *Was he disappointed in not having enough time to visit publishers about his books?*

Before she could ask, LP said, "Listen! Miracles do happen." "Final boarding now, Philips party, please proceed to boarding terminal two," a voice bellowed through the airport terminal. LP quickly gulped down the last mouthful of beer and stood up, placing several one-dollar notes on the table as a tip before reading "In God, We Trust"; he thought, *Right, but everyone else pays cash!*

They rushed over to the airline assistant, were allotted their seats, and went down the ramp, where they entered a now full aircraft, ready for takeoff. They were the last to enter before the captain instructed, "Arm all the doors."

By the time they were seated, the engines roared as the aircraft taxied across the runway for takeoff. LP shut his eyes and sunk back into his seat, letting out a huge sigh of relief. He made it with Ingrid in and out of New York over Easter and delivered the Scroll, but one word still begged the question: Why?

BOOK 4

ARCHAEA RISING

33

APRIL 2014

ARCHAEA RISING

Armies on the move soldiers of Archaea
moving from the north
their weapon rising
a silent reaper
from depths below
breaking open oceans
releasing their weapon
of mass destruction
returning their world
to reign for a billion years.

"Wake up your mumbling in your sleep," Ingrid said as she nudged LP's shoulder to wake him up.

"I'm not asleep. I'm just having one of those moments when I start predicting the future, and what I see I don't want to talk about right now."

"Well, leave me in the dark as usual, but I warn you, snap out of these negative thoughts, or it'll send you crazy," Ingrid said, while turning to him and giving a reassuring hug.

Feeling her warm body against him, he started to relax and let go of those thoughts that dogged his mind.

Sunrise was approaching as first light filtered through the bedroom window. It was time to get up like every other morning to capture the perfect sunrise.

"OK, are you coming. Sunrise in ten minutes, let's be quick about it," whispered LP.

"You can't take your time about anything. Go and we'll talk later."

LP quickly changed into his board shorts, put on his runners, grabbed a warm flannel and sprinted out the front door clutching his camera case in one hand, and in the other his iPhone and car keys for his Holden Cruse. Ice on the rear window, and cold wind pushing against his face was a taste of what to expect when he arrives at one of the beaches of Caloundra.

His car was not completely covered from the cold morning air in the carport. He kept a bucket of water just opposite the car for moments like this. He picked up the green bucket and tossed its contents over the trouble spot with a mighty splash, but it wasn't enough to remove all ice. It just needed a quick wipe and a bit of scrapping to remove any trouble spots for seeing in reverse. Now LP was ready to back out from his driveway, camera ready on the passenger seat, and iPhone on speaker as he turned the ignition on.

Changing colours of sunrise always got him excited, as he rushed to one of his favorite beach locations to capture the moment. It would take three minutes to get there. Enough time to go over in his mind what he was going to say to Ingrid over breakfast, and explain what Archaea is, was, or whatever, and not frighten the living daylights out of her. Caution may be the better tack and explain it away as dreaming. The last thing she'd want here is a lecture of biblical proportion connecting the creation story of God removing Adam's rib to create woman. Then compare it to bacteria and Archaea becoming one, billions of years ago, being the source of all multi-celled life forms on Earth over time - you may well call them the creator - but at the same time the opposite could be true.

The question Ingrid may well ask, *Where did they come from in the first place?*

His answer won't please her. *From space. Hitchhikers of the galaxy, that can remain dormant for hundreds of thousands of years in the most extreme conditions, including meteorites.* That may well be the real creation story. They harbour no disease, no pathogen nor virus.

LP stopped his car at Dicky Beach car park with a few minutes to spare before sunrise. He quickly walked down to the foreshore feeling the wet sand sink between his toes. Early morning, weather permitting, not only revealed the changing colours of sunrise. This morning, reflected a golden glow reflection before his feet, stretching back across the ocean. After his photo shoot, he found it the best way to kick off any day, with a morning walk along the beach to boot. Not everyone can do it. But when you have the opportunity, one should take advantage of it, with a camera or iPhone, capturing the moment forever and share it.

Ten minutes after sunrise LP was back driving home, but not before going to the top of Queen Street looking inland to see what the Glass House Mountains looked like - clear blue sky, mist or overcast. He would decide if it's worth taking the twenty-minute drive to his other favourite spot for snapping photos, walking the mountain trails, and climbing the not so hard mountain peaks.

Storm clouds on the distant horizon engulf the peaks, so he proceeded to drive home along Sugarbag Road, and back up his driveway within two minutes. Parking his vehicle in the carport, LP then went straight inside with his phone and camera in hand.

Ingrid called out to him. "Bacon and eggs are almost ready. Are you using Photoshop or eating now?"

"Just give me a sec. I'll upload the pics I want to edit and post on Twitter for later."

LP walked from his laptop that dominated the kitchen table, strewn with scribbled notes on A4 sheets of white paper. A second glancing eye would see typed pages of his latest novel spread out in chaotic order. It looked like you'd need to be a mind reader to figure out what he was doing.

If Ingrid had her way, she would wipe her hand across the table and bin the lot of it. However, that was not going to happen while LP could get his way, by pointing out there's a perfectly good table on the veranda for eating off.

And he would say when Ingrid complained about wanting her kitchen table back. *When you stop using the outdoor table for planting miniature cactus, I'll stop using the kitchen table as an office.*

Stalemate. Nothing would change. They're both too pigheaded to comprise.

"Come on, I'll make room on the outdoor table, but you better get the bacon & eggs off the barbie, before it goes cold. I've turned it off," said Ingrid.

LP placed breakfast in front of Ingrid, and he sat down with his food, and said, "I'm one step ahead of you, eat it while it's hot, and I'll tell what I was on about earlier this morning.

In between scoffing down mouthfuls of food LP started to explain,"Well, I'm not going into it too much, but Archaea is a single-cell organism,'*that*'joined together with bacteria forming multi-cell organisms. Archaea that remained singled-celled, went about transforming an inhospitable world that looked like Venus today, along with Caynbacteria into something habitable for multi-celled life forms like us. Archaea can still be found in the most extreme conditions on earth - in hot springs, sulfur plumes, puma-frost, and active volcanoes above and below the ocean. And up until 1978, these single-celled organisms were unknown to scientists. Only after 1990, were they recognised as a separate kingdom, classified like plants, animals and fungi."

"Hang on, what's the problem with that? That's in the past?" Ingrid said with a distorted look on her face.

"That's right, 3.5 billion years ago, and they're on the march to take back their world," replied LP.

"How can that be relevant now. Get your mind off this shit," Ingrid said with a dismissive tone in her voice.

LP replied, "Just two words - Global Warming." "Are you still on about that?"

"Yep, and you've got your head in the sand. You should read more."

"Stuff you, and take your food with *ya!*" she screamed.

LP stood up from the table, pushing his chair back with such force it bounced over the balcony rail. He didn't speak, just scoffed down a last mouth full of bacon, and figured he should keep his mouth shut. Ingrid put her head down and continued eating. She was not happy. LP walked inside sitting down in front of his laptop with Photoshop opened. To take his mind off what just happened, he started editing his morning sunrise shots for posting on Twitter. When Ingrid was in a better mood he would try to expand on the subject about micro organisms, and why they could end the world we know.

After uploading his best sunrise photo on Twitter for his followers, he figured it was time to give his old mates a phone call, and fill them in about Archaea, as well, his plan to climb Mt. Beerwah. Maybe they'll be more receptive to what he's got to say.

Bear was first in his contact list. A quick touch on his iPhone and he answered, "How the fuck are *ya?* When are *ya* coming down to Sydney next? We'll get on the piss and do some gambling."

"I'm not ringing about doing that. What do you know about Archaea?

"Can you bet on it?" Asked Bear.

"Possibly your life, if the powers to be get it wrong," LP snapped back..

"Fuck no, what are you on about this time. Are still paranoid. I thought this all ended after you left New York. You delivered the Scroll and it was up loaded as foretold back on New Year's Eve. It's over, there's nothing more any of us can do, it changed nothing, it's still a violent world with crazy weather all over the place."

"My concern is not for myself, it's our kids and grand- kids to have a better future or should I say, a future! We need to meet." Bear was starting to get curious. "Why, tell me now what else do you know?"

"No, let's meet at your old beach house and I'll fill you in why we need to return to the mountain as well. I"ll reveal what I know, and only then. I'll let you know when, after I speak to Brownie, Kato and Mason."

"They're not going to climb the mountain. Certainly not Brownie. He thinks it's his Dreamtime ancestor." Bear said in a raised voice.

"We'll see. I'll phone you again after speaking to everyone." LP replied.

Next, LP would do the ring around, contacting the old gang and explain what's on his mind. He would say Bear will be coming up from Sydney, as well, to climb Mt Beerwah.

Assuming that Bear was on board, LP was sure they would all agree to meet at their old haunt. LP only had to lock the time and date.

LP looked at the front door as a loud bang demanded attention. Before he could get up from in front of his laptop, Mitchie his youngest son strode in carrying his tool box, looking like he was in a hurry to be somewhere else.

"What's the panic," asked LP.

"I'm packing my bags. Loading up the vehicle and I'm out of here."

"Out of here to where?" LP asked with a surprised look and a stare.

"Port Hedland in Western Australia. That's where big money can be made over in the Pilbara region." Mitchie replied with confidence.

"Who's going with you?" LP asked.

"No one! One of my mates is already over there earning the big bucks. So the sooner I get there the better."

"Hang on, have you got a job lined up?" "Nope!"

"So, you're going to drive five thousand clicks across Australia and hope you'll get work. Are you sure that's a good idea?"

"You're to conservative, *'old man'*. Where's the old risk taker, the visionary, the adventurer?" Mitchie said while shaking his head.

"I've still got it, so I'll be your navigator, I'm coming too." LP replied.

There was silence for a few seconds as those words sunk in, and then Mitchie laughed with a surprised look on his face.

"OK, be ready in five days. We're crossing Australia in six days from East to West, down to South Australia, up to Uluru, onto Alice Springs, and up to Kathrine. Then across the top end to Broome. And if I've timed it right, then it's only another six-hour drive south, and we'll hit Port Hedland."

"I'll find my old road maps, and check out if you're on the money or your calculations are out. Where we're travelling we won't get much of a GPS signal, so I'd rather rely on my old paper map of Australia."

Mitchie was OK with that, and walked away heading for his bedroom to start looking at packing, while LP went out to his vehicle, opened the glove box and grabbed out a folded map. He went back inside and on the kitchen bench, opened the map to mark the route and check if his son's calculations were correct.

Ingrid shouted from the balcony. "Who were you talking too?" "Mitchie, he's leaving home and I'm going too," replied LP. "Talk sense, what's going on?"

"I just told you. And when you're in a good mood I'll explain what's happening, and when you come inside I'll show you the map."

He could see on Ingrid's face, she was still grumpy as she folded her arms, and gave LP a stare that could kill from where she was sitting on the balcony.

LP thought, *It's time to be tactful. Walk away and not talk about what he was on about earlier at breakfast. Nor try to explain why he was leaving in five days to cross Australia without her. Just not good timing.*

34

Friday on his mind came around fast enough for LP, going over everything they'd need for their road trip to the red centre, and across the top end. LP's son insisted that they check out Uluru previously known as Ayers Rock, four hours south of Alice Springs in the heart of Australia. This wouldn't be the quickest route to take to get to Port Hedland in six days.

"OK '*old man*', are you sure you got everything packed back there. You know I would have helped, but I've been working all week." Mitchie said, as he walked behind his vehicle, checking everything was secure before closing the canopy windows of his Holden 4x4 Rodeo tray back.

"Take care of our son and get him there safely or don't bother coming back," said Ingrid.

You could tell in her voice, she was still pissed off with LP's attitude earlier in the week, because he still hadn't explained what he was on about regarding Archaea, or talk much about the trip across to the West Coast.

"See you in a week love, and I'll phone to let you know how we're travelling when we've got reception." LP replied.

Ingrid walked to the driver's side door and gave her son a big kiss on his cheek, and said. "Stay safe, and ring me before you listen to your father's advice."

LP laughed off that last comment, as Mitchie pushed the gear stick into first gear as LP started to rattle off a checklist - two food bins, two five litre containers of water, fishing rods, carton of beer, bedding, tarp, poles, ropes, table, gas stove, camping chairs, phones, wallets, jack, fuel drum, tools box, and the cooler with cold food from the fridge, with a few chilled beers on top.

"Did you fill up the Jerrycan?" Mitchie asked.

"No, it's half full. We'll fill it when we fill up next, and if we've forgotten anything, there's no turning back," replied LP.

Mitchie drove out of the driveway and gave a wave to his mother, and LP stretched out his hand and gave a thumbs up as they left home. Heading west they would travel past the Glass House Mountains, LP's second home when it comes spiritual enlightenment.

Two and half hours into their journey they drove across a railway line, stopping directly opposite the rail crossing at a pub on the outskirts of Dalby. There they would down a cold beer, before, changing drivers. *The Bun*, the nickname for this pub had the longest town name in Queensland. By the time they try to pronounce it, the publican would have two beers poured.

Kaimkillenbun pub was your typical hotel design from when Cobb & Co. Coaches, and men on horseback would stop for accommodation, a cold beer and food. The two story building had surrounding balconies, with overnight rooms upstairs for travellers, and the public bar downstairs.

LP and his son walked into the public bar and asked for two schooners of cold beer on tap. They sat at the bar and chatted about where to stop overnight. It wouldn't be upstairs. They were travelling on the cheap, and tonight would be under the stars further west, and there was still enough light for another couple of hours of driving before sunset. They took their time knocking down their cold ales, but Mitchie wanted more beer, a carton of Corona to be to his liking. But not there, grog would be cheaper in Dalby. They finished their beers and said thanks to the publican and walked out the way they came in. Through the front door and two steps down to their vehicle parked out front.

Mitchie was up for more driving. He wasn't tired and drove off to find a bottle shop in Dalby. After angle parking in front of Liquorland, he then went in to buy a carton of Coronas. Mitchie got back behind the wheel, still keen on driving, and let '*old man*' be a tourist for now.

They headed west with a fair amount of traffic coming their way from workers ending their shift, most likely from the hundreds of coal seam gas wells that had been drilled throughout the district. It was now dark on the outskirts of St. George as they looked for a spot to pull off the highway and set up camp. LP pointed to a cutting in the bush, and Mitchie left the bitumen driving twenty metres into an open clearing of scrub. It was eight o'clock and they weren't going to bother setting up the tarp over the rear of the vehicle. Just remove the table, gas stove, camping chairs, and cooler making enough room for two to sleep in the back, on a form mattress under the fiberglass canopy. But a problem presented itself. They had to find a hunk of wood to prop up the tailgate because the tray back was short for the mattress. They needed to prop it to allow for the mattress to fit. If not, their feet would be overhanging by a foot. Mitchie spotted a solid tree branch not far from the vehicle, walked over and cleaned it up with LP's axe, and positioned it under the tailgate as support.

Mitchie dropped the axe next to the cooler then pulled out a cold Corona and asked, "What are you having?"

"I'll have one too. Grab a couple of stubby coolers from the consul while you're at it." LP said.

They didn't bother with cooking a meal because they got KFC on the way through town.

Sitting and relaxing beneath a cloudless night sky, stars shone bright. Bush abounded with red dirt under foot, as they melted into their surroundings. This was just a taste of what's to come. This is the real Australia. Not the city lights and hustle and bustle, but highways with little traffic that stretch in a straight line for hundreds of kilometres.

After a quiet drink under the stars, surrounded by silence, LP folded up his chair and pushed it under the not so white vehicle covered in red dust, and climbed up under the canopy and settled down for a good night's sleep. Mitchie decided to knock down another beer and listen to some music before crawling into bed.

During the night, the barometer dropped to almost freezing. Daybreak couldn't come sooner for them, as LP started to stir.

He stretched out his hands and started worming his way out of his not so comfortable makeshift bed, and planting his feet back onto red dirt. Looking around he spotted his shovel learning up against the corner of the bullbar. He picked it up and continued walking into the bush to make a bush toilet. A hole in the ground and then cover it with dirt. One thing LP was very wary of was snakes, especially after the snake attacked Mason, his old mate, on their road trip in the early seventies. LP was wiser from that; pay attention to your surroundings, or if you're unlucky, you might get bitten on the arse while doing your morning constitutional. LP placed the shovel next to his axe so not to forget it when packing up. He then started preparing to make bacon, and eggs on toast.

By the time Mitchie crawled out of bed, breakfast was ready as he handed him a plate, saying, "Get this in *ya*! And we're on our way as soon as we pack up."

Well, their is old saying: *We' ll hit the road;* was an understatement. Wallabies and kangaroos littered the road as road kill. Eagles soared above looking for a feed, on the stretch of road to Cunnamulla Mitchie had to zigzag along.

They reached their next destination without too much drama since there was little traffic on the road, and fewer animals feeding on the side of the road in daylight. Most of the animals killed at night were from road train bullbars striking them dead.

Stopping at the Roadhouse on the outskirts of town, Mitchie filled up for the first time, and just in time as the fuel light flashed; *fill tank*. Seventy three dollars later, and checking the trip meter for how far they could go on a full tank was - 840km. Before leaving Cunnamulla, they took a quick drive around town. It was known as the centre of the largest known body of underground water in the world. Cunnamulla is an aboriginal word meaning - long stretch of water, and the Warrego - river of sand, is the river, along with the Artesian water supply that made the mulga country viable for European settlement. The town became the home of the largest sheering shed in the world, sheering half a million sheep in a year. And in recent times for the statue of a *bushie*, looking thoughtful as you drive into town; named -The Cumnnamulla Fella.

Next destination Broken Hill. Arriving at 7:00pm at a Big Ten caravan park in Broken Hill, they proceeded to book in and find a campsite for the night. At least hear they could shower and freshen up and use the cooking facilities at hand, which they did. The next morning they were back on the road again heading towards the South Australian border. They wouldn't be going to Adelaide but would take the fork north to Port Augusta. Arriving there, it was time to stock up on supplies, mainly alcohol from the local bottle shop - Coronas were on the hit list, and a hot chook for lunch from Woolies across the road.

Mitchie asked LP to open up his map, after loading their supplies in the back of the vehicle. He reached over and pointed to Coober Pedy on the map, and said, "We can make it before sunset, you do some driving. I'm having a Corona."

Seven hours of driving lay ahead with Mitchie's music blaring. Stopping every couple of hours to change drivers, the navigator would look for something to drink as they crossed paths, reaching in the rear window, and digging deep, he'd find the coldest beer in the cooler.

They arrived at 8:15pm, later than Mitchie calculated, and booked in at the tourist caravan park on the outskirts of town. It also had a restaurant with pizza on the menu. That solved where to sleep and eat, in one go.

The next morning they packed up early, after LP heated up a can of cream of chicken soup to share for breakfast. Mitchie wasn't in the mood for sharing. He wanted something stronger - black coffee to get his brain into gear. Before driving out LP walked over to reception and handed over the amenity keys. The owner of the park may well have been the local tourist guide, pointing at a map on the wall, places of interest to see before leaving town. He told LP to walk in the front entrance of the resort in the main street, you couldn't miss it. Then turn left and you'll see stairs leading down to underground workings of an old opal mine. It's well worth looking at, and it's free to enter. And check out the underground church across the road.

They took on board local advice, and did a quick tour of a maze of tunnels under the resort. Memorabilia of yesteryear was displayed over the walls, and rusty digging equipment was roped off for safety.

Next, LP strode across the road, leaving Mitchie walking around checking tyre pressure, and lifting the bonnet to check fluid levels. Mitchie wanted to make sure everything was right for their next leg of their journey.

Mitchie shouted out to LP as he crossed the road, "By the time I check over the vehicle, be out of there. Make it quick or I'll leave you behind."

Under a pile of red dirt that was a roof on a church, LP pushed open a solid door, opening to a small entrance leading to another door. He turned the door knob, and gently pushed, and started to walk down the aisle until he was standing in front of the church alter. It reminded him of a grotto from many a movie watched. It was starting to give him goose bumps. It was like been transported back in time. Here was one man, a priest performing a ritual started two thousand years ago. As LP cast his eyes around, he realised there was no one else there, just him and a priest at the alter head down reading.

He thought to himself, since they were alone, he could ask the question to the meaning of life, in this sanctified place of worship. So what does LP blurt out when the priest stopped what he's reading. He asked, "Do you pull a better crowd than this on Sunday?"

"Yes, fifty yesterday, and if you have any more questions sit down there, and I speak to you later," while pointing to a pew.

LP missed his opportunity to know more. He didn't know why he asked such a silly question, and didn't have time to wait to know what else could be revealed there. Mitchie was waiting outside, anxious to get on the go, and if LP didn't hurry up, his son might be true to his word, and leave him behind. LP turned, walking out, cap in hand, sunglasses on, thongs flapping and a T-shirt blazoned with a New Zealand map and a Kiwi bird on it. At that moment, he thought what he must have looked like to the priest; *a Kiwi tourist, not a potential convert.*

LP stepped back into the passenger seat, and before he could click his seat belt on, they were heading north out of town, onto the main highway. Destination Uluru, but first they needed to fill up at the BP Roadhouse on the outskirts of town.

After paying, they were back on the road with clear blue sky ahead of them, and to the west, thunder heads were brewing. Looking left and right as they left Coober Pedy behind; what they witnessed resembled a crater-like scared landscape as far the eye could see, with mounds of dirt looking like miniature pyramids.

Their destination looked within reach after a few hours of driving, but they mistook a table-top looking mountain for the sandstone monolith - Uluru, on the horizon.

LP looked at his map and said, "That's not Uluru its Mt.Conner and over to the west is Walpa Gorge. Uluru's not much further."

"Well, the old map has come in handy, since we can't get any GPS signal out here!" said Mitchie.

Mitchie kept a sharp eye on the road as a wonder of nature seemed to swallow them as they entered the national park. Now in the heart of Australia; the rock overshadowed their vehicle at the base of Uluru. Mitchie was keen on climbing it, but after reading about the rock and the aboriginal trustees, it was clear they wouldn't be climbing Uluru today. It was closed for climbing indefinitely.

Mitchie was disappointed. They took the long way around to get to Port Hedland. If it wasn't for sight-seeing, they could have cut a thousand kilometres of their trip by firstly heading north to Mt.Isa, across the Barkly Highway and onto Katherine to cross the top end along the Great Northern Highway.

Mitchie may have missed the opportunity to climb the red rock, but LP wasn't going to miss snapping some photos at sunset. They'd spotted a car park when entering Kata Tjuta National Park encompassing Uluru renamed in 1958, which would be perfect for photos. They headed back the way they came, not before exploring around the base of Uluru, that still, some tourist company's call - Ayers Rock, named after the South Australian of the time, Premier Sir Henry Ayers, and discovered by Ernest Giles an explorer, in 1872. If Giles had been able to speak the local language, the indigenous people, the traditional owners, would have told have told him: *The rock has been here as long as they have, going back to Dreamtime. It didn't need discoverin'.*

LP and Mitchie entered a cave entrance, what looked like a wave rock overhang protecting aboriginal drawings, going back possibly tens of thousands of years. Not touching anything, LP got up close and snapped a couple of photos he hoped he could reproduce as prints on canvas when back home.

They stopped at the car park where dozens of vehicles were parked. Light drizzle popped up the brollies from tourists standing against the fence line, trying to get a clear shot of the changing colours of the rock on sunset. As LP grabbed his camera and umbrella, he overheard one couple saying, "Pity about the rain."

LP saw it differently. It's not often in this part of Australia you get much rain, let alone a rainbow striking the rock. That's exactly what LP captured. A rare moment that connected him to aboriginal folklore of the; *Rainbow Serpent.* LP left the car park with Mitchie driving to the caravan park on the outskirts of the National Park, fifteen clicks back down the road from Uluru.

On arriving LP's plan was to freshen up, eat and hit the sack early, then get a head start on all the tourists next morning. Mitchie plan was to stay up and knock down a couple of

Coronas, and see if he could attract some female talent walking by their somewhat messy campsite.

Still dark when LP woke, to be exact, 4:30am. He tried to wake his son to no avail. What he'd find out later, Mitchie hooked up with a fellow female tourist and had a late night.

Leaving his son sleeping in the back, LP jumped in the driver's seat and headed out of the car park, with Mitchie somewhat cramped in after LP put all their gear back next to him.

Arriving back at Uluru, but a different car park for sunrise, with walking trails lit up by low posts with solar lighting revealed paths to follow in the dark. One thing LP was unsure about: Dingoes, the native Australian dog roamed this place, and have attacked tourists in the past.

LP didn't want to waste time thinking about what may be lurking in the dark. He walked the dimly lit trails looking for a perfect vantage point for a sunrise shot. What one of the trails led

to, was a large elevated viewing platform. LP decided that was the best spot to set up, so he headed back to the vehicle and grabbed his camera gear. He tried to wake his son, but no go.

He then returned to the deck, and walked up six steps, turned left, and positioned his camera on his tripod up against the front handrail, ready for what Uluru is famous for - the changing colours of the rock.

Tour buses were starting to arrive as LP looked back to see if Mitchie had stirred, but no sight of him yet. Tourists poured out of those buses, as well, hundreds more arrived by cars, and you don't have to guess where they were heading. Well, within minutes the platform creaked with eager photographers crowding the viewing area. LP had laid claim to his corner, as tourists jostled shoulder to shoulder to snap a memorable photo of sunrise at the rock. LP readied himself, for the moment, to capture the sun striking the rock from the east as he pointed his camera west. It was still overcast and it would be later than sunrise, before the sun broke through low storm clouds.

Mitchie by this time still hadn't risen, and LP couldn't go back for him, or he'd lose his position, and he didn't want to leave his camera and tripod unattended, even if he could push through the crowd.

The moment arrived as cameras clicked and the crowd was not disappointed. LP had captured a wonder of nature, as the colours of the red rock changed before his eyes. Whitish grey cloud streaked across the rock framed against a background of blue sky.

LP hoped Mitchie would wake up, and at least, look out the tray back window, because it was his idea to go the long way around, just to see Uluru. And this moment was spectacular, and he missed it.

Pushing his way through the crowd LP headed back to Mitchie's vehicle and found him still asleep.

"Mitchie wake up. Last chance to see the rock."

With no response, LP placed his camera gear on the back seat, and drove out of the car park heading for Alice Springs, leaving Mitchie to sleep in. He'd check on him in a couple of hours.

After travelling east along the Lasseter Highway, then turning north onto route 87-Stuart Highway, he veered off onto an expanse of red dirt, after seeing only - desert, bitumen, and the odd backpacker van go by. He steeped out of Mitchie's vehicle, and thumped on the side window to wake his son up. It was his turn to drive.

Mitchie shouted, as he looked out the canopy window, "Stop the banging."Where are we?"

"Not Uluru, you missed sunrise. We're on the way to Alice. You drive." LP shouted back.

Mitchie wriggled his way out of a warm bed. Taking stock of where he was, and said, "OK, let's keep on the move. We wouldn't want to break down here. It'll cost a fortune to get us out of trouble."

Mitchie took control behind the wheel, accelerating, blasting a red dust cloud in the distance as tyres spun onto bitumen.

Alice Springs looked like a two stubby trip for Mitchie if he had his way, but *'old man'* would not be happy seeing him knock down a Corona while driving, so that was not going to happen. With cloud cover still overhead, kept the temperature down to bearable for locals. Air conditioning now on for them was a cool change from the *Outback* heat. Entering Alice Springs, they were confronted with the local prison on the left, with a billboard: *Welcome to Alice* - in front of barbed wire fencing, and on the right, the airport.

LP commented, "Local cops take seriously any minor breaches of the law. I know you can't drink alcohol in public places, or you'll get arrested. So don't rip the top off a Corona until we're out of town, when I'm driving, or you could end up behind barbwire or on a plane back to where you come from."

"Got *ya*, let's fill up," Mitchie said.

LP pointed to a Shell *servo*, two intersections down the road. Green lights showed the way. Mitchie turned right and pulled up next to the diesel bowser. They both stepped out. Mitchie to fill the vehicle. LP to find a toilet. He was busting for a leak. Next he walked inside the front entrance to pay for the fuel. As LP walked outside he heard Mitchie '*revving*' the engine, prompting him to jog over to an impatient driver ready to plant his foot down on the pedal, and get on the move for the next leg of their journey.

Mitchie said, "Take a look at the map, '*old man*' we're taking a shortcut across the Tanami Desert, and we'll save a thousand kilometres and make up a day's travelling time."

LP's first thoughts were, *It's a dirt track except for a couple hundred kilometers of bitumen.*

LP figured he would be wasting his breath trying to persuade Mitchie from taking the Tanami Track. What was agreed upon when they started their road trip was, to leave Alice Springs, head north to Tennant Creek and then on to Katherine, before tracking west, across the top end of Australia.

What was unfolding was the unknown? No phone reception, no recovery gear, and not enough fuel to make it to Halls Creek, and back onto bitumen after a thousand and forty kilometres across the Tanami Desert track. The best fuel consumption they had got so far, was eight hundred and forty clicks from a full tank. It was not going to be enough, but Mitchie pointed out he had a long-range fuel tank, and good for another one hundred twenty kilometres. Plus they had the Jerrycan.

By the time LP shuffled opened his old map and checked if Mitchie was right, he just realised something important, when

Mitchie mentioned the Jerrycan - they'd forgotten to fill it up. It was only half full and only good for another eighty kilometres. They argued over the map and change of plan, as well, blaming each other for not filling the Jerrycan. Mitchie was already on the outskirts of town and he wasn't turning back.

Mitchie"s four-wheel drive would have to be very fuel efficient. On LP's calculations they wouldn't have a drop to spare before making it to Halls Creek.

LP reminded Mitchie, "You can't run a diesel vehicle bone dry, or you'll have to bleed the fuel line, let's turn back and get more fuel. We won't make it."

"You worry too much *'old man'*. We'll be able to get more fuel on the Tanami Track before it turns to dirt. The map shows a roadhouse at Tilmouth."

LP was still concerned with the change of plan, but as Mitchie approached the turn off for the Tanami Desert, LP said, "Let's do it." One hundred and sixty six kilometres later, they entered the roadhouse at Tilmouth, but it was closed. No one was there. It wasn't a township, just an old abandoned fuel stop surrounded by desert.

LP said, "I guess the old map was older than I thought. We'll stop here tonight and go back to Alice and fill up again, and this time fill the Jerrycan."

"Nope, we'll keep going. The map shows an aboriginal settlement about another hundred clicks down the track. We'll get fuel there." "The maps that old, the aboriginals will have gone on walkabout by now. It'll be deserted." LP said, with a concerned look on his face.

LP was not happy anymore, and could not persuade his son to wait until morning. Before leaving the old roadhouse LP went to the back of the vehicle, and pulled out a couple of cold beers. One for now, and one for later while Mitchie drove.

It was a two stubby trip, when, in the distance, they spotted a sign, you couldn't miss.

Last fuel for 740 km. The sign was the size of a roadside billboard with a large arrow pointing right to a smaller dusty track.

Mitchie said, "I told you. Nothing to worry about." "Really, look at the gauge. It's dropped under three- quarters.

There better be fuel there. Not abandoned like the last place." LP said.

Just a few kilometers down the road they entered the local indigenous township. Nothing flash but looked not abandoned. Homes could do with a lick of paint, but what stood out was their own Centrelink building for collecting government benefits. It was the best kept building they had seen in the township so far. Who ever worked in that green corrugated building, certainly would need air-conditioning on a hot summer's day.

LP made the comment, "That tin shed's spotless. I reckon when Centrelink people come out on pension day, they bring cleaners. I doubt if anyone else here would do it."

"Forget about the building. Look for a bowser." Mitchie said. It was still twilight, but time got away on them. It was six thirty when LP spotted an aboriginal man standing next to a small general store. Mitchie pulled up next to him, and looked out from his window that was down, and asked, "Where do we get fuel around here?" The answer was not what they wanted to hear, "Hey bro, no fuel here now. Come back tomorrow." "OK… tomorrow," Mitchie answered.

As he engaged the clutch and pushed the gear stick into first gear, he drove away slowly, not to stir up a dust storm.

Mitchie turned, glancing at '*old man*' saying, "I'll back track our way out of possible trouble. We're the only two white fellers here, from what I can see. We can't stay here tonight. It's an aboriginal settlement for locals only. I didn't see any signs about camping or accommodation, did you?"

One word summed up their situation, "Nope." LP replied. Mitchie drove back the way he came, and turned right at the sign that warned them of the danger ahead. LP looked on the map, did the sums again and said, "We need to find a rest stop and set up camp, and go back early tomorrow for fuel.

"I'm not turning back. We can make it." Mitchie was starting to sound like LP's old mate Bear - always over confident.

Minutes later, LP yelled, "Turn now."

Mitchie swerved off the track and stopped in front of a small sign that read: *Truck rest area. For your safety, no camping.* He thought that was odd, with an arrow pointing north, and below it, 33km. Nothing else was there, just red dirt.

LP needed to convince Mitchie they had to stop somewhere, but definitely go back for fuel. People die in situations similar to what they're about to get themselves into. They were ill prepared for what lay ahead, and what was fast approaching, tracking their way was a thunder storm. Lightning, in the distance, lit up the night sky. It was the worst time to travel with wallabies and kangaroos feeding on the side of the track eating sparse dry spinifex as tumbleweed blew across red dirt.

This storm had been building up since Coober Pedy, tracking slowly north to Uluru, and now it seemed it was going to bucket down on them. If that happened, the track would turn to mud. Stuck they would be, until rescued, and that could be a very long time, since they didn't tell anyone, they had changed their route, and now heading further into the Tanami Desert.

Mitchie drove away from the sign in the direction indicated. They might be light on recovery gear, but the Shu-Roos on the bullbar were working a treat. Mitchie's headlights acted like spotlights as ears pricked up from the high pitch sound coming off their vehicle only some animals could hear. Literately, wallabies bounded from the edge of the dirt track where they were feeding, away from what was bearing down on them. What the Shu-Roo's couldn't stop was the big reds hopping across the track in full flight. Only the bullbar would stop them, and that still would cause considerable damage to Mitchie's pride and joy. Luck was on their side. They reached the next rest stop without hitting any animals. Only two giant roos came out of nowhere. Mitchie's quick reaction slamming on the brakes avoided certain impact, and with the storm now tracking west, it was one less thing to contend with.

Eyes fixed on the new sign as Mitchie pulled off the track onto more red dirt. They looked at each other and couldn't believe what they were reading on a larger sign: *Truck rest area - For safety no camping.* This time arrows pointed north and south. Go back 33km or forward 73km.

Although there were no facilities like, toilets, BBQ or shelter, just a vast expanse of emptiness and the black night, peppered with white dots above. Mitchie wasn't going any further.

Mitchie spoke first, "We'll make camp here until daybreak."

LP pointed to the sign lit up by the headlights and said, "Look again at what's sprayed on it."

"ICU" Mitchie replied. "Fuck! this place is giving me the spooks already. After we eat I'm locking myself in the front of the *fourby.*"

LP was still going to sleep in the back. They had no weapons except their short handle axe and a large carving knife.

Mitchie picked up the carving knife and headed for the front driver's side door, stepped in, supposedly, to lock himself away from anything out there.

LP stepped up into his makeshift bedroom under the vehicle tray back canopy, with stars above to the horizon. As he wriggled up to put his head on a dusty pillow, he dragged the axe alongside. If anyone was going to try to drag him out by the feet, he was coming out wielding the axe.

As he lay on his side, he wiped red dust from the side window, and watched the stars give off a twinkle of light. His grip on the axe was tight. And to get his mind off the immediate danger, his thoughts turned to what to do with his book - *Image of the Past*, not the possible danger they were in. His conclusion seemed to be, bury it, leave it behind, and move on. He figured he'd spent enough time and money on it. Even though he was passionate and motivated to write it. He figured it was time to stop.

After drifting off to sleep, it wasn't long before something unexpected happened. Suddenly, he felt a tap on his right shoulder, sitting now upright. In shock, he looked out the back, and the tailgate lights were on. He pushed his way out holding the axe. Quickly, he went to check on his son to find out why - the headlights were blaring out to nowhere at twelve-thirty in the morning.

"Mitchie, Mitchie wake up, did you turn the lights on?" The window was down, and the carving knife rested against the passenger seat. LP reached in and switched off the headlights.

Again, LP yelled, "Did you turn the lights on?" Silence...

LP pulled the key out of the ignition as he stood next to the driver's door, and dropped it on the floor, and checked that his son was breathing. He could only hope the battery was not drained too much, and Mitchie's vehicle would crank over in the morning. LP couldn't make any sense out of what just happened. Maybe his guardian angel woke him, or his fortune telling skills were no so rusty after all, and still worked even when asleep. LP climbed back in under the canopy and plonked his head on a dusty pillow while gripping his axe tighter than before, just in case there was trouble out there lurking in the dark.

Sunrise started the morning with a display of red and yellow colours on the horizon as LP opened his eyes. He was up beat, after a restless night. He didn't really sleep much after turning the lights off. He stepped down from the back of the four-wheel drive and walked over to the driver's door and gave Mitchie a shake on the shoulder. "Wake up sleepy head. I bet you don't know what happened last night. I'll fill you in while I finish making something to eat."

"Nothing I hope. What are you making." Mitchie asked, while wiping his eyes, stretching his arms, and giving out a big yawn.

"Help pack up, so we can get a quick start after we eat what smells good." LP said.

LP opened the driver's door and picked up the key off the floor. Pushing it into the ignition he asked Mitchie to kick over the engine.

"Why? We'll waste fuel. You said pack up."

"Just do it. We need to know if it'll start. I'll explain later." Luck was on their side, as Mitchie's vehicle started to crank over with a blast of black diesel smoke from the exhaust, then he turned the engine off.

LP explained to his son what happened while he slept, and finished packing up, ready to head off while munching down a bacon and egg sandwich.

Both were back in the vehicle ready to head off when, LP said, "I've got something to do. Give me a sec."

He reached over to the back seat and grabbed one of his books - *Image of the Past.*

"I've just got to get the shovel out of the back."

"You should have thought about having a shit earlier. You're holding us up. Hurry up, and you don't need to take a book to read." Mitchie said.

LP started to dig a hole, but the ground was like concrete, as the shovel bounced off baked red dirt. He managed to get to a depth of ten centimetres. There he placed the book wrapped in alfoil, with a note in it, for anyone, if they found it. He filled the hole and kicked a dry cow pat over it, then went back to the running vehicle and hopped in, after placing the shovel back behind the cooler where he got it from.

They were on their way with Mitchie taking the morning shift on traversing the Tanami Track. As agreed they would change drivers every two hours or so. The driving was not so boring as they had to work the track, to avoid the corrugation from the dirt road not been graded for quite while. They owned the road, left and right and just let the vehicle drift when it hit loose sand. It was a bit like driving on the beach to Double Island Point.

There was no wrong side of the road out there, just more dirt stretching beyond the horizon that didn't seem to end, with patches of spinifex and the odd burnt out abandoned vehicle. They keep a sharp lookout for kangaroos, and wallabies that jump out of nowhere, or poisonous snakes, like, death adders waiting for the unwary to strike when stopped. Free range cattle posed a danger as well.

And surprisingly camels roamed the track too. Time ticked over in the morning without incident, while changing drivers at a cattle grid, and then a couple of hours later at a gold mine, with its own air strip for fly in fly out workers. No luck for diesel there only aviation fuel. LP continued to check the fuel gauge. Running the vehicle without air conditioning conserved fuel, and driving the vehicle with the revs between twenty-two and twenty-four hundred RPM, helped too. These measures should help get them closer to Halls Creek, and with a bit of luck arrive at the BP roadhouse to fill up.

"Look ahead we've got another sign, and the fuel light's on. I'll stop at the sign, and put the last bit of diesel in from the Jerrycan. I'm sure we're going to make it. There's still fuel left in the reserve tank," Mitchie pointed out.

In front of the sign, left no doubt why other signs read: *For your safety, no camping.* They were on the road to Wolfe Creek, known for its meteorite crater, but more so, for what happened to Joanna Lees's boyfriend. The cops still haven't found his body. People can just disappear out here and never be seen again.

LP and Mitchie stepped out of their four-wheel drive and surveyed the landscape. More desert, a dry creek bed, and more abandoned vehicles, and no shelter from the blistering sun.

Having assessed their situation, it looked like they were still in the middle of nowhere, low on fuel with another two and a half hours before reaching Halls Creek.

Mitchie pulled the Jerrycan forward from the back of the tray back while LP removed the fuel cap, then Mitchie started pouring diesel in, ever so careful, not to spill a drop.

LP was quick to put the fuel cap back on before taking over driving. He was trying to be upbeat about what they got themselves into, but had doubts if they'd make it to Halls Creek.

Mitchie placed the empty Jerrycan next to the cooler, and then grabbed two beers out before stepping back in next to *'old man'*. Mitchie's mouth was dry, and any amount of beer or water wouldn't wash the taste of the Tanimi Track from his mouth, but he'd give it a go. Even trying to peel the red dirt from his tongue by dragging his teeth on it, didn't help. With the windows down for most of their desert journey, dust entered the cabin, and was painted red, and you couldn't keep it out unless you wound the windows up, and that was not going to happen until they hit bitumen, and fill up, then they can turn the air- conditioning on and close the windows.

LP slowly accelerated trying not to spin the wheels and create a dust storm for more dust to choke on. It wouldn't be long before reaching their destination, and still no vehicles had passed them on the track all day, but up ahead may be their first encounter. It looked like a stationary vehicle. It could be another burnt-out wreck or someone stopped and in trouble. As they got closer, it looked like someone trying to wave them down for help, or could it be something more sinister.

"LP said, "I don't like the look of this. When we get up close I'll decide to stop or not. Remember what the signs indicated: *Don't stop.* Keep that in mind as we assess the situation."

LP slowed, as he approached an old Toyota Land Cruiser that had seen better days. What he could make out was three blokes, not aboriginal, but looked like young lost backpackers, and most likely clueless to what lay ahead of them.

Mitchie could see they were definitely backpackers in need of help, as one guy rolled a tyre away from the back wheel.

LP pulled up alongside them, and said, "Looks like you lot have got yourselves into a bit trouble out here."

"Yah, you have pump." His accent left no doubt who these guys were - German tourists. "We need for other wheel. It low too." "No, No" LP said, as he stepped out of his vehicle and inspected the other back tyre. It was half bagged out. "Can't help, turn back. Where you're heading you won't make it."

"We have fuel for three hundred K's. We good. Just need air." LP was not getting through to this lot, so he added, "Turn back, you need fuel for seven hundred K's. You die out here,"

while pointing in the direction they were going - Halls Creek.

LP had enough of this bunch of losers. Said no more, and stepped back behind the driver's wheel. Mitchie was already back in the passenger seat with his seat belt on.

LP looked back through his side mirror, and said, "We better report this lot to police when we get to the roadhouse. Who knows what their liable to do next?"

With no phone reception, the backpackers were on their own, and so were they, until they got within range of a communication tower. Mitchie pushed on keeping a close eye on the fuel gauge as they approached their destination, but it wasn't long before the red light came on, flashing; *fill tank.*

LP eyes focused on the red flashing light, and said, as he took a deep breath, "We're going to make with some diesel to spare."

Entering what they thought was a township turned out to be just a few houses, pub, roadhouse, police station, and school. LP pulled into the BP Roadhouse and stopped at the diesel dowser.

Mitchie wasted no time in filling up, as LP walked into the roadhouse and paid. Mitchie took over driving out onto the Great Northern Highway, after LP hopped in with two meat pies to share, he'd bought whilst in the roadhouse.

35

TIME TO RELAX

Back on track and hard bitumen their next stop would be Derby, and find somewhere to set up camp for the night. It would take at least six hours to get there. Mitchie reminded LP about contacting the police, and he said, "OK, I'll ring, when I finish my pie"

On a straight stretch of road across the top end of Australia, seemingly to have no end beyond the horizon, LP glanced down and picked up his phone, to find the phone number for the local police, and phoned. A woman answered, who he guessed was a cop and proceeded to tell her about the backpackers out on the Tanami Track.

Her question was, "Do they have water?"

LP's reply was somewhat sarcastic, "How would I know." "Backpackers, huh," she answered back, and then there was silence from the other end of the phone.

LP thought that was a bit rude. Possibly the signal dropped out, or maybe they get a lot call outs to tourists who just don't grasp how big this country is, and get themselves into trouble. You can travel on some byway's long distances without seeing anyone, for hours or days can be unnerving. Even the local aboriginals sometimes get themselves into trouble out on these arid desert tracks throughout Australia, and need rescuing, let alone tourists who have no local knowledge at all.

Six hours later after a couple of driver changes, LP had taken over driving at the turnoff for Derby at around 8:00pm. It wasn't long before they entered the township after a short drive. Mitchie gave directions to pull into the local caravan park. LP followed his navigator's instruction, and parked outside reception to book in. LP opened the driver's door stepping down onto a concrete pathway leading to a blue door. He knocked briskly, and was greeted by chap in P-Js answering the knock. "It's too late too book in. Find somewhere in the park and set up camp. Fix me up in the morning."

LP thought, *He's a trusting soul.*

LP and Mitchie were pretty tired after taking turns driving over fourteen hours from the Tanami Track to Halls Creek and onto Derby. Knocking down beers along the way didn't help. They both had a headache.

They pulled out some of their gear and made room to sleep in the back of the vehicle.

The finish line was getting close, after their challenging road trip with just another six hundred and fifteen K's south left to go, once they get to Broome. They survived the Tanami Desert, and Mitchie's Holden Rodeo never missed a beat, travelling over five thousand K's in six days, without punctures or overheating.

Next morning, they will be in no rush to get out of town as reception didn't open until 7:30am. Mitchie was up first and made a fresh brew of coffee, and opened a tin of spaghetti to share for a change. LP climbed out of his not so comfortable bedding still covered from the red desert dust. Everything needed to be washed, but that would wait until settling in at Port Hedland.

After something to eat Mitchie started up his vehicle, and they went for a drive along the main street of town. Then headed for the town jetty to check out if they could fish. No locals were fishing, as it was low tide, and the jetty looked like it was not good for fishing off at that time. They headed back to pay at reception and make tracks for Broome, just two hours away.

Arriving at Broome on the West Coast of Australia, Mitchie was excited at seeing the ocean again after so much dry land, and the first thing he thought of; *I want to fish.* Town Beach was not near the town, but was also the meeting place for the local aboriginals who were congregated under a large tree as the temperature hit unbearable. What Michie thought was unusual, or more to the point; a West Australian police four-wheel drive vehicle drove off the bitumen, and literally parted a group of about thirty locals in the shade of a large fig tree. One of the coppers spoke to some of them through the driver's side window. Out of earshot, Mitchie, while standing on the sandy beach, thought what he might be saying: *Drink here or cause any trouble to tourists, and we'll arrest the lot of you.* LP and Mitchie turned away from what was unfolding under the tree. It reminded LP of the Baobab Tree they stopped at on the outskirts of Derby.

It's about power and control. Nothing much has changed. You just don't see the chains.

Before British colonisation it was a ceremonial site for the indigenous local population. There, a tourist sign now told the story of what was an infamous part Australian history called: *Black Birding,* the forced removal of aboriginal men, from their traditional hunting ground, then sold into slavery. Old black and white photos depicted them chained together around the neck, with the Baobab Tree in the background, an aboriginal sacred site. LP's thoughts turned to his mate Brownie, thinking: *If he saw this, he'd want to hunt down those responsible and enact Aboriginal payback. But of course, he's two hundred years too late.*

Mitchie looked at LP and said, "What do you think. Are you keen on fishing? I want to try my new rod."

"What did ya say?"

"Fish,"

"Sorry, I was thinking of something else." LP replied. "Come on take your mind off everything. We made it. Let's just relax and unwind after six days of grueling driving," Mitchie said while pulling out his rod and tackle box from the tray back.

"Well, let's not relax too much." LP said, as he pointed to a yellow sign on the sand reading: *Recent croc sightings in the area BEWARE.*

"Ah, no wonder no one's in the water for a dip. I thought it was a bit strange, with those aboriginal kids only playing on the rock groin." Mitchie replied.

LP glanced back over to the shady tree, and watched a cop drive his vehicle slowly back over the gutter, leaving the local aboriginals standing on a patch of green grass. No one was arrested, but you could guess; they were warned, drinking alcohol in a public place will get them arrested, even if was their sacred site. The cops drove out of the car park without giving all the backpacker vans a second glance parked near the foreshore, as they headed back the way they came in.

LP grabbed his rod too, and both cast out using lures for bait, and waited for a bite. It wasn't long before movement from the water got their attention, as a dog jumped in, and of course, dog paddled, further out near their lines. Then another splash, as some guy dives in and follows the dog out into deeper water. There was hardly any swell, more like at a still lake stretching to the horizon - until now.

LP couldn't believe what he was seeing, and said, "Must be a backpacker who can't read signs."

"Backpackers huh." He'll need rescuing soon just like those Germans out on the track." Mitchie replied.

They reeled in their lines. It looked like the only thing they were going to pull in today was a backpacker, a dog or a croc.

After packing away their fishing gear, they headed back into town to buy more beer, and find somewhere to knockdown a schooner of the local brew. At the bottle shop LP paid for two cartons of Coronas and a bag of ice. He asked the attendant, "Hey, mate, where's the best place for a beer around here with a view over the ocean?"

He answered, while a security guard watched on, "Just go round the corner, and back up the main street. You'll see Castaway Resort. Out the back is a beer garden. Check it out. It's good for a coldie and the ocean's right in front of *ya*, mate."

After taking on local advice LP walked out past security, and placed six beers in the cooler with a bag of ice on top. He then put the remaining cartons next to the cooler, and followed the directions. Parking opposite reception, they walked in past the front desk at Castaway. Mitchie waved to the young girl there, and said as he walked past, *'old man'* "I'll have a Corona with lime, your shout."

LP walked around to the bar area as Mitchie went over to the edge of the beer garden overlooking the Indian Ocean. No problem finding a table, no one else was there, other then bar staff back where LP was ordering what his son wanted, and pouring LP a drop of the local brew. *'Swan Lager,'* the barmaid suggested. "It's what *'westies'* reckon is the best beer in the world."

LP had some bad news to report after talking to another barmaid while holding two beers. Placing the beers on the table he said, "You wouldn't believe this. The roads closed to Port Hedland."

"What the hell happened? Mitchie asked.

"You saw me chatting to the barmaids."

"Yeah, it looked like you were trying to crack onto *em*."

"Funny ha ha. No, there's fires burning on both sides of the highway south. One of my so-called girlfriends said, her boyfriend works on a road gang, and he can't make it back tonight. I'm off to check out what's the standby rack rate is if we stay here? We'll get an early start in the morning."

LP booked in for $140 overnight twin share. He figured it was good value for a luxury resort.

He walked back to Mitchie and gave him the good news, "We're staying here." After finishing his beer LP went back to their vehicle and drove into the resort, parking out front of their new home. They removed what they needed for overnight into their new luxury accommodation. Somewhat upmarket to what they were use too: Sleeping rough across Australia. LP was going to take full advantage of this delay in reaching Port Hedland. He grabbed two stubbies from the back of the four-wheel drive, and shouted over to Mitchie, "I'm having a coldie in the pool. Come over. I'm cooling off,"

Mitchie joined him in the pool, and chilled out with a cold ale in hand. Minutes later, Mitchie grabbed the attention of a barmaid in ear shot, "Schooner of Swan and a Corona, thanks. Put it on room 120."

LP had something to say about that, since he was paying. "Next shout. Go back to the cooler, and don't clock up anything more on my tab."

It wasn't long before their space was invaded by a couple young blokes that were staying in the resort. Mitchie struck up a conversation with them, and learnt a thing or two about them.

They were backpackers with a taste for luxury, and had plans for tonight. What would transpire later was the young ones would head down to the backpacker hostel for a wet T-shirt contest? LP was invited, but he passed on that.

LP was more interested in snapping a sunset and sunrise before leaving Broome. First, he shared a meal of noodles & beef stir-fry with his son. Mitchie's cooking skills were improving to the point that he might actually be able to fend for himself.

It wasn't long before there was a knock on the door, and Mitchie was off with his new-found mates to check out Broome's night life, then later head over to the local backpacker haunt for some fun, and maybe get to know the winner of the wet T-shirt contest.

Sunset wasn't until after 7:00pm so after the boys left, LP walked around the headland from where Castaway Resort was located. Finding the best vantage point, he positioned his tripod with his camera ready to snap the setting sun. Smoke from fires burning down south acted like a lens filter, to produce an image, like looking at a planet through a telescope.

Next morning, LP will be up before sunrise and anxious to get on the go, but first he would have some sunrise photos taken from the resort. After he finished his photo shoot and walked back up from the flat sandy foreshore, he called out to Mitchie,

"Get up lazy bones, let's get on the move to Port Hedland. "Let me sleep in. He moaned" That didn't cut it with *'old man'*.

"Come on, we can't waste time, and you can fill me in on what happened last night. You got in pretty late."

Mitchie didn't have much to say about out on the town, except, "You should have been there. Those foreign backpackers got big tits, especially the winner. I got to dry her off."

LP responded, "Sounds like I should have gone with you and your mates last night, but I would have missed sunset. Let's now try focus on getting to Port Hedland without any more distractions or delays. I'm driving, and I'll book out. I'll meet you at the front desk. Hurry up."

I've just gotta brush my teeth. Don't rush me," said Mitchie.

LP thought, *Son you would test the patience of a saint.*

He walked out the door. Started the vehicle and pulled up outside reception. Looking confident and refreshed LP walked up to the young receptionist, and commented, "This place is like heaven compared to we've been staying over the last couple of days.

"She smiled and said, "Have a safe journey. I'm in heaven everyday. Where you're travelling along next, will look like hell, from what one of the bar staff told me."

LP pushed their room key forward, picked up the receipt as Mitchie joined him from their overnight stay in paradise. Although, it looked like a clear run to Port Hedland, with blue sky above; it was deceiving. A north-easterly wind pushed smoke from the burning fires down south. Within a half-hour of travelling they were confronted with still smoldering scrub.

The receptionist was spot on. It looked like hell on Earth. Tree stumps glowed with red amber's looking like guide posts along a highway to nowhere, while smoke washed across parts of the roadway. Undeterred they pushed on along a straight stretch of road for hours, without a bend in sight. Another hazard to overcome, boredom and fatigue before reaching their destination.

They could tell they were close to Port Hedland when they entered an intersection you'd normally see driving into any capital, not a seaside township, but from this small township, developed the largest port in the world, exporting gas and iron ore around the globe.

LP pointed at the road sign above the highway and said quickly, " Turn left."

They arrived. They made it, and so too Mitchie's vehicle in one piece.

That afternoon Mitchie settled into his new abode. A small bedroom that needed painting, in a share house with four bedrooms. A filthy toilet, that LP scrubbed out before using. It was so bad it should have been condemned. The squalid kitchen was not much better and in need of a *reno*. One good thing was a full length covered patio at the back of the low-set house. Seven other workers would share the facilities, while they dream of earning the big money offered in Port Hedland.

Twenty-four hours later Mitchie dropped LP at the town airport for boarding a Qantas flight to Perth, then he'd connect with the red-eye flight, so called because it takes off at 11:30pm and arrives at Brisbane at 5:30am the next day.

LP said his good-bye and gave Mitchie a big hug, reminding him he was only a phone call away.

LP didn't leave Perth Airport. No time for sightseeing, he just checked in and waited for his flight. At 11:00pm, the boarding call for his flight brought him to attention and quickly followed other passengers onto his flight. He plonked himself down in the left aisle seat 53-D, after placing his carry-on luggage above.

Just before take off one of the young, pretty cabin crews greeted LP and said, "After we level off there's more room to stretch out up front. Business class is not full."

He figured she thought he was a bit cramped, after seeing him angle his left knee into the aisle and looking somewhat uncomfortable. Being helpful, she suggested moving up front, when the seat belt light turned off after takeoff.

36

NOSTRADAMUS'S PROPHECY

As the plane taxied down the runway, it reminded LP of bumping down the tarmac at JFK airport leaving New York behind in 2012. Thoughts returned to the question he asked himself back then; *Why! Why New York? Why, did the Scroll need to be delivered and be in water? Why, did he need to be there over Easter?* Part of the questions now could be answered, but others not: Why, fulfill the prophesy's from a sixteenth- century soothsayer that coded his writings and made no sense to most people or scholars, but hundreds of books have been written about him, and his visions of the future coded in quatrains.

Ding, the seat belt turned off. LP looked down to business class, watching the stewardess about to push a silver beverage-food trolley forward. He stood up, stretched his legs, and walked down the aisle, before she started serving passengers. He spotted a row of seats empty and shuffled himself along to the window seat. As he sat down he grabbed a throw rug, and pulled it over his somewhat out stretched body taking up all three seats, thinking: *Now this is comfortable.*

As he drifted in and out of sleep, his mind connected with his deeper self, that he now calls Lewis Philips, the writer, the visionary who sees the future, getting him out of many a life's threatening situation, and along with foresight, making decisions came easy.

What turned over in his thoughts relating to New York, was; for what reason did he need to be at Ground Zero in the first place, and deliver the scroll?

The site of destruction that had befallen the twin towers in Lower Manhattan, fits a quatrain of Nostradamus. LP thoughts were muddled, jumping from one line of thought to another. But what resonated, beyond leaving a copy of the Scroll at Ground Zero, and boarding the Staten Ferry, and dropping a second copy of the Scroll into the Hudson River to flow out into the Atlantic Ocean, still puzzled him. The fact that a quatrain related to LP's presence in New York, could justify for him, why travel there in the first place from Las Vegas, rather than, go back to San Francisco for sight seeing.

Firstly, Nostradamus, in his coded writings mentioned the new city that scholars believed was New Amsterdam - now known as New York. The quatrain goes something like this -

> *One will travel from the east*
> *and stand in the shadow of towers*
> *he will be marked on the face*
> *with a gap between his teeth, and bald.*

LP fitted the description above. He travelled from the east to the new city (New York) was bald, and had a gap between his teeth and a birth mark on his left side of his face.

Another quatrain was interpreted by scholars of medieval literature to predict the destruction of the World Trade Center twin towers. And there he stood at Ground Zero were once the towers stood tall casting shadows. It was an eerie feeling, an uncanny fit, that Nostradamus predicted, now it seemed to include LP. Was it coincidence, fate or chance, that LP stood at Ground Zero, half a world away from home?

His answer for why New York, was becoming clear. The image he now called Zero (the beginning of time) that became part of the Scroll coupled with the mantra, seemed to have some magical power when the image appeared while whispering the Mantra and looking at the Scroll. It seemed to unleash the power to connect with something greater than self - The infinite universe. Some say, Mystics and Prophets taped into what some describe as universal thought, connecting with future events, because it's happened else where in other worlds; parallel universes, and thus give warning to avoid disaster if heeded.

It's a long bow to draw, but LP was drawn to the conclusion that whatever we perceive God as: The true God, the eternal God of creation; or something else, is part of, but may well be beyond existence as we think, and thus uncomprehending to the human mind. The Scroll he figured is the prophet for our time, and LP delivered the Scroll to Ground Zero, and he thought this would bring peace and healing for those that lost love ones from the fall of the towers. Add in the symbolism of Easter, becomes a potent mix for renewal and forgiveness. And why did the Scroll need to end up in water? Well, LP assumed it was symbolic of baptism, to clean the earth of the poison of destruction, and now; one of the copies of the Scroll is immersed in one of the great oceans of the world flowing out from the Hudson River. LP's plan when arriving back in Australia was to allow another copy be taken out by the current into the Pacific Ocean from Dicky Beach. And with a trip across Australia unbeknown to him when in New York, he would again travel from East to West, this time across Australia to another new city, and cast another Scroll, this time into the Indian Ocean.

LP hadn't mentioned to Mitchie why he was so quick to volunteer to be his co driver across Australia, as it fitted in with taking the Scroll across the continent to Port Hedland, and leave it to flow out from the harbour as the tide was going out into the Indian Ocean.

More thoughts captured the memorable moments he enjoyed with Ingrid before returning to Australia via their five-day stopover in Los Angles to see Disneyland, Warner Brothers Movie World and Hollywood after leaving New York.

Ding, as the cabin light came on with the pilot saying, "We are starting our decent shortly, and touch down in Brisbane is on schedule. The weather is fine. Please fasten your seat belts. Cabin crew prepare for landing."

Four weeks went by before LP heard from his son unexpectedly. He answered his phone in bed, having decided to hit the sack early after not picking the Melbourne Cup winner that paid big time. His psychic skills were starting to let him down these days.

So, to help a good nights sleep; he knocked down a couple of Buds before retiring. That didn't help much either.

He was just starting to think about how Mitchie and him survived the Tanami Track, and made it to Port Hedland. All was good now, or that's what he thought, until the phone rang, hearing his son's voice.

'*Old man*', Mitchie here, "I've run into a bit of trouble." "I'm listening, but do realise, it's dark over here, and I'm in bed. First, I won't put you on speaker, for your mother to hear what you're about to say. You do remember her. She's worried sick about not hearing from you. Now what's up?"

"It's not what's up. It's what's down. I went for a fish. I've hit a sink hole at Pretty Pool, and the vehicles down to it axles like in quicksand." Mitchie said.

Pretty Pool is a spit of sand and mangroves jutting out from Port Hedland. It's a recreational area for fishing and driving on the beach. Venture further south, and it's an optional clothing beach.

"Have you phoned a tow truck mob," LP asked.

"Yes, one bloke came out while there was still plenty of light, and said he wasn't going anywhere near it."

"Look up to the roadway, I saw plenty of houses with four-wheel drives parked out front. I drove down to Pretty Pool in your vehicle on the Sunday morning while you were sleeping in. Go up and knock on a couple of doors and see if anyone will help you. As well, watch out for crocs. There were signs up on the road saying there were recent sightings."

Mitchie was getting frustrated with *'old man's'* advice. He phoned to let him know what was happening, not get a lecture.

"I can't talk anymore, the water is up to the doors, and I'm trying to salvage what I can. My phone will be the last thing I take out, when I pull the cord out of the cigarette lighter, then it'll be dead. And if I don't hurry... me too." Then there was silence. The phone disconnected.

LP shouted out, "Ingrid, I've just heard from Mitchie, and you better be sitting down when I tell you what's happening."

It was a restless night for both, hoping their son was OK. There was no other way to contact him. They didn't know who he was working for, or even a contact number where he was staying. His phone was their only link to him.

Next morning, after Mitchie was able to charge his phone, he phoned his father to give him the bad news. "The vehicle was swamped - it went under twice."

LP asked, " What are you going to do now?"

"I could do with five hundred dollar. They're slow payers on the new job site. I'll need it to pay the tow truck guy and get some new wheels.

"You'll need more than loose change for that."

"No, I'm getting a skate board to get around on until the insurance payout."

"Son, your living on the edge. I'll transfer the money today. Fix me up when your on top of things."

"OK, talk to you soon."

Just as LP hung up another call came through. He could see it was Bear, "How's it going. Still planning to climb Mt. Beerwah? "Yep, twenty third. Make sure you're fit enough to make it.

LP replied.

"Twenty third of what?

"January, that when the sun sets on the peak of Mt. Beerwah. That's when you'll find out what I've learnt from the Scroll."

"How's that bloody Archaea thing? I've done some homework. It's a fucking disaster just waiting to happen. Bloodly hell! What else have you unearthed about it?" Bear asked anxiously.

"Probably no more than what you'd find in Wikipedia. The only people who could shed some light on it may be climate scientists. It needs a peer review paper linking Archaea as a hot bed for global warming, as well, fossil fuels. Climate change deniers have sway for now, but they need to pull their heads out of the sand. Join the dots. Analyse the data and get on board with the rest of the population fixing the problem" LP answered.

"OK, that's a mouthful. I'll keep researching if I can find out more about these resilient ancient inhabitants of Earth, and let you know what I come up with, and how to keep these buggers buried for another billion years," Bear said.

"What I need to know, now. Are you good for 23rd? LP asked. "All been well I'll see you then," responded Bear, with a bit of a chuckle.

LP was happy to hear Bear was on side, now it was time to contact Mason at his Masonic Retirement Village, before he became part of the sedated retirement lot. He figured a face to face call will get a positive response. A phone call would be too easy to fob him off.

"Hi, could you let your CEO know I'm here to see him, thanks."

The receptionist replied. "And you are, and do you have an appointment?

"Just tell him it's LP. Your boss knows me."

LP was glad it wasn't the same receptionist Bear gave a hard time too, when he last asked the same question long ago. Hopefully, the old dear would be part of the retirement crowd, and recovered from the hard time Bear gave her back then, when he threatened to kill her if she didn't show them to Mason's office.

The young receptionist looked at LP, and nodded, then proceeded to walk with him to Mason's cedar paneled office door, knocking twice, then opened the door and let him in.

"Hi LP what's happening? Mason asked.

"Just letting you know Bear arrives on the 23rd. to climb Mt. Beerwah. I'm just here to make sure you're in."

"Last thing I heard the old bugger was using a walking frame to get around, but if he's in, I'm in."

"Good, bring your climbing boots. I'll be in touch." LP replied.

"Would it be too much too ask why are we climbing Brownie's mountain?

"Yes, you'll find out then. Just be there. 23rd. January. Put it in your diary," LP said.

Mason asked one other question before LP left. "Why is there some misunderstanding relating to the numbers and New Year's Eve?"

As you know, the numbers you revealed back at the ancient aboriginal site after you were struck by that deadly snake, and almost died, were 0101100000. We understood it to be the first day of the New Year - midnight - 0000, the year 2010. That being New Year's Eve 2009. That's where some mistook the date to be New Year's Eve 2010. Once it was explained that 0000 in railway or military time is the start of the next day, as well as midnight, then there is no issue. Anyway, New Year's Eve 2010 turned out to be pretty eventual as well. There was no mistake with the upload and download of the Scroll. No confusion if you take into account railway time. LP continued saying. "And you heard what happened on New Year's Eve 2010, so I won't repeat myself."

Next it was a phone call to Brownie when LP got back home from seeing Mason.

"Who is it. Speak up, you're breaking up, Brownie here." LP walked outside, but reception was still crackly. He shouted,

"It's LP, are you good for the 23rd. January for the climb up your Dreamtime relative.

The line dropped or he hung up from LP's sarcasm. LP wanted him there, because they'd been through so much relating to the Scroll, and wanted his mate's strong connection to the Dreamtime spirits of The Glass House Mountains. He would try to ring again. This time get straight to the point, before he hung up or dropped out.

That left Kato to contact. LP scrolled through his contact page and pressed on Kato's name.

"G'day mate, what's up?" was Kato's first comment.

"Are you up for climbing Mt.Beerwah on the 23rd. January?" "I'm up for an operation. Could go pear shape on the 1st February, so if anything going to kill me, it might as well be the mountain.

I know the way up. I'll be the guide as far as I can make it. Then you're on your own."

"I can't ask for more. I'll talk to you before then." LP replied with a sigh of relief.

LP rang Brownie again ."Where the fuck are you. You keep dropping out."

"Just driving on the outskirts of Charleville, thousand K's west of Brisbane.

"No wonder I can't pick up reception. Hey, all but you have given the thumbs-up to climb the mountain on the 23rd are you in?

"What mountain?" Brownie replied. "It better not be Mt. Beerwah."

"I'll leave you guessing. You'll need to be there to try to stop us, or be with us." LP answered.

"I'll see you then. What month? And we'll see who's climbing the mountain."

"January." LP replied.

Not exactly the response he wanted from Brownie as he, disconnected, but he' ll be there, LP thought.

Finally, he had his mates almost on side for the climb. With Brownie's secret knowledge to connect with his Dreamtime ancestors. Mason with his Masonic beliefs that puts him on a path to connect with his - immorality. Bear's never give up attitude, and Kato's climbing knowledge of the mountain should be enough to see LP reach the peak to make known - *For what I see, you' ll see. For what I know, you will know.*

The secret revealed within the Scroll LP had discovered was not what could be learnt, but what could be bestowed upon those with an open heart, peace, and forgiveness.

37

THE ARCHAEAN ANCIENT KINGDOM

LP"s view was not dissimilar about scientific consensus relating to climate change, and was somewhat in sync with experts in the field of studying global warming. Overwhelming they agree through peer review publications, and come to the conclusion - man made carbon emissions are contributing, and increasing the risk of further adverse climate change that will impact on civilisation throughout the 21st. Century. LP calculated in two other possibilities - global dimming from a three kilometre layer of greenhouse gas in the atmosphere, and methane producing Archaea seldom mentioned in mainstream thought relating to climate change. LP formed his own view, not peer reviewed, but still valid if researched - The greatest risk to our way of life are the ancient ones - Archaea. And warming oceans, already on the rise, and changing wind patterns in the northern Pacific, as the perma-frost melts in the Arctic accelerating the problem.

The awakening of Archaea and the thinning of the Arctic ice shelf will exacerbate global warming, and is a potent mix that will cause a rapid rise of methane in the atmosphere, thirty times more potent than carbon. Natural carbon sink holes can't absorb the burning of fossil fuels fast enough, let alone the release of unsustainable amounts of methane as well. With the planet's eco-system out of balance with the natural order of things of past centuries, methane, from thawing tundra, the ocean floor as oceans warm, due to the lower layer of the atmosphere radiating heat back to Earth, scientists refer to as; *the greenhouse effect,* a recipe for disaster.

Climate scientists have been vilified by skeptics and climate-change denialist. LP figured unless the fact that 97% of peer review research by scientists, in their field of expertise relating to factual current data, is accepted relating to global warming, and not negated by propaganda (fake news) peddled by media (social media) on behalf of big business, nothing will change. He hoped social media would get the truth out, and negate the influence of media barons who rely on advertising dollars from corporations, and hence vet any negative reporting that may impact on their clients. It's not their business to save the planet only report news that sells papers, hold viewers to the six o'clock news, and deliver a profit at the end of the day to shareholders.

It seemed obvious data relating to global warming has been suppressed and you could only hope the truth would get out somehow. It looked like even 100% consensus will not sway those with power and influence. What the public needs to do is get behind the facts, and protest for change, relating to scientific data from experts in their field of study (climate change) who overwhelming agreed through peer review publications, there is a real threat to civilisation as we know it.

LP's research on global dimming didn't negate global warming. What it meant is the sun is going through a period of lower solar activity, which would have plunged the world into a mini ice age, similar to the one in the middle of the last millennium, if not for carbon build-up in the atmosphere.

What has occurred more so in the northern hemisphere is the build-up of greenhouse gasses in the lower stratosphere.

Good for plant growth, but bad as the ocean warms, and the North Pole, in particular, melts, not so good news. What this also means as glacier's retreat and tundra in the north becomes exposed, algae like blooms will become more prevalent. The ancients; from the Greek word: Archaea are returning, and their contribution is methane, more potent than burning fossil fuels. If left unchecked will return the world to their kingdom like billions of years ago.

LP thoughts rolled back to 2010, a time of extreme weather, not only in Australia but throughout the world. It was Earth's most turbulent weather since 1816. The Amazon experienced its second one hundred year drought in one hundred years. With unabated clearing of the rainforest, the ability for it to remain a major factor in absorbing carbon, is under major threat through land clearing and burning. Its role in this complex biosphere is clear. It takes out two billion tons of $Co2$ out of the atmosphere a year. But due to drought in 2005 caused a net five billion tons to enter the atmosphere. The Amazon as well stores carbon dioxide in soil and biomass equal to almost fifteen years of human causing emissions, which may well be released if global warming measured by carbon in the atmosphere exceeds 350ppm (parts per million). It's already hit 400ppm in March 2015 in some parts of the world.

Pakistan was hit hard by flooding that killed thousands of people and displacing twenty million citizens.

Moscow scorched under its worst heat wave in late June. Extreme heat wave conditions in the Arctic is making it hotter than cities across Europe and North America.

2011 fared no better with drought, wildfires, famine, and earthquakes to name a few - Christchurch, New Zealand, and even worst, in Japan an 8.9-magnitude earthquake caused a tsunami engulfing Fukushima and taking out its nuclear power plant. It was estimated 15,000 people died.

Drought throughout East Africa impacting, Kenya, Somalia, Ethropia, Erithea and Djbouti in June and July caused wide spread famine accounting for deaths of tens of thousands of children.

The Philippines was hit hard in December, by a severe tropical storm bucketing down so much rain in such a short time, caused widespread flooding, and a death toll in the thousands.

In April tornadoes ripped through the Alabama region, causing severe damage and many deaths. And on May 22nd. another tornado destroyed the town of Joplin, Missouri.

2012 played out with more severe weather, fires storms and earthquakes.

In January of 2013 Cyclone Oswald struck the North Queensland coast, causing extensive property and crop damage North Queensland as well as major flooding. Severe flooding occurred after Mexico was hit by hurricane Ingrid, and in North America, Oklahoma bore the full impact of a severe tornado killing twenty-four people, destroying homes and infrastructure in May. Typhoon Haiyan more destructive and larger than Hurricane Katrina in 2005 caused a four metre storm surge in November resulting in wide spread damage to roads, water sanitation and infrastructure. The storm displaced millions of people and killed hundreds in the Philippines.

LP's view of these so-called natural disasters are not so natural. They are more intense and more often. Looking back over the past fifteen years and comparing statistical data going back over the past one hundred years, showed an increase in extreme weather, even taking into account the scientific view relating to Australia going through a one hundred year cycle of more dry than wet. This assessment was too simplistic in explaining away drought and wildfires as the norm. They were happening too often and more chaotic in nature - not only in Australia but throughout the world.

Without exception, 2014 brought more flooding in places like the Solomon Islands, Bosnia and Pakistan to name a few.

Typhoons hit the Philippines, earthquakes in Yannan Provence, China, and throughout the world billions of people were sensing something was wrong, and could be seen, expressed in anxiety and violence as the temperature rises. The climate looked like spiraling out of control. If you join the dots, you'd get; Global Warming, caused by man made burning of fossil fuels - creating the perfect storm.

News reports attributed heat waves in 2015 killing close to fifty five thousand people throughout the world. And it was predicted, heat wave activity will increase ten fold by the year 2100 if global warming is not abated.

2016 gave no reprieve from famine, earthquakes, fire storms, tornadoes, cyclones and typhoons across the globe.

38

STARS ALIGN

23 JAN. 2016

News on TV, in newspapers and social media were reporting on an astronomical event that will not be seen in the night sky again until July 2020, and who knows when on the 23rd of January again. LP was now joining the dots relating to the Glass House Mountains and the sun setting on the peak of Mt.Beerwah.

From Bulcock Beach vantage point at the mouth of Pumicestone Passage, LP spent many an evening there over the years capturing sunsets across Pumicestone Passage; looking to the Glass House Mountains on the horizon, in the laid back beach-side town of Caloundra. Those mountains formed from volcanic plugs, remnants of volcanic activity twenty six million years ago. Or as Brownie tells it from aboriginal folklore.

His mob lived by the sea, but retreated inland as the great waters swallowed up the rivers and streams. They took sanctuary in the deep forest. But there, Beerwah, Tibrogargan, Coonowrin and his brothers and sisters who were turned to stone after Tibrogargan turned his back on his son, Coonowrin, for disobeying him, by not helping his mother who was pregnant, and his siblings get to higher ground. Coonowrin only thinking of saving himself, caused the Rainbow Serpent of Dreamtime to turn them into stone, as a warning to all.

Now, LP had another story, and it goes like this -

In the beginning, he and his mates were entrusted with a Scroll at an ancient aboriginal ceremonial site in outback Australia, that involved the numbers, zero and one. Zero and one relating to a date in time, an image that some could see, and the secret knowledge that would unfold over time.

It was only in 2010 after the upload of the Scroll on New Years Eve that LP discovered the sun set on the peak of Mt Beerwah on the 23rd of January looking from Bulcock Beach. Another coincidence relating to numbers. But now, aware that the planets were aligning on the 23rd January 2016 as well as a full moon, things started to fall into place relating to something he had sketched many years earlier - A triangle drawn over a drawing of the setting sun on the peak of Mt. Beerwah exactly fitting over the sun. It was an equilateral triangle measuring twenty three millimetres. This sketch foretold the alignment of - Planets and Sun, as well as a full Moon rising on the 23rd January 2016. It was becoming clear these events were more than coincidence. And what was becoming clearer based on signs in heaven above, and on Earth, encompassed one thing - The peak of Mt Beerwah. Not only did the sketch reveal something new. It also revealed a facial image on whatever angle you moved the page. It was a strange drawing LP had done, since he didn't intentionally draw the image. It just appeared as a ghostly aberration.

What had been on his mind for more than a year was to reach the peak of Mt.Beerwah, and make known what else could be revealed from the Scroll? That time was approaching. All would be revealed on 23rd. But obstacles arose causing LP to contact his mates, days before they planned to climb to the summit.

Bear wasn't impressed when he heard the news, since he'd already booked his flight, and wanted to know what date, he could change his ticket too. LP told him to hold off booking another flight just yet, because his daughter was about to arrive from Cairns on the same day of their planned climb, and he had to pick her up.

What he didn't tell everyone, Ingrid reminded him their granddaughter's birthday party was on the 23rd. This was about to become an issue on reaching the summit by sunset, and being there when the planets align.

It was made perfectly clear by Ingrid; he was to be present for their granddaughter's party, and pick up their daughter from the Brisbane airport that morning. There will be no time for going off with his mates climbing Mt. Beerwah.

LP tossed over in his mind how he could get a compromise out of Ingrid, and still reach the peak of Mt. Beerwah as the sun set on the 23rd. January. Impossible he concluded, but he had a light-bulb moment: *Pick up his daughter at the airport, drive to the car park at the base of the mountain. Walk and climb a third of the way and leave his latest book - I Am The One, Lewis Philips with a hand- written message on the inside cover for someone to find.*

He hoped when someone removed the shrink wrap and read the message inside, it would go viral through social media for all the wrong reasons. It needed something more added. But it would get his book noticed and potentially a book deal beyond been self published. All he needed was someone to take it up the mountain.

He'd already penned a few words on a yellow post-it note, and stuck it on the cover before shrink wrapping. It read:

> *Whoever picks up this book,*
> *please take it up the mountain*
> *and leave it there.*
> *Thanks,*

So if he couldn't climb it, he was going to be there one way or another. What he would do is ring around to get a flight over the mountain on sunset. Helicopters no go, but he managed to contact a pilot whom he had flown with before in a Waco replica 1938 single engine open cockpit bi-plane. It seated two in the front and one behind for the pilot.

Rodney remembered the last time he flew with him, and gave instructions on what time to be at the airstrip. Weather permitting, take-off would be 4:45pm. The forecast was for thunderstorms in the afternoon. Rodney only gave a fifty, fifty chance of taking off from the tarmac if the weather didn't improve, as well, he would be pushed for time with an engagement party to attend later.

The day arrived to pick up Nicky from the airport, about a one-hour drive from the Sunshine Coast. Ingrid and LP would pass the Glass House Mountains on the way to the airport, following the Bruce Highway and turn off for the domestic terminal. Minutes from the airport the phone rings.

LP pressed speaker and answered, "Hi Nicky, are you at the pick up area?"

"Almost," she answered.

"We're just about to pull up in the black Cruse. I'll flick my lights on." LP said.

No time for small talk, Nicky quickly opened the back passenger door, threw her carry-on case in, and followed, slamming the door shut.

"Let's get out of here. It's bedlam," she said, "Love you for doing this. You know I could have caught the bus."

"Wouldn't have it. Anyway, I've got a surprise for you." LP replied.

What is it? Nicky asked.

"I'll tell you when we get to the base of Mt. Beerwah." LP said. "Mum, what he up to?"

"I'll let him explain," Ingrid said.

"It's not dangerous so long you follow me and don't touch anything you're not suppose too." LP said while looking at Nicky in the rear vision mirror, giving her a reassuring wink and smile.

Ingrid was not sure what he was up too either, but it better not interfere with their granddaughter's birthday party, or she'll not be happy.

The pick up area had only one rule. Don't park and wait. Just pick up or get fined by over-zealous traffic controllers. Forget about road rules it was every man for himself or woman. Road rules went out the window there. The only thing that mattered was, pull over, pick up, and get out as quickly as possible.

"Hang on," *LP* said in a loud voice: *While thinking it's like driving dodgems at the local theme park.*

He accelerated from the gutter swerving to miss in coming and out going traffic chaos, and headed back onto the highway heading north. First stop Mt. Beerwah.

Mother and daughter chatted while LP drove, tossing over in his mind his plan when they reached Mt. Beerwah.

"Anyway, what happened about Mitchie's vehicle? Nicky asked. "Insurance crowd are slow on paying out. Its been eight weeks and still no payout. We'll know more next week." Said Ingrid. After crossing the Pine River bridge on the outskirts of Brisbane, traffic congestion was still heavy. By the time they approached the Steve Ewin Way, to fork left, it wasn't long before they passed the car park at Mt Tibrogargan. Turning left at the next intersection, and sharp right at an old 'homestead' and they'd be almost there. Little traffic now, just woodland with a sprinkling of homes, cattle properties and macadamia plantations; a photographer's paradise to drive through. While passing Mt. Coonowrin on their right, suddenly LP crossed to the opposite side of the road braking hard on loose gravel. Cattle had moved up close to the fence line twenty metres from the roadway. He quickly stepped out from behind the wheel with his Olympus camera in hand, and trodded his way through long grass, while keeping a sharp eye out for any surprises - snakes under foot, and spider webs at eye sight level. The cattle were inquisitive and approached closer. LP aimed his camera, and clicked off in rapid fire to capture a perfect shot of good breeding stock, with Mt. Coonowrin in the distance.

Back in the Navara LP said to Nicky, " That would be a top photo to paint. I'll send it to you."

"Thanks Dad, I've almost finished painting the one you texted last month. You know it's nicknamed - Crookneck." She opened her phone and showed him the painting she was working on.

LP nodded and said, "Looking good, I'll buy it when finished." Twisting bends on narrow bitumen lay ahead as LP accelerated away whipping up a trail of dust behind him.

"We're almost there. The mountain turnoff is just past that macadamia plantation, where the dirt road forks." LP said with confidence.

LP stopped in front of a sign depicting what you can and can't do when climbing the mountain, or walking the trails.

He turned to Nicky and said, "It's your birthday on the 23rd of March, so just in case we don't catch up then, here's a birthday surprise. We're going to climb up part of the mountain. I know how you love hiking, and then, in the arvo we'll fly over Mt Beerwah on sunset. It's an early birthday present for you. How goods that?"

"I can see how we'll walk the mountain trail, but fly over it, in what?"

'If I tell you, I'll spoil the surprise. Let's do this first." LP said.

What he didn't say as well, was, why he put his novel titled: *I Am the One*, in his small backpack along with his camera and bottled water. He would fill Nicky in on what he planned to do, after they walked and climbed the trail to a location that presented a challenge, to climbers to proceed to the peak. There he would explain what his intentions were, then and only then.

Ingrid said to her daughter, as she, and LP started to walk away. "If it gets dangerous don't listen to your father, turn back." "It won't be a problem Mum. I've done plenty of back-packing on trails in Asia. You wouldn't want to know about the obstacles encountered there. Don't worry." Nicky replied, as she gave her mother a reassuring hug before walking away.

Nothing was going to stand in LP's way. He was following through in getting his book with the message written on the inside cover to the peak. The hand-written message contained inside the cover made a statement; *for what he knows, you will know,* but there's more to be revealed in his book. All he needed to do was get it noticed in a big way, one way or another.

Even though LP buried the original book titled; *Image of the Past,* in the desert hoping that would end it - it wasn't over. He was motivated to write again and continue his story in Book 3 book titled: *I Am The One - Lewis Philips*, detailing his journey of discovery relating to the Scroll, spanning four decades. Firstly, travelling down south to Bells Beach with his mates for a surf contest in Australia, while been perused by bikies that wanted to kill them. Bear and Brownie confronted the Bad Meadows bikie gang on a lonely stretch of highway; outnumbered big time won, the battle. George disappeared mysteriously after been shot by Herbertsin, a crooked cop. Red was never seen again after his canoe capsized in rapids at Big River, after discovering a gold nugget weighing over three kilos. Cassa, LP's albino mate didn't make it out of Asia alive. And Kato, inventor, hindered by government once authorities found his invention saved eighty percent off power bills, was always the skeptic. He kept LP grounded and not let him get too over excited with his mission in life; to finish what was started back at the ancient aboriginal site in *Outback* Queensland; *to save and deliver the Scroll.*

LP's journey to New York to stand at Ground Zero and deliver the Scroll, in the end, didn't go exactly as planned.

Mason helped with advice with his connection to Masonic beliefs, and how to achieve his brand of glorious immortality.

Without Brownie's Dreamtime connection with the legend of the Glass Mountains, LP would not be standing before the mountain to climb it.

LP travelled through many parts of the world, but his journey always ended back at the mountain. Now destiny awaits again.

LP and Nicky trekked through dense forest, following the trail to a place on the mountain LP had visited many times before. He knew the lay of the land to that point. Three hundred paces from the car park to a clearing, and BBQ area, then another seven hundred before a full assault on the mountain.

Brimming with confidence, LP pushed on followed by Nicky, after stepping up some well placed stones, where fresh water trickled down. And there it was, the peak in sight, with low cloud moving across the top of the mountain.

LP said to Nicky as they stepped onto flat ground, "We can't stay long. Read that sign over there."

Nicky repeated what she saw, "Beware, rock falls, do not wait in this area."

LP went on to say, "Let's make it quick. I want you to take a short video of why I'm leaving this book here. And hopefully someone will pick up the book and take it up the mountain."

He pulled out his camera and book from his backpack, and handed Nicky the camera while he held his book in his right hand. LP then said, "Nicky turned the camera on to video and when I say start, click the left hand top button to record."

As Nicky was about to film, three strangers approached from where they had just walked. LP thought, *This could be good or bad. Are they Herbertsin's cohorts or just blokes out to climb the mountain? Paranoia was stating to set in. He needed to act fast.*

"Hey guys, are you planning on climbing to the peak," LP asked cautiously.

The answer was what he wanted to hear. All three answered, "Yes."

"Can you do me a favour. Take this book to the peak and leave it there," asked LP.

They looked puzzled as they watched on, as LP explained why he was doing what he was doing, as Nicky filmed. He then handed the book to one of them entrusting its contents to reach the peak before sunset on the 23rd. January 2016. LP and Nicky walked back the way they came, with LP hoping what he had put in play would make a difference, in a world he saw spinning out of control.

In eye sight of his vehicle, he heard Ingrid shout out, "Hurry up. About time, We've got a birthday party to attend, and help prepare some party food for the kids. Are you satisfied now? I don't want to hear any more about the mountain?"

"Not quite satisfied. You well know. I have a second surprise. Me and Nicky are going to fly over the peak of Mt. Beerwah on sunset. Happy Birthday for the 23rd.

"What's dad on about?" Nicky asked.

"I'll let him explain."

"I've booked a flight for both of us in a 1938 Waco open air cockpit bi-plane. This is your birthday present for March. We'll fly over the peak of Mt.Beerwah on sunset after your niece's birthday party, weather permitting. How goods that?" LP said with a confident smile.

"I'm up for it." Nicky replied with a wide grin.

Everything was starting to fall into place, and it looked like he and his mates wouldn't need to climb to the peak after-all.

LP hoped this would be enough, by just leaving someone else to take his book up the mountain, and when opened, reveal what was hand-written in the book for all to know, and get some publicity for his book.

LP placed his backpack back on the back seat leaving the rear left door open for Nicky to get in. He was back behind the wheel and heading home, happy that his first part of his mission was completed.

Later, if the pilot gives the OK, Nicky and LP would be flying over Mt. Beerwah on sunset. Mission accomplished. So he thought.

LP was starting to get impatient. As much as he wanted to be there for his granddaughter, his thoughts were fixated on flying over Mt. Beerwah on sunset. Time was running out. It was nearly four-thirty in the arvo with thunderstorm heads brewing in the north, and south west. BOM weather radar on his phone confirmed storms approaching from the west, and it looked unlikely they would clear, for take off from Caloundra airstrip. Luck would be on their side. The weather gods shone on them as they stood on the tarmac, with their pilot, as they looked for clear sky over the Glass House Mountains. No radar or weather report would dictate a decision by the pilot. It was his call based upon the weather conditions as he saw it at that time. LP and the pilot remained on the tarmac waiting until the sun broke through storm clouds on the horizon, while Ingrid and Nicky exchanged small talk just inside the hanger. It was forty-five minutes before the setting sun could be seen through the low menacing storm clouds.

"Right, we're good to go." Rodney, their pilot said.

He instructed his passengers to climb up and squeeze into the front cockpit with just enough room for two people.

He then followed and positioned himself in the rear cockpit and would fly the plane from there. Instruments in front of LP and Nicky were disengaged, but the pilot still warned not touch anything, or he could lose control of the plane. Rodney waved over his mechanic to give the propeller one big heave down to crank over the engine, that sounded like a car backfiring as it started to roar. Moments later, they were in the air heading a straight course to Mt. Beerwah. The storm clouds had now dissipated somewhat and within five minutes they were flying around the mountain, and over it, as the sun sunk below the distant horizon. LP got what he wanted. An incredible sunset full of colour, and Nicky was really excited at witnessing a spectacular display of nature, as thunder and lightning strikes could be seen to the south and north as Rodney turned the plane around, pointing it in the direction of Caloundra Airstrip. LP continued to snap photos by holding his camera in reverse and hoped he'd capture the amazing colours of sunset and engulfing storm.

There was no room to turn around in the front cockpit. It was just guess work if he'd capture anything worthwhile for posting on Twitter or Facebook. After looking at one photo as the plane was about land, it looked like they were not alone at that moment in time.

Landing with a smooth touchdown and taxiing down the runway brought their day to a magic ending. Nicky was over the moon, a full moon at that, with what she had experienced, and LP was thankful everything ended almost to plan.

They thanked Rodney for a great flight, and he replied, "I should be thanking you. I've never seen a more spectacular sunset ever in all the time I've been flying over the Glass House Mountains. Email me a couple of photos. I'd love to add then to my Facebook page."

39

THE MOUNTAIN CALLS

Six months passed, and nothing was reported about finding LP's book on the peak of Mt. Beerwah, with the message enclosed. Something must have gone astray. Did the guys entrusted with LP's mission fail to leave his book at the peak? Did they turn back and keep the book, or maybe it was thrown from the mountain? There was one other possibility, two giant eagles soured above the mountain every day, and something shiny might attract then, and possibly one of them took it back to their nest.

LP decided on a new time to climb the mountain to see if he could find out what happened to his book. He contacted all his mates and told them the new date - 23rd. January 2017. Lock it in, he said to them all.

The new plan, had finally come together, and he would find out if the young blokes had delivered his book back in 2016, and left it on the peak to be found.

LP's mates all met on Sunday, at Bears old beach house the day before the climb. Not so old since the renovations started. All knew how to get there with a short drive along the beach to the small township at Teewah. LP greeted Bear, first with a firm hand shake and a hug, next Brownie, Kato and Mason.

386

Together they would end what was started all those years ago at the Bora Ring in *Outback* Queensland.

Bear did some reminiscing and said, "Love this old place. It's full of stories."

"Yeah, like the time we had that confrontation with Nutter and his mad bikie mates, Mason said.

Bear answered pointing at the doorway, "I thought we weren't going to make it out alive as I summed up the situation that day. From what I could see we were outnumbered ten to one."

"But mate, you were fearless confronting Nutter." LP responded.

"I had Nutter bluffed and put on a pretty impressive front. That just gave us enough time to get out of there, and catch up with Brownie waiting in the back street before the house exploded."

"Better late than never," Brownie said with a bit of a chuckle. "And you did a pretty good job on the *reno*."

"Pity Red's not here, he'd like hearing that story again, and seeing what you did to the old place since last here" LP said.

Bear responded in a soft voice. "I still feel responsible for losing Red down the rapids at Big River. I got the gold nugget, but it wasn't worth it in the end. I shouldn't have got him involved. If I hadn't picked him up in Melbourne and taken him on a gold hunt, he'd be still alive today."

"Don't be too hard on yourself, Red was a risk taker, if it wasn't then, it would have been somewhere else." LP said

"Yeah you're probably right, now what the plan." Bear asked. LP went through his idea on how to proceed, but wanted input on making sure all would make it to the peak. If everything goes to plan he figures they'll make the news big time.

"LP you should be more up front with us. Is that all you want to do," asked Brownie. He knew that there was no way of stopping LP from going ahead with whatever he was on about, so he figured he'd better tag along and keep a watchful eye out at his ancestral home.

"No there's more, but not to worry I'll handle it." LP said to everyone.

"This is not an easy climb at our age. In our younger days not a problem, but now we'll be pushing it." Bear said.

Mason had something to add. "You've seen the news reports lately and just about every second week someone's taken off the mountain by state emergency rescue guys."

Kato spoke up while sitting on the lounge room couch, "I've climbed it when the mountain was closed after the rock falls. It's easier now, but still dangerous if you don't know what you're doing. LP if you want to be on the peak by sunset on the 23rd we'll need to allow an hour for the accent and fifteen minutes to get back down."

"That doesn't add up." Mason pointed out.

LP ignored his question and nodded in agreement, then speaking to everyone, "Firstly, I'll point out how it's going to go down or should I say, go up!" When we reach the peak, we'll find my book, second, we upload the evidence of Herbertsin shooting George to social media, third, upload the Scroll and mantra too. Finally, explain what was hand-written on the inside front cover of the book, then capture a sunset photo. Simple as!"

LP had been taking sunset photographs across Pumicestone Passage from Bulcock Beach looking to the Glass House Mountains for the past seven years. His patience would pay off one day, on the 23rd. January and snap the perfect sunset photo as the sun set on the peak of Mt. Beerwah. But this time he'd be standing on the peak on the 23rd. Sunset at 6:42pm and allowing for fifteen minutes as the colours of sunset change, would still give them time to descend with enough light.

Kato spoke next to answer Mason's question, "I agree, I've timed it. It's possible to get down the mountain in fifteen minutes, but we'll need extra time to do all the things you said LP. We'll need to leave fifteen minutes earlier. Delaying decent after sunset is pushing it. It will be dark as we walk back the last seven hundred metres, so we'll take small LED torches, the latest innovation in lighting. At the hardest part of the decent will be made easy, as LP pointed out, by wearing denim shorts, and we'll need to be on our arses sliding down, digging in our climbing boots on rock to stop us tumbling down. It's almost impossible to stand and descend after passing through the limestone cave, and without light, too dangerous."

Bear scratched his head, looked over at LP and said, "What book? What's it doing on the peak?"

I don't want to go into it now. All will be revealed soon enough, LP replied.

"OK, but I don't think I've got the right gear for climbing." Bear didn't have proper climbing boots nor denim shorts. LP wanted to reassure everyone, "clothing and footwear wasn't a problem, just cut the legs of your jeans, and runners are OK for climbing."

The next day, Monday the 23rd. they all bundled into LP's 4x4 off-road vehicle, leaving Teewah Beach behind and headed for a turn off, from bitumen onto dirt, leading them to Brownie's ancestral home, the forest surrounding Mt. Beerwah, mother of Dreamtime folklore.

Brownie, Bear, Kato, and Mason were silent. LP could sense that his mates doubted why they needed to climb Mt. Beerwah. He hoped they wouldn't back out on what was agreed, even though they all had their health issues, could give them good reason not to go with LP.

LP slammed on the brakes stirring up a dust storm. In front of LP's Navara was another sign, this time depicting what you can and can't do when climbing Mt. Beerwah. Nothing had changed since he was last there with Nicky. The mountain was still open for climbing, and being a weekday, few other people would be climbing, especially in the late afternoon.

Bear was first to break the silence. "Are you sure this is a good idea. Look at the photo, that's no rock fall. It's boulders tumbling down where we're supposed to climb."

LP responded, "Yep. We've been through worst shit before, remember back when we lost George, and the rock fall back then. That's past, and we are now in the future and it's been cleaned up now. The mountain is open for climbing."

Brownie had a question on his mind. "Hey bro, do we worry about Herbertsin anymore, after what happened at New Year? What if he's gotten wind of what we're about to do today."

"Forget about him. It's been over seven years since he wanted to kill us. If he thought, he could, he would have done it long ago. I've got the evidence of him shooting George. Today is his day of reckoning. I've got it on a memory stick with me now, plus the video on my phone to upload later. That's our insurance, our get out of jail free, and his ticket to jail." LP replied with confidence.

Kato was at the back of the vehicle pulling out what was needed for climbing. Five bottles of water and ten metres of climbing rope and shackles, if needed.

All had their smart phones, climbing boots or runners, and wearing denim shorts as LP requested. They were prepared for the climb. Before LP locked the Navara, he grabbed his small backpack out. It just had room for his iPhone, book, a copy of the Scroll shrink wrapped, and squeezed his water bottle in, then gave the key to Brownie for safe keeping. They then headed single file along a narrow pathway engulfed in forest with sunlight filtering through. Three hundred paces brought them to a clearing with table, chairs and BBQ covered by an awning. From there they could see the peak as low white cloud slowly drifted across. As well, two eagles soared above the summit.

It reminded LP of the Great Eagle in the rock face of the Grand Canyon, that kept a watchful eye on the first peoples of the Americas. He hoped this was a good omen.

"Let's push on," said LP, while pointing to another track leading into more dense forest. This part of the climb he knew well. The incline was starting to get steeper and LP could hear heavy breathing behind him. It was already becoming a struggle for some of them.

LP raised his hand and said. "We'll stop for a few minutes and catch our breath."

The guys looked relieved - crouching down catching their breath and lowering their heart rate.

"OK, take a few deep breaths, not much further to the next clearing, and then we can take another break. Let's go" LP commanded.

Now they were within sight of their quest, as clear water trickled down the last forty stone steps. They could see the next clearing as they looked up at sheer rock, their next obstacle to assail. Kato's knowledge would come in handy now. He'd climbed this part of the mountain many times before.

LP said to Kato, "You lead, you know the way best." Leaning forward with the climbing rope over his right shoulder, Kato leads the way up. No need for rope yet. If needed it would be on the descent.

Kato was now in sight of the cave opening, and turned his head to those behind him and said, "Not much further guys to the limestone cave. It's just ahead. When we enter we'll rest again."

Kato was really pushing himself. He knew he couldn't make it to the summit. He was going to keep the rope with him at the cave. The entrance would be as far as he's going. He questioned why he was doing this at all. But he knew - mateship. He would wait until they came down and help, with the rope if need be.

They entered the cave, all looking up, seeing creamy stalactites hanging from the cave ceiling like daggers. It gave them all an eerie feeling as they looked around the walls, depicted in aboriginal drawings from Brownie's ancestors.

Brownie was not only feeling the strain of the climb. He was spooked. He knew he shouldn't be there. It's a sacred site for his mob. And he now knew; he should have taken heed of the warning from the custodians of this place. The sign also read in front of where LP pulled up. *In respect to the elders and folklore of the mountains, please do not climb.*

Brownie called out to LP, "Sorry mate I can't go any further or bad shit is going to happen. We'll end up like *Tibrogargan* - stone dead."

"Bullshit. Your taking Dreamtime to far, but it's your call. If anyone else wants to turn back, go with Brownie," LP answered.

Bear who was tough as old boots but was feeling the pain. This climb had challenged what he thought he was capable of. In the old days, he was fearless, but age does weary him. What he thinks he can do, his body is no longer up to it. He will turn back as well.

That left Mason to have his say. LP looked over to him and asked, "What's your excuse for not following me?"

"Don't second guess me. I've followed you this far. We all have, and I'll follow you to the peak. I'm not exhausted. I feel great. I've been working out in the gym at the Masonic Retirement Home after work."

"That's good, but if you change your mind, I have a selfie stick for a live feed on my phone. I can do this alone if I have to.

Now, I'll be quick. Sunset is approaching. What I have to reveal is about immortality." LP replied Bear butted in. "I knew you were fucking crazy."

"Let me finish," LP shouted. "At times I'd have to agree but hear me out." He then continued in a soft calm voice.

"You know what we've all been through in saving the Scroll." They all nodded in silence.

"You all have seen the image within the Scroll." Again, they nodded.

"And we all know about the mantra relating to the Scroll." Again, they nodded.

"Well, I've looked into the centre of the Scroll revealing the facial image, and whispered the mantra daily since returning from the Teewah Beach houses, after what happened back on New Year's Eve," said LP.

Bear blurted out. "Yeah, shit happens, Herbertsin and his cohorts are still out to get us?"

"Stay with me on this, I have something important to repeat. Before whispering the mantra one morning."

> *May the healing spirit of g0d*
> *through the enlighten One*
> *rest upon y0u*
> *and all who you*
> *come in contact with*
> *in peace.*

LP continued. "I had a feeling of dread, and of my mortality and a feeling of nothingness. Then there was a flash of intense white light that saturated my whole body as I started to whisper the Mantra. At that moment, I connected with my immortality. Not this mortal life, but the knowing. The part of God, my soul, will go back to God. I have no fear of death, because I've been blessed with the knowing. *Not scripture. Not faith. Just the knowing.* It's just impossible to fully explain in words - I only have belief."

Mason said. "That's a big call, but I believe *ya*, I too yearn for glorious immortality along with my Masonic brethren."

LP had something else to add, "What I discovered relating to the mantra is it has twenty three letters in the first line and twenty three words in total."

"OK, another coincidence with numbers. We'll talk about that later. What actually are you going to do when you reach the summit? Is it about Herbertsin?" Bear asked

"Yes and no. The memory stick in my pocket is not just insurance it's payback time for Herbertsin. I have a copy ready for a live feed on my phone to social media, as well, deliver a message for all the world to hear."

Mason, we're running out of time. We'll push on to the summit. It's only a half-hour before sunset," LP said.

He instructed the guys to head back down, but they would defy him, including Brownie, who may well bring the wrath of the mountain upon them all, if he didn't appease the ancestral spirits of this ancient land: *Leave this sacred place now.*

LP and Mason started walking deeper into the cave, exiting through a large crevice to a tall stand of forest on the mountainside. They traversed up along to the edge of the cliff face with just enough rock under foot to get a foothold.

Kato's rope would come in handy now, but there's no turning back, LP thought.

Looking ahead LP pointed to another worn track leading further up, and twisting around to who knows what? What confronted them was the edge of another challenging rock face. Looking up from that vantage point, they could see the summit only few more minutes climb away.

LP struggled to concentrate on his footing. One wrong step would send him over the edge, if he didn't blank out thoughts of what he was going to do, when he reached the summit.

Mason shouted out. "Face the rock. Don't look out, just look at your feet and grip the rock face, and move one foot and one hand at a time. They shuffled along making it to the peak. There they stood looking out over a panoramic view of the coast and mountains, with the setting sun soon to drop behind the mountain range in the distance. Now, LP had little time to waste. He reached into his small backpack, moved his bottled water aside, and pulled out his iPhone and a copy of his book.

Mason looked at what LP was doing, and asked? "What's first on our do list?

LP replied, "I plan to kill two birds with one stone."

Mason replied, "Look above, I think you might need more than one stone. Those eagles soaring above look like trouble if you ask me." "What I mean is I'm going to reveal the message hand-written on the inside cover of my book. It should have been revealed by now by the guys, I entrusted my book too. Can you see anything up here that looks like this book cover?

Mason looked around and sighted nothing at first. Then he spotted something over in a crevice of rock at the edge of the peak. Mason took a couple of paces to the edge of the mountain, and pushed his hand down and grabbed it with his thumb and fore finger, and pulled it out carefully, handing it to LP.

It was LP's book he entrusted to the young blokes. It was still in shrink wrap, and LP wanted to add to what was already hand-written, but time had run out.

"Well, let's get on with it, hand me your phone, and stand side on to the sun. It's just dropping behind clouds on the horizon," Mason said, with an anxious tone in his voice.

"Are you expecting a call?" Mason looked at who was trying to contact them.

It was Bear.

"What's up? Are you off the mountain yet?" Mason asked. "Shut up." He yelled. "Listen, Herbertsin's just passed the cave. He's on his way up with help. Can't you hear it?" Mason pressed end.

"Bloody hell, it's Herbertsin, hear that noise, he'll be here in a *sec*. Start talking I've got a live feed now. I doubt if he's here to rescue us."

LP raised his right hand, with his shrink-wrapped book in hand, standing straight as the sun was setting on the 23rd and said, "*Take more notice of;*"

and with his left finger, he made the sign of *V+1* and continued to say.

> "*And in my name … ,*" LP paused.
> "While I have your attention, I'll add; *Protect children nor exploit their labour. Don't own slaves nor be a slave to money. Desert people release your slaves, now!*"

"Is that it." Mason asked, as swirling rotor blades woofed above.

LP stood silent as though in a trance, then shook his head, looked up and spotted Herbertsin holding a handgun, pointed at him from the helicopter side opening.

Panic set in: He steeled his thoughts, *They always shoot the messenger!* Looking defiant, he yelled out. "Give it your best shot arsehole." Not that Herbertsin could hear him.

We'll Brownie was right, bad shit was about to happen. Eyeballing Herbertsin; LP stretched out his right arm in defiance as Herbertsin took aim. At that moment, the sun reflected off the shrink wrap, like a laser beam, blinding the pilot momentarily, losing control, as Herbertsin fired a bullet past LP.

There was no escape, once the pilot regained control. But like the eagle legend from the Navajo people of the Grand Canyon, so too, two giant eagles gave a watchful eye over their domain: Mt. Beerwah. This other big bird; blades swirling with deafening noise needed to be taken down. LP could see what the pilot couldn't; two eagles soaring on a thermal current, with wing spans of almost two metres, about to attack anything they saw as a threat to their domain.

Herbertsin was their prey and swooped in on him, clawing and pecking Herbertsin's head, before he fell from the side of the helicopter, landing before LP's feet.

LP placed his foot on his body and said to Mason, "Send the feed about Herbertsin. Then I've got something more to say."

"OK, sent, I'm ready, what next," Mason asked.

"Hand me my phone, thanks… Done! I've sent the photo on Instagram of sunset."

LP changed back to Twitter to send the final message to his followers - *The end is the beginning, life renewed. Download the Scroll, whisperer the mantra, and connect with, what I see, you will see. What I know, you will know.*

LP closed his phone case and said, "I think that's enough for today. Let's catch up with the guys, and get down this mountain before worse shit happens. I'm leaving the book where you found it, after I write what I revealed today about V+1. As well, I'm leaving a copy of the Scroll."

"Mason, you do know what I mean by the Roman numerals?"

"Well, actually no". Mason said, with an inquisitive look on his face.

"It's the fifth and six commandment from the Old and New Testament - Thou Shalt Not Kill. Depends which book you're reading. Both are correct. Let's get off this mountain. You go first; I'll follow, just in case Herbertsin's copper mates are waiting back at the car park for me. Otherwise their liable to arrest us all."

"OK, but when are you coming down?"

Grinning, LP replied, "Don't worry about that, I have a plan."

Mason backtracked down the mountain, while a drone descends. LP reaches up and grabs his delivery. Straps on the wingsuit and takes a running leap off Mt.Beerwah.

LP flashes past the cave where Mason had caught up with Bear and his mates, and they look in disbelief as giant eagles act as wing men.

The weather was not improving, as lightning and rain intensified after the sun set on the peak of Mt. Beerwah -01:23.

The updraft carried LP and the eagles all the way to Wild Horse Mountain, 123 meters above sea level. After releasing his shute, he pulled back on the cords and landed just opposite the stairs leading up to the tower. The eagles landed, perching themselves high on a tree branch.

After stepping out of his wingsuit, LP walked up the stairs as darkness from storm clouds engulfed the tower, while thunder vibrates through it.

The next flash of light sees only the person wearing a Driza-Bone waistcoat and hood; standing with his hands on the central platform, as lightning so intense stretches like a wall of white bright light that spans the horizon from Brisbane to Mt. Beerwah, then more lightning strikes the communication aerials atop of the tower.

One moment he's there, the next he's gone as the eagles take flight back to Mt. Beerwah.

Past-Present-Future are one.